**For early access, extra content, and updates, follow me at:**

Website: http://www.thefalsehero.com/

Patreon: https://www.patreon.com/MichaelPlymel

Facebook:

https://www.facebook.com/michael.plymel.79

Twitter: @Michael_Plymel

Discord: https://discord.gg/Wc2cYpPMt3

Reddit: https://www.reddit.com/r/TheFalseHero/

# Patrons

## Divine Class

ArkSkwyre
The last Survivor of The 423rd Royal BattleMech
Division
Jacob Strack
Eduardo Mejia
joel southard
max wells
Michael  Kilousky
Red Phoenix
Brennan C


## Heroic Class

Allen Boesl
ImNotRevy
Justin Novack
Kconraw
SnowFairyAsuna
YouStillTryin
Rissien
Hunter Malachai
Galleu
Sinclip
Gabino Reyes
Matthew Robison
Justin
Moheebi3abc
Jeffrey D McArthur
jay

# Master Class

Andrew Gallegos
Chocotaku
Coywolf
J B
Ricky Lalley
Jon Bryant
Nathaniel Jablonski
Amanda Smith
Timothy
James Burrett
Aolgar SilverStar
Andrew Thomas
Stephen McIver
Bruce Johnson
Anfernee Gonzales
Illiterate Scholar
Adam
David M
Saleh Alazmi

# The False Hero

## Volume 8

# Michael Plymel

# The Story So Far

## Volume 1

After being summoned to a new world, Lutz was quickly labeled as the prophesized False Hero and sentenced to death. By some miracle, he escapes his fate and flees.

After quickly adapting to the game-like mechanics, he begins to hunt the strength he needs to survive in this unforgiving world. He's a big of a jack-of-all-trades but has powerful Wind Magic and excellent spearmanship.

His first stop is a city just north of the kingdom's capital, Silvia. There, he meets his first true companion in his new world, Laya. Lutz rescues her from slavery and begins to train her in magic.

The 19-year-old elf girl doesn't look any older than ten, but her small frame is contrasted by her killer instincts. She specializes in Wind Magic and uses her mid-ranged chain sickle to hound her enemies.

Together, they cross paths with Marquis Adel and get pulled into his scheme to save the city of Silvia from its fate at the hands of its corrupt ruler. They manage to slay him, avenging Laya's destroyed village in the process.

## Volume 2

After fleeing north from Silvia, Lutz and Laya eventually need to restock their bags, so they stop at the city of Reim. It's no better off than Silvia, and he ends up getting dragged even deeper into its mess.

It's at this city that he meets his next two companions, Alisha and Belle.

Belle was a slave alongside Alisha, and together, they killed their old mistress and fled, trying to survive on the streets. She has powerful Fire and Water Magic, plus various support spells. But she lacks confidence in close combat, so she has to rely on her teammates to defend her.

Alisha is a beastkin, with cat-like ears and tail. She's incredibly protective of innocent people but also a fierce predator on the battlefield. The only thing that's holding her back is the [Curse of the Forsaken], which drains her stats and lowers her skill points.

Now a party of four, they hatch a plan to bring down Reim's mayor and put an end to the rebellion that had taken over the city. Things don't quite go as planned, but in the end, the worst-case scenario of an all-out bloodbath was avoided.

# Volume 3

Lutz's ultimate destination is the elven lands. So after leaving Reim, he travels east, beginning the long journey across the vast Orakian Kingdom.

While Lutz maintained his single-minded focus on surviving, there was someone else with an equally powerful goal. Princess Lumina de Eldridge left the castle in search of Lutz, determined to find out if he is truly the hero she's looking for.

She deduces his ultimate destination and matches his pace eastward, heading toward the elven lands.

At the same time that Lutz and Lumina began their trek east, the Orakian army made its move, invading the lands of Chaos. Led by Lumina's eldest brother, Crown Prince Rhys, the fifty-thousand strong army seeks to end the conflict once and for all, using the strength of the other three summoned heroes: Cedric, Rolf, and Collette.

If all of that weren't enough, trouble is brewing back at the castle. The kingdom's most powerful noble has his eyes set on the throne, and he'll use anything at his disposal to get it, even if it ends up causing a civil war.

It's during this time of turmoil and uncertainty that Lutz and Lumina finally meet once again. But their reunion is cut short and the two of them are teleported away.

Though there were points of danger, Lutz manages to protect Lumina. During their journey to reunite with Laya and the others, the two of them come to terms with their turbulent past, forming a deep bond in the process.

After quite of a bit of fighting, they meet up safely and foil the plan of a group of vampires who had been terrorizing the region.

In the end, Lumina decides to go back to the castle, claiming that she has important business.

So, it's just the four of them once again: Lutz, Laya, Alisha, and Belle. They continue east, down the final highway that separates them from the elven lands.

# Volume 4

The party travels to the eastern edge of the Orakian Kingdom. As usual, they're completing a batch of guild requests with no reward to help those who have been abandoned by their own country.

One of these quests puts them close to a dungeon, The Twisted Spire. Desperate to grow stronger, Lutz leads the girls inside, where they face monsters and challenges befitting the dungeon's reputation.

While climbing the tower, they run across four slaves: Kalyn, Geralt, Ina, and Devin. Lutz frees them from their battle-hungry master and gives them the strength they need to survive on their way out of the dungeon.

The party continues to climb, finally reaching the final floor. The wyvern they find there is a rather disappointing final boss, but to their surprise, a hidden path leads toward a hidden floor above. Inside, they find a secret boss that guards the dungeon's final door.

After defeating the construct, they step into the hidden room and find a powerful orb. That orb seems to control the flow of mana within the dungeon, as if it were acting as a heart to keep the energy moving to where it needs to go.

However, even more surprising is the vampire they find in that very room. Tylith von Phyress, sister to Vampire Lord Ashton, had been trapped there after the party she followed through the dungeon leaves without her.

After a brief confrontation, the vampire princess joins Lutz and the others as the group levels up by defeating the tough bosses near the top of the dungeon.

When their grinding is complete, all five of them leave The Twisted Spire, heading back to the town of Resta to the south.

Once there, the group decides to take a small vacation at a nearby hotspring. Although it was meant to be a relaxing experience, Lutz takes it upon himself to transform the natural spring into a resort to give the economically depressed town a landmark to attract travelers.

During their stay, High Priest Melina begins terrorizing the region, gathering Forsaken and executing them. One of her victims is Resta's mayor, Wilhelm. The biggest problem is that Melina herself is unknowingly creating the Forsaken with her Unique Skill, [Touch of Chaos].

Unwilling to let her ravage the countryside, Lutz and the girls step up to challenge her. During the fight, High Priest Melina absorbs power from a mysterious orb within the Great Cathedra's Oracle Chamber.

The power is corrupting her, even changing her very appearance to that of a demon. With no other recourse, Lutz destroys the orb, then slays the High Priest within the Oracle Chamber. Unfortunately, the Great Cathedral's connection to the Goddess is broken at the same time.

Although the threat posed by Melina has been dealt with, the long-term consequences of destroying the Great Cathedral is still unknown. Lutz and the girls have no choice but to move on before the weight of the Orakian Empire falls on them.

And so, they close the last of the distance between them and the elven lands, eventually arriving within a stone's throw of the forest that marks the beginning of the elven territories.

Turns out, the elves weren't very happy to see them.

# Volume 5

Lutz and his party finally stepped foot into the elven lands, only to be greeted with weapons. Fortunately, the elves are a reserved people and didn't attack outright. Rather, Lutz allowed his group to be taken into custody and transported to an Elder, one of the people in charge of an elven enclave.

The trip was mostly uneventful, though they did meet a group of Dryads who spouted some mysterious words about visiting a place known as the Ancestral Glade, then vanished as quickly as they appeared.

Shortly after, they met Elder Saevel. Lutz showed the aging elf his Unique Skill, [True Blessing of the Goddess], and for the first time since coming to this world, he finally managed to secure himself at least a little goodwill without an ounce of bloodshed.

That said, Laya did take part in a battle against a powerful elven warrior named Galan. Though she had to pull out one of her aces, she managed to secure a victory, ensuring no elves would question her place among Lutz's party.

With their new freedom, Lutz visited an elven blacksmith, where he crafted new weapons for his party, including a mysterious chain sickle with the name [Arc of the Crescent Moon]. How it came to have a name, nobody knows. But its power can't be denied.

Next, they headed off toward the Ancestral Glade, where some elves believe the spirits of their ancestors reside. There's a being there who's said to be the mother of all Dryads, known as the Astral Dryad.

After some annoying tests, Lutz managed to meet her, where he learned that before the devastation 10,000 years ago, the world once has an advanced and prosperous civilization. The Astral Dryad left many mysteries with her words, but more importantly, she taught Lutz how to dispel the [Curse of the Forsaken]. Now, it's only a matter of time before Alisha is cured.

She also tasked him with a mission: Save the forest from a disease that's destroying the trees and other life on the far eastern edge of the elven lands. So, with a goal in mind, the party heads further east, where they arrive at a battlefield.

The demons from the Forsaken Wastelands have been assaulting the elves, precisely where the disease has begun to spread through their forest. Lutz and company get to work figuring out how to solve it but are interrupted by the arrival of a dragon.

The creature was fleeing from a horde of demons, but Lutz manages to rescue it. Though the creature passes out and remains asleep for some time. During its nap, Lutz manages to figure out the disease and comes up with a way to stop it. And just as the final operations for his missions in the battlefield are coming together, the dragon awakens.

After a conversation with the dragon, Freisheldrith Zaldryre—or Frei as Lutz calls him, they learn that an Archfiend has taken hold in a mountain not far from the elven encampment. It's there that the army of demons launches its assaults, and if left alone, the Archfiend plans to summon a horde of fiends.

Hearing this, the Prime Elder, Rena, decides to take action. But Lutz can't wait for them to mobilize. He takes the dragon and his group to the mountain, where they infiltrate the demon's base.

After making their way to the center, they meet the Demon Lord. But he isn't the reason they came all this way, so as Frei battles him, Lutz and the others enter the room where the Archfiend Vrazruk awaits.

Although they don't manage to slay him, they do force Vrazruk to flee thanks to the mana-draining poison they acquired while solving the disease that was destroying the forest. Finally, they destroy the orb that was being used to power the teleportation circle.

With their mission complete, everyone heads back to the elven encampment. However, Frei departs back to his homeland, telling Lutz to stop by if he's ever in the area.

Just after, Lutz receives a telepathic message from Lumina. Turns out, another army of fiends has invaded Orakio's capital city of Roshar. The fearsome creatures have broken through the city's walls and now rampage within.

With no other alternative, Lutz activates the teleportation artifact linked to the one he gave Lumina back when they last saw each other.

Just like that, the False Hero finds himself back at the castle, where everything first began.

# Volume 6

After teleporting back to the castle, Lutz and the girls were thrown into a hectic battle for control of Orakio's capital city. Working together with Lumina and Elise, they hatched one plan after the next, trying to turn the tide back in their favor.

Lumina herself stepped onto center stage, taking the role of Prime Oracle and putting on a display of power to gain control of the command post—and therefore, the troops.

While Lumina played her role, Lutz and the girls set out to rescue survivors and eliminate fiends. They were so successful that the Archfiend himself stepped onto the battlefield to confront Lutz. But rather than turning into a battle, the Archfiend invited Lutz to meet with the Lord of Chaos. Of course, he refused.

The battle wrapped up shortly after the Archfiend left. Although the losses were high, the capital managed to withstand the siege.

After the battle, Lutz decided to investigate the Assassin's Guild to get information on the Great Heroes who leads the guild, Rolf.

His plans caused him to run into a strange foxkin girl, Rin. With her somewhat reluctant help, Lutz manages to become a gladiator at the coliseum.

It's there that Lutz has his first run-in with a real assassin, though it was the girls who actually confronted him.

Lutz managed to learn where the Assassin's Guild was located, but he couldn't just drop out of the arena and finish his business with them. Not while Rin needed him.

Though it was an ordeal to get her to talk, Lutz did eventually learn why Rin was fighting in the arena. She was looking for Kiah, a nine-tailed beastkin she was protecting.

The Assassin's Guild had kidnapped Kiah, so Rin joined Lutz for the final confrontation with them.

After the battle, Lutz realized Kiah isn't just a beastkin but a completely different race called a Kyuubi. Kiah said a lot of mysterious stuff, as if she had knowledge beyond the people of the world.

In the end, Rin and Kiah left, going back to their homeland in the beastkin nation of Belfast.

As for Lutz and the girls, they went to destroy the teleportation circle the fiends used to warp near the capital. But when they arrived, Vrazruk appeared and ripped Lutz's heart right out of his chest.

Somehow, Lutz survived even that. Though how is still a mystery.

And during his ordeal, Lumina was having one of her own. She had cast [Scry] on the three heroes and saw that each had the Unique Skill, [Blessing of Chaos].

The worst part was that Collette now knows that Lumina figured out their secret.

# Volume 7

After nearly losing his life to the Archfiend Vrazruk, Lutz and the part retreated, hiding at the cabin where Lutz fled after his initial escape from the dungeon. The place brought a flood of memories back to him, prompting him to place the entire cabin into his [Inventory] before leaving.

Hearing that Lumina's under threat from one of the Great Heroes, Collette, Lutz decided to pick her up and bring her to a dungeon to grind her some levels. But before that, he decided to join the party being thrown in honor of her new position as Prime Oracle.

Of course, he ended up dancing with her. And it was a lot of fun.

On their way to the dungeon, they stopped by Belle's hometown, where they met their family. Although the initial meeting was a bit rough, it didn't take long before they started getting along. They even decided to hire Belle's family to run the shop they started in the capital city.

After power leveling in the dungeon, Lutz and most of the girls reached the highest level they could attain there, level 72.

Next, they made the trip to Silvia, the town where Lutz first met Laya. He paid a visit to several people from his past, like Baldrick the blacksmith, Marquis Adel, Karina and Edwin, and even Miri, the girl who started a church in his name.

As usual, the party finds themselves pulled into another mess, with an unknown group seemingly trying to destroy the prosperity the city has recently enjoyed. With a bit of time to spare, Lutz decides to investigate.

He expected the hand of Chaos to be at work, but no matter how much they searched, they couldn't find a trace of fiends.

Eventually, they realized that the supposed plot to bring the city down was nothing more than a petty noble scheming against Adel.

Using that noble, Lutz was able to set up an event for Miri's church, where a fake image of the Goddess would appear and defeat an Archfiend to give her church a large boost in popularity.

But it didn't go as planned. Rather than a fake Goddess, the real one showed up. She told Lutz that he needed to seek the Dragon Lord and gain access to his Mana Node.

At the same time, the Goddess finally revealed to the people of Silvia that Lutz was her chosen hero. He had finally gotten the acceptance he desired, but it was just one city. Those who weren't there to witness the event would be understandably skeptical, making it hard to spread that acceptance to the rest of the world.

After tying up some loose ends, Lutz and the girls drop Lumina and Elise off at the castle, then start their journey south, toward the Dragon Isles.

# Prologue

## ----- Viola -----

My hand reaches out, sliding a key into the lock attached to the beautifully crafted door. After an audible click, my other hand wraps around the knob and gives it a twist. With a gentle push, the wooden door swings soundlessly on its hinges, revealing the ornate room that even a queen would find pleasing.

However, I've long since become accustomed to such a sight, so my eyes glide right over the beautiful array of plants and decorative ornaments. Instead, I focus on the object in the room that was the reason for my visit in the first place. A young girl, looking no older than 12 or 13.

"W-where am I...?" she asks.

"Finally awake, I see. That's good. We can get started, then."

"Started? You're a human lady, aren't you? Who are you and where did you take me?" The girl looks behind me, but all her blue-green eyes see is an empty hall.

Her matching hair is a bit of a mess, seeing as how she just woke up from a sleeping potion. Since she suddenly found herself in an unknown room, it's no wonder she hasn't prioritized fixing her appearance. Perhaps she would even have tried hiding her elven ears, as is often the case for her people when they're outside their lands. Of course, such an action would be useless. We already know she's an elf.

*Maybe that's why he bought her in the first place.*

After pondering uselessly on the reasons for his decision, I make a motion toward the young girl.

"Follow."

It takes a bit of coaxing, but the elf eventually relents. She has nowhere to go and no idea where she's at, so in the end, all she can do is obey the orders of those who reside at her new home.

A long hall sits outside her room, just as richly decorated as the chamber in which she awoke. If I were to tell this elf that the mansion belonged to a king, she would likely believe me.

It doesn't, though I suppose some would argue that my answer is only semantics. However, having lived here for nearly a year now, I can't imagine a king even coming close to the power and authority possessed by this mansion's owner.

A flight of stairs and another long hall later, we arrive at a door similar to the one that caged this elf girl. By all accounts, a new visitor would expect a high noble or royal to reside within. But even that expectation wouldn't do the room's occupant justice.

"Enter." A confident voice calls out without even waiting for me to knock.

I do as he commands, and his finely furnished room appears in my vision, with blood-red carpets lying atop the waxed, dark-brown floors. Sharp, angular decorations and other eye-catching coverings only add to the elegantly brutal theme, making the room reminiscent of a recently vacated battlefield.

I bow before my lord. "I brought her."

"Excellent." He puts down the quill he had been using and looks at the elf. "Quite the rare catch. Though we'll have to do something about that appearance of yours. I didn't trade one of my prized artifacts for an elf girl with unruly hair."

"A..." The young girl takes a step back. "...Vampire!?"

She dashes toward the door, but I've already locked it. Next, she tries the window, but after pulling the curtains aside, she realizes that we're several stories high. Despite that, she tries to open them. She fails, of course. I've already locked them, too.

Her attempts to break the glass end in another failure, as they're tempered beyond what a simple elf girl can break. Having no way to escape, she turns back, first to me, then to our lord.

"Are you quite finished?" He asks.

"W-what do you want from me?"

"I guess you could say I'm a collector, of sorts. Art and artifacts are only a matter of course. But what I truly desire are rare specimens. And what more can a vampire ask for than an elf?"

As a human girl who woke up in this very vampire's mansion nearly a year earlier, I know well the fear that's openly painted on the elf's face.

"My lord," I say to break the short silence. "You can leave her appearance to me. I will make her presentable."

"Of course, Viola. I trust you will choose the appropriate outfit to match her distinct elven features."

"You can count on me."

"As for you." He turns his gaze back to the elf. "From now on, I expect you to refer to me as 'lord'. And if you find yourself with me in the company of outsiders, then 'Lord Ashton' would be more appropriate."

"Ashton!? The girl's eyes widen. Are you...!"

"Aston von Phyress, Vampire Lord of the Coven of Dusk. Pleased to meet your acquaintance."

----------

"Here it is." I stop in front of a shop. "You'll be visiting this general store often Ruri, so you should memorize its location quickly."

"Yes, ma'am," Ruri replies obediently.

It's only been a single day since the young elf girl, Ruri, arrived at Lord Ashton's mansion, but once she realized she was at the heart of one of the Great Clans, she understood she had no chance to escape.

All around Ruri are vampires, the very race her people have been battling for nearly two thousand years. The only reason she hasn't become food for them already is because of her new position as Lord Ashton's servant.

"Oh, this is unusual," the shop owner says when we walk inside. "Even Lord Ashton must have had a hard time getting his hands on an elf."

"Yes. They're very protective of their young, so I can't imagine how they managed to kidnap her."

"I would say she's lucky to have been picked up by him, but considering how many of his servants end up disappearing..."

"Indeed. It's the fate of those who displease him."

"You must be quite the hard worker, Viola. Been what, a year? Can't remember any other servant that lasted as long."

"It's simply due to my desire to stay by his side. I suppose he finds such conviction agreeable."

"Guess so." He pulls a sack out from behind the counter. "And you were a noble girl back when you were living with the humans, right? Someone like you won't embarrass him, what with your fancy etiquette and all."

"That is true. I can serve him without issue, even when among the other Vampire Lords."

I take the bag from the counter, then nod to Ruri. The girl places the pouch of coins where the bag used to sit, and the shopkeeper takes them with a smile.

"Feel free to stop by again if you need anything else."

"Thanks. I'll consider it once I'm given my monthly wage."

With that, we leave the store. The man who runs it is one of the more agreeable vampires. He doesn't seem to care about much, as long as we keep bringing coin for his goods.

The same can't be said of many others. As Ruri and I walk down the street, many vicious eyes fall on us. Without doubt, their fangs would seek our flesh in an instant, if we weren't sworn to Lord Ashton.

"This way." I step into an alley. "It's a convenient shortcut to our next stop, but don't take it without me, got it?"

"Yes, I understand."

The reason I warned her against taking the route appears before us. A vampire walks in our direction, his eyes narrowing as we draw closer.

Although none dare lay their hands on us out of fear of Lord Ashton's wrath, the dark corners of the city can still be dangerous. If a vampire thinks he can get away with it, then there's nothing stopping him from doing as he pleases.

At least, that should be the case. However...

"Move aside," I say to the crimson-eyed man. "We are servants of Lord Ashton. Any who hinder us will be met with his wrath."

"A bold lie, girl. One I don't blame you for trying, but do you really think I'll let such a feast simply walk away?" His eyes fall on Ruri. "I think not."

"Then you leave me no choice." My arm comes up, and a beam of fire erupts.

"Gah...!" The flames slam into the vampire, knocking him clear off his feet.

He crashes into the side of the alley, but I don't relent. I let the full force of the spell run its course, until the last ounce of power flows from my palm. The vampire's body remains pressed against a stone building, despite the force of my magic no longer pinning him.

*No, he's not being pressed against it. He's still standing!*

The man lowers his arms, which had been crossed before him to shield his body from my [Scorching Ray]. His skin sizzles, and his sleeves are all but burnt to nothing. But his face shows no fear.

*Vampires usually flee when faced with opponents stronger than themselves. The fact that he's not running must mean…*

"That hurt, girl." He steps toward me as he speaks. "A pain I will be returning!"

"Ruri, run!" I catch the vampire's fist, then pull him off-balance.

At least, that was my intention. But I'm a far more capable mage than warrior. The same can't be said of this vampire.

"Haha!" He easily overpowers me and lifts me by my collar. "You're weaker than I thought!"

Taking a glance behind me, I see Ruri still standing there, frozen in fear. At a young age, elves are taught to fear vampires, so it's only natural she would stiffen when faced with the murderous intent of such a fearsome creature.

"I think I'll have a taste of you first." His smile widens, revealing his vampiric fangs. "Before moving on to the main course."

*"Lord Ashton, please…!"*

The vampire pulls me close, completely focused on my bare neck. His fangs inch closer, as if in anticipation of the first drop of blood to sate his thirst. I can only squirm in his grip, my eyes shut for what's to come.

Despite my eyes being closed, I can still clearly see the bright flash of light. Immediately after, my body seemingly becomes weightless as a sense of vertigo overtakes me.

When my eyes reopen, I'm staring up at Lord Ashton's expressionless face, cradled in his arms.

"Lord Ashton!" I can't help but yell out.

"Seems you've run afoul of a miscreant, Viola. How rare for you."

"My apologies, Lord Ashton. He was too powerful, even for me."

"I see that. Level 53. High enough to have made a name for himself, which makes it all the more strange that I do not recognize him."

"Who are you!?" The vampire stands, having been blown away by Lord Ashton after his teleportation.

"Oh? You dare question me?" Lord Ashton's eyes come alight. "Maggots like you should know your place."

"Maggot!? I'm one of Vampire Lord Theron's top generals! I won't let you off for that insult, even if you beg!"

"So that's it. Theron was a fool to have picked such an incompetent general."

"Bastard! Nobody speaks of Vampire Lord Theron in such a way!"

The man takes a step toward Lord Ashton. Just a step. After that...

"W-what...!?"

"What's wrong? Don't tell me this is all you're capable of."

"F-fear!?" He gulps. "This is ... [Hypnosis]! But the only ones capable of such powerful Dark Magic are...!"

"Vampire Lords," Ashton finishes for him.

"W-wait, so that girl was telling the truth!? I'm sorry, I didn't know! A-actually, I came with an important message, Lord Ashton! Lord Theron wishes to..." The general suddenly shuts his mouth, as if the fear suddenly became too much.

"I don't care what wishes Theron has. Though perhaps I will entertain his whims if he sends a more fitting messenger. As for you..."

"N-no...!"

That's the only word the general manages to get out. Immediately after, his head slides from his shoulders and falls to the ground, severed.

Lord Ashton finally puts me down, and I unfortunately find myself standing on my own two feet again.

"Are you injured?" He asks.

"No, you arrived just in time."

"And the girl?" He looks to Ruri, who's still frozen like a statue.

"Untouched."

"In that case, all is well."

He walks toward Ruri, and the elf girl takes a step back as the powerful Vampire Lord closes in on her. Of course, there's no escape, and she soon finds herself a single pace from him, gazing up at his youthful face.

"Let's end the shopping here for today," he says. "We have other tasks we need—"

Lord Ashton goes silent and turns his eyes back down the alley. However, he's not looking at the body that lies slumped on the ground. He's peering at a seemingly empty point in space.

But it doesn't remain empty for long.

"Ashton," a vampire's deep voice calls his name without a shred of reverence. "Even you cannot slay my generals without retribution."

"Ah, Theron. How convenient of you to teleport in with such timing. It saves me the trouble of hunting you down to ridicule you for your poor choice in subordinates."

"Always with the smug attitude. You can guarantee I'll be seeking the highest of compensations for slaying my general."

"A payment I'd be happy to pay, were his death unjustified. But in this case, your plea for restitution will fall on deaf ears."

Theron frowns. "And why is that?"

"Because your general sought to take that which belongs to me." Lord Ashton looks to me and Ruri.

"Tch. When did you get your hands on an elf? Whatever. He was a fool anyway, and I have important matters to discuss with you."

"Oh? I do remember your general saying something of the sort."

"Ashton, our lord wishes to speak to you. It seems you won't be participating in the war against the human country of Eshia."

"What other scheme could hold more import than our invasion of the human land?"

"We've received word that the False Hero may yet live and that he intends to travel south, to the beastkin lands. Our lord has a plan, and you are the one who will bring it to fruition."

"The False Hero..." Lord Ashton shows us a rare look of surprise. "Fine. I will meet with our lord and discuss the details. I wish you well, Theron."

With that, Lord Ashton releases his unfathomably powerful magic, and the world vanishes as he teleports us back to his mansion.

# Chapter 1: Home

## ----- Lutz -----

"Looks delicious," I say. "But you don't always have to make my favorite when you cook breakfast."

Laya takes a seat next to me. "And you don't have to make mine."

"Hahaha. You got me."

The cabin's interior currently only has two occupants. The other three girls left even before the crack of dawn, heading to a nearby town to buy a few supplies, leaving just me and Laya to enjoy a bit of downtime.

We still have plenty of food and other daily goods, but we decided it might be a good idea to make short stops by various towns and villages as we travel, rather than buying supplies in bulk from major cities.

Not only do we prefer to avoid huge crowds, but the smaller towns are the ones struggling the most. If we can spend some of our coin at their shops, then we can at least inject a bit of money into their local economy. It may not be much, but it's better than nothing.

While the girls are visiting, they'll be gathering info. Belle's especially good at that, and she'll be using her talkative personality to find out if there are any groups of monsters harassing the people in the area. Taking them out would barely be an inconvenience for us as we are now, but it'd mean the world for the ones who are at risk of losing their lives to them.

Even though Laya and I decided to stay behind, neither of us would be happy just lazing around. There are plenty of things that we can do, and we plan to finish them while the other girls are taking care of business. To be more precise, there are domestic chores that need to be done, and this is the perfect time to work on them.

After breakfast, of course.

Without Belle and Alisha, the atmosphere in the cabin is far more subdued. In fact, throughout the entirety of our time eating breakfast, Laya and I don't speak a single word.

It's not like it became awkward to the point that neither of us wanted to be the first to break the silence. It's simply that we can sit in peace and simply enjoy the pleasure of each other's company without the need to fill the air with noise.

That's not to say the other girls are loud to cover up any deficiencies they may feel. It's just that Laya and I share a natural affinity for peace and quiet. Just being in each other's presence is enough for us, so there's no need to fill it with frivolous conversation just for the sake of it.

Maybe it's because she was the first person I truly got close to in this world, or maybe it was the weeks we spent alone before any of the other girls joined us. Perhaps it's even that we're just the most compatible within our group. Whatever the case, there's nobody I feel more comfortable being with than Laya. Even though she hasn't said it directly, I know she feels the same.

"Delicious," I say as I swallow the last bite.

"Thanks." Laya finishes the same time as me.

*Jeez, you always have to match my pace when eating, don't you?*

The truth is that she's not the only one paying attention to how quickly the other is eating. Somewhere along the line, I began doing the same. Because of that, Laya and I always finish our meals at the same time.

*It's weird, right? Maybe that's why we're both too embarrassed to mention it, despite doing it every time...*

With my plate in hand, I stand from the table and walk toward the kitchen. It's not much of a kitchen, but it serves the purpose.

I've expanded the cabin a bit since its first renovation, but it's still not large enough to be considered a proper house. I plan to keep building onto it, but it's hard to find time for major projects when we're traveling all day.

I stop just in front of a sink. Of course, Laya's right beside me, her plate also in her hands. She sets it down at the same time as I do, and they end up stacked together on the small kitchen counter.

Since Laya cooked this morning, it's my responsibility to do the cleaning after. That leaves her free to relax for a bit while her food settles, but this is Laya. Taking it easy might as well be a crime in her mind.

The cookware used to make breakfast appears on the counter, brought to me by Laya's hand. They were already soaking outside where she did the cooking, so washing them will be a simple task.

After that, she retrieves a cloth from her [Inventory] and gets to wiping down the table. No matter how many times I see her dedication and work ethic, it always makes me shake my head, knowing I can't match her.

*Well, I can try, at least. No way I'm gonna become a bum who relies on her to clean up after me.*

My hand reaches out and falls atop the purple crystal that sits just above the marbled sink. After filling it with my mana, water begins flowing from it. The steam that rises from the clear, blue liquid makes it obvious that the water is scalding hot.

Thanks to my crafting skills, I was able to combine Fire and Water Elemental Crystals. Separately, a Water Elemental Crystal will produce fresh water when given mana, while a Fire one will produce a flame.

But when crafted together, they make a stream of hot water. It's perfect for something like a sink to wash our dishes and hands. I even have plans to craft a giant crystal into a bath, but I'd like to add a bathroom to the cabin first.

*That should definitely be my next addition. Maybe I can even make a shower. I wonder how hard it'd be to make a shower head and get the pressure just right for it to flow properly...*

I finally dip my hands into the pool of water in the sink. Were it the me back on Earth, the heat would be too much to wash dishes in, but as I am now, I feel nothing but satisfaction as my hands soak in the burning hot water.

Being able to use such hot water makes getting the dishes clean a simple task, and the fact that they're made of mithril means I can scrape them with an amount of force that would break any glass or ceramic dinnerware from Earth. Not that I need to, but it's just an option available to me.

The cleaning goes by in a flash, and when I'm done, I set the dishes aside to dry. I would put them in my [Inventory], but they'd never dry in there since time doesn't flow inside it. On that note, I've found that another interesting perk of having a nearly infinite storage space at my disposal is that we don't need to make space for things like cabinets or closets.

"Good job, Laya." I look around the cabin and see that it's spotless, as usual.

"Mmm."

"Belle and the others seem to have made it to town, but we've still got some time before they get back. I figured we could finish a few more tasks while we wait. Any requests?"

"Clothes."

"Yeah, I saw that coming. In that case, I'll come out with you and keep you company. I've got something to work on, so I might as well do it by your side, right."

"Yes." Laya nods as she speaks, which is actually a rare display of desire for her.

Stepping outside, we're greeted by a grassy plain with gently rolling hills. Animals cover the ground and sky in a way that I would never see on Earth. Some I can sort of relate to ones I'm familiar with, such as the squirrel-like creatures that dart away at the sound of the cabin door opening. But others are too strange for me to find a direct comparison, making me wonder a bit about their natures.

*Maybe one day I'll have the leisure to explore all the little details that make this world unique.*

For now, I'll have to make do with watching them from afar, as I have important tasks that need to be completed. Every day is like a rock that has to be placed in order to build the mountain I need to survive. I simply can't afford to go wandering around each time something catches my eye.

"Well, here's my batch." My clothes appear from nowhere, falling into the basket beside Laya.

"Thanks."

"Sheesh. I don't mind washing them, you know?"

"No."

"Same answer as always, huh?"

"Forbidden."

"I know, I know. But it just doesn't sit right with me."

"It's fine since it's something we decided."

Since there's nothing I can say against the girls' unanimous decision to forbid me from laundry duty, all I can do is accept it. Of course, it was Belle and Tylith who spearheaded the opposition, making one ridiculous claim after another that I don't care to repeat.

In the end, I was excluded from the rotation. But at the same time, they always tell me to add my clothes to the wash pile when laundry time comes around.

It's not fair, I tell you.

Laya's already sitting next to a wash basin, soaking the clothes in the soapy water within. I can't help with the laundry, but I can at least set up the clothesline for her.

*Hmm I wonder if a really weak [Inventory] ring that barely slows down time would be a good place to store our wet clothes as they dry.*

*But would they get moldy from lack of airflow? Maybe I'll test it with a sock.*

*No, make it two socks. Wouldn't want to end up with an odd number of socks if the experiment fails.*

As the thought runs through me, I take out a chair and set it next to Laya's. As usual, she's hyper focused on her task, as if getting out every stain in our clothes were a matter of life and death.

Of course, that's one of her good points. Nobody else has such laser focus on the details like her.

"New project?" Laya asks, sneaking a peek at the gems and other materials I brought out onto the table.

"Kinda. It's more of a continuation of one I set up but never finished."

"Spell Orb imbued with Water Magic?"

"That's right. If I combine these Water Elemental Crystals with this gemstone, I can create a Spell Orb that specializes in Water Magic."

Laya takes another glance at the table just as I gather up the gem and crystals, placing them in a ceramic bowl. After channeling pure Fire Mana in my right hand and pure Wind Mana in my left, I place my hands on the bowl's opening and let the flames heat the contents.

The heat emitted by my right hand is enhanced by the constant supply of oxygen by my left, creating a small but intense inferno within the ceramic bowl. It's so effective that it basically becomes a tiny forge, capable of quickly smelting a small amount of material.

After heating the gem and crystals up to a suitable temperature, I cast [Transform] on the malleable contents and forcefully turn them into a goopy mixture. The materials mix together into a sort of soup, with their chemical structures becoming interlocked with each other.

Normally, [Transform] is a temporary effect. But when outside influence is applied to a transformed object, it can force the transformation to become permanent. It doesn't work well on living things, but inanimate objects don't have the same resistance to the effect.

"Hot." I remove my hands from the bowl, revealing the glowing contents.

Next, I take the bowl and dump the soup into a tube, where the contents slide down and into a spherical container.

That'll do it, I say after cleaning the bowl and setting it back onto the table.

"Hands." Laya holds her own out as she requests to see mine.

Giving in, I place my hands into her own, palm up. "Sorry, they got a bit burnt again."

"It's fine. But I'll say it again. You need to find a better way to heat up your materials." She casts [Cure], and her warmth fills me.

"If I did that, then I'd lose this moment each time I melted some Elemental Crystals down."

Laya looks torn between wanting me to stop burning my hands and having the chance to heal me after. But as is usual for her, she makes the choice that's in my best interest.

"Unfortunate," she says. "But necessary."

"Guess I don't have a choice, if that's what you want."

I have plans for the Spell Orb I just crafted, but rather than working on that right now, it's more important to keep Laya company while she's doing laundry. So, I pull out one of the [Minimap] enchanted orbs I have and begin studying it, looking for ways to improve its functions.

Compared to a lot of other things I could be doing, this is low on my priorities. But it doesn't take much focus, so it's a good choice for an early morning task.

And more importantly, it keeps me right here by Laya's side.

After another good half-hour of relaxing time together, all the chores are finished. Of course, there weren't any problems thanks to Laya's meticulous attention to detail.

Fortunately, we finish at just the right moment because before Laya and I have to look for another task to fill our time, a familiar feeling appears nearby.

Turning, we watch as an empty space of grass is suddenly flattened by three sets of feet, each appearing from seemingly nowhere.

"We're back!" Belle says with her usual energy.

"Master, Master! Goblins!" Alisha matches her friend's pace, though her words are a bit harder to interpret.

"We should start from the beginning, Alisha." Tylith's mature response settles the excited little catgirl just a bit.

"Well," Belle says, "it's like this. We bought some supplies from town, and I asked around as usual. Turns out, a group of goblins settled in a nearby cave. They're still manageable, but you know how goblins get when left alone."

"Yeah." I nod, having heard the stories. "A dozen can turn into a hundred before you know it."

"Right. So, I told them we'd take care of the little problem. We were going to do it ourselves, but I figured you and Laya would be about done with chores and wanted to come along."

"Actually." I bring out the newly crafted Spell Orb. "This is the perfect opportunity."

# Chapter 2: Home Defense

## ----- Lutz -----

*"Enemies engaged."* Laya's voice echoes through our minds.

*"Good work. Bring some to us."*

*"Mmm."*

The left side of the screen in front of me begins to fill with red dots, each of which trail a green one. They're heading directly toward the center of the monitor, where multiple green dots sit. Of course, red indicates enemies, while green is my party.

And even though I called the object everyone has their eyes on a screen, it's actually a magically enchanted artifact. It's roughly the size of an average computer monitor and is completely flat, so it does resemble what people on Earth would describe as a TV screen.

However, there are no channels and no other forms of input to change what the artifact is displaying. It can only show the mana sources of any creatures within range, along with a general image of the terrain. It's enchanted with my [Minimap] skill, after all.

*"Cabin in sight,"* Laya says.

With my hand atop the Master Orb's surface, I alter the flow of mana, and the cabin door opens. *"Targets spotted. Requesting evasive maneuvers."*

*"Understood."*

After her reply, Laya leaps onto an [Air Step]. She stays low enough to the ground for the goblins chasing her to think they still have a chance to catch her but high enough that she won't be in the line of fire for what's coming.

"Alright." My hand still sits on the Master Orb. "Initiating combat procedures."

The magical energies that circulate within the cabin coalesce at a spot just next to the open door. As they gather, they weave themselves into a spell formation. The entire process takes less than a single second, and when it finishes...

"Large caliber, ready!"

A chunk of ice about the size and shape of a full-size, folded umbrella shoots out from the cabin wall at tremendous speed. In a blink, it closes the distance to the oncoming goblins, skewering one before it could even process the appearance of the [Ice Lance].

It doesn't stop there. The powerful spell pierces straight through the monster with barely a loss of momentum. In its path is another goblin, who meets the same fate as the first. After a third falls, the spell zips out of sight, still carrying enough force to slay anything in its path.

"Wow!" Alisha looks on with a smile. "It's like a goblin shish kabob!"

"Um, Alisha," Belle says. "I don't think goblin meat would make for a good snack."

"Eh? Really?"

"Belle's correct," Tylith says. "Vampires who've quenched their thirst on goblin blood typically only do so a single time. From what I hear, just remembering how they taste is enough to eliminate all thought of feasting on them again."

While I listen to the girls' conversation, I prepare for my second assault. There are still two dozen or so goblins, but I don't want to wipe them out too quickly. This is a test run for the cabin's offensive capabilities, after all.

"Machine gun, engaged!" At my words, four spears of ice shoot out from the cabin's wall, one after the next.

Unlike the first, these are only the size of butcher knives. Their speed is also reduced along with their size, but that doesn't mean they're weak.

"Ah." Tylith makes a sound. "Four more corpses. The accuracy is high, even when casting in quick succession."

"Yep." I nod, my hand still on the Master Orb. "The cabin is enchanted with [Detect Presences], which lets it lock onto targets. Helps with quick, precise aiming."

"This cabin is becoming more of a dungeon with each passing day."

"Who knows, maybe one day it'll be classified as such. If only I could figure out how to spawn monsters…"

"You just want to grind without having to go to a dungeon," Belle says.

"Oops. You figured me out."

Alisha raises her hand. "And it means I can fight whenever I want!"

"That's our little predator for you."

The goblins are finally closing in on the cabin, which means the one they're following is also getting close. Since the door's wide open, Laya elegantly leaps through it without even touching the ground. Or the cabin floor for that matter, since she's still leaping around on her translucent steps.

As soon as she passes the doorframe, I shut the door behind her. She eventually comes to a stop beside us, her eyes already focused on the screen with red dots showcasing the monsters' location.

Goblins are rather crafty monsters, even forming crude societies, often led by a powerful goblin leader. Powerful compared to the rest of the pack, that is. Even the goblin leader is considered mid-rank, so all they really have going for them are their numbers.

Though from what I hear, there are rare instances where a Goblin Lord will show up with a horde of greenskins. When that happens, it's not uncommon to find many goblin leaders in his pack, with the Goblin Lord being several steps above even them. But in this case, we're not dealing with something like that.

"They've got to be beating on the cabin wall with their crude weapons," Belle says. "But I can't even hear it."

"The [Barrier] spell will hold for a long time against monsters this weak. Since it repels attacks, they're not really making contact with the wall. But..."

I disable the spell. As soon as it fades, the thunking of their clubs hitting the wooden cabin wall fills the air. It'd be a fearsome sound if we were an average family barricaded in our home, but as we are now, it's just noise.

*Hmm. It's oddly satisfying, like thunder or the sound of a fan. I think I could sleep to this...*

*Unfortunately, I don't think the girls would agree to having a pack of goblins beating on the walls at night. In fact, now that I think about it, the idea just sounds really dumb now.*

*I'll just keep that thought fully to myself.*

"Alright," I say. "I think we've heard enough. Definitely wouldn't want to sleep like this."

The girls give me strange looks, but none of them make any remarks.

"Anyway," I continue. "Let's thin out the herd a bit. Auxillary canon, fully charged!"

The sound of roaring water erupts, creating a backdrop to the beating of the goblin's clubs against the cabin wall. The [Maelstrom] appears at the spot with the most monsters, and I make sure that it's large enough to encapsulate then all.

Although the second-tier Water Magic specializes in crowd control more than raw damage, that doesn't mean it's weak. In the center of the hurricane-like spell, the forces are enough to shred the average monster to pieces. So, it's not surprising to see several red dots vanish as soon as the [Maelstrom] springs to life.

It can only go in a straight path once cast, so the sound of the roaring water slowly recedes as the spell flies off into the distance. As it goes, so does the sound of the goblins' clubs. Not because the spell took care of them all but because goblins aren't as dumb as an average monster.

"They finally realized they're outmatched, huh. Guess that means playtime's over."

Along with their relative intelligence comes the ability to understand when they're facing opponents they can't beat. It's actually one of the more annoying aspects of exterminating a goblin infestation because as soon as the pack begins to flee, they scatter, making it hard to wipe them all out.

*You really think I'm going to let you escape?*

"Main artillery, fire!"

As soon as the goblins break away from the cabin, a massive blade of water appears. The crescent-shaped, third-tier Water Spell is as long end-to-end as the cabin's wall is wide. Without exception, each goblin beating on the side containing our front door is cut down in an instant.

A few others had gone around to the other walls, but that doesn't mean they can escape. Three casts of [Ice Lance], and three fresh corpses. With that, the small group of goblins has been eradicated.

"Awesome," I say as I remove my hand from the Master Orb. "That was even more fun than I thought it'd be."

"Mmm. A fitting home."

"Yeah," Belle says. "But we gotta talk about all those strange phrases you said before each attack. Do I even want to know what a canon or machine gun is?"

I look at her. "I'll have you know that many men dream of being able to say those words just before launching attacks like that. And of course you want to know what canons and machine guns are. Because they're awesome."

"I'm gonna go with a big 'no' on that one."

"I want to know, Master! If it goes swoosh and bang like magic, then it sounds like fun!" Alisha's arms move around energetically as she speaks.

"Hah." I give her a thumb's up. "I knew I could count on you!"

"Yeah! Main auxillary fire, charge!"

*Um, what exactly are you asking for, Alisha?*

Ignoring her excited command, I zoom out the screen on the cabin's built-in map. Although the detection range extends out even beyond the cave system the goblins are using as their base, the entire area is cloaked in darkness.

The artifact only records the terrain information after it has been physically close enough to do so, and we're currently too far out for that feature. So, the screen isn't picking up any of the goblins that are still hiding in their caves.

"Still needs some improvements," I say. "But the cabin is becoming quite a force in its own right."

Tylith looks at the Master Orb. "Never thought I'd see such a capable recreation of a Dungeon Orb. Even if it lacks the power and connection to the Mana Network, it's still an amazing creation."

"I'm happy with it, though I'd like to figure out how to add more autonomous functions to it."

"A tall order, but I'd have said the same about the Master Orb as it is now, before you created it."

"Just gotta take it one step at a time. I've got some training on spellcrafting from the Astral Dryad and some powerful orbs to study that we took from various members of Chaos. Not to mention what I learned from my visit to the Dungeon Orb at The Beast Warrens. The answer to further improving my Master Orb lies in those three things."

I take a look behind the [Minimap] enchanted screen. A shelf protrudes from the wall, containing many half-spherical indentations. All the indents are empty except for one, which holds my recently crafted Spell Orb.

It's that Spell Orb which contains the first, second, and third-tier Water Spells that I used to wipe out the group of goblins. By connecting it to the network of mana that flows through the cabin, I can control it from the Master Orb. With this method, I can power the magic with the mana held within the cabin, rather than my own body.

By crafting and adding more Spell Orbs to the cabin, I can enhance its functions and expand my list of available spells. There are limits, as my crafted orbs are weaker than what I can cast using my own magic. But depending on how far I can push this magical technology, there's a chance this cabin can be a useful tool to us in the future.

"Well, I'd say the test run was a success, at least. I was going to suggest we take a look at the outside walls to see if those goblins managed to cause any damage, but..."

"Self-repair," Laya says.

"Yeah. Guess we'll have to test its defensive strength another time. Perhaps on a tougher group of enemies, since I doubt goblins would ever be able to break past these mana-enhanced walls."

"You mean the corpses of the Treants you used to build them," Belle says.

"Semantics. Besides, what better building material than a body of wood that's already used to holding mana?"

"Don't semantics me. And there are magical trees, you know. The regular kind, not the monster kind."

"Yeah, but this was way more convenient. Those magical trees are tucked away in faraway lands. Though I bet the elves would let me harvest a few as a reward..."

"Protective," Laya says.

"Yeah, which is why I didn't want to ask when I had an easy alternative. The Astral Dryad could probably conjure some up for me, but owing her a favor would be..."

A few of the girls give me dry looks. They simply don't understand the depth of her brattiness, but I have a feeling they'll learn it one day.

"Anyway," I continue. "Let's just wipe out the rest of the goblins the old-fashioned way."

"Alright!" Alisha leaps into the air. "Battle!"

"Yep. It's good to exercise in the morning, so let's enjoy ourselves, shall we?"

The cabin vanishes back into my [Inventory], with me and the girls landing softly on the dirt ground that it used to rest upon. In our hands are our weapons, while our lips curl with the anticipation of battle.

# Chapter 3: The Edge of the Empire

## ----- Lutz -----

"It looks about the same as any other city, huh?" I look around the street we're walking on.

"Not exactly the same," Laya says.

"True. This one definitely has a somber atmosphere to it. With how big this city is, I expected more hustle and bustle."

"Mmm. Problems with the beastkin?"

"Maybe so. But the beastkin land to the south is Belfast, which is also at war with Chaos. I don't see why these two countries would be fighting each other right now."

"Old disputes won't fade easily."

"Ah, that's true. In fact, times like these are perfect for people who are looking for things like revenge."

We just stepped through the gates a few moments ago, paying an entrance fee that was definitely too large. They even had the audacity to hassle us during the process. But I held my tongue because I wanted to check this particular city out since it's the last major one before we enter the beastkin lands to the south.

I was curious about what kind of state it would be in due to its close position to another country filled with an entirely different race of people. I had hopes that I'd see a mingling of the two races here, getting along better than cities at the center of the kingdom.

But it seems that was too naive. Although I'm not sure what's causing it, the atmosphere here is heavy, as if the people are preparing for an attack that they're not even sure is coming.

"Hmph." Tylith releases her trademark sound. "The air may be tense, but that won't stop us from enjoying a nice meal."

"Yeah!" Belle agrees. "We put lunch off so we can try the food here, and I won't let something like these people's bad mood get in the way!"

"It appears our little cat-eared companion agrees." Tylith eyes Alisha, who looks to be on the verge of drooling already.

"Keep it together, Alisha. We're bound to find a street with restaurants soon."

"Ah! I'm not drooling!" She denies it, despite nobody having accused her of such. "But if it's food, then it's that way!"

Alisha points down a side street. With her animalistic senses, it's obvious she'd pick up on the smell of cooked food before anyone else. It's definitely because of her enhanced senses and not at all because she's a voracious carnivore.

As expected, Alisha's nose knows where to go. After walking only a short ways down the side street, even I pick up the smell of food cooking over an open fire.

We haven't done any fighting today, but we did run a long distance, so we worked up quite an appetite. The delicious aromas wafting from the shops and stalls is enough to stir my hunger, so I'm not surprised to see the girls eyeing them with anticipation.

"So many choices." Belle looks from one restaurant to the next.

"And yet there can only be one," I say.

"I vote a place that has good chicken."

"Ah! But what about Mr. Burger!?" Alisha asks.

"Hmph. Isn't it obvious that a bloody steak is the best choice?"

Seems Laya doesn't have anything particular in mind because she doesn't voice an opinion. As for which option we intend to go with, there's always an easy way for us to decide.

Tylith's hand slowly rises. "Seems you two really wish to engage me in battle. Who am I to stop you from walking straight into your doom?"

"Bold words," Belle says. "Especially coming from the one with the most losses among us."

"Don't think that the days of your superiority over me will continue forever. I've unlocked the dark powers that will allow me to seize victory at my own discretion."

"Oh, really. Then let's put those new powers to the test right here and now."

"I-I'm fighting, too!" Alisha steps up to the two girls, forming a triangle on the side of the street.

Each of them prepares their weapons of choice, yet they keep them hidden from their opponents' view, awaiting the right moment to bring them out and use them to attain victory.

After a tense moment of absolute stillness, the silence is broken by their warcries as each of them release their hidden armaments.

"Paper!" Tylith looks at Alisha's hand. "As expected of you!"

"Awww, why did you choose scissors! They're mean!"

"Not to worry, Alisha." Belle motions to her balled fist. "I won't let her win so easily!"

"Hmph. One of each means it's a stalemate. But don't think you can stall my victory forever!"

Laya and I watch on as the three girls do their usual routine. The first one to win two rounds will be labeled as the victor, but because they've gotten so good at predicting each other's moves, the games can sometimes drag on for minutes at a time.

As Belle said, Tylith is exceptionally poor at this game. Though that's only compared to the others, Alisha included. If she were to go up against anyone else, it would likely be a slaughter.

"Victory!" A single girl raises her hand into the air. "I can taste the chicken already!"

"How confounding...! To think my dark artes would be bested yet again!"

"Yay, chicken!" Alisha seems completely unphased at having lost.

"Good job." Laya congratulates Belle on her victory.

"Thanks! If there's one thing I'm confident in, it's knowing my friends better than they know me!"

"Isn't that just because you're nosey?" I ask.

"How rude! It's not nosey! It's because I have a caring personality!"

"That so? Well, I will admit..." I give her a pat on the back. "It's nice having people who care."

"A-ah, well that's only natural…" She looks away, her cheeks a bit rosier than normal.

"Since you won, we're at your mercy for the choice of lunch today. Chicken is actually my favorite, so I was rooting for you from—"

"Hey!" A deep voice cuts me off.

Turning, I see three guardsmen with scowls on their faces. We felt them moving around, but we didn't take any actions to avoid them.

First off, we're fully hiding our identities. Anyone with cat ears or vampiric, red eyes is using [Transform] to hide them. Meanwhile, our mana signatures are covered by my recently crafted Spell Orb that allows us to alter how it feels to anyone with the [Sense Mana] spell.

By all accounts, we should appear as a normal group of humans, although a wealthy one.

But it's not like we were just being careless. The simple fact is that we're sick of looking over our shoulder each time there's a slight hint of danger, especially now that the Goddess has given us her blessing in front of the entire city of Silvia.

Besides, calling a group of city guards dangerous is laughable. As I am now, I have enough power in my pinky finger to obliterate the entire city garrison. The same could be said for the girls, meaning there's absolutely no threat to us here.

So, even if we were to get harassed by guards, all we would feel is annoyance that we were interrupted on our lunch break.

But to our surprise, the guards aren't looking our way. Rather, they're stomping toward a young man and woman on the other side of the street. By the looks of it, they're a couple who've come here to eat.

From a quick inspection, I can't find anything strange about the couple. They're wearing decent clothing and are an average level. Neither of them have weapons, and I can't detect any mana signatures that could be a hidden artifact or the like.

Curious, we watch on as the three guards stop in front of the couple. It's obvious now that the two people are terrified, especially the girl, who's hiding behind the young man. Already, I can practically feel the hair bristling on Alisha's body, but she waits patiently, her eyes locked on the scene before us.

"You!" one of the guards yells. "You dare show your face around here!? Cowards should stay out of sight so real men don't have to look at them!"

"I-I already told you," the young man says. "I'm not a fighter. There's no way I could join the city guard and be sent off to fight in the beastkin lands…"

"That's why you're a coward! And if it weren't for men like you, I wouldn't have to be in this city right now! I'd be fighting by Lucas de Salemon's side, gaining glory on the battlefield! But because you and the rest of the sniveling cowards are too afraid to even sign up for patrol duty, I'm stuck walking these boring streets day after day! Yet you have the guts to say I'm overreacting!?"

"I … never said that. I just asked if–"

"Enough! I won't hear it again!" The guard takes an aggressive step forward. "Looks like one beating wasn't enough. But don't worry, I'll knock that cowardice out of you no matter how many times it takes. It'll be a good show for your little girlfriend, too. Maybe afterwards, she'll want to know what it's like to be with a real man."

The man tells his girlfriend to leave, and she takes a few steps back. But the young woman's path is blocked as the other two guards circle around, cutting off her escape.

"This time," the guard says, "I'll make sure the healer has his work cut out for him."

The guard's fist flies out, heading straight toward his victim's face. The young man brings his hands up, but he has no real way of defending himself against someone twice his level and outfitted in combat gear. It'll be a one-sided beating.

At least, it would be if his attacks could reach him.

"Don't bully people!" Alisha yells, the guard's fist in her grasp.

"Who the hell're you!? Looking for trouble, girl!? Then I'll–gah!"

Alisha delivers a soft kick to the guard's midsection. Although she held back to an insane degree, it was still enough to send the troublemaker flying.

There's a thud as he hits the ground, then a groan as he slowly stands back up. Despite hitting him in one of his most armored spots, Alisha managed to dent the metal on the man's cheap breastplate.

The people of this world understand that strength can't be determined at a glance, but that doesn't mean there aren't clues that can be used to estimate a person's power.

Among the ways to gauge strength, age is one of the most obvious. Nobody would look at the 13-year-old Alisha and guess that she's actually powerful enough to stand against an Archfiend. But sometimes, the expectations the people of this world rely on are completely betrayed.

"An ... adventurer!?" The guard says after getting his feet beneath him.

"You're not wrong," I say. "But you're still missing the mark. Though I don't care enough to explain everything to you."

I see the guard's eyes flicker to his two allies, but they've already been dealt with in a similar fashion.

"Now," I continue. "You said some very interesting things just now, so I'm going to need a few answers from you. Most importantly, who is Lucas de Salemon, and why is he attacking the beastkin?"

"F-fool!" He finally seems to regain some confidence. "So you don't even know who you're messing with!? Hah! Maybe I'll accept your apology if you beg!"

"Right, right. Just spill it already."

"Sir Lucas de Salemon used to rule the lands south of here before those filthy beastkin invaded! That's why now's the perfect time to take them back, while they're at war with Chaos!

"As for who he is..." The guard's smile widens. "Of course he's the father of the Great Hero summoned by none other than the Goddess herself, Sir Cedric de Salemon!"

"Yeah, I figured, considering the surname."

"You ... figured?" His confidence begins to wane. "You knew, yet you still attacked the guards under his direct command!? Are you insane!? He'll have your head for it!"

"I've had far more powerful people than him come after my head. As you can see, it's still attached, and I don't plan to let it go any time soon."

"T-then, what are you going to—"

His words are cut off when I lift him off his feet. He struggles, landing several kicks, but I barely even feel them.

Next thing he knows, he's flying through the air. Like before, he smacks into the ground and ends up in a heap. But this time, he's joined by his two companions.

"I hope you have a nice journey." I raise my hand toward the fallen men.

"Magic!?" The guard scrambles to his feet, as do his two companions. However...

"Guh...!" They all collapse at the same time.

Their eyes move from me to the source of the [Shock] spell that just paralyzed their bodies. Laya stands with her hand still outstretched, looking down at them as if eyeing bugs that she intends to squash.

"On the ground where you belong, worms."

A pattern appears beneath the guards. It's one that many people have likely never seen, but those who have would never forget.

"Teleportation!?"

That's the last word the guard gets out before he and his two companions vanish from sight.

*Guess now we know why the people of this city seem so frightened. Being harassed by your own city guards doesn't seem ideal for fostering a healthy community...*

"What...?" The young man looks at the spot where the guards vanished.

"Don't worry about it," I say. "You won't be seeing them for quite a while, assuming they ever make it back."

"Where ... did you send them?"

"To the capital city of Roshar. It's about two weeks by foot, so even if they start walking now, it'll all be over by the time they get back."

"Over? What are you going to do?" The man shows a hint of fear.

"Nothing super crazy. Just go meet that hero's father and prevent him from starting a war with the beastkin."

"That's not crazy!? Who exactly are you!?"

"Me?" I think back to the Goddess' words when she told me that I needed to gain the people's faith. "I'm this world's one true hero, Lutz."

# Chapter 4: Fate of Steel

## ----- Lutz -----

"This is … terrible," I say.

"Master…" Alisha looks down at the city with sad eyes.

"Wasn't expecting our first visit to a beastkin city to end up like this."

"If what the people in the other city told us is true," Belle says, "then this city is contested territory, often changing hands between humans and beastkin. It's no wonder that it's in such bad shape."

"Yeah. Getting conquered over and over is bound to take its toll on a city. And since Lucas de Salemon just recently took it by force, I guess this is the result."

The city gate we saw had been blown open, no doubt by mages during a siege. After that, there was likely a bloody battle, as the section of the city just beyond the gate was nothing but rubble.

We're currently leaping far above the city, so we have a clear view of just how widespread the destruction is. It seems no neighborhood escaped unscathed, with entire buildings having collapsed in some sections.

Whether the mass destruction was from battle or simply to frighten the inhabitants, I can't say for sure. But no matter the reason, the result is obvious. Most of the homes below are empty, making me wonder what their former inhabitants' ultimate fate was.

*Hopefully they managed to escape. But … perhaps that's wishful thinking.*

Even though the beastkin homes are empty, that doesn't mean that they're all gone from the city. Many of them wander the streets. The problem is they're bound in chains and are being led around by human soldiers.

When we saw that, Alisha wanted to go cut down the soldiers right then and there. But I managed to calm her just enough to prevent a full-scale battle from breaking out.

When I explained that fighting our way through the city would only increase the chance of the captured beastkin getting hurt, she understood what we needed to do.

"When we meet Lucas de Salemon," Alisha says, "he's going to pay."

"I'll leave him to you. But at least let me talk to him a bit."

"Yes. It would be good if he confessed to his crimes first."

We already know where he is. At least, where he likely is. During our short reconnaissance before entering the city, we saw an extravagant mansion, probably used by the city lord. Compared to the other buildings, it seemed to have miraculously escaped damage.

Though more likely, it had less to do with miracles and more to do with the man who conquered this city. Cedric came from a noble family, and they ruled a land on the southern border that was conquered by beastkin.

The guard I teleported to the capital said this was their territory before they lost it to the beastkin country of Belfast. That means the mansion isn't just a random noble's home. It's likely the one their family used to live in when they ruled this territory.

Now that his son has been chosen as one of the Great Heroes, Lucas has gotten bold, using the sudden boost to his reputation to raise an army to retake his former land. I've never met the man, nor have I heard anything about him other than a few, recent details. But I already know what kind of person he is.

*Using his new power for selfish gain when the world is on the brink of destruction…*

*Yeah, sounds about right for the father of one of those rotten heroes.*

"Okay," I say. "Let's descend."

"Plan?" Laya asks.

"Nothing fancy. We're gonna barge right in and meet with Lucas."

"What about the beastkin, Master?"

"We'll be asking for their unconditional release in exchange for sparing the soldiers' lives."

"Most of their lives." Alisha's already in her scale mail armor, sword in hand.

We hit the ground just in front of the mansion. There aren't any guards at the door, but there are many of them relaxing on the grounds, enjoying their victory against the beastkin.

When a mysterious group suddenly drops from the sky, of course it would raise alarm. So, it's no surprise to see many of the men jump to their feet.

"Who are you!?" one yells.

"I highly suggest you sit back down," I say to him.

"Hey! That girl's a beastkin!"

"Listen to Master. Or else."

"Tch! Like we'll let you just do as you want!" He looks at the soldiers around him. "Capture them!"

"I warned you."

A [Shockwave] flies toward their commander, originating from Alisha's sword. Even though she's not yet buffed by [Protector], her stats have grown enough that the skill is a death sentence to any average person caught in its path.

By the standards of the humans who aren't off fighting against the fiends, the commander is no slouch, with his level being several steps above the men around him.

But it's not enough.

"I-impossible...!" That's the last word he'll ever speak.

Seeing their leader cut down in an instant, the other soldiers can't help but second guess their attack. Many of them stop in their tracks, while the ones that don't join their commander on the ground before they can even reach us.

"A vampire...!" one of them yells.

"And even an elf!? What's going on!?"

"Adventurers! No other group can be so diverse and powerful!"

"Adventurers from the beastkin lands? They aren't supposed to get involved in wars!"

"What other explanation can there be!?"

While the men argue over who we are, we make our way up the steps, stopping in front of the mansion's door. Turns out, it's not even locked, so we let ourselves in.

The soldiers cautiously follow us, but they stay at a safe distance. No doubt they can't be seen deserting from battle when a group is heading straight for their lord. Were we to be defeated, the ones who ran would likely be executed for their cowardice. Such is the way of this world.

During the commotion, a few soldiers ran off to inform Lucas. That's convenient for us, since it means we can skip past the surprise and get right to the point.

I expected him to gather his men and meet us in the mansion's hallways, but it seems he wants the meeting to take place in the room he's been in since the beginning.

We reach that door, soldiers behind us and many more waiting inside. There are over ten men for each one of us, and I can feel the mana of the rest of the soldiers converging on the mansion at this very moment.

No doubt, Lucas wants to intimidate us with the hundreds of men he has under his command. But if it's only in the realm of hundreds, then it can barely even be considered a challenge for us as we are now.

I finally push open the door, and a luxurious room fills my vision. Seems even the beastkin lords prefer to live in comfort because the furnishings look right at home in the noble estates I've visited over the months.

However, none of that interests me right now. My focus is entirely on the man we came to see.

Lucas sits in an ornate chair, flanked by a dozen of his most powerful men. Several times that fill the rest of the room, while the ones behind us pile in, completely surrounding us.

"Adventurers," Lucas says. "Whether it's humans or beastkin, you're not allowed to involve yourselves in war. I hope you aren't too attached to your jobs, because after today, you'll be stripped of your Guild IDs. If you live long enough to regret your decision, that is."

"You're right that we're adventurers. But I don't care about things like whether or not we're kicked from the guild."

"Taking your supposed ideas of justice into your own hands is more important than being an adventurer? I'm surprised you lasted more than a month, as those with such idiotic ideals are often ousted quickly."

"You're one to speak. As soon as you gained the authority from your close relations to one of the Great Heroes, you sought your own form of justice by taking back your old lands."

"Hah." Lucas gives us a sneer. "Those at the top aren't shackled by the same collar that binds your ilk. If you had learned that lesson sooner, then perhaps you wouldn't be in this predicament."

"Oh trust me, that lesson was made very clear to me as soon as I was summoned to this world. But there's one thing you're wrong about. It's not us who's in danger here. It's you."

"Summoned to this world...?" Lucas' sneer slowly fades. "Brown hair, silver overcoat, spear, little elven companion...!"

"Ah, you finally figured it out."

"You're the damn False Hero!"

At his announcement, the already tense atmosphere seems close to boiling over. Men who were already prepared for a battle with an uncertain outcome now turn grim, as if the hope of a peaceful resolution had just been snatched from beneath their feet, sending them tumbling.

With the hostility having turned to desperation, it's a miracle the soldiers don't attack immediately. But perhaps because they're in the presence of a Great Hero's father, they hold onto some slim hope that this meeting between us is a form of destiny that will result in my defeat.

As for Lucas, the man isn't just a confident leader. He has the strength to back up his arrogant attitude. Although he can't compare to something like an Archfiend, he would probably be a good match for the king.

When surrounded by people much lower level than himself, having that much strength is bound to go to his head. At some point, he likely began conflating his higher numbers to his personal skills and ability, forgetting the privilege provided to him by his position at the top of this world's hierarchy.

I've seen the same arrogance many times in video games from people with better gear or optimized builds that they copied from online guides. When defeating opponents who aren't min-maxed like themselves, they often claim to be the better player, even if they were afforded a huge benefit from their numerical advantages.

Perhaps that's why instead of fear, Lucas only shows us an arrogant smile.

"I was already destined to rise to the rank of Duke," Lucas says. "The highest noble class. But if I defeat you here, then even the king won't be able to refuse tying my great family to his own. I do believe Princess Lumina's hand would be an appropriate reward for Cedric, given our generous contributions to the war against Chaos."

"You…" The casual tone in my voice is gone, replaced with a deathly whisper. "…Really shouldn't have said that."

"To think…" Laya says.

"…you would dare…" Belle continues.

"…even dream…" Alisha adds.

"…of such sacrilege!" Tylith finishes.

"The hell's got you so worked up?" Lucas asks. "Don't tell me you have a thing for—!"

His words end abruptly, with his jaw clenching so hard that his tongue wasn't able to get out of the way of his teeth before they slammed together.

As blood drips down his chin from his injured tongue, Lucas looks to the hundred or so men around him. Without exception, each of them are locked in place, with the only sound coming from them being the clanking of metal as they shake in fear.

"Hy … [Hypnosis]…!" Lucas manages to squeeze out. "Impossible … so many…!"

"You think this is all?" I ask. "I wonder how the hundred or so men in the mansion's halls and grounds outside are faring right now."

"No, you're lying…!"

"Hah…" I let out a sigh. "This is why dealing with conceited idiots is tiresome. Whatever…"

After my words, someone steps forward. They walk with purpose, with each step hitting the wooden floor like a war drum counting the seconds just before a battle begins.

Lucas is still sitting in his ornate chair, frozen in fear. It's all he can do to look up at the approaching figure's face when they eventually reach him, casting what now appears to be a very dark shadow as they loom over him.

"Because of you…" Alisha says. "Because of you, my people had to suffer again! Always! There's always someone like you who only knows how to hurt others!"

She raises her sword, and it seems to ring with a deathly toll. "But don't worry. Because for every person who offers only misery, there's another willing to rid the world of it. And today … that person is me!"

"W-wait, you can't—"

Lucas isn't even able to beg for his life before Alisha's sword falls. Despite her anger, the young catgirl has no desire to make anyone suffer, no matter how twisted they may be.

Her blade pierces Lucas directly in his heart, bringing an abrupt end to his life.

With their lord slain so easily, the soldiers visibly lose all will to fight. Most of them were recently conscripted and aren't even real soldiers, so having to face a group powerful enough to waltz in and take out their general is far too much for them.

However, there's still one more thing to do before Tylith and I release them from [Hypnosis].

"Listen closely!" I say. "Because I won't be repeating myself. Any soldiers who leave the city and go back north will get to keep their lives. Those who think to carry off any loot or mistreat any beastkin on their way out … well, you'll be joining your lord shortly after."

Finally, we cancel the Dark Magic that has bound the hundred soldiers around us, along with a hundred more in and around the mansion.

Like a dam that's suddenly collapsed, a tidal wave of men flood the room's only exit, seeking to be the first out the northern gate and back to the safety of the city they came from.

"Girls, let's split up and ensure that any soldiers who think my words an empty threat learn a quick and deadly lesson."

Since the door and halls are crowded with fleeing soldiers, the five of us shatter the nearby window and leap out, fully prepared to make examples out of any men bold enough to refuse my generous offer.

----------

My hands grip the collar placed on a middle-aged beastkin woman's neck. It's loose enough on her that my fingers have no trouble fully wrapping around the poorly crafted metal.

There's a soft groan as the lock that holds the collar together is stressed to its limits by the force of my pulling. A second later, it snaps, sending pieces of metal falling to the dirt. The rest of the collar follows after, the shackles that bound her now twisted into ruin.

"Any injuries?" I ask.

"No..."

"That's good. If you go to the elf right over there, she'll give you a few supplies. It's not much, but it'll fill you up."

"Why..."

"Why?"

"Why!? Why couldn't you arrive sooner!? My daughter... they ...they...!" She turned and stumbled away, almost in a daze.

"I'm ... sorry..."

In everyone's favorite stories, the hero always arrives in time to save the people in need just before things go terribly wrong. But life ... life isn't always so accommodating.

"Master. It's okay. You're doing your best."

"Alisha ... thank you."

"There you go, sweety." Belle's soft voice comes from beside me. "No more scary collar."

She tosses the shackles onto the growing pile at her feet. Thanks to her excessively high level, even a mage like Belle can easily tear these steel collars in half with her bare hands.

"Mommy," the little beastkin girl says. "Is Daddy going to be free, too?"

"Daddy is ... daddy is going to be away for a while."

"Eh? How long?"

"A ... very long time."

The mother ushers her child away, trying desperately to hide the pain on her face.

*Dammit. Why is it always the innocent ones who have to suffer because the people with power always want more?*

We've been freeing, healing, and feeding the unfortunate beastkin who weren't able to flee before Lucas broke through the city gates. It's been well over an hour already, yet more people are still arriving, collars on their necks or injuries on their bodies.

We were met with a lot of suspicion at first, but when I showed them the body of the general who brought them all this suffering, they understood. The fact that Alisha supported our words also helped, though just having a beastkin with us doesn't necessarily mean we're going to have an easy ride here in their lands.

Just like humans, there are good and bad people in every society. Anyone we meet on our journey through their lands will naturally be on guard against a group that contains humans and a vampire, no matter what Alisha says.

Even the elves, who are notoriously loyal to their own kind, treated us as prisoners when we first arrived on their border. The best we can hope for from the beastkin is to not be attacked outright.

*"I'm returning."* Tylith's voice echoes in our minds.

*"Okay, the coast is clear."*

I feel a convergence of mana behind me, directly in the center of the teleportation circle Tylith created about an hour ago.

Since we wanted to help these people as much as we could, I sent her to the city north of here to buy some extra supplies. It's the very same city that Lucas gathered his men from, so it's only right that they be the ones who help these people get back on their feet.

I did tell her to pay a fair price, of course. The shopkeepers had nothing to do with Lucas' decision to invade the beastkin country of Belfast, so just stealing from them would make us no better than the man who caused this situation in the first place.

"How was the trip?" I ask after Tylith reappears.

"I believe the journey was exceedingly beneficial." She steps into a wide-open spot. "Behold the bounty obtained to rid this city's inhabitants of its hunger!"

A small mountain of food appears in the clearing, taller than Tylith herself. Each piece is a type of vegetable or fruit that has an outer layer which can be peeled, otherwise she would have never thrown them out onto the ground.

As for the more delicate food like meats, they appear atop a proper table, stacked up so high that I worry a strong breeze will topple them. Another table appears, along with a random assortment of edibles that don't fit in any of the other categories.

All in all, it's enough to feed hundreds, maybe a thousand. Although, even that won't fill the bellies of all the beastkin in this city for long.

"Hmm." Tylith taps her chin. "I seem to be out of tables. I suppose I'll bring out the rest once some of this has been handed out."

"There's more?"

"I bought twice as much as you see here. Enough to feed two thousand or so."

"Great job. That'll probably give them enough for a week if they ration it out. Hopefully, it'll be enough time for more help to arrive."

"Is there anything else we can do, Master?"

"I'd like to offer some gold to help rebuild the city, but even I can't just throw around that much coin."

"Then what about donating some to the church?" Belle says. "They'll make sure it gets to the hands of those who need it."

"The church, huh? Yeah. Yeah, I think that's a good idea."

Eventually, the beastkin who need their collars removed dwindle, then disappear entirely. There are still many who need to be fed, but Laya and Belle stay behind to distribute the mountains of food on the tables.

As for me, Alisha, and Tylith, we head toward a nearby church. The human army left the building untouched, though whether they did the same for the clergy is still a mystery. But it won't remain a mystery for long.

The doors are already open, as if inviting the desolate people inside to fill their heavy hearts with spiritual hope. As we step inside, we do in fact see a group of priests tending to the unfortunates. They don't have much to offer other than words, but it's clear that many have come here for that reason alone.

"You must be the adventurers who freed the city," a dog-eared priest says after catching sight of us.

"Yeah, that's us."

"The Goddess works in mysterious ways. The humans brought great tragedy, but they also brought salvation." He looks to Tylith. "Seems the rumors of vampires and elves were true. How strange to see all the races gathered into a single group."

"Just how things turned out. But enough of that, we're here to give you some things to help the city."

"Supplies? We'll take any you have to offer." He looks at our empty hands. "Did you park a cart outside?"

"No, we don't use carts." An apple appears in my hand, which I hold out to the priest. "Show me to a room with plenty of empty space."

"Fascinating." He takes the apple. "Please, follow me."

As Belle suggested, we offload the rest of our recently obtained supplies at the church. They'll have the reach and authority to spread it amongst the people who need it, something we don't have the time to do effectively.

The priests who are here to help distribute the food and gold can hardly believe their eyes. Having such a massive stock of supplies suddenly filling the room must have been quite a shock, as they stand frozen like statues.

"Who are you?" the original priest asks. "No such magic as this should even exist."

"I'm..."

I haven't told any of the people here who I really am. It seems my identity isn't well known in the beastkin lands, probably because the humans didn't spend nearly as much time spreading the name and likeness of the False Hero to their long-time enemies.

But it's not because of my reputation that I haven't told anyone in the city. It just seemed that using this disaster as an excuse to spread my name as a hero would be in bad taste. These people have gone through true suffering. There's no way they'd want to deal with someone looking to boost their reputation at a time like this.

"Master, please tell him. She said it was for the sake of the world, didn't she?"

"Alisha... you're right. I hate the idea, but you're right. I need their faith." I shake my head. "No, that's not right. This world needs someone to believe in, someone who can lead them to victory. And whether I like it or not ... that person is me."

"While I can agree with your reservations," Tylith says. "You must be willing to reach your hand out so those who seek salvation can take hold. You may sometimes end up getting burned, but that's why we're here, isn't it?"

"Yeah." Alisha nods at Tylith's words. "We know the truth, and that's all that matters, right?"

"I guess ... I guess you two are right." I turn toward the priest. "My name is Lutz, though you might know me by my title of False Hero. I was summoned by the Goddess herself to put an end to Chaos, and I intend to do just that."

"What...!"

As expected, the priests are in disbelief after hearing my introduction. Back when I was first summoned, it was common for people to attack me after hearing who I am, but things are different these days.

It's obvious that I'm far too powerful for even this entire city to defeat. After all, I routed the army that breached their gates and occupied the city. What could the remnants of these defeated people hope to do to me?

"Anyway," I say. "Do whatever you want with the supplies. We're done here, so we'll be leaving the city."

The priests watch on with uncertainty as the three of us walk out to the prayer room where the beastkin are still giving their thanks to the Goddess for sparing them. Or perhaps they're asking for more help to survive the coming hardships.

Either way, there's nothing else for us to do here. We don't have time to see to their each and every need, not if we want to make it to Dragon Island and meet the Dragon Lord before the war against Chaos is lost.

"Wait!"

Turning, I see the priest walking toward us down the main aisleway.

"Are you ... really him?"

"Yeah, I am. Check it out when you get a chance. Brown hair and eyes, silver overcoat, little elven companion. Take a good look and decide for yourself later."

"I ... don't understand. The Goddess would never lie to us. So why would the enemy of the four races save this city?"

"Not everything is as it seems, priest. The Goddess is fighting her own battle, and her opponent is crafty enough to put out a false prophecy."

"That's...!"

"Believe what you will." I turn to the nearby church door. "Let's go."

We leave the man still standing undecided, and the mid-afternoon sun hits us as we step back out into the open air.

Laya and the others haven't handed out all the supplies, but we just leave the rest for the city's residents to pick through on their own. We take the tables, though. But I at least put the food on a blanket instead of the ground.

Just like that, we leave the city. It was a bittersweet beginning to our journey through the beastkin lands. But at least we managed to improve the lives of many downtrodden people.

"So, where to next?" Belle asks, obviously trying to get our minds to focus on what's ahead of us instead of behind us.

I open up the map in my hand. "There are a few villages on the way to the next major city. I figured we could stop by and explore the beastkin culture a bit."

"Yeah!" Alisha happily agrees. "I want to see all the things I remember from my childhood again!"

"Mmm. It'll be interesting to see how it differs from the human lands."

"I'm in agreement," Tylith says. "With my venture into your homeland, I'll have a good grasp on each of the four races cultures."

"It'll be amazing!" Alisha rushes ahead of the group. "Hurry, hurry! I wanna see it!"

"Well," I say. "Don't want to keep our resident catgirl waiting, do we?"

With a quick cast of [Gale], our speed rises to such a degree that a cross-country trip becomes a simple matter.

And so, our journey through the beastkin lands truly begins.

# Chapter 5: Lock and Key

## ----- Lutz -----

"Really?" Belle says. "Another dungeon?"

"Dungeons are important. How else are we going to get stronger?"

"Well, yeah. But we just got out of one barely a week ago! And what happened to exploring the beastkin's culture!?"

"Don't worry, don't worry. I already said we're not going to conquer it right now, didn't I? We're just going to take a look … and maybe step inside for a bit and see what it has to offer. At most, we'll conquer the first floor to see what kind of monsters and loot are inside."

"Yeah, right. I can hear it now. Just one more floor, just one more floor. Soon enough, we'll be at the Dungeon Orb!"

"Haha…"

"That's not a denial!"

"I believe it would be a beneficial trek," Tylith says. "If we can obtain another 20 or so levels in a matter of days, it may give us all the strength we need to save the world."

Laya shakes her head. "I'm against it. The Goddess requested for us to meet the Dragon Lord and gain access to the Mana Network. I believe that should be our top priority."

"True. I suppose we don't know how much longer we have before the human defense crumbles and the fiends run rampant through the world. But that just makes me more anxious to increase our levels as much as possible."

"Mmm. But if we place a teleportation circle here, we can return after meeting with the Dragon Lord. I believe that to be the correct option."

"As much as I want to grind," I say. "Laya's right. The Goddess wouldn't tell me to meet the Dragon Lord without good reason. I'm really just curious about this mysterious dungeon."

"Yes. I admit that I'm intrigued, as well."

"I know right!? A dungeon that not a single adventurer has even been able to enter? Really makes me wonder what secrets it holds inside! Normal enemies that are as strong as bosses, hidden super guardians powerful enough to push us to our limits, and god-like treasure the likes this world has never seen! There are so many possibilities!"

"Drool."

"I-I'm not drooling!" I wipe my mouth, just in case. "Ahem. Anyway, as interesting as it sounds, we'll only take a peek for now. Though if it lives up to even an ounce of my expectations, we'll be returning soon."

"If we can get inside."

"That's true."

Before we parted ways with Lumina, we discussed other dungeons that may help us reach the next pinnacle of power, should we need it. The Beast Warrens we conquered is one of the most dangerous dungeons in the Orakian Kingdom, so we picked her brain about potential places we could grind next.

Of all the ones we talked about, the one we're heading to now caught my interest the most. The only thing known about it is the shape of the building that houses the dungeon. But even that left many lingering questions, as it's supposed to be small and simple, as far as dungeons go.

Even though nobody's ever stepped foot inside, it's still recognized as a dungeon without any doubts. First off, the walls are completely indestructible, which is a tell-tale sign in itself. But even if that weren't enough, the dungeon text sitting above the only set of doors would suffice.

Of course, as the only one who can read dungeon text, I'm hoping I can find a clue on how to open the doors after reading it. And since the dungeon is virtually on route to Dragon Island, stopping by to check it out is a no-brainer.

"Master, I see something!" She points toward a nearby hill.

I follow the direction of Alisha's finger. "Alright! We're here!"

We rush toward the building peeking out from behind the hilltop. By we, I mean me and Alisha. The other girls aren't nearly as excited, though I have a feeling Tylith is simply trying to appear casual.

When we reach the top of the hill, Alisha and I look down over the landscape, taking in the sight of the mysterious dungeon.

"Black stone," I say. "No windows or anything, just smooth walls. Even the ceiling is flat and bare."

"Eh? Is it really a dungeon, Master? It's so tiny."

"I know what you mean. It looks a little too tall for a one-story building and too short for a two story. Either way, there's not much room to fit a dungeon inside it."

"Could it be that we'll have to go underground?"

"Maybe so. Really, that's the only logical conclusion, unless it does something really crazy like teleport us halfway across the world to fight in some strange land."

"Wow! We might go somewhere that far away!?"

"Who knows. It's just a possibility we have to keep in mind."

During our conversation, we make it to the base of the dungeon, where a set of double doors teases us. The other girls arrive shortly after, and we all stare at the mysterious building that houses a dungeon nobody's ever been able to enter.

The others find me staring at a spot just above the door. The dungeon text I'm looking at captivates me to such a degree that the words I intended to say don't come out, leaving my mouth hanging open.

I can feel the gazes of the girls burning into me as they each wait for me to read it out loud, but it takes one of them to speak up to break me from my stupor.

"Well," Belle says. "Are you going to share it with us?"

"Ah, sorry. I just ... I didn't expect this. Not at all..." I swap focus, looking to the girls. "The dungeon text says, 'Door to the Heavens'."

"Wait! Isn't that the place the nine-tailed foxgirl told us to find!?"

"Yeah, Kiah. She said she'd tell me whatever secrets she knows if I found this place. And ... here it is."

"Detour?" Laya asks.

"Sorry. I really want to know what's inside, so I was thinking of meeting with Kiah."

"Mmm. She's close, so it won't take long."

"Yeah." I check my [Minimap]. "Rin's dot is only a few hours east of here if I pull out all the stops."

Tylith nods at my words. "You mean if you enchant your gear for maximum speed and use teleportation to cover large distances."

"Exactly. Without a teleportation circle, the spell's distance is greatly limited, but it's enough to cover a full day's walking distance for a normal traveler. And with my insane speed while leaping through the air, I can get there in less than three hours."

"And getting back will be an even simpler matter, as long as you place a teleportation circle here before you go."

"Exactly, which means I can be back here with Kiah in just a handful of hours. I'd say it's a worthy detour, considering the potential this place has now."

The other girls give their nods, so we make a quick change to our plans. I'll be going east to fetch Kiah, while the girls stay here.

Since it takes more mana for each person I teleport, it'll be quicker if I go alone. Besides, the only person who can really keep up with my full speed is Laya, with Tylith not far behind.

But since I'll just be rushing there without pause, there's no reason for all of us to go. Instead, the other girls can use this chance to enjoy a bit of downtime or do some chores. After all, I won't be leaving them here without a place to relax.

My hand comes up, and the clearing that sits just beside the so-called dungeon becomes a temporary yard for the cabin we call home.

The ground isn't perfectly level, but Laya immediately steps inside and uses the Master Orb to activate the [Earth Wall] spell. A foundation lifts the cabin just high enough to keep it level and prevent any stress points from causing wear and tear on its joints.

"Alright," I say. "With that, you girls should be good for a few hours. Of course, message me right away if anything happens."

"What a worry wart!" Belle says.

"Worry wart, worry wart!" Alisha happily echoes her friend's words.

I shake my head, holding back a sigh. "Yeah, I should have seen that coming. Anyway, I'm off. See you all in a few hours."

"Bye-bye!" Alisha sees me off with a smile.

The other girls do the same in their own ways, then I turn to the east and activate [Teleport].

----------

My feet touch the ground for the first time in about half an hour. Thanks to my recent grinding session, my stats have grown enough that the [Air Step] spell lets me stay in the sky for nearly forty minutes. And since the cooldown is so short, the time I spend walking on dirt is close to zero.

However, despite my spell having already come off cooldown, I don't step back into the skies. The reason for that is simple. I've arrived at my destination.

Or to be more precise, I'm close enough to it that it'd be better if I walked the rest of the way.

*Man, they really built their homes this far from civilization, huh?*

*They really must be hermits, like Rin said. Though I guess I can't blame them, considering they need to protect Kiah.*

As of now, I haven't actually seen any of their houses. There's still nothing but a thick forest around me, which is a great natural barrier against any groups looking to explore or settle the area. And I know from my recent trek through the skies that a tall mountain range protects the other side of their hidden base.

But that's not the only way these people protect their home.

"Stop!" a voice calls from the depths of the forest. "Drop any weapons and present your hands!"

I do as the voice asks, though there's no weapon to drop since they're all in my [Inventory]. Still, I make a show of looking as innocent as possible to hopefully earn a bit of their trust.

Even though only one of them spoke out, I can feel the mana of four others hiding nearby, no doubt pointing weapons straight at me. They also have me completely surrounded to ensure they maximize their advantage in case it comes to a battle.

As I hoped, I get the chance to put a face to the voice as the one who called out to me leaps down from the branch of a nearby tree. She's a foxgirl with sandy brown hair, dressed in a familiar looking garment that looks more like a ceremonial robe than a battle outfit. Though the one this girl is wearing seems like a step down compared to the robe Rin wears.

"This domain is forbidden to outsiders," she says. "Leave."

"Yeah, I knew it was forbidden. But I can't just leave without at least checking out your so-called domain."

"You knew!?" Her posture immediately turns hostile. "How did you hear about us, and what was your reason for coming here!?"

I turn my head, taking in the sight of two more female warriors stepping into view, their weapons drawn. The final pair stays hidden, ready to surprise me in case these three can't handle me alone.

Of course, I'm not going to let this turn into a battle. Hopefully.

"I came here to fulfill a promise with Kiah."

"How do you know that name!?"

"Rin told me."

"Rin...! So she was speaking of such things while in the human lands!"

"Well, Kiah was there with us, and she approved of everything Rin told us, so I don't think you can really be mad at her."

"Silence! We'll get the truth from you soon enough." She readies her sword. "You will be coming with me."

"Sure. That's convenient, actually. Though I'd rather tag along as a guest instead of a prisoner."

"Fool. That decision belongs to me."

"Well, something tells me you may have a contender to your title of decision maker soon."

"Huh? Speak in a way we can understand, human!"

"I was just saying that—ah, it's too late."

Another person drops down from a nearby tree, landing just a few paces from both me and the foxgirl I've been talking to. Unlike the others, this new person doesn't have their weapon drawn. Rather, she looks relaxed, as if there's not a single threat, despite the tense atmosphere.

"I didn't think you'd pay us a visit so soon," the new girl says. "But did you have to send such a vague telepathic message? I was fortunate that our protector was able to point me in your direction."

"Hey, Rin." I give my friend a wry smile. "I knew she'd help you find me, and it ended up working out in the end, right? Oh, and to be honest, even I didn't expect to stop by today."

"This visit was a surprise, even to you? Then does that mean something sudden spurred your arrival?"

"Yeah, though it's probably best to save that for when we meet with Kiah."

"Rin!" The noisy one shouts. "Who is this man!? And why does he expect to be given the honor of meeting with our great protector!?"

"My apologies, Liz. Surely you recall that I received help in finding and rescuing our protector, do you not?"

"Yes, I remember. Are you saying this young human was that help you spoke of!?"

"Indeed. Without him, I would likely have failed in my mission to bring her home."

The other foxgirl, Liz, looks back to me. Despite having Rin speak up on my behalf, the scowl on her face tells me she hasn't changed her opinion one bit.

"Fine," she says. "He can enter our domain. But don't think I trust you or anything! I'll be watching your every move!"

"Please don't look too much. I'm a little shy."

"I don't care about that!"

Rin shakes her head. "Give up, Liz. You won't win. Now, please follow me. Kiah is waiting."

Rin turns and begins to walk casually through the forest. I follow, with Liz and the rest of the foxgirls bringing up the rear.

*This is turning out to be a very interesting trip.*

Last time I saw Rin, she explained that her and her companions were known as Battle-Maidens. They exist solely to protect Kiah, one of the Immortal Beings, which explains why the foxkin here are several steps above what I'd expect to encounter in the human lands.

As for Rin herself, she was chosen as the Valkyrie, a position that makes her Kiah's personal protector. It's only given to the most capable and devoted warrior of each generation, and I have to agree that she was a great choice.

After a short trek through the forest, the foxgirls and I step out into a wide clearing. Unlike the wild woods behind me, the grassy plain I'm now walking in has every hallmark of civilization I can think of.

Buildings fill the area, both massive in size and unique in their construction. Made from a kind of white stone, they remind me of the documentaries I've seen on places like ancient Greece. Stone pillars holding up roofs, walkways topped with arches, and chiseled designs carved directly into the stone.

Bricked paths lead from one building to the next, though the stones used are far more colorful than the white rock seen in the major constructions. It's hard to tell the size of the city at a glance, but it must have dozens of huge buildings, if not more.

Along the paths walk a variety of foxkin, some with white, poofy tails and others with long, black ears. Each of them is distinct in their own way, but they're all foxes, just like Rin. Oh, and there's one more similarity they share.

"Uh, Rin. Could it be that your home is filled with nothing but girls?"

"Ah, right. I suppose you weren't aware. Only female foxkin are allowed to reside in our domain."

"Okay. But that leaves me with a lot of unanswered questions."

"Hm? Such as?"

"Ah, actually ... it's probably best I don't dig too deep."

"I see. Well, if you decide otherwise, simply ask."

*How exactly would I ask about how you maintain a population this size without any men around?*

I ignore the lingering questions and return my focus to the city around me. Or rather, my eyes are drawn to the foxgirls who have finally noticed that I'm being escorted by a group of their guards.

I expected them to look at me with contempt, as Liz likes to do. But it feels more like they're appraising me, as a merchant would do when trying to decide if an item is worth purchasing.

It makes me feel a bit uneasy, like I'm a piece of meat they intend to slice up and serve at a dinner party. Other than that, I can't sense any hostility, despite their domain supposedly being off limits to outsiders like me.

"Finally taking one for yourself, Rin?" a passing foxgirl asks.

"A-as if!" Rin gets uncharacteristically loud. "You know the rules!"

"It's a shame," another says. "The Valkyrie isn't allowed to partake."

"Yes, it'd be bad for our great protector if the Valkyrie were unable to fight for months on end."

"Guess that means he's for us. What do you girls think about him?"

"A bit scrawny for my tastes," a third says.

"Oh? But he looks healthy, if a little young."

"Then I'll wait and see what he has to offer before deciding. I wonder how capable he is as a warrior."

"If he came here alone," another voice says, "then he must be quite strong."

"And it's rare for a human to visit. I wonder if he'll end up being popular simply due to his exotic nature."

Their conversation continues, with Rin pointedly ignoring them as she leads me down the city streets. Because she's ahead of me, I can only see a bit of her cheek, which has turned a light shade of red.

*So that's how they keep their population going. It's a bit … well, I guess it makes sense, but it's still discomforting.*

Ignoring the vultures, I return my focus to the amazing architecture that surrounds me. Now that I'm up close and personal, it's obvious what some of the buildings are used for.

The homes are still made of the same white stone, with eaves held up by thin, stone pillars. But the roofs are tiled red, similar to what I normally see in human cities, though the shade and texture of the red tile is obviously different, even from a layman's perspective.

Scattered through the city are other buildings, with shapes distinctly different from the houses. Some of them are much larger, with domed roofs that allow for large, open spaces inside. The design of these other buildings is far more detailed and intricate, with carved pillars and stone statues adding to their architectural beauty.

*That one looks like it might be a temple of sorts. And that one's definitely some kind of arena.*

*As for that one … w-wait! Why aren't they wearing any clothes!?*

I quickly turn my head away from a group of foxgirls standing outside a particularly popular building, but not before a few of them catch me staring wide-eyed at their birthday suits.

"Oh my," one says. "Looks like I'm having a feast after dinner tonight."

"Save some for me," another says. "You weren't the only one he was looking at with those hungry eyes, after all."

*No, there was nothing hungry in them, I swear.*

I try to convince myself of that fact as I face forward, completely ignoring my surroundings.

*I didn't know I was in such dangerous territory. Even a dungeon can't compare to a place where people walk out of the bathhouse nude without a care.*

After another short trek, we finally arrive at the object that's looming over the entire city. It caught my eye as soon as I left the forest, but I've been ignoring it since I knew Rin would bring me here. Kiah is nearby, after all, and she's the one I need to speak to.

The gigantic pyramid that acts as the centerpiece of Rin's city towers before me, the many thousands of square-cut rocks that make up its structure eclipsing even me in height, while being as thick and wide as they are tall.

*I've never been to any of the pyramids on Earth, but...*

*...This one would definitely be a match for any of them.*

There's another interesting fact about the pyramid, which helps explain why the Battle-Maidens around here are so much higher level than most of the people in this world.

"Rin, you have a dungeon in the middle of your city?"

"Yes. Our protector laid claim to this land long ago and built many of the structures nearest the dungeon with her own hands before ever obtaining her first Valkyrie."

"Ah, so that's it. She made this isolated place her home, then turned it into the city it is today by getting all these foxgirls to settle here."

"Yes, though we stay here of our own accord. Kiah is too important to leave unprotected."

"I agree with you there, though I still wonder how someone like her can be both so powerful and vulnerable at the same time."

Rin peers at me from the corner of her eyes. "Perhaps she will explain her situation to you, if you ask."

"Yeah, I think I'll do that."

Our destination isn't actually the pyramid-shaped dungeon. Rather, it's the temple sitting at its base. It rests on a raised platform, with marbled steps leading up to a walkway flanked by elaborate pillars that hold up the path's thick ceiling.

Liz and her other warriors stop at the base of the steps, and she gives me one last frown as she watches me climb them.

We walk for a while, passing by one finely carved pillar after the next. Finally, we reach the end, which is capped off by a pair of gigantic, stone doors. Like the rest of the temple, their architectural design is several steps above everything else in the city, making me curious how the building's interior looks.

I don't have to wait long to find out, as the doors open seemingly on their own, giving me a view of the inside. As expected, everything I lay my eyes on is a work of art, as if crafted by a master artisan.

Carved stone, beautiful illustrations, intricate pottery, and more. It's like stepping through time and into the holy temple of a Greek god. Except the one this place was built to worship isn't some mystical, unseen creature. She's real, and she's looking right at me.

"Welcome, John Lawrence Locke," Kiah says. "I hope my residence has met your expectations."

The little, nine-tailed foxgirl shows me a playful smile as she sits atop what can only be described as an altar of worship.

*Yeah. I guess an Immortal Being like Kiah is god-like enough to have worshippers, huh?*

# Chapter 6: From the Jaws of Death

## ----- Lutz -----

"Hello Kiah," I say to the little kyuubi. "If you want to know my feelings on your home, I'll say that I was quite surprised at how different this city is compared to everything else I've seen in this world. But it's really cool, like an ancient land lost to time."

"Hehe. Thanks. I built the original structures myself. Since the world was so primitive at the time, I decided to go with an aesthetic that matched. After many thousands of years, I grew to like it so much that I never updated the city to match the times."

"So that's why it feels so different. I think it makes your domain unique and memorable, so I'm glad you kept it."

"Yes, I'm inclined to agree." Kiah hops down from her altar. "Since you're showing yourself before me, am I correct to assume you found it?"

I watch on as her pitter pattering comes to an end, with her stopping a casual speaking distance from me. Rin and I are the only two in the room, and I have a feeling that Kiah wouldn't be so friendly if any of the other Battle-Maidens were here right now.

"I did. Though the 'Door to the Heavens' didn't look like I imagined."

"Reality often diverges from expectations. But all you can do is accept what you see, else you'll only find yourself wrapped in lies weaved by your own hand."

"It's tough hearing philosophy from a girl who looks six years old."

"I may look young, but you'd be surprised to hear my true age."

"Your status says 47, but that's obviously a lie. You said just a minute ago that you've lived here for many thousands of years. Did you edit your status to trick the [Scry] spell, like I do?"

"Incorrect. My status is accurate. I have truly lived for 47 years. At least, for this body's incarnation."

"This incarnation? Are you saying you can somehow change bodies?"

"You're not wrong, but the details are likely not as you suspect. Since I promised to reveal some secrets to you should you find the 'Door to the Heavens', then I suppose I'll start with some of my own."

Rather than continuing, Kiah looks to Rin. The stoic foxgirl is her current Valkyrie, a position meant to guard the kyuubi and do her personal bidding.

"As you wish." Rin turns to me. "Every 1,000 years, our protector … perishes."

"Wait, what?" I can't help but vocalize my disbelief.

"Do not be alarmed. Although her body may die, it becomes a vessel in which her soul is incubated. Precisely one year after her demise, she emerges from the shell of her former body, reborn anew. However, for the first 50 years of her new life, her strength is limited. Her body cannot handle the immense power that she used to wield, and so she must be protected until the day she matures."

My fist lands in my open palm. "I get it now! A cycle of rebirth! No wonder you're so weak!"

"How rude!" Kiah puffs her cheeks. "I may be vulnerable, but haven't you ever heard the phrase 'knowledge is power'!?"

"Haha, sorry. It just kind of slipped out. Guess I've gotten used to dealing with bratty Immortal Beings like the Astral Dryad."

"Oh-ho. So you're on such good terms with her? I'm a little jealous! It's been a few hundred years since I've visited her, so maybe I'll drop by once I regain my full power."

"Let me know when you decide to go. I'd definitely like to tag along. In fact, I can teleport us there anytime, since she let me keep a teleportation circle near her glade for quick travel."

"Interesting." She looks to Rin. "Have you ever wanted to visit the elven lands?"

"I can't say I've given it much thought. But Lutz's elven companion did strike me as pragmatic, which is a trait I admire."

"Then it's settled! We'll visit her together soon!"

Kiah looks satisfied at the conclusion. Something tells me she gets bored sitting around this city for 50 years while her body matures, so she's likely looking for an excuse to venture somewhere interesting.

"Dangerous," Rin says.

"It's fine." Kiah waves her hand dismissively. "I'll be accompanied by one of the Goddess' chosen heroes. Not to mention he's gotten much more powerful than the last time we met."

"Is that so? It's only been a couple weeks. How could you gain so much strength in such a short time?"

"Dungeons are amazing," I say. "Oh, speaking of power, I'm surprised Kiah hasn't taught you the Lost Magics yet. They're spreading through the land, so it's not really a secret anymore."

"That's true," Kiah says. "I didn't want to inundate this world with Arcane Magic before it was ready. Those particular spells are the key to unlocking the secrets of magic's true potential."

"Yeah. With the ability to sense and manipulate mana, things like Mana Springs can be used to power spells and artifacts with strength far beyond what a normal mage could hope to achieve."

"Correct. And it is through such advancements in technique that society will grow and evolve, as it did in the past. It will foster an age of great wealth and magitechnology, but also great war."

"That's pretty much unavoidable." I shake my head. "Human nature won't vanish, no matter how much a society flourishes. There will always be people who hunger for money and power, even if they have more than they could ever need."

"We have the Goddess guiding the world this time, but whether or not she can prevent another devastation is yet to be seen."

"The Astral Dryad has the same doubts, but I'm reserving judgment until I learn more." I turn from the two girls and face toward one of the temple's walls. "But are you just going to ignore that?"

There's nothing but highly ornamented stone and various decorations in my line of sight. Rin's obviously a little confused about what I'm looking at, which isn't surprising considering she can't sense mana.

What I'm really watching isn't a physical object in my line of sight, it's a source of mana that entered my detection range even before I stepped foot into this temple.

"It's just another Drake," Kiah says. "They've made themselves a nest in the mountains nearby, so they wander close from time to time."

"Oh, so it won't attack?"

"I never said that."

"Hey, start explaining things properly!"

A smile appears on Kiah's lips. "What's the fun in that?"

"I swear, you Immortal Beings are all the damn same..." I make a show of sighing. "Anyway, what's going to happen if it attacks? It's strong enough that people may actually die during the battle, you know?"

"Yes. However..." Kiah returns to her altar and takes a seat. "That's simply the fate of those who live by the sword. Would you have me pamper them, to remove all the challenges and risks that come with life? Do you really believe that would make them happy?"

"That's ... no, that's definitely not a healthy relationship. All the burden would be on you, and they'd just end up being needy children all their lives. But it doesn't have to be so extreme. You may be weak right now, but you can still help out, even if it's just letting them know that the drake is on the way, right?"

"Hmm? But I don't need to help this time. You're here, aren't you?"

"Hey, who's over relying on who now?"

"It's fine if it's you, though~"

Another sigh escapes my lips as I turn to face Rin. "Well, should we warn the others and get ready, just in case?"

"Yes. Let us meet with Liz to explain the situation."

"Her again? Guess I better prepare to be scowled at some more."

"Liz is the captain of our defense squad. She was chosen precisely because of her intimidating personality. Though she has the strength to back it up."

"Since I can't argue against that logic, I have no choice but to accept that my immediate future is destined to be filled with a pair of eyes burning a hole in me."

For some reason, Kiah hops back down from her altar. When I turn to look at her, I see an eager smile on her lips, making clear just what she plans to do.

"Jeez. You climb onto your throne to act all wise, but when the action starts, you want to come down and watch. Make up your mind."

"Heh. It's fine if I have it both ways, right?"

"I'm saying precisely that it's not fine!"

"Alright, alright. I'll refrain from sitting on my throne the next time I drop some wisdom on you. Happy?"

"No, nothing about what you just said makes me happy…" I turn toward the temple's only door. "But let's get this over with so I can find out what's behind that mysterious 'Door to the Heavens'."

Rin leads the way back outside. When I entered Kiah's temple, I thought Liz would go back to her post, but I guess I was too naive. She must have decided that waiting for me to come back out was a more valuable use of her time because she's standing at the base of the stairs, scowling at me as I descend them.

"You better not have been rude to our protector, human." Liz starts off with an antagonizing remark, as expected.

"Only a little. I can't help but stir the pot a bit."

"Grr! Rin! What did he say!?"

"My apologies, Liz. The conversation was private, so I cannot repeat it. Besides, there are more immediate matters that need to be resolved."

"Like what?"

"A Drake is approaching. According to our protector, this one is quite powerful."

"Another Drake? Hmph. Those creatures never learn. My squad will slay it just as easily as the others."

After her words, she turns to the girls around her, the same ones that had me surrounded back in the forest. There's a small discussion amongst them as they work out a few details, then Liz turns back to me.

"You better not harass any of the other girls while I'm gone."

"Hm? How could I do that? I'm coming with you, after all."

"What!? Human, you may think yourself strong, but Drake's are some of the most powerful monsters outside the dungeons. You're a fool if you think to treat this battle as a mere spectacle!"

"Could it be that you're worried for my safety?"

"A-as if I would ever worry over such a thing!"

It seems I really struck a nerve because her face flushes with anger. At least, that's the reason I'm going to tell myself.

*Yep. Definitely anger and not anything else.*

I guess the time for talking must be over because Liz organizes her squad and prepares to head out. Rin leads the way, though I'm secretly the one pointing her in the right direction. Kiah's with us, too. Liz protested when she realized that the one they're supposed to be protecting wants to watch the fight, but because the Valkyrie is by her side, she couldn't say much about it.

Since the landscape around their city is flat and rocky, there aren't nearly as many obstacles to block our vision like there were in the forest. Thanks to that, it's only a short while before we catch sight of the monster that's threatening enough for some of the Battle-Maiden's most powerful warriors to face.

Drakes are related to dragons, just like Wyverns and Salamanders. Wyverns are relatively small, with wings that make them capable of flight, while Salamanders are long and slender, with a very lizard-like body.

But unlike those two, the Drake before me is far more similar to Frei's Silver Dragon form before he turned humanoid. Its body is thick, with powerful hind legs and a huge jaw. Although it's on all fours, it would definitely look similar to something like a T-Rex if it stood up, minus the baby arms.

"Stay here, human." Liz gives me an order before turning to Rin. "You fighting?"

"No, I will be guarding Kiah."

"Good. I wouldn't want anyone else stealing my glory." She swaps focus to the Drake, stepping ahead of her squad. "You know the drill, ladies. I'll draw its attention to give the four of you a chance to strike unhindered. Any questions?"

Nobody raises any concerns, so Liz takes off into the sky on a series of translucent steps, heading straight to the Drake. As for the other Battle-Maidens, they split into pairs and take off in opposite directions, setting up a flank.

"She sure is confident," I say.

"Liz was one of the contenders for the position of Valkyrie, alongside me and one other."

"Ah, makes sense. She's actually a higher level than you, so I was wondering who would win in a duel."

"Victory would be difficult. But strength isn't the only factor when deciding on the next Valkyrie."

"If I had to guess, I'd say you were chosen for your temperament. Nothing seems to phase you, and you always look at things objectively."

"Yes, that was the main reason I was picked over the warriors who can best me in single combat. But age is also a factor. Liz is 4 years older than me, so by the time I reach her age, I will likely be stronger than she is currently."

"Ah, right. That's true, too. So you have more potential because you're stronger than all the Battle-Maidens your own age."

"Correct."

"Interesting. Ah, but it looks like the battle's about to start. I wonder if they can really win..."

According to [Scry], the Drake is level 51, a frighteningly high level compared to most monsters. Since Liz is only level 42, the power gap may be too much for her to overcome, even with the help of her squad, who are in the mid to upper 30's themselves.

*I wonder why the powerful warriors back in the city weren't gathered to help slay the Drake.*

*Could it be that the older warriors leave things like this in the hands of the younger generation so they can grow?*

It's important for people to be given the freedom to win or lose. A parent who hovers around their child like a helicopter will only stunt their growth in the long run. But it's still a little concerning, considering the strength of their opponent.

*Ah, the Drake looks really angry. Or maybe that's just how they all look...*
*Either way, it'll definitely attack anything that gets in its way.*

The one that does get in its way is Liz. She hops down in front of the ferocious Drake, her sword pointed directly at the beast's face. Seems the monster doesn't like having a creature a fraction of its size threaten it, as the Drake charges directly at her without missing a step.

Of course, this was their plan all along. As soon as Liz becomes its target, she swaps to evasion. Being small definitely has its advantages, and Liz uses them to their fullest, nimbly avoiding the Drake's massive jaw.

Her squad doesn't miss the chance Liz gives them. Four Battle-Maidens land on the Drake's large back, each thrusting their swords into the monster's body.

However...

"The scales are tough," I say. "I once fought a Salamander that was much stronger than me, and it took a while to crack its scales so I could do some real damage."

"Yes. It's the same for Drakes. Once they're shattered, the Battle-Maidens will target the weak spot until the wound becomes too much for the creature."

"A solid strategy, but it's like dancing on a knife's edge until it begins to slow from the injury. I know that from experience, as well."

The battle continues for a while longer, with the foxgirl squad striking with their swords when the opportunity arises. Liz throws out spells after her teammates attacks in order to regain the monster's aggro, but what surprises me is finding out that the Drake can cast magic, too.

I don't mean monster skill, I'm talking about real magic, just like the four races. I've seen other monsters do it before, like the Naga that Lumina and I fought back when we got forcibly teleported. But it's still a rare sight.

"Wow, she's really determined to win," I say.

"Liz has always been a prideful girl. It's one of the reasons she's never ... never produced an heir." Rin pointedly ignores my gaze.

"That so? I don't see how pride factors into something like that, though."

"It's because she refuses any man who can't defeat her in battle."

"Ah, I see! Though I wonder if that's just a convenient excuse."

"Who knows..."

For a while, it looks like Liz may actually be able to win. But perhaps we all underestimated this Drake's intelligence because unlike a mindless beast, it won't be fooled by the same trick time and again.

When Liz's squad comes in for another attack, the Drake releases a [Flame Pillar] directly on itself, engulfing it and the four Battle-Maidens who sought to deal it yet another blow.

"Retreat!" Liz yells.

Three of the warriors dash out from the roaring flames, their bodies charred from the intense heat. But the fourth foxgirl was directly in the center of the blast. Rather than dashing out, she leaps haphazardly out of the spell, landing directly in front of the Drake's face.

Wounded and dazed, the Battle-Maiden stares up at the gaping maw that's seeking to put a quick end to her life.

"I won't let you!" Liz pushes her companion out of the way.

She got there just in time, but that also means there's no time left for her to escape.

Rather than giving into fear, Liz thrusts her sword directly into the Drake's throat. She must know that she's done for and decided to deal a critical hit in order to give her people the best chance of defeating it after she's gone.

*Huh, I don't hate that.*

"[Accel]."

"I..." Liz says in shock. "I'm alive...?"

"Hey. Things were looking pretty bad, so I hope you don't mind if I join."

"You're...! How!?"

Liz eyes my adamantium spear with wide eyes as the weapon effortlessly holds back the Drake's massive fangs, the shaft jammed in its mouth to prevent it from snapping its jaw shut.

Although the monster towers over me like a lion does a typical housecat, the laws of physics here don't play by the same rules as they do on Earth. When I apply force on my spear, it's the Drake who's pushed back, its clawed feet scraping along the rocky ground.

"How's it feel to be on the other side of the strength curve?" I ask the monster.

It only answers with a growl, the hot, stinky breath climbing right up my nostrils.

"Ugh. Disgusting!"

As I wrinkle my nose, the heat coming from its mouth quickly rises. The darkness of its throat begins to light up red, and it only gets brighter with each passing second.

*Ah, I've seen this before.*

The Drake releases its fire breath directly in my face. At least, it tries to. But the five [Shimmering Shields] I create between me and its throat don't let a single flicker of the flame through.

The spell specializes at defending against magical attacks, and that includes monster skills like this flame breath. And since I can create up to five shields in any shape I want, blocking off its throat is a simple matter.

After the flames die down, I yank my spear from its mouth. "Now, let's have some fun, shall we?"

My weapon whirls, and with each time it passes by the Drake's face, scales shatter. Blood follows my spear tip wherever it goes, spraying through the air and splattering onto the rocky ground.

The Drake rises onto its hind legs, pulling its face away from my attack range. But the spear isn't my only weapon.

"[Shardstorm]." I say the name of my recently acquired fourth-tier Water Spell.

A frozen orb half the size of my body erupts from my extended hand. Shards of ice as large as my [Ice Lance] spells fly from the sphere in nearly every direction, leaving only enough space for me to stand unaffected.

The orb of icy death approaches the Drake, which has already been punctured by over a dozen shards, right in its soft underbelly. The sudden appearance of such a powerful spell makes the creature recoil, nearly falling onto its back in its attempt to get away from the oncoming sphere.

But it's too slow. The frozen orb reaches its body, where the spell's true power comes to life. Shard after shard pierces the Drake's underbelly at point blank range, sinking dozens of deadly projectiles into its flesh.

The dragon-like creature roars in both anger and pain, but the spell refuses to relent. I watch on as the orb continues its deadly assault, with the Drake's body becoming a pin cushion filled with icy shards.

Finally, after what must have felt like forever to the Drake, the [Shardstorm] spell comes to an end, the frozen orb becoming nothing but mist that evaporates into the air. When it's over, the powerful monster lies on its back, blood streaming from dozens of wounds.

And yet, it still lives.

*Guess it's not a dragon-class monster for nothing, huh?*

*I'll just finish it quickly. No need to let it suffer.*

I hop high into the air. Higher and higher. So high that even the Drake looks like it could be a typical housepet. I ready my spear, pointing it toward the ground, then cancel my [Air Step].

Air rushes by me, filling my ears with the sound of a freight train. The rocky terrain below grows more distinct at the same time, with the Drake's body getting larger as gravity pulls me back to the ground.

In a flash, my spear reaches the Drake's head, the tip coated in the magical energies of my [Gale Stab] Weapon Skill. The combination of all the forces combined makes this one of the deadliest attacks I have in my arsenal. So, I'm not surprised when my weapon goes straight through the monster's thick skull and pierces the ground beneath it.

"And that should do it," I say as I pull my spear free from the recently deceased Drake.

Turning, I see Liz standing in the same position she was in when I rescued her. Except now, she's gaping at me, her eyes wide with surprise.

"You...!"

"Me?"

"You ... defeated it so easily!? A Drake that powerful!?"

"I'd say it's on the weaker side compared to the bosses I fought in my recent trip to a dungeon." I walk back to Liz's side. "You didn't get hurt anywhere, did you?"

"W-what are you doing!?" She gets noisy when I get close to check for wounds.

"I'm just looking. See? My hands aren't even touching you."

"A-ah...!" She lets out a sound I didn't expect, then turns her face away.

"Seems like you're alright. Then I'll just focus my healing magic on your allies." I release [Cure All], and a white light flows from me. "With that, everything should be taken care of."

"Are..." She still refuses to look at me.

"Are?"

"Are you ... going to stay the night?"

"Uh..."

"I-it's not like I'm asking you to, or anything...! I was just curious!"

"I see. Well, I have something to do after this battle, so I was going to leave the city." I look to Rin and Kiah. "But I have friends here, so I'll definitely be back sometime."

"Is that so? Then ... I'll be waiting..."

Liz turns and runs off toward the Battle-Maiden that nearly got chomped by the Drake.

"Oh, my." Kiah's voice echoes in my head. "I didn't expect you to swoon Liz. What a naughty child you are."

"Shut it! I don't want to hear that from the one who refused to help! This is all your fault!"

*"Hmm. I suppose having one of the Great Heroes provide a generation of new children for us would be a fantastic idea. It's settled. John Lawrence Locke, you have my blessing."*

*"I don't want your blessing for something like that!"*

As usual, dealing with the Immortal Beings is nothing but a headache.

But there's never a dull moment.

# Chapter 7: Heaven's Gate

## ----- Lutz -----

"And so," Kiah says. "To fulfill the promise I made, I will be going with Lutz to reveal the secrets he wishes to know."

As soon as Kiah finishes speaking, a commotion erupts outside the temple, where the Battle-Maidens have gathered. She just explained the major details to everyone here, like the fact that I was summoned by the Goddess, and that she promised to show me what's inside the 'Door to the Heavens' once I found it.

They're understandably anxious, since their protector is still in the stage of her development where she's too weak to defend herself. But Kiah is practically their deity, so they can't exactly force her to do anything. Besides, the Valkyrie is going with us, so it's not like she'll be completely unguarded.

Still, that doesn't stop some of the Battle-Maidens from voicing their objection.

"Protector," a Battle-Maiden says, "it's too dangerous to leave the city as you are!"

"I agree! You were already targeted once. Who's to say they aren't waiting for another chance to strike!"

"Please reconsider!"

The crowd gets noisy, with many of the foxgirls protesting against Kiah's plan to visit a faraway place where she'd be vulnerable. Among the people gathered, one in particular has been silent. But it seems she's finally heard enough because when she looks to me, I can practically feel her losing the will to hold her tongue.

"Silence!" Liz yells. "It's rude to speak all at once in front of our Great Protector!"

"Liz." One of the other Battle-Maidens breaks the short silence. "You can be our voice. As a former Valkyrie candidate, perhaps she will listen to you."

"I intended to address her on this issue from the beginning." Liz gets down on one knee, facing toward Kiah. "Great Protector. Please be safe on your journey."

"What!? Liz, you wish for her to go!?"

"You didn't bear witness to the battle, so you simply don't understand. Our Great Protector is safer by that man's side than within her own temple."

"No way! Even if he defeated that Drake, there's no way he's more powerful than all the Battle-Maidens combined!" She turns to Liz's companions, who also saw the battle. "Am I right?"

The four foxgirls turn from her gaze, obviously unable to agree with her. That shocks not only the one who asked but also the rest of the warriors gathered here.

"Liz speaks the truth," Kiah says. "The strength of the Goddess' chosen hero is not to be underestimated. Worry not, I will be safe."

From the looks on many of their faces, they do keep worrying. But since the matter has been settled, nobody else speaks up with any complaints.

It seems Kiah likes to make a scene because rather than going somewhere private and silently teleporting away, she makes a show of getting close to me as we stand at the top of her temple's stairs.

Rin doesn't have much understanding of Dark Magic in general, so she must assume we need to be touching to teleport together. Otherwise, I doubt she would be latching onto me so tightly like she is now.

I'm not going to correct her, though.

"Rin…!" Liz's voice is just barely loud enough for me to hear over the silence. "I won't lose to you this time…!"

*What exactly are you fighting over?*

Ignoring her comment, I wave goodbye to the crowd of foxgirls below. I wait for Kiah and Rin to do the same, then release the teleportation spell I've been holding at the ready.

----------

"Welcome back." Laya's the first to greet us.

"Thanks. It's good to see everyone again."

"I feel the same," Rin says. "I'm glad we get to meet again so soon."

"Me too!" Alisha raises her hand. "I don't like it when my friends leave~"

"Unfortunately, I have responsibilities that cannot be ignored, no matter what."

"I understand. But it'd be nice if you could join Master's party so we can talk whenever we want."

"Hmm." Kiah looks thoughtful. "If it's long-distance communication, then that's within my current power."

"Really!? Then we can speak anytime!?"

"For you, I shall allow it!"

"Yay~"

"Jeez. Why are those two suddenly getting along so well?"

"Perhaps they are more similar than they seem, Belle." Tylith turns to me next. "Did you run into trouble?"

"Ah, yeah. I was gone for a bit longer than I expected because of a little incident."

"Was combat involved?"

"Was that a lucky guess?"

"Hmph. I can smell the lingering scent of battle on you, even now."

I raise an eyebrow. "Uh, not sure how you can smell something like that."

"Ah, I smell it too, Master! It smells like blood, sweat, and blood!"

"Hey, why is blood being said twice? You know what? Don't answer that."

I turn to the cabin and place the entire thing back into my [Inventory]. Such a massive object suddenly vanishing sparks Rin's interest, but I leave it up to the girls to fill her in on the details.

As for me, I'm far too excited about what we're about to see behind the 'Door to the Heavens', so I lead the group to the mysterious building while listening to Belle explain to Rin about how I'm creating my own dungeon.

"Interesting," Kiah says just as we step in front of the door. "It seems you've already begun to unlock the secrets lost to the world from before the Devastation."

"I learned a bit from a few places and am just putting some ideas into practice. It's still an infant compared to the real thing."

"Progress must begin somewhere. And with the Immortal Beings providing you with such invaluable knowledge, perhaps your progress will accelerate exponentially." She looks at the door ahead of us. "Especially after you see what's inside this building."

"Well don't keep me waiting, then."

"As you wish." Kiah places her hand on the door.

It's just solid, black stone, with no visible mechanism to open it. Within the door and walls runs a massive amount of mana, which is what gives them their indestructible property. Even with my full power, I can't hope to put even a scratch in the stone.

I'd run into a similar problem, were I to try to disrupt the flow of mana to make the door vulnerable. The current of energy is so overwhelming that it's just not feasible.

However, none of that seems to matter to Kiah. With her hand on the smooth stone, I feel her mana begin to move and circulate into the door, as if her mana we're harmonizing with the energy inside the stone.

In only a couple seconds, a grinding sound fills the air as the massive stone that makes up the building's entrance begins to move. Each of the two double doors parts, making a tantalizing crack between them that gives me just a glimpse of what lies inside.

The rumbling continues, and that crack grows wider, the darkness within evaporating as the sun's light illuminates the interior.

Kiah leads the way inside, followed by Rin, then me. The girls file in after, until each of us are within the dimly lit building that most people assume is some kind of dungeon.

I wasn't sure what to expect. I wouldn't even have been surprised if it was a dungeon, perhaps the most powerful one in the world. The 'Door to the Heavens' could simply be a reference to the fact that anyone who beats it would obtain the ultimate power, making them as strong as they could get without actually becoming a god.

However, another part of me wondered if it was some sort of gateway to the Heavens, like a teleportation circle that can take us to meet the Goddess in her own domain.

But from what I'm looking at, I'm starting to doubt either of those two possibilities, especially the dungeon one. The reason for that is...

"Is this," I say as I look around, "some kind of reception room?"

"Ah, good eye," Kiah says. "It is indeed a waiting room of sorts. In the past, a receptionist would sit behind that desk and direct guests to the appropriate part of the facility."

"Facility? So this building is some sort of office where people work?"

"Hmm. That's not quite right. Although people did work here, calling them mere office workers would be doing them a huge misjustice."

"Then what? What kind of stuff went on in here?"

"I believe it would be easier to explain if we went a little deeper into the facility."

Now that my eyes are adjusted to the dim light, I take a good look around the room. Unlike the stone outside, the interior walls are made from a sleek, silvery-blue metal. They're so well-crafted that I wouldn't doubt anyone who said they were made with modern Earth technology, like laser precision cutters.

Hanging on the walls and adorning the room in general are various contraptions. A few are quite obvious in their function, such as a desk that sits against the far wall. But others aren't so easy to figure out.

*Is that ... a ceiling light?*

My eyes are fixated on the ceiling, where a small protrusion puts out a faint glow. It reminds me of those emergency lights that come on once a building has lost power, providing just enough light to see without consuming too much energy.

While I'm looking around the room, Kiah steps up to a sleek, black rectangle hanging on the wall. She reaches her hand up to it, but...

"Curse this tiny body." Kiah turns to her Valkyrie. "Rin, please..."

"As you wish." Rin lifts the little nine-tailed foxgirl, gently cradling her.

"Much better." She touches the black rectangle.

The dim room is further lit up by the light now leaking from the formerly black object. It's not just glowing like a light bulb, though. It's displaying words, like a television screen.

With the exception of Kiah, none of the others here can read what's on the screen, since it's written in dungeon text. Not wanting to keep them in suspense, I read out the words on the monitor.

"Warning. Facility is under emergency lockdown. Access will only be granted to those with administrative clearance."

"Emergency lockdown?" Laya asks. "What kind of emergency is there right now?"

"There isn't one," Kiah says. "Not anymore, at least. But there was a major emergency about 10,000 years ago."

"Devastation."

"Yep! This facility has been in lockdown ever since, which is why the door wouldn't open."

"Does this mean you have this 'administrative clearance'?"

"I do! It was granted to me by ... well, let's call him a very dedicated man."

"Then, that door..." Laya looks to the only door in the room, other than the one we entered from.

"Working on it." Kiah runs her finger along the screen.

Some sort of menu appears, and after going through a few options, she makes a selection. Immediately after, the door opens.

Kiah motions for Rin to put her down, then trots over to the opening. "Follow. It's going to get interesting from here on."

"It's already interesting," I say. "Which only makes me more excited for what's to come."

One by one, we file through the door and into a hallway. Like the reception room, the walls are finely crafted from some kind of silvery-blue metal, with more strange objects adorning the walls. Although I have no idea what most of them do, a few are emitting light, letting us see well enough to navigate the hall.

We pass by a couple doors, along with another passage that branches off the main corridor. But Kiah ignores them and continues onward. Eventually, we arrive at one, final door. Like the first room, there's a black rectangle just out of her reach, forcing Rin to lift her once again.

The same scene plays out, with Kiah navigating through the menus until she finds the option she's looking for. With the press of the digital button, the door opens, and like every time before, Kiah leads the way inside.

"What...?" I look around in amazement. "This room ... is it full of laboratory equipment?"

"Correct," Kiah says. "You see, this building was once the most advanced magical research facility in the entire world. It was here that many of the most cutting-edge advancements were made near the end of the previous era.

"However, even they weren't able to prevent the Devastation that befell them. Or perhaps it's more precise to say that it was facilities like this that brought that disaster upon their world."

"Amazing..."

"Indeed! I knew you'd find this place fascinating! But don't get too surprised because I have yet to even begin my explanations." Kiah gives me one of her devious smiles. "John Lawrence Locke. How would you like to know the truth long lost to the people of this world?"

"The lost secrets of this world," I say. "Yes, I would really like to know. I've been curious about them for a long while."

"Then..." Kiah brings out a table from her [Inventory], along with a chair. "Let's get comfortable, shall we?"

The table is large enough for everyone here to sit around, so we bring out our own chairs and place them at our desired spots. Unsurprisingly, Laya and Alisha decide to flank me, while Belle and Tylith sit together nearby.

As for Rin, she's standing behind Kiah, keeping watch over her like she always does. Though I'm not sure who she's protecting her from in this impenetrable facility.

*Yeah, she definitely reminds me of a certain princess' battle-maid.*

Since everyone's gotten into their positions, I take out a pitcher of freshly brewed tea, still steaming from when I made it yesterday. Belle's the first to pour herself a cup, with Kiah not far behind. The rest of us pass the pitcher around afterwards, each filling a cup to the brim.

"Delectable." Kiah gives her thoughts after taking a sip. "The perfect accompaniment to a tale that hasn't been told in millennia. But first, tell me what you already know of the time before the Devastation."

"Only that the world was far more advanced than it is now, but I didn't expect it to be at the level of this facility. Also, I heard the planet was all connected through the Mana Network, though I'm still not sure exactly what that means."

"Put in a way you will likely understand, the Mana Network is a vast computer, powered by many mana springs from all over the planet. It's this network which acts as the hand of God, using its immense power granted to it by an unimaginable amount of mana at its disposal."

"How many mana springs are we talking about, exactly?"

"In its fully powered state, the Mana Network consists of 1,024 mana springs, roughly half the world's total."

"W-what!? There are that many!?"

"Yes. This planet is much larger than this one continent, after all. Didn't you realize that from your [Minimap] skill?"

I look at my map and zoom out. I told the other girls before that the known world is only a fraction of the planet and that there's still much to be explored. But the technology available to the people here just isn't advanced enough to explore beyond the ocean's horizons.

"I did notice this continent is only a small part of this world," I say. "Does that mean there's another land mass somewhere out there?"

"Indeed. An entire continent exists beyond the ocean, filled with people hardly any different than the ones here."

"You're kidding me..."

"It's no jest. The Phoenix watches over them, guiding them in her own way. Ah, the Phoenix is an Immortal Being like the Astral Dryad and Dragon Lord."

"And like you."

Kiah looks conflicted. "Perhaps. Though am I truly immortal if my lifespan is finite? Sometimes I even wonder if the me that's born is the same as the one who perished."

"I ... guess you have a point. But if you have the same memories and personality, then I'd like to think it's still you."

"My father was adamant that I would be the same person, even through my rebirths. He claimed that my soul was simply being transferred between bodies while I was in my incubation stage, though I have no way of proving that myself."

"Your father?" Even I can hear the surprise in my voice. "You have such a thing?"

"Perhaps it would be more accurate to label him my creator. I was born in this very lab, after all."

"What!? You aren't a natural being!?"

"Oh, no. Me, along with all the other Immortal Beings, were each a product of humanity's magical experimentations."

"Experimenting? On what?"

"What else would a highly advanced race want? Immortality, of course."

At Kiah's revelation, a few pieces of the puzzle click into place. Even back on Earth, there were those fascinated with the idea of living forever. It was still just a sci-fi fantasy, but there were people who froze their own living bodies in the hopes that someday in the future, they could be awakened and have their lives extended.

*Of course the people who lived in such an advanced society would want to live forever.*

*Considering the success they had by creating the Immortal Beings, it looks like it wasn't just some sci-fi fantasy, either. They really did defeat time itself...*

"So this father of yours," I say. "He worked in this magical research facility?"

"Yes. He was world renowned for his knowledge when it came to immortality. He and his partner, whom he would later make his wife, were the two head researchers here."

"You said humanity created the Immortal Beings. You didn't say anything about the other three races. Does that mean..."

"Ah, you caught that, did you? While the other three races existed before the Devastation, they were scarce. For every demi-human—as they were often called back then—there were 1,000 humans. That's bound to be the case, since the other races were also created by humanity near the end of their civilization."

"So it's as I thought..."

"Eh? You knew, Master?"

"No, but I had a few clues which gave me some ideas. I mean, what are the chances that people would randomly develop animal ears and tails? That definitely sounds like some kind of genetic manipulation."

"Correct," Kiah says. "The beastkin were the first of the extra races created by humanity. It may not surprise you to hear that they were made as weapons of war by humans seeking to create super soldiers by combining the genetics of humans and animals."

I nod in understanding. "Yeah, that sounds like a logical first step. And the part about them being weapons is equally unsurprising."

"Even though their creation was only somewhat successful, it gave way to a number of experiments, which eventually led humanity down the path of playing God. Though rather than warriors, the next race they created was their first attempt at reaching for immortality."

Kiah looks to Laya, who seems completely undisturbed about finding out her entire race was created by humans. She rarely shows her emotions, but even I'm surprised that she hardly has a reaction to the revelation.

"Does that mean my race's extended lifespan was a result of human research into immortality?"

"Precisely. Though in the end, the researchers weren't satisfied with extending their lives by a mere few hundred years, hence why they continued their research."

"Then…" Laya looks to Tylith. "Is that when they made the vampires?"

"If so," Tylith says, "then it was a futile effort. Elves and vampires have the same lifespan."

"Ah, about that. The vampires weren't created by humans." Kiah looks between Laya and Tylith. "They were made by the elves."

"What!?" Laya and Tylith both yell in shock.

"You see, the creation of different races was quite controversial. Since the beastkin were weapons of war, it shouldn't come as a surprise that when they finally began to obtain some rights as a distinct people, they had a difficult time integrating into human society.

"So as to not make the same mistakes with the elves, human researchers gave them a mild temperament, one that would make them easy to control. For generations, it worked. They remained as malleable subjects who provided invaluable data to the scientists.

"But humans were still new to playing as gods. The elves' mild nature may have made them docile, but it also gave them a strong bond with their own race. And the humans underestimated how much that would cost them."

Laya looks conflicted. "So my people's natural cohesion is a result of humans seeking to control us…"

"Correct."

"But how did that lead to the elves creating vampires?"

"Because one particularly brilliant elf managed to gain the favor of the researchers. He was given access to information and machines that allowed him to learn the methods the humans used to create his own race. And he used it to … alter the genetics of the next generation of elves."

"Wait!" Tylith says. "Are you saying that vampires weren't just made by elves, but they actually are elves!?"

"Indeed. Despite your races' differences, you are actually one and the same. Though whether you can still be considered such is questionable. After all, the elf made many changes, such as altering the vampire's mild temperament to one that seeks violence.

"That was what ultimately led to the elven rebellion that freed his people, but it also caused a shattering of the elven race, with the two factions being too different to get along as they once did, hence the long-standing hatred between your people."

After a long and extraordinary explanation, Kiah finally stops long enough to take another sip of her tea. Even I wasn't expecting such a fantastical tale of the two races' histories, so I can only imagine how Laya and Tylith must feel about it.

"This…" Tylith says. "This changes nothing for me. Whether we were once the same race doesn't matter. I will still seek peace between our people."

"Mmm. But perhaps knowing the truth will give us some ideas on how to fix our shattered relationship."

"That's a good attitude to keep," Kiah says. "Ten thousand years is a long time. Enough for evolution to blunt some of the sharp edges that once led to the division between your races. Perhaps now, a compromise can be found."

"I've still got a question," I say. "You said humans created the other races near the end of their civilization. But how exactly did they get wiped out?"

"Mana radiation."

"Mana … radiation?"

"Some spells are forbidden. Not in the way that Dark Magic is today. I mean some spells are simply too dangerous to use, less they cause devastation on a scale that can destroy civilizations."

"And … someone used one?"

"Yes. After the other three races obtained their freedoms, the world became a bloody battleground. Many more creatures were created during this time. The monsters that roam the land, the demons in the far east, and even the dragons."

"War…"

Back on Earth, nuclear weapons were considered powerful enough to destroy the world if enough were used at once. There was even an understanding that if one major power were to use them, the others would send their own nukes in response. It was known as mutually assured destruction, and there were certain times in history when it almost came to that.

If the people from the past civilization had access to similar power in the form of magic, then perhaps it was only a matter of time before someone pressed the button and sent the world back to the dark ages.

"I get it now," I say. "Playing God, losing control, and world-ending wars. It definitely fits. And the only things that survived were self-sustaining creations, like dungeons and research facilities like this."

"Yes. Their automated systems kept them functioning. And since they gain their power directly from mana springs, they can operate like normal, even without human intervention. As for living creatures, they were forced to stay underground for several thousand years, until the mana radiation had sufficiently dissipated."

"Is that why the Goddess came to this world? Because of all those disastrous events?"

"Ah, no. The Goddess is … well, it'd be best to refrain talking about her without her consent. If you want to know the truth about how she came to rule this world, you will need to ask her yourself."

I nod, deciding not to push the issue. "Alright. You gave me a lot of interesting information on other topics. But there's something you skimmed over that interests me more than anything else."

"The Mana Network," Kiah says.

"Yep. The Goddess herself told me that it's essential to winning this war, so I'd like to know more about it."

"Like I said, it's equivalent to a large-scale computer system, one that can operate independently, based on its settings. Though anyone with enough control over it can bend it to their will and use its functions for themselves."

"And it can do things like give people Unique Skills, right?"

"That's only a fraction of its power. In fact, it is the Mana Network which controls the entire leveling system that exists in this world. From giving experience through kills to awarding skill points on level ups. It's all the work of the Mana Network."

"Seriously!? So each time I kill a monster, the network knows and gives me experience!?"

"Actually, it gives you a fraction of the monster's mana, placing it within your Mana Core. That's why more powerful monsters award more experience, because they have more mana."

"But how? Is it watching everything with some unseen eye?"

"In a way, yes. After all, each Mana Core is connected to the network."

I place my hand over my heart, where my Mana Core rests in my chest. It's not a physical object, but more of a collection of mana that circulates in a spherical shape. Though it is something that can be affected by mana, including shattering it under the right circumstances.

*So that's how the Mana Network tracks everything. We all have chips inside us that are connected to the network.*

*Then, could it be that the faith I need to get from the people isn't actually for me and is instead for the Mana Core inside me to strengthen my connection to the network?*

There are still a lot of details that are unclear, but I could probably talk with Kiah all day and still have unanswered questions. Since most of the information I wanted to know has already been revealed, I swap focus and begin to look around this ancient laboratory.

The devices here are far beyond my ability to understand. I can't even imagine how they work or what they do, much less how to operate them. But it'd be a huge waste to just ignore them when we're likely the first humans to step foot in here for 10,000 years.

Besides, I have an Immortal Being with me. She can probably answer nearly any questions I have about the devices in here.

Kiah watches my face. "Interested? Although most of the devices in here are tools for measuring or examining various samples, there are a few special pieces of equipment that you will likely enjoy hearing about."

"Yeah. I'd be grateful if you could show me around a bit."

"Then let's take a tour!"

We all stand and send the items back into our respective inventories.

As she promised, Kiah leads us around the room, explaining some of the more interesting items. Most of it goes over the girls' heads, and to be honest, even I have a hard time grasping some of the things she says.

But I at least have the advantage of understanding some basic scientific principles thanks to my years of schooling on Earth. Because of that, I'm able to pick up on some meanings even if I don't fully understand them.

Eventually, we wind up exactly where Kiah began the tour. But there was one oddity that she seemed to completely skip over.

"What's in that room?" I point toward a particularly secure looking door.

"Ah, that's…" Kiah looks hesitant. "Even I can't access it, but that room is where my mother and father performed their most advanced experiments."

"You can't get inside, even with administrative clearance?"

"No. Only a handful of people could open that door, and for good reason. Regardless, there should be nobody left in this world who can access it now."

"I see…"

"But! I can open this one! And the most interesting items are inside!"

Kiah walks up to a second door, one that looks far more like the others in this facility. After the usual lifting and keypad method that she and Rin have done several times now, it opens.

The room looks like another laboratory of sorts, but the equipment is vastly different. Gone are the tables full of various small instruments, replaced with large cylinders made of clear glass which line the walls, leaving the center of the room quite barren by comparison.

Kiah walks up to one of those glass cylinders. "This is where the genetic manipulation took place. Creatures of all kinds were once grown in these cylinders, bringing to life the various life forms that now inhabit the planet."

"So the other three races, the demons, the dragons, and even the monsters that roam the world. They were all made in these tubes?"

"Yes, though not these specifically. There were other facilities like this, some of which still remain today, in various conditions."

"Isn't that kind of dangerous?"

"It wasn't, not while the people of this world lacked the magical technology to operate them. But with the introduction of the Lost Magics, that will eventually change. Though I'd say we still have a few hundred years before they reach a point where anyone could make use of facilities like this."

"I see. But it's still a little worrisome."

"Fear not. The Immortal Beings will watch them closely."

"Um, Master…"

Everyone looks to Alisha and notices her pointing toward a corner of the room. Our eyes follow her finger, and all of us end up gaping in shock at what we see, with the exception of Kiah.

Belle turns to me. "What are you looking at!? It's rude to stare, you know!"

I turn my head away. "Hey! I wasn't expecting *that*!"

Kiah walks up to the cylinder. "A doll. One that has yet to receive a host."

"A doll? What's that mean? Or more like, why is there a naked girl in that cylinder? I can't even feel any mana from her."

"If you look closely, you'll see these devices are different from the others. That's because these weren't for genetic manipulation. They are for placing creatures into stasis."

"Stasis? Like putting them to sleep?"

"Yes. And while asleep, they do not age. It was a product of humanity's research into immortality, but it's useless to be immortal if you're asleep. Though it still has its uses."

"Okay, but why is there a girl in one of them!?"

"Mother and Father must have had plans for this body. But…"

"The Devastation."

"Yes. Now, it's a mere leftover from that time. However, coming here has confirmed one of my suspicions."

"And what's that?"

Kiah looks at an empty cylinder, just next to the one the soulless girl is in. "Last time I came here, there was a body within that stasis device."

"A second body? But … it's empty now."

The little, nine-tailed foxgirl looks to me next. "Indeed. Because that body has been put to use."

"W-wait, what are you saying…?"

"John Lawrence Locke. Your soul now resides within one of the most advanced magitech bodies ever created. You have become this world's sixth Immortal Being."

"You're … kidding me…"

# Chapter 8: The Sixth Immortal

## ----- Lutz -----

"I'm ... an Immortal Being?"

"Ah, perhaps I'm getting a little ahead of myself," Kiah says. "Whether or not you have a mechanism to maintain immortality is yet to be seen."

"A mechanism? What's that supposed to mean?"

"You've surely noticed from your encounters with me and the Astral Dryad, haven't you?"

I think back to what I learned about the Astral Dryad. She was always mysterious, rarely letting me know when she was serious and when she was messing around.

But perhaps she's like that for a reason.

*She did say that she and her Ancestral Glade are inseparable. And she can only maintain her glade on top of a Mana Spring.*

*Does that mean...*

"The Astral Dryad must need an immense amount of mana to maintain her immortality," I say.

"Who knows~" Kiah gives me a mysterious smile. "I definitely wouldn't reveal her secrets without her permission."

"I see. But as for you, it's obvious. Your rebirths."

"Correct. And the other Immortal Beings have their own ways of extending their lifespans. However, Mother and Father weren't satisfied with these restrictions. They sought true immortality that wouldn't leave them vulnerable for decades every thousand years or other inconveniences.

"Plus, Father wanted a way to transfer his own consciousness into such a perfected body. Hence why he turned his focus to the dolls, like the one you now occupy."

I look down at my own body. "And you're wondering if they managed to make one that's truly immortal before the Devastation?"

"I have a fairly good idea on where Father was on his research before the world ended, and I'm quite certain he didn't manage to perfect his creation just yet. Perhaps in another century, he could have."

"A century? He was a human, right?"

"Ah, yes. But there is a spell which slows the aging process, which allowed humans to live over two hundred years. However, there was no way to turn back time, which is why Father placed his hopes on obtaining a fresh body to occupy."

"That's a lot of stuff to take in. But if he didn't finish making the perfect body, then shouldn't mine be flawed?"

"Perhaps. But 10,000 years have passed since that day. There's no telling what has changed since then."

I look around the room. "Changed? This facility is empty, right?"

Kiah doesn't respond. When I turn back to her, I see her simply staring at me with an unreadable expression.

*Could it be that one of the other Immortal Beings likes to visit here?*

*If it's one of them, then it's possible that they could have been continuing the research left behind by Kiah's parents.*

Since the little Kyuubi doesn't seem keen on providing an answer, I drop that line of thought.

For now.

"In any case," Kiah says, "that body of yours should last at least a couple thousand years, so even if you're not immortal, you will certainly outlive even the elves many times over."

"That's ... a lot of time."

"It seems that way now. However, your perspective will change after the first millennia or so." Kiah makes a thoughtful face. "But forget about it for now, because there's another important matter to discuss."

"What is it?"

"We need to settle on your new title!"

"My ... what?"

"Your title! If you're going to join the ranks of the Immortal Beings, then you'll need a proper title to go along with it!"

"Uh, is that really so important?"

"Of course! It means you'll be recognized as a demi-god to the people of this world!"

"I could ... do without that kind of worshiping."

"I was thinking," Kiah continues, ignoring me. "How does The Plunderer sound?"

"What kind of title is that!?"

"Well, you basically plundered that body, right?"

"No! It was a gift! From the Goddess!"

"Hmm. I'm not convinced~"

*These Immortal Beings...!*

It's already bad enough that I can't beat the young-looking Astral Dryad, so there's no way I'm going to let myself lose to someone who looks like a little kid. So, I quickly reach for a way to turn the tables.

"Heh." I let a confident smile form on my lips. "If it's about how I acquired this body, then there's a far more appropriate term."

"Oh? Then let's hear it."

"From henceforth, you shall refer to me as ... The Conqueror!" I look down on Kiah with my smug expression.

"How..." She makes a strained face. "...Embarrassing."

"Why!? It's way better than yours!" I look around the room for support.

Several pairs of eyes turn away just as they meet mine, revealing what they think of my new title. However, not all hope is lost.

"Yes," Tylith says. "A title befitting one who ripped immortality from this world's shattered past."

"Ah, it's really cool, Master!"

"See!?" I look back to Kiah. "What do you have to say now!?"

"Oh yeah." Kiah uses her knuckles to knock on the side of her head. "I forgot that new titles are voted on by the Immortal Beings before they're accepted."

"What!? When did that become a thing!?"

"Just now." Kiah giggles. "You're the first in 10,000 years, after all."

"Don't just change the rules when it's convenient!"

"Ah, I forgot to tell you about this interesting device." Kiah pitter patters her way over to a strange machine.

"Get back here! We're not done yet!"

She completely ignores me, stopping in front of a box secured to the wall with metal tubes coming out the top, which seemingly vanishing into the ceiling. It looks like an electrical box, like the one in homes that contain all the circuit breakers, except it's just solid metal with no way to access whatever's inside.

With heavy steps, I walk beside Kiah and look at the metal box.

"This device holds specialized magic instructions which can be turned on or off. In other words, it acts as a switch for various functions. Interesting, isn't it?"

"No. You just wanted to use it to escape." I give her my unfiltered thoughts. "But it does remind me of something. You said that the Mana Network controls the leveling system in this world. Does that mean if the Great Cathedrals were destroyed, the system would collapse?"

"Oh, no. The Great Cathedrals are just relay points. In other words, they are for sending instructions from the Mana Network to the world. But that's only the case for manual instructions. Its autonomous functions would only go offline if most of its 1,024 Mana Springs were disconnected."

"So that's why the Goddess wasn't worried about destroying them. I also heard that she could rebuild them later, and since Chaos is trying to gain control of them to overrun the world, she actually wants them gone."

"Yes. It would be the easiest way to hinder their plans."

"In that case, do you think I should get rid of them? It'd mean the fiends wouldn't be able to extend their territory since they can only go so far from the Great Cathedrals they control."

"That's a decision that you alone should make." Kiah hesitates. "However … I wouldn't simply assume the fiends' advance would be halted, even if you destroyed them."

"What do you mean?"

"The one who leads Chaos is … the word brilliant seems insufficient…"

"The Lord of Chaos? Is he that capable?"

"…" Kiah turns from me. "I believe I've fulfilled my promise. This lab brings back many memories, some good, others not so much. But I've had my fill for one day."

Now that I know that she was born in this research facility, I can see why she'd have mixed feelings about it. After all, she was created as a subject to test methods of creating Immortal Beings. That kind of childhood must have left some scars.

*Guess the Astral Dryad must have gone through something similar.*

"Let's get out of here, then." I lead the way to the door.

Since the facility is in lockdown, the doors close on their own after only staying open for a short while. Because of that, Kiah and Rin are forced to repeat their door opening ritual several times on the way out.

Even though we first arrived at this facility around noon, it's now late in the afternoon, leaving us with only a few hours of sunlight left. The time I spent rushing to get Kiah, plus the battle against the Drake and exploration of the facility ate up a large chunk of the second half of the day.

However, the same won't be true for the trip back to Kiah's city. I did leave a teleportation circle there, after all.

"We'll see each other again soon, right?" Alisha looks at Rin and Kiah.

"I'm sure of it," Rin says. "Even if Kiah can't get involved in this conflict due to her immature body, we can still provide some assistance, if needed."

"Yay! So we can stop by and say hello anytime!"

"It's not often we receive visitors, so don't expect a warm welcome." Rin's gaze falls on me.

"Yeah." I nod. "But at least they're girls, so it should go a little better for them, right?"

"Hey." Belle speaks up after hearing my words. "Why does our gender matter? No, wait! What happened while you were gone!?"

"Nothing. Nothing happened."

"I can smell your lies from across the continent!"

"Would you like to know?" Kiah asks. "Your companion here had some very intimate encounters during his short visit."

"I-intimate!?" Belle's face flushes.

"Hey!" I yell. "There was nothing like that at all!"

"Oh?" Kiah smiles. "How many nude bodies did you see in my city?"

"Nude bodies!?" Belle's head snaps in my direction. "Well!? How many did you see!?"

"It doesn't count!" I say. "They had just stepped out of the bathhouse!"

"And what about Liz?" Kiah asks. "Didn't she say she wants to sire your child?"

"Lutz." A calm voice quietly calls my name.

"L-Laya. It's not how it sounds!"

"Distractions are bad. Please focus on our objectives."

"O-of course!" I try to sound as confident as possible. "There's no way I'm going to let something like that derail me!"

"Hm?" Alisha tilts her head. "Does this mean … more harem?"

"It doesn't sound like it, Alisha." Tylith speaks while avoiding everyone's gazes.

As expected of an Immortal Being, Kiah had to end her visit here with a clear victory. If both of the immortals I've met so far are this competitive, then it makes me wonder just what's in store for me when I meet the Dragon Lord.

*He better not be a rascal like these two…*

Since I feel like I'd lose again if I tried to sneak in a last second miracle, I can only cut my losses.

"Well," I say. "I'm taking them back to their home. My mana's already recovered from the previous teleportation, so I've got enough mana now to teleport there and back without having to wait between casts."

"Mmm. No more sidequests."

"I swear," Belle says. "Everywhere you go, you have to make another girl swoon. Six isn't enough for you?"

I look at the four girls in front of me. "Uh, I'm guessing you're counting Lumina, but if you're saying six, then…"

"Elise, of course."

"Yeah, I figured…" I turn to Rin and Kiah. "You two ready?"

"Yes." Rin gives me one of her usual, short answers.

Kiah nods, so I release the teleportation spell I've been holding at the ready, and the world's light vanishes.

# Interlude 1

## ----- Lumina -----

"And done!" My hand comes up, holding a vial filled with a greenish-yellow liquid.

"Congratulations, Princess."

"Thanks Elise! It's exciting to explore new hobbies!"

I bring the vial closer and give the liquid an inspection. It has the consistency of a thick pudding and is such a strange color that I'm quite certain nobody would mistake it for a healing potion.

However, it is a potion. Just not one that will heal wounds. More of the liquid sits bubbling within the small cauldron placed on the table before me, ready to be put inside their own vials.

I place my newly crafted potion into my [Inventory]. "I didn't think it'd be so fun to have my own atelier."

"Potion making is a complicated profession, but I believe someone of your intellect will perform admirably."

"Thanks. Though I'm quite a cheater, as Sir Lutz would say."

"Indeed. I didn't imagine you would request Sir Locke to rank up your Alchemy skill using his daily Party Management upgrades."

"Yes." A smile finds its way to my lips. "The expression on his face was priceless."

I take a look around my new atelier. It was an old storeroom before I had it converted, but it now contains shelves lined with ingredients, a chest of empty bottles, a cauldron for mixing, and more.

As it was recently put together at my request, this is its first use. And also my first time crafting potions in a proper atelier.

I've been so busy since returning to the castle that I haven't been able to take any time for myself. But recreation and relaxation are an important part of a healthy lifestyle, so I specifically requested to have this day for myself.

That said, it's not like I plan to lounge around, and since I have other objectives to accomplish today, I quickly empty the cauldron into a dozen more vials, placing each into my [Inventory].

"That should do it," I say with a nod. "And now that I've performed my first test run, I can start making potions for the orphanage and Sir Lutz's new shop, The Elven Crossroads."

"I'm sure it will work out splendidly, Princess."

"I hope so. Being able to provide useful medicine to those who need it would bring me immeasurable happiness."

"That goes without saying. But please keep in mind that the ingredients you have stored in your [Inventory] aren't immune to the effects of time. It would be best to use the perishables before they go bad."

"Yes." I hold up my hand and look at the [Inventory] ring on my index finger. "This new ring slows time more effectively than my old one, but it can't compare to the original spell."

With my mission here accomplished, Elise and I exit the atelier, locking the door behind us. The ingredients in the room are only the cheapest and most common stock, with all the useful ones kept safely within my [Inventory]. But it's still good to keep the alchemical lab locked when not in use.

"Shall we move on to our next objective?"

"The carriage is already prepared to depart, Princess."

"Excellent. Then let's not keep them waiting any longer."

With my new position as Prime Oracle came a lot of responsibilities. But it also gives me the freedom I need to move around as I please. Part of that is simply due to my close connection with the Goddess. But another part is Father loosening the leash he kept on me for my entire life.

I'm not the only one who's had a sudden surge in personal freedom. My second brother, Lyle, has also been given free rein to do as he wishes. Within reason, of course.

Since Father's restrictions were the ultimate cause of the frustrations that led to Lyle being accused of high treason, he had no recourse when I confronted him about the whole situation. Hence, Lyle is now able to participate in hunts to increase his level.

However, the monsters around here are so weak that it'd take him ages to reach a level high enough to step onto a true battlefield.

I sit down on my carriage's plush seat. "Perhaps we can bring Lyle to a dungeon. Rhys, too. Leveling them up will ease my mind to no end."

"We can easily defeat the monsters in The Beast Warrens' early zones, so that's a possibility. But traveling there is the problem."

"Yes. Though if we send a mage to place a teleportation circle, we will have easy access."

"True." Elise smiles. "Seems like Sir Locke's casual use of the Dark Artes has finally rubbed off on you."

"I have no choice but to admit that the spells are too useful to avoid. If it means saving this world, then I will use anything at my disposal."

"Then perhaps a trip to the dungeon can be arranged."

After a rather short ride, we arrive at our first destination. The carriage pulls into a stall specifically built for me, which sits just beside an open gate.

Elise and I walk through that gate and onto a large yard. As soon as we step foot on the premises, we're swarmed by the occupants.

"Princess Lumina! Princess Lumina!" a young child yells out as he rushes toward me.

"Idiot," a young girl says. "She's the Prime Oracle now."

"Hey! She's still a princess, too!"

As usual, the orphanage gets lively when I arrive. The kids here have almost nobody who will even pretend to care about them, other than the ones who oversee the orphanage. So, when the princess of their kingdom shows up to tell them stories, it puts a sparkle in their eyes that seems to wash away the despair.

Even if I came here with a purpose, I can't disappoint these children's expectations. The thrill of adventure lives in nearly every person, and that goes double for kids whose imagination is the only way for them to experience a world outside their orphanage.

The story of how I stepped into the infamously dangerous dungeon, The Beast Warrens, grabs their attention in a way I've never been able to do before. When they hear of the wolf that stands on two legs and towers over even the tallest of men, the young boys can scarcely contain their excitement.

However, I don't have time to recall the entirety of my trip through the dungeon, and it's best to leave more for later visits. So, after recounting our first few battles, I give the children the usual treats and tell them to work hard on their studies.

This is normally the point where I would leave, but I've got one more mission to accomplish before I can go.

"Where's Kurt?" I ask one of the caretakers.

"In the sleeping quarters, as usual."

"I assumed as much. Then let's go to him. I believe it'll be better than asking him to make the journey to us."

The orphanage is rather large, thanks to the royal family's donations. But there's simply no way each child can have something like their own room.

So, four separate rooms were constructed, separating the kids first by gender, then by age. This allows each group to sleep comfortably around those most similar to them.

Of those rooms, the one where the older boys sleep is rarely empty. That's because there's one particular child who prefers to stay inside during the day, rather than go out and play.

Normally, I'd knock before entering a bedroom. But there's no expectation of privacy with a communal sleeping area for orphans. Besides, the door is already wide open, so I step right through.

"Good morning, Kurt."

"Hello, Princess Lumina." He gives me a small bow but remains seated with his back against the wall.

Normally, such an action would be considered rude when greeted by the kingdom's princess, but the thought doesn't even cross the mind of the ones here. The reason for that is simple.

My eyes fall on Kurt's left leg. Or rather, where his left leg would be, if he had one. However, there's nothing but the empty fabrics of his shorts.

Nobody is sure how, but Kurt sustained an injury before being picked up by the orphanage. Unfortunately, the infection was too much for the cheap potions the orphanage could afford at the time. It was before the royal family got involved, after all.

In the end, Kurt lost his leg. But at least he managed to keep his life. Though how much such an existence is worth to him is questionable, as exemplified by his somber attitude.

"Are you feeling well today?" I ask.

"I guess so. Not any worse than yesterday."

"That's good. You have to look on the bright side of life, no matter how bad things get. There's no telling when your fortunes will change, after all."

"Sure…"

"Hey Kurt, I brought something for you." A sparkling, blue potion appears in my palm. "I think drinking it will lift your mood."

He takes the potion from my outstretched hand. "Um, what kind of potion is this? It looks really expensive."

"Don't mind the cost. Just try it out."

He uncorks the lid and takes a whiff. Most potions have a bitter taste, so he was probably expecting a pungent odor. But the one in his hand is remarkably sweet, as are all the ones crafted by Sir Lutz's hand.

Kurt guzzles the contents all at once. "It tasted pretty good. But why would you give—"

His words end with a wince, and his hands move to his hip, where the stump of his left leg sits.

"I-it tingles…!" An uncomfortable expression clouds his face, but it doesn't seem to be filled with pain.

As he squirms, the fabric of his shorts begins to move, seemingly of its own accord. It rises from the ground, as if suddenly filled with something physical.

Soon after, pink flesh peeks out. More and more appears, growing to match the length of the right leg sitting just beside it.

When the growth comes to an end, all the occupants within the communal sleeping room stare in amazement at Kurt's newly regenerated left leg.

"W-what!?" He can't help but voice his shock.

"Congratulations, Kurt. You're whole again."

"No way! I was told potions that regrow limbs are super rare and expensive!"

"Indeed. But I have a companion who is rather generous with Restoration Potions, so it's only right to share."

He gets down into a proper kneeling position, his forehead touching the wooden floorboards. "I'll work hard for the rest of my life to pay you back, I swear it!"

"Raise your head, Kurt." I wait for him to comply. "The only reward I seek is to see you become a fine young man, so please put your efforts toward your studies."

"P-Princess Lumina…" Conviction enters his eyes for the first time since I met him. "I-I want to become the best alchemist in the Orakian Kingdom!"

"Oh? Then I suppose we should supplement your education with some extracurricular courses."

"Yes, please!"

After having his leg restored, Kurt is understandably excited to go show it off to his fellow orphans. When I give him leave, he runs out of the communal sleeping room, heading outside where the others are playing.

"Something tells me he'll be spending far less time indoors," Elise says.

"Yes. Children should be enjoying their time in the sun."

Elise gives me a wry smile. "How old are you again?"

I pout at her cheeky question. "Just because I'm 12 years old doesn't mean I need time to play."

"Right, right. I'll keep that in mind."

"I'm being bullied…"

As we walk back outside, we hear the excited yells of kids who are watching Kurt run around for the first time in years. Not wanting to disturb their fun, Elise and I make our escape back to the carriage.

"Onto the next destination," I say to the driver.

The wheels begin to turn, and the clacking of the wood rolling over stone fills the inside of the carriage.

Our next stop is in an adjoining district, so the trip is rather short again. Among the market streets, the one we are visiting today is known for its high quality, while still being accessible to commoners.

It may lack some of the extremely rare items found in the nearby noble's district, but nobody can claim this street to be anything but high-class.

After we come to a stop, Elise and I step out of the carriage and see exactly what we expect. The storefront is decorated with an exotic, blue-green design that sticks out among the more traditional decor around it, while the lettering above the door that lists the shop's name hammers home its unique nature.

"The Elven Crossroads," I say. "Naming it after the supposed source of their wares does spark interest, as can be seen by the number of patrons inside at this very moment."

"Yes. A formidable strategy. Perhaps Sir Locke has a knack for marketing."

"Something tells me it's just his natural penchant for surprise shining through."

The guard at the door gives me a bow as I pass. We've come here several times now, so he's grown used to seeing us.

As for the ones inside, they're a bit shocked at having their princess step into the same shop they're browsing. But I ignore their wide eyes and step up to the counter, where a young woman stands.

"Hello, Celine," I say to Belle's older sister. "It seems the store is busy, as usual."

"Yeah. We can't catch a break! It's like night and day compared to how it was at our old village!"

"When Sir Lutz is involved, things usually end up at an extreme, one way or another. Regardless..." I pull a basket of vials out of my [Inventory]. "This is the first batch of potions I crafted this morning. I'm curious how well they'll sell here."

"Oh, we'll definitely add them to our stock! Should we advertise that they were made by the princess's own hand?"

"No. I want an objective sense of their worth so I can determine what the market desires."

"Understood. In that case, we'll simply put them on display with the other potions." Celine pulls the basket to her side of the counter.

"Heads up," Celine's older brother says. "The thief is making his move."

"Thief?" I sneak a peek in the direction the two seem to be focused on and see a man making his way to the shop's exit.

"We've gotten pretty good at spotting them," Celine says. "But we don't want to accuse anyone of stealing when they could just be browsing, so we always wait until they make for the door."

"Ah. With your high levels, I suppose catching them is no problem, even if they have a head start."

"Yeah," Celine's brother says. "But pardon me, Princess, as it's my job to apprehend them."

He steps out from behind the counter to get into position to chase the man. However...

"Please wait," I say. "This is the perfect opportunity."

"For what?"

"To test this." I grab one of the vials from the basket.

Turning, I see that the thief is boldly walking out the shop's door, as if he didn't just pocket an item from one of the shelves. Since the guard is mainly to prevent violence, he's completely unaware that the man who just walked by him is stealing from under our noses.

However, this is precisely how they wish to run their store, as it allows them to prevent false accusations from overzealous guards.

I make my way to the exit with haste, then look down the street. The man is walking briskly now, looking to mesh into a nearby crowd to complete his escape.

But no matter where he goes, he won't be able to flee. I've memorized his mana signature, after all.

"Stop, thief!" I call out to the man.

He turns, his eyes meeting mine.

That's the precise moment my arm whips out, hurtling the vial directly at his face. It smacks into his forehead, releasing a loud crack as it shatters on impact.

The greenish-yellow goop splashes all over his face and even splatters the area behind him. However, not a single other person on the street gets even a drop on them thanks to the [Shimmering Shield] I placed around him.

The Water Spell only works on magical effects, allowing normal objects to pass straight through. But since potions are imbued with mana, the liquid qualifies as magical. Little goopy globs can be seen slowly dripping down the barrier and toward the road below.

As for the thief...

"Alright!" I yell. "It worked!"

Elise walks to the man, who's lying flat on the road. "Princess, I regret to inform you that the reason the man isn't moving has nothing to do with the paralyze effect within the potion. You simply knocked him out cold with your vial."

"Eh!?" I rush over. "No way!"

I check the man and see that he is indeed unconscious. So, I do the only obvious thing. I grab him by the collar and shake him vigorously.

"Wake up! Don't just pass out on me when I'm testing my paralysis potion!"

"Ugh..." He comes to, thanks to my command.

It certainly had nothing to do with the violent shaking.

"W-what!? My body is…!"

"Hmph. And there we have it." I stand and look down at the paralyzed thief.

"Good job, Princess. I think…"

"There was no need for the addendum."

Since the potion has been properly tested and the thief apprehended, we leave the rest to the city guard. After I give a short statement, of course.

*The nice thing about being the princess is that my word is essentially law. Though that can be quite scary, too…*

"Anyway," I say. "Let's get back to—"

I stop my words when I notice something strange.

"What is it, Princess?" Elise looks around for signs of danger.

"No, it's nothing dangerous. It's just that Father's mana suddenly vanished."

"He's hiding his mana? But why would he do such a thing?"

I remove a [Minimap] enchanted artifact from storage. He can hide from the [Sense Mana] spell, but he can't hide from Sir Lutz's Heroic Skill.

I track his dot on my artifact and see that he's leaving the castle. He has two others with him, both of whom are hiding their mana. But I have them tagged, so it's obvious that the other two are his personal guards.

*Where is he going without his usual retinue? And why is he hiding his mana?*

"Elise. Want to go for a walk?"

"Princess, getting involved in his affairs is ill advised."

"I know, but I have a feeling that this is something important."

"In that case, of course I will follow you."

I send a telepathic message to my own guards, telling them to await my return. They argue, of course. But we leave them behind, regardless.

Following my father's dot on the [Minimap] artifact, we find ourselves outside a rather shoddy building in a bad neighborhood. There are only a few reasons why the king would come here in secret, and most of them aren't good.

However, I put aside my reservations and sneak inside the building. Actually, it's Elise who does the sneaking, while I follow her commands.

She was trained as a master infiltrator, so a task like this is par for the course, as Sir Lutz would say.

There are only two others inside. With my father and his two guards, that brings the total to five. They're all gathered in a single room, where a rather old man sits, alongside a middle aged one wearing a thick cloak with the hood down.

The two strangers don't appear the least bit anxious to be having a secret meeting with the world's most powerful ruler. In fact, since Father was the one who came to meet them, it's almost as if the two strangers are the ones with all the cards in their hands.

Since Elise and I are hiding our mana, we can't cast [Scry]. So, all we can do is focus our hearing to eavesdrop on their conversation.

"...your help in securing my kingdom," my father says.

"I told you two decades ago that I was retiring from my position as the royal advisor," the old man says. "Yet you wish me to return now, just because things are getting difficult?"

"I know I'm being presumptuous. But it's not just me who needs you. It's the entire world. If I lose the crown, I'm confident the kingdom will fall. And with it, the world."

"Hmm." The old man looks to the man wearing the cloak. "Why don't we leave the decision in his hands?"

"That's..." Father matches the old man's gaze. "No, I suppose I have no room to argue."

The cloaked man stands, and I see that his height nearly matches my father's. In fact, his features look quite similar, as well.

"Long time no see," the man says. "I heard the crown was a bit too small for that big head of yours, so did you end up having it reforged?"

"It fit just fine the moment it was placed on my head."

"I wonder if the artisan actually crafted it as an artifact to fit the ego of any who wear it, then."

"..." Father takes the insult with a stoic face.

"Don't give me that look. It's our first time meeting in two decades, isn't it? We should be celebrating, dear brother."

*B-brother!? But Uncle Leon was...!*

"Elise," I say telepathically. *"I'm going in."*

*"Understood."*

I waste no time walking into the room the others are gathered in, unleashing my mana and casting [Scry] at the same time.

As expected, the cloaked man is indeed Leon de Eldridge. However, that should be impossible.

"You were followed!?" the old man says.

The king turns and takes in my face. "Lumina!? What in the blazes are you doing here!?"

"Father, please tell me how it is that Uncle Leon is here today. After all, records state that he was executed after the civil war two decades ago."

"That's..." The king looks back to his brother. "...A long story."

# Chapter 9: Carriage Ride

## ----- Lutz -----

The sky's natural shade of blue has finally given way to a mixture of orange and purple as the sun finishes its daily trip over this particular section of the planet, leaving us with less than an hour of sunlight left in the day.

In the end, I decided not to destroy the Great Cathedral that resides in this beastkin country of Belfast. I left a teleportation circle at the magitech research facility, so it won't be hard to warp back there and rush toward the Great Cathedral, if needed.

But I figured I could wait until I at least spoke to the Dragon Lord and unlocked the power of my Unique Skill, [True Blessing of the Goddess], before making a decision. After all, it can't be undestroyed.

Even though it's nearly dark, that won't stop us from continuing south for several more hours. When we're leaping through the sky, things like darkness are only a minor annoyance. Besides, our high level somehow enhances our senses.

We can see like a cat in the dark, and our hearing and smell are just as keen. Even on a moonless night, the scarce starlight is more than enough for us as we are.

But even without our improved senses, we essentially have a sixth sense in the form of the [Sense Mana] spell. The chance of us running into any kind of trouble is so small it's basically non-existent at this point.

However, the same can't be said for most of the people in this world. Many of them are low enough level that the average monster or soldier can threaten their lives.

That fact is made evident by the scene that's playing out on the highway below.

"Master?" Alisha looks to me. "Which ones are the bad guys?"

"That's a good question."

"I want to find out!"

"Might as well." I meet the eyes of the other girls, and they nod. "Then let's see who's riding in that carriage and why they're being chased by a small army of soldiers."

We begin our descent toward a carriage that's moving at full speed, escorted by guards. However, the dozen men are no match for the hundred or so soldiers pursuing them.

Since a carriage is obviously slower than a horseman, it's only a matter of time before battle breaks out. Fortunately, there's still a small gap between the two sides, giving us an opening to figure out what's going on before we jump into action.

"Alright," I say as my feet touch a solid surface for the first time in a quarter hour. "Let's see what these beastfolk have to say first."

"Ah, I'll do my best, Master!"

"Mmm. Counting on you, Alisha."

"Right!"

"Enemy attack!" A man's voice calls out from nearby. "They've landed on top of the carriage!"

I look around and see many of the guards repositioning to surround the people who boldly landed atop the carriage.

We're those people, of course.

They're obviously desperate to protect whoever it is that's riding inside, so they don't hesitate to send a barrage of spells our way.

"How uncouth," Tylith says. "At least attempt to judge the disposition of new arrivals before attacking."

"Desperate." Laya consolidates her thoughts into a single word.

"True. In that case, I shall withhold judgement for now."

The spells have all played out their effects. We dodged them, of course, but only because we don't want to dirty our outfits. Even if they hit us, we would hardly take any HP damage, if this were a videogame. That's just how far below us the average soldier is now.

"Ineffective!?" the same man yells. "We can't let them get to her! I'll engage, get her onto a horse and get out of here!"

The guard stands up, even as his horse gallops at high speed. With a kick, he leaps from the saddle, landing on top of the carriage with us.

Among the men here, he's by far the strongest. Though saying that would be like a professional baseball team talking to a high school's star player and complimenting him on his skills.

It may be a true statement, but sometimes, being the big fish in a small pond doesn't really mean much.

"Rebels!" the man yells, his voice fighting against the rushing wind and rattling of the carriage. "You'll perish here!"

"We're not rebels!" Alisha yells back. "We just want to talk!"

"Silence! I won't be lulled into carelessness!"

"Aww…! Just be a nice person and listen!"

"I'll hear your grievances once you lie on the ground defeated!"

Despite his hostile words, the man doesn't engage. The reason is obvious, as his goal is actually to buy time for his men to get whoever it is they're protecting out of the carriage so they can flee on horseback.

Since it seems like that'd end up as a headache, I motion for Laya to take care of it.

As always, she immediately jumps into action, her movements showing no sign of excess or inefficiency. Before the guard can even take a single step, Laya has already vanished from the rooftop and entered the carriage, just before one of the horsemen could reach it.

"Scoundrels!" He attacks, probably to prevent anyone else from following Laya.

"Is it time to play?" Alisha intercepts him with ease.

The rest of us wait patiently while Alisha and Laya take care of their tasks.

This scene is something that I couldn't imagine just a few months ago. Standing on top of a fleeing carriage and facing off against the captain of their guard, all while a small army closes in from behind.

But I've been through so much crazy stuff that it just seems like a typical start to another sidequest.

The guard up here with us must have realized just how outmatched he is because he gives up on trying to take Alisha down. Instead, he moves toward the edge of the carriage, as if he plans to leap down and through the door, as Laya did.

However, the girl in question makes her return before the man can enact whatever plan he had in mind. Seeing her suddenly jump back to the roof only makes his expression turn grave, as if he believes Laya had just completed an assassination mission.

However, the truth is...

"Noble beastfolk girl," Laya says. "Fled from a nearby city."

"She's fled?" I ask. "Why?"

"Civil war."

"You've got to be kidding me!" I turn to the guard who's still up here with us. "You! Explain! Why is there a civil war in your country!?"

"You ... don't know!?"

"It's because we don't know that we said we want to talk."

He finally seems to realize that we don't plan on fighting them. Or rather, he knows by now that if we wanted to, we could wipe all of them out at any time. The fact that we haven't already just lends weight to our words.

"There's no time to explain," he says. "We're being hounded by rebel forces as we speak."

"Yeah, I noticed. Guess it's time I have a chat with them, too. I feel like things would get messy if we all went, so you girls stay here."

"Okay! Have fun, Master!"

"M-Master!?" The captain's voice fills my ears as I take to the skies.

*I'm sure the others will sort out his misunderstanding.*

Even in the short time that we were talking with the first group, the other soldiers managed to close a lot of ground. Not having a carriage means their horses can gallop at full speed, and they've used that advantage to the fullest.

*So he's their leader, huh? Not bad. But I have to wonder why someone as strong as him isn't off fighting the fiends.*

Unlike Earth, the captains and generals in charge of the troops are typically stronger than the ones they command. This is a world where the numbers on people's status screens are vitally important, so it's a convenient way to judge who's capable of leading a charge into battle.

Fortunately for me, most of the powerful warriors were stuck on the front line when I was first summoned. That gave me the chance I needed to grow stronger without getting swarmed by soldiers I had no chance of defeating.

This beastkin general is certainly one such man. In terms of strength, he would put up a good fight against King Edgar, if things like equipment were equalized.

Such a powerful person should be on the front lines, since this beastkin country, Belfast, is at war with Chaos. Yet here he is, participating in a civil war.

*No use thinking about it. I'll just get some answers after I put a stop to this slaughter.*

I begin my descent toward the approaching soldiers. Like everything else in this world, horses have levels and gain stats like Agility. So it's no surprise that they can move quicker than the ones on Earth, which are limited by the heavy hand of physics.

However, for high level people like me, they can still be considered slow. Even the captain of this small army could probably outrun his own horse, but he still decided to ride, likely for several reasons. It's tiresome to run at high speed for long distances, for instance.

But because it's rather obvious that anyone who can keep pace with these fast horses must have at least a certain level of strength, the captain and his nearby men immediately recognize that I'm no random kid. After all, I did just drop from the sky and fall in line with them while hopping atop my translucent steps.

"Hey," I say casually. "I've got several questions for you."

"Who sent you!?" The captain doesn't even entertain my intended line of questioning.

"Man, I'm getting really tired of people just doing as they please. Can't we get to the point already?"

Of course the captain has no idea how to respond to my words, so he does what soldiers often do when met with any sort of opposition. He attacks.

"Take this you little ... huh?" He looks at his empty hand.

"Nice sword." I examine the captain's weapon, which now rests in my grip. "Thanks for the gift."

The sword vanishes into my [Inventory].

"H-hey! Where'd my weapon go!?"

"Hm? Your sword? Well, you were holding it out to me, so I just assumed you were offering it as a gift."

"Who'd give their weapon to the enemy!?"

"Oh, was I mistaken?" His sword reappears in my hand. "I'm not against giving it back, if you'll stop your attack on the carriage."

"I knew it! You're a rebel! To think they'd be working with the humans!"

"No, I just got to your country and ended up dragged into this mess. I have no idea what's going on, actually..."

"Fool! I won't be tricked by your lies!" He looks at his fellow soldiers, who've already surrounded me. "Capture him!"

"What a pain..."

Weapons of all kinds appear, fully encompassing me in a wall of steel that closes in like an iron jaw. Some have even leapt from their horses, seeking to cut off my escape by attacking me from above.

Without fail, each of their weapons scores a clean hit on my body.

And pass right through.

"What!?" The captain watches as my body swirls into mist.

"Looking for me?"

His head swivels forward, where I leap from one magical step to the next ahead of their charging army, now safely out of range of their weapons.

"What kind of foul magic is this!?"

"[Shadow Step]. Heroic-Class Dark Magic."

"You have access to such powerful spells!? No, wait! You used it while still maintaining your [Air Step] spell...! Dual casting!?"

"Technically, [Shadow Step] is a buff, so it's possible to activate it even while using another spell, as long as you buff yourself with it beforehand."

I give him the short version of how [Shadow Step] functions, since it's rather unique as far as spells go. When buffed with it, it gives the caster a limited amount of uses for as long as the spell lasts.

When activated, it allows me to teleport a short distance, while leaving behind a shadow clone. It even has a fake mana signature, while mine is hidden for a few seconds. It's great for assassins, though I just think the spell is fun.

*With this, the men should realize how outmatched they are and be more willing to talk things out in a civil manner.*

*After all, who would be reckless enough to go all-in on an opponent who's obviously giving them a chance to–*

"Attack!" The captain's voice interrupts my thoughts. "We can't allow this man to live!"

*Well, who could have seen that coming...*

Since they've been galloping at full speed the entire time, they finally managed to catch up to the carriage carrying that noble beastkin girl. When my party sees that the soldiers show no sign of giving up their pursuit, they retrieve their weapons and get into battle formation.

It's an interesting sight, seeing them standing atop that speeding carriage. Anyone on Earth would have been thrown off long ago, but the bumps seem to have no effect on the girls.

As the land around here is wide and flat, it allows for the horsemen to easily flank the carriage with their superior numbers.

Meanwhile, the noble girl's guards can only watch with grim faces as the soldiers set up the noose.

"Girls," I say as I land beside them. "Let's show these guys just what kind of mistake they're making."

"Mmm. It will only take one spell."

"Yeah, but ... go easy on them, would you? We still don't know what's going on."

"Of course. Only a few should perish."

"Hey, try for zero. Zero."

Laya's not the only one channeling. Belle and I are preparing our own spells to ensure we have enough firepower to end this battle before it starts.

With the soldiers finally converging on the carriage from nearly every angle, we unleash our magic.

Belle's spell roars to life, appearing just behind the carriage in the shape of a giant wall of flames. However, it's no mere [Flame Wall] spell. The fire washes over the land, moving forward at an incredible pace and burning everything it touches.

This is her recently acquired fourth-tier Fire Spell, [Flame Wave]. It creates a moving wall of fire, and even though it passes quickly, it can burn most normal monsters to ash in an instant.

Those flames engulf the horsemen trailing the rear of the carriage, who release frenzied shouts alongside the cries of their horses.

On the carriage's left side, I release the very same spell as Belle, and I'm treated to yet another sight of horsemen getting washed over by a wave of fire.

As for the final girl, she doesn't have Fire Magic. So, she relies on another spell to protect the carriage's right flank.

The fourth-tier Wind Spell, [Windstorm], rages before her, with several small tornadoes ripping through the approaching line of cavalry. With Laya's magical strength, an average person would be ripped to shreds when buffeted by those powerful winds.

And yet...

"No casualties, I hope," I say as I look around the carriage. "But that might be a bit optimistic. Still, we lowered the strength of our magic so much that—"

*crack*

A loud snap rings out, and the carriage's roof suddenly tilts hard to one side. Since it's still moving at high speed, whatever broke causes a cascade of other disasters as the whole carriage takes a dive into the dirt road and starts tumbling.

However, even before it makes its first flip, I'm already inside. The noble beastkin girl was thrown from her seat, but she's otherwise unharmed. That might not be the case for long, depending on how badly the crash gets.

So after whisking her into my arms, I leap through the window, leaving the tumbling carriage behind.

Laya mirrors me, also exiting through the window. The reason she followed me into the carriage was because the noble girl wasn't the only one inside. She has an attendant, a young woman whose level isn't much higher than an average townsperson.

That attendant now lies on the ground, brought to safety by Laya's decisive actions. As for the noble girl...

"Hey," I say to her bewildered face as she lies in my arms like a princess. "Pretty exciting day, isn't it?"

# Chapter 10: Resolution

## ----- Lutz -----

"Ah…!" The noble beastkin girl begins squirming in my arms.

"Hey, don't wiggle when you're being carried." I set her down as I speak.

She takes a few steps back, looks for her attendant, then dashes to her. After peeking around from behind her attendant's back, the girl finally seems to catch up on her current situation.

Her broken carriage lies nearby, having tumbled down a small hill next to the roadway. The horses took a beating, but we've already cast [Cure] on them, so they'll be fine soon.

Beyond that, her guards have formed a loose ring around us, facing outward. They've already realized we're not enemies, so their focus is completely on their pursuers.

Speaking of those soldiers, many of them lie on the ground next to their fallen horses. Our spells were powerful enough to knock them around like toys, but we used [Manipulate Mana] to lower the strength enough to spare their lives.

Though it seems some were unfortunately killed. Either they had a bad fall from their horses, or they were simply so weak that even our reduced magic was enough to take their lives.

*Well, I did my best to stop them. This was the path they chose when they decided to go to war.*

The reason we used such high tier magic was two-fold. First, the spells have massive AOEs, so it's perfect for blasting things like a flanking army. But it also shows the soldiers just what kind of power we have at our disposal.

The show of force was enough to cause the small army to hesitate even though they still hold a huge numerical advantage. Although the ones unaffected by the spells surround our little group, they don't attack immediately.

Their captain steps forward from the encirclement. He was caught in one of the AOEs, but since we reduced our power so much, it wasn't strong enough to knock him around like we did for most of his men.

"You demons," he says. "Where the hell did you come from?"

"She's from Orakio." I point to Belle. "And she's from the vampire's Great Clan, the Coven of Dusk. She's from the elven enclave of Aescela, while our little beastkin is from your very own country of Belfast. As for me, I came from a planet called Earth."

He listens with an increasingly incredulous face as I list off the places where each of us were born. As I pointed to each girl, the men seemed to realize that we're not just a group of humans but a full representation of the four races that inhabit the known world.

Even the noble girl and her guards give us strange looks, as the situation was too hectic for most of them to pick up on our diverse backgrounds until now.

"Adventurers!" The general yells. "You'll be barred from the guild and hunted down for joining in this battle!"

"Yeah, yeah. I've heard it before. Still don't care."

"Tch!" The general looks around and sees that his little army has gotten into position.

He wasn't just engaging me in discussion for fun. The men we knocked around with our spells needed time to regroup, and he was buying that with his words.

It was an obvious tactic, but it doesn't matter to me how many small fries he has surrounding us. If it were an army of thousands, it'd be a different story. But if it's just a couple hundred, then there's not really a threat to us.

While he gathered his men, the girls and I were also preparing. We stepped through the encirclement of guards, putting ourselves between them and the general leading the pursuers.

"You." I point to the general. "I challenge you to a duel."

"You ... what!?"

"A duel. If you win, we'll quietly let you capture these people. But if I win, you leave them in peace."

"You expect me to duel you when I have hundreds of men at my command? Are you a fool?"

"Oh, I forgot to mention. You don't have to fight me. You can pick any one of my companions. And, you can fight alongside nine of your best men. Surely the ten strongest among you can defeat a single one of us, right?"

"Ten against one…" The general looks over my party. "And I get to choose who to fight."

"Yep. Me or any of the four girls in my party. Take your pick."

The general starts to actually consider my offer. He motions over several men, and they start talking amongst themselves. They likely think we can't hear them, but with our enhanced senses, we can just barely pick up their words.

"What do you men think?" the general asks. "Attack or accept the duel?"

"We have over 200 men here, and there are only 5 adventurers. Do you really think they can defeat all of us?"

"Half the men are barely more than trainees. They'll be useless against powerful opponents."

"So we fight 5 of them with a hundred men or duel one with ten. And since we can pick our opponent, the odds might just be better to accept the duel."

"If they hold to their word," a third man says.

The general nods. "After we defeat our opponent, we'll capture them and force their hand."

"In that case, I think we should accept."

"I agree. With our ten strongest, there's no way we can lose. But which one should we pick?"

The men look our way, their eyes running over the girls. It's obvious that I'm out of the question, especially after my display when I stole the general's sword. So, one of the girls will end up doing battle against them.

*Good. The information Alisha shared with us ended up being right.*

I didn't ask for a duel simply out of the blue. Before we left for the beastkin lands, Alisha explained a few things to us so we'd be prepared for the journey.

One of the things she told us was that beastkin love to duel. Sometimes, an entire conflict will be settled by the armies' generals fighting in solo combat, rather than having a pitched battle to determine the winner.

It's simply one of the quirks of beastkin society, and I'm glad I was able to leverage it to my advantage here today.

"The vampire's out," the general says. "Too risky."

"Agreed. The elf's the youngest. Should we challenge her?"

"No. She may look young, but elves age differently from us. I'd wager she's older than the boy, and if she uses one of their famous chain sickles, it might be bad since we don't have experience fighting against them."

"So it's the human girl or their beastkin companion, then."

"I've decided," the general says loud enough for everyone to hear. "We'll accept your duel. And our opponent will be…"

All eyes trace the path of the general's finger, and Alisha finds herself being stared at by hundreds of warriors.

"I get to play!" The catgirl grows excited.

"Congratulations, Alisha," Tylith says. "I hope you enjoy the battle."

"Thanks!" She steps toward the empty space between us and the soldiers.

"You definitely chose well," I say to the men.

"What do you mean we chose well? Are you being sarcastic?"

"No. I meant exactly what I said. After all, right now…"

"…I'm the weakest!" Alisha finishes my sentence.

"Why are you saying that with a smile?" The general asks. "That's not something to be proud of!"

"Eh? But Master said it's fine, so there's nothing to be mad about, right?"

"Of course there is! A warrior should always strive to be the strongest! Being proud of weakness will only lead to defeat!"

"Are you proud, even though you're so weak?"

"Kuh…! This girl's got quite a mouth on her!"

The ten men who're dueling Alisha—if we can still call it a duel with these conditions—have also made their way to the no man's land between our two groups.

From the expressions of the spectators, it seems they're really looking forward to the battle. As Alisha said, these kinds of events are as big a part of beastkin culture as noble gatherings are to the ones who rule the human kingdoms.

Humanity relies on soft power to decide on who gets to be in charge, like someone's noble lineage or the amount of coin they have. On the other hand, beastkin are more straightforward. If one can defeat their opponent in a duel, they earn the respect of the others, which gives them access to higher positions and opportunities.

It's by showcasing their strength that they open new doors for themselves. But that doesn't mean just anyone can walk up and challenge the king for the throne. There are rules to follow and expectations to meet, but I'm still a little fuzzy on the details.

"Oh, right. You'll need this." I toss the general his sword, which was still sitting in my [Inventory].

He catches it with a practiced hand. "With this, our victory is all but guaranteed."

He tosses his other sword back to the soldier he had borrowed it from.

"Now," he continues. "Let's fight!"

"What do you think?" Belle asks. "One minute? Or maybe two?"

"One," Laya says.

"But she loves to play around, so there's a chance—ah, the first one fell."

"It's true she likes to play, but she's in a duel with her fellow beastkin. There's a certain honor to this battle, so I don't believe she'll toy with them."

"That's true. She does look more serious than usual. Oh, that's number four. They're getting really desperate now."

"Why can't we hit her!?" the general yells. "She's just one little girl!"

"Hmph. These fools really expect to pressure someone like Alisha. Even without her [Protector] activated, these men are far too weak to challenge her."

"Mmm. They're learning that fact now."

"Seems beastkin share some cultural aspects with vampires. Battle is a way of life for us, as well. Though it's closer to an assassination attempt when one of us seeks to rise in our hierarchy, rather than an honorable duel. Ah, there's number seven."

"How could we be losing!?" The general sounds really desperate now. "No choice, I'm going all out! You two, get ready to strike at the opening!"

"Looks like he's sacrificing himself to give his last two men a chance," Belle says. "May the heavens bless his soul."

"Hey." I take a peek at Belle. "Why are you saying it like he's about to die?"

"Well his body may live on, but don't you think getting utterly humiliated in front of your men like this is a deathblow to his pride?"

"Well ... you have a point." I look back to the battle. "And now he's on the ground."

"Mmm. Two more and—no, zero more. It's over."

The fighting finally ends, leaving just one person standing in the clearing between the two opposing groups.

Of course, that person is Alisha.

She trots back over to us. "I won, I won!"

I give her hair a nice ruffling. "Good job, Alisha. Does that mean you earned some honor?"

"Eh, this duel was a bit abnormal, so I don't think it will really earn me any respect. They think I'm an adventurer, so in their mind, I'm just being a bully. Besides, only those who are in the right position should be able to ask for a duel in the first place, like a general calling out the opposing general."

"I see. Guess I've still got a lot to learn about your people. But I'm glad to finally be here so I can experience their culture for myself."

"Yeah! I'll teach you lots and lots!"

One by one, the men Alisha defeated get back to their feet. From the looks on their faces, I'd forgive someone for thinking they just lost everything they hold dear. But the truth is the only thing Alisha took from them was their pride.

"So," I say. "Are you going to live up to our agreement?"

"Blasted boy," the general says. "This duel is so far outside tradition that nobody would punish me for throwing out the result. But I have my own pride. The day is yours."

He turns and waves to his men. Immediately after, they begin the retreat. However, the general turns back to me one more time.

"I'd suggest staying away from Velia. The city is under siege by thousands of troops, and the one in charge of the assault isn't the kind of person to entertain a duel request from adventurers. You'll be facing every single man on the open field if you go."

"Thanks for the advice. I'll keep it in mind."

With that, the general and his men retrieve their horses and fallen men, then start the journey back south, likely going back to the city of Velia where the siege is taking place.

*Well then, this is turning into quite the sidequest.*

# Chapter 11: Velia

## ----- Lutz -----

After watching the retreating army's backs for a while, the guards finally relax, and I hear the scraping of metal as many of them sheath their swords.

"My pr–" The guard captain stops his words and glances at us for a brief second. "My lady, we should hurry and flee. There's no guarantee how long they will continue their retreat."

"But what about Brother and Father!?"

"The reason your father sent you from the city was because he knew the battle was lost. Going back now would only mean you'd fall into enemy hands once the city falls."

"No...! How did it end up like this!? Everything was fine until just a few days ago...!"

"I'm sorry, my lady, but this is simply the way of war."

The young beastkin noble turns her face down, not wanting to show the despair that fills it.

Now that I've got nothing else to focus on, I finally take the time to get a good look at her. She's about Alisha's age, with black cat ears and tail, and although she's on the run, she's wearing an extravagant dress, even by noble standards.

Of course, I [Scry] her and see that she's indeed 13 years old, just like Alisha. I check her name, along with all her other information, but I don't see anything particularly interesting about her. She doesn't even have a Unique Skill.

The noble girl finally lifts her face, and her eyes fall on me. In them, I can see a glint of hope shining through the despair.

"Um ... you're strong, right? Please, I'll pay whatever price you ask, just please save my brother and father!"

"My lady," the captain says. "Even if they're powerful adventurers, they can't battle an army of thousands. Especially with that general leading them..."

"Riona..."

"I suggest you give up and seek safety. As long as you survive, our cause may yet live on."

The noble looks at me again, and I can see that glimmer of hope slowly fade.

"Master..." Alisha says softly.

"Yeah, I know. This city," I say loud enough for the noble girl to hear, "it's to the south, right?"

"It is..."

"Then you're in luck. We're heading south."

"Then...!"

"If we're going by the city, then we might as well stop by and say hello to this general Riona, right? Who knows, maybe she'll see the wisdom of ending the civil war with peace instead of blood."

"Unfortunately," the captain says, "that's far too optimistic. Riona follows orders to a fault. She won't end the siege unless ordered by her new king."

"Ah, so the old king got booted out, huh? That's rough."

"Y-yes..." The noble girl looks particularly distraught about it.

"Anyway. I'm still going. Until I see the strength of the army, I can't make any promises. But it's kind of my responsibility to take care of things like this, so I'll try to find a way to solve it."

"Your responsibility? Aren't you adventurers?"

"Yeah, technically. Though it's not our main job. By the way I didn't catch your name."

"Ah, my apologies." She gives us a curtsy. "I am ... Emily de Esmund. A pleasure to make your acquaintance."

"Yeah, same here ... Emily. I'm Lutz, and this is..."

I motion to one of the girls, starting a round of introductions. Since everyone already knows about Laya and Tylith's races, there are no long explanations needed.

Finally, it's time for the last girl to introduce herself. Normally, she'd be one of the first to excitedly spout out her name, but she held herself back this time to ensure she'd be the final one.

"Hello, I'm Alisha. I was born in Belfast but spent almost half my life living in Orakio. It's good to meet you, Emily!"

"It's rare for a beastkin who lived so long in human lands to prosper so," Emily says. "I suppose being a powerful adventurer has its benefits everywhere."

"Yeah! But I didn't do any prospering until I met Master! In fact, I was a slave!"

"Ah? You still refer to him as Master, despite not being a slave anymore?"

"Master is Master."

"I … understand." The look on her face doesn't show a hint of understanding. "In any case, I truly appreciate your offering to help. If you can turn the tide of this war, then you will surely be rewarded with riches beyond your imagination."

"Eh? We don't really want any, though?"

"You … don't?"

"No. We just want to help people. It's our responsibility!"

"Responsibility…" Emily looks between us. "You keep saying that, but why is it your responsibility to aid in a civil war in the Belfast kingdom?"

"It's not just this kingdom. It's the whole world! We're going to save everyone, right?" Alisha turns to me.

"It's impossible to save everyone. But we're going to save as many as we can."

Emily still doesn't understand, but it's fine to leave them with lingering questions. After all, we're not the only ones holding back.

*"I wonder why she gave us a fake name,"* I say telepathically. *"I wonder if her family is famous in Belfast."*

*"Well she is on the run,"* Belle says. *"She was probably warned about giving out her real name, and that goes double if she's famous or something."*

*"True. Guess that makes sense."*

*"Keiko de Ballard,"* Alisha quietly says the noble girl's real name. *"Why does that sound familiar?"*

*"You recognize it?"*

*"Maybe. But it's been so long since I've been to my homeland, and I was so young when I fled that I didn't really know much outside my hometown."*

*"Well it's not a big deal. It doesn't change what we need to do, and once we get to the city, maybe we'll find out more."*

Although we've decided to check out this sieged city, there's no way I'm going to slow down to the speed of these guards. We still have our main objective of meeting the Dragon Lord, which takes priority over almost anything else right now, so a long detour is out of the question.

But we can't just leave this beastkin noble behind, since having her vouch for us would make this sidequest much easier. Because of that, there's only one way to make it to the city without wasting time, while also bringing this young noble girl with us.

"Okay," I say. "Who's going to carry Emily?"

"Ah, I'll do it!" Alisha raises her hand.

"Makes sense. She'd probably be more comfortable in your arms."

"Yeah! And it'll give us a chance to talk about things!"

"True, true. I bet you have a lot of things you want to ask."

"Hehe~"

"Then it's settled."

"W-wait!" Emily gets loud. "Why am I being carried!?"

"Because we've got a tight schedule and can't afford to go at the leisurely pace of your horses."

"Eh? Horses are quick, right!?"

"It's all about perspective. Anyway, if you want to save your brother and father, then the condition is that you let us carry you to the city quickly."

"Ah…"

"I can't allow that," the guard captain says. "Having her carried off by an unknown group is out of the question."

"Then you can come, too." I figured he would speak up, so I already prepared my response. "I'll carry you."

"W-what about me?" the attendant asks.

"Sure, why not. Tylith?"

"It seems my assistance is needed once again. Then by all means, prepare yourself for my embrace."

"And there we have it. The three of you can come with us. Otherwise, you'll have to find another way to save the city."

"I'm … I'm going!" Emily—or rather, Keiko—says. "I can't allow Father to fall into his hands!"

As expected of a civil war, it seems there are a lot of circumstances going on that are massively impacting the lives of many people. I've gotten a taste of the political struggles that permeate the upper class of this world's kingdoms, but I don't have the time or patience to deal with them within the rules they live by.

*It's going to be interesting to see the looks on their faces when a powerful third party suddenly appears and stirs the pot.*

*I wonder if I can make some good connections while I'm at it. If this noble beastkin really is from a powerful family, then it could be a good chance to spread my reputation.*

*But first things first...*

I walk up to the captain. "I don't like this any more than you, but you chose this path."

He sighs. "I'm already prepared."

"Hmph." Tylith walks up to the attendant. "I'm sure you'll find the trip a comfortable one."

"Um. Thanks..."

"Emily, Emily! Are you ready!?"

"S-sure. Alisha, wasn't it? Thank you for carrying me."

"No problem!" She lifts the noble girl, then turns to me. "Ready, Master!"

"Alright. Then to the south we go!" I leap up onto an [Air Step].

The girls follow my lead, and before anyone knows it, we're cresting the top of the few trees that sprout from the mostly flat landscape.

"W-w-w-what are you doing!?" Emily yells.

"Eh?" Alisha looks at her with a confused face. "What's wrong?"

"What do you mean what's wrong!? Why are we going so high into the sky!?"

"But this is normal for us, right?" She looks to me.

"Yep. Don't worry, she probably won't drop you."

"You aren't doing a great job at alleviating my anxiety when you add a probably to your statement!"

"Ah. Haha..."

It seems like the trip's going to be a bit noisier than usual, but at least that means it won't be boring.

"Okay," I say, ignoring the noble girl who gave us a fake name. "Onward to have some fu–I mean to save the city!"

"And his real reason for accepting reveals itself," Belle says. "Not that we didn't guess it already."

"Less talking and more leaping through the sky. Unless you want to be left behind!"

I take off to the south to see about putting a stop to the bloody civil war in the beastkin country of Belfast.

And to enjoy a little adventure, of course.

----------

"We're as close as we can get," I say as my feet touch grass for the first time in a quarter hour.

"It's a miracle we managed to get this close to the city without being spotted." The captain of the noble girl's guard puts a few steps between us after I set him down.

"It's not a miracle. This is just the result of our ability to sense mana at such a long range. We can easily find the areas where there aren't any troops so we can get as close as possible without being spotted."

"[Sense Mana]?" Emily says. "That's one of the Lost Magics. Are you carrying an artifact enchanted with the effect?"

"No, I can cast it without artifacts. But that's not important right now." I check the [Minimap] in the corner of my vision.

Thousands of red dots fill the map, forming a complete circle around the blue dots that occupy the city. The mass of color makes it look like there's a lake surrounded by a raging inferno, though the soldiers seem to be concentrated outside the western wall of the city, making me wonder if the troops have gathered there to prepare for a coordinated assault to breach the city's defenses.

If that's the case, then the battle will turn bloody unless the ones within the walls surrender. It's not a situation I want to deal with, so I need to find a solution before things get out of hand.

*If we had to fight this entire army, things would get pretty bad.*

*Especially because of that one warrior. Riona, I assume.*

Thousands of troops are concentrated here, many of them far stronger than most soldiers I encountered in the human lands. There are even a couple hundred that we can't take down with a simple spell or attack. If they were to group up and support each other properly, they could put up quite a fight.

Among them, a few dozen are even strong enough that I can't help but wonder why they're here and not off fighting the fiends. Although they can't compare to an Archfiend, they're in the realm of warriors that could actually face one and not be killed in an instant.

It's troops like them that are kept in reserve to counter an Archfiend when they step onto the battlefield. When they gather into a party of dozens, they may actually be able to defeat an Archfiend.

But their general, Riona, is another story. Without a doubt, she must be one of the strongest warriors in Belfast. I can assume that with some certainty because this Riona is the strongest person I've felt so far, other than exceptions like Prime Elder Rena and Vampire Lord Ashton.

The only one who's close to her in strength is a single person within the city, likely the defender's general. But the sheer difference in the number of troops between the two sides makes the outcome of the battle obvious, were they to fight.

Even I wouldn't want to face this army. Although I don't think we would be defeated, fighting them in the open field wouldn't be easy, even with our strength.

I felt it back when we rescued the dragon, Frei, from the demons. We fought an army to save him, giving us a taste of what it means to stand against a tide of warriors focused solely on only a few.

There was no way to dodge all their magic or arrows, and each time we cut one enemy down, two more were waiting right behind him. Little by little, our mana and stamina were draining, and even though the wounds from each individual attack were small, they began to add up.

Without a doubt, if we had tried to stand our ground against that army back then, we'd have been defeated.

The same situation could play out again. We're stronger now, but the army surrounding this city is one that has undoubtedly fought on the front lines against the forces of Chaos. They've likely battled things like Archfiends, so they probably have a plan to take care of powerful warriors like us.

That said, if it came down to it, I don't have to play by their rules.

*But why are they here and not fighting the fiends? Just what is going on in this country?*

"How are we going to get inside?" Emily asks, dragging me from my thoughts. "D-don't tell me we're going to leap so high into the sky that mages and arrows won't be able to reach us..."

I tear my eyes away from the [Minimap] and look to the frightened beastkin girl. "You really don't like heights, huh?"

"It's scary when there's nothing but air beneath your feet, isn't it!?"

"Not really?" I look to my party and don't see a bit of agreement for Emily on their faces. "Anyway, we won't be leaping into the city like that. If we're spotted, it might cause a frenzy. I don't really want to deal with that. Plus, we'll have a swarm of guards on us wherever we land in the city. That'd be a pain. Even if you vouch for us, I can't see anything but problems all the way until we finally make it to your father."

I look at some blue dots on my [Minimap], their brightness showcasing their high strength. "Speaking of him, I'm going to assume he's one of the leaders of your faction's resistance here in the city. Knowing how beastkin society is structured, that means he has to be pretty strong right? So in terms of strength, where about is he compared to the rest of the people in the city?"

"You're correct to assume my father is in a high position here," Emily says. "As you claimed, most beastkin leaders have the physical strength to match their rank, and my father is no exception. In fact, he's undoubtedly the strongest warrior within the city."

"The strongest, huh? That makes this easy, then."

"How so?"

"Because there's a source of mana in the city that's head and shoulders above the rest. In other words, I know exactly where your father is right now."

"You can sense him, even from this distance!?"

"Don't look so worried. I'd never use this spell to do something like assassinate people I don't like. Well, not very often, at least."

My joke doesn't ease the look of apprehension on the noble beastkin girl's face. But there's not much I can say to convince her, so all I can do is prove my words with my actions.

*I just hope I don't have to turn on her...*

There's no guarantee the noble girl's faction is the good side in this civil war. It could be that the former king was overthrown for a reason, and I may end up as his enemy by the time we figure out what's going on. Though it could also be that neither side is good or evil, just a different shade of grey.

Even though my [Minimap] shows the sieging army as red dots, indicating them as enemies, that's only because I'm currently seeing them as my opponents. If I were to swap my line of thinking, then the color of the dots would swap to match, since the Heroic Skill works off my own perception.

It's for that reason that I can't rely on the color of a dot on my [Minimap] to tell me who's good or evil in an objective manner. I can only use it to see people who I've decided are enemies or allies.

There are even ways to fool the [Minimap], such as a spy who's pretending to work for my allies. Duke Bradley's dot was blue when I first saw him at Lumina's ball, and it was only after I realized who he was that it turned red. That's because I subconsciously changed the color of his dot by assuming him to be an enemy. Otherwise, it would have stayed blue.

That doesn't mean the [Minimap] doesn't have its own autonomy. People who are openly evil, like a group of bandits, seem to get automatically tagged as red, even before I lay my eyes on them. Though the details on how it decides who to tag red or not are still a bit fuzzy to me.

"Well, no use standing around in this empty field," I say. "Let's get going."

"Going where?" Emily asks.

"It'd be easier to show you. Tylith, care to take some of the load off my shoulders?"

"Of course. This is my specialty, after all."

Since we all just landed in this small, grassy area, we're tightly packed together. That means we're close enough to each other that Tylith and I can activate our spell as soon as we finish channeling.

"Get ready to say hello to your dad."

"Again, how—" Those are the only words Emily can get out before the world's light vanishes.

Since the distance we need to go is so short, the teleportation spell doesn't last long. In what feels like just a couple seconds, we reopen our eyes, taking in the sight of a large room filled with men.

The first sound I hear is their voices, though we appeared in the middle of a conversation, so there's not much context to what they're saying. That doesn't matter though, since they quickly quiet down once they realize a group suddenly teleported into their room.

The voices don't stop, though. It's just that instead of continuing their conversation on what to do about the army outside their gates, they decide to start yelling at us about all kinds of things.

Who are you, how did you get here, and several other questions are lobbed at us. But I ignore them all and motion to Emily. The girl's a bit dazed at the sudden teleportation, but it seems she's finally regaining her senses because she zeroes in on the one I suspect to be her father.

"Keiko!" The man yells in shock. "Why are you here!?"

"Father!" She runs through the guards who have us surrounded, stopping at his side.

"How? No, why did you return? I told you to flee, didn't I?"

"Yes, Father. But we were being hounded by hundreds of soldiers. Escape was impossible, and we only survived thanks to the arrival of Sir Lutz and his companions."

The man turns to me. Like his daughter, he has black cat ears. I assume he has a matching tail, but it's hidden from my sight at the moment.

Either way, he looks far different than I imagined. I thought he'd be a big, burly warrior with thick arms and a permanent scowl on his face. But the truth is that if I saw him walking the halls of a castle, I'd likely assume him to be a butler or attendant, not a high noble—were it not for the fact that he's wearing powerful enchanted gear, that is.

Although we shocked him with our arrival, he seems to have already recovered and has assessed the situation with a keen eye. To me, that kind of cool, calculating attitude is more dangerous than pure strength.

Before Emily's father can speak up, the guard captain steps forward. He gets on one knee, bowing to the nobleman.

"Please accept my deepest apologies, Your Majesty. I failed to bring the princess to safety."

"No, it wasn't a failure on your part. The fact that they knew of your mission to escort my daughter can only mean one thing. There's a traitor among us."

Silence falls over the room. Without a doubt, the nobles, warriors, and tacticians within this room are the leaders of this battle against the army at their gates. Having one of them be a spy who's actually working for the enemy must be a huge revelation.

But there's only one thought going through my mind at the moment.

*So...*
*...She was a princess all along.*

# Chapter 12: The Beastkin Way

## ----- Lutz -----

"Lutz, was it?" the beastkin king says. "It appears you keep company with quite an odd group."

"Yeah, I get that a lot." Several faces frown at my casual tone.

"From my daughter's words, it appears as though you arrived just in time to rescue her from the pursuers. How convenient."

"F-Father. What are you suggesting?"

"What better way to get a group on the inside than to save the king's daughter. Wouldn't you agree?" He directs his last statement to me.

"You've got a point. But there are a few flaws in your logic. Should I point them out or do you want to try your hand at them first?"

"I'm well aware that using such a suspicious group would be antithetical to an infiltration plan similar to what I'm suggesting. Though perhaps they believed a simple claim like a group of well-intentioned adventurers more likely to succeed than a group of beastkin, considering we're in the midst of a civil war."

"Ah, so you'd be more suspicious if a party of powerful beastkin were to rescue her, since they could just be soldiers from the army that has this city surrounded. Makes sense. Though that's not the only reason why your argument is weak."

The beastkin king stares at me, his eyes telling me that he's going through a myriad of information in order to figure out what other reason I'm talking about. Unfortunately for him, it's not something that he's likely to ever consider due to how strong he is.

Among the men in the city, he's definitely the strongest. The only one who could really challenge him in a duel would be the opposing army's general, Riona.

And us, of course.

"I have a few ideas," the king says. "But they seem too weak to use as foundations to prove your innocence. So let's hear what you have to say."

"It's simple. If we wanted to wipe out the soldiers in this city, then there's nothing that could stop us. Even you."

"Outrageous!" an important-looking soldier yells. "My Liege, let's toss them into a cell until we know the truth!"

"No," the king says without hesitation. "It's better to exhaust our options for diplomacy before taking action."

*Well, he's already a step ahead of a certain king with a tendency to make rash decisions.*

"In that vein," the king continues, "I'd like to know what makes you so confident that a single group of adventurers like yourselves could indeed defeat us. I alone can face most S-Class adventurers and win, yet you speak so confidently of victory, even while surrounded by nearly a thousand of my men."

"First off, let me apologize for my rude behavior until now. I must admit that I was testing your temperament to see what kind of man I was dealing with. But it seems you're quite an understanding ruler, which is good to know.

"Secondly, the reason I can be so confident is simple. I know your strength, along with that of all your men in the city. I don't mean that in a general fashion. I can accurately assess all of them with the use of the Lost Magic, [Sense Mana].

"You." I point to the king. "You are the strongest one amongst your men, without a doubt. Followed by him, then him, then…"

I continue to point at soldiers and other beastkin, accurately listing them in order of their strength. Since there are nearly two dozen men in this meeting room, it becomes quite a long process.

"Finally, you're bringing up the rear." My finger points to a scholarly looking young man. "And that concludes my tier list."

Their silence tells me that none of them have any logical arguments against the hierarchy of strength I laid out. Of course, that's to be expected since I have access to all their status at a glance.

"You're well informed," the king says. "Though whether it's from prior knowledge or an artifact enchanted with the Lost Magics is up for debate. Regardless, I would first like to know your reason for testing my temperament, as it's widely known among the citizens of Belfast that I tend to abstain from conflict."

"Well, I don't know anything about you since it's my first time in Belfast. And since I'm only passing through, I didn't do much studying. So, when I was suddenly face to face with this country's king, I wanted to know what kind of person you were.

"As for why specifically I chose this course, it's because I'm a busy man. I don't have time to play political games if I want to put a quick end to the civil war in this country, so I opted to test you by trying to push your buttons to see if you'd get mad."

"Because you're busy!?" that same soldier yells again. "You were rude to the king of our country for such a simple reason!?"

"Hey, cut me some slack. There are a lot of things I need to do before I can save the world."

"His head is even bigger than Rei's!"

"Hmm." The king lets out a thoughtful sound.

"Father," Keiko says. "I believe you should consider his words. I saw his beastkin companion battle ten of the strongest soldiers who pursued us, and she won easily!"

"Strength does not equal righteousness. But I suppose we should allow them to stay in the city, if they wish it. They did come to your rescue. Though it would have been better if you had continued to flee instead of returning here. Regardless, don't expect to be privy to the details of our defense against the siege. Though I certainly won't stop you, if you wish to join the fight."

"That's not good enough," I say. "I don't have time to sit around for who knows how long while this siege continues. I'm going to put an end to it today."

"Today?" The king gives me a look of surprise. "No matter how strong you are, even you can't face an army of thousands."

"Maybe. And I also can't afford to wipe out the army. We may need them in the battle against Chaos after this civil war. That means I need to perform a surgical strike. In other words, I'm going to go after Riona."

"Slay the general? Certainly, that's a valid strategy, but she won't fall so easily."

"I know. She's too strong for even me to take out in an instant. But I don't plan on killing her. At least, I really hope it doesn't come to that. Which is why I need your help. I want to know how this country ended up in this civil war, why you were the one forced to flee, and who this Riona person is. With enough information, maybe I can find a solution."

"You're asking for a lot of detailed information, considering you're an outsider. Didn't I just tell you not to expect to be part of my meetings?"

"Yeah, but I ignored it. Anyway, I feel like we're just going to go in circles if this continues, so I'll just come right out and say it." I point my finger directly at the king again. "I challenge you to a duel."

"Preposterous!" the same important-looking soldier yells. "You think just anyone can demand to duel the king of Belfast!?"

"I'm not just anyone. If you manage to defeat me, then I'll tell you who I am and why I can speak to even a king as an equal."

"Nonsense! Only the Great Heroes can consider themselves equal to royalty!"

"Hmm." The king makes the same thoughtful sound.

"Your Majesty! Don't tell me you're actually considering it! Remember what happened last time you accepted a duel!?"

"H-hey!" Keiko yells. "That was uncalled for!"

"It's quite alright," the king says. "He has a point. But as the one being challenged, I can choose to deny him after hearing his request. So, what is it that you want, if you win the duel?"

"Just the information I mentioned and your cooperation with ending the civil war. That's all."

"And if I win, you'll tell me about yourself. Though I'm interested in who you are, there's no guarantee anything you'll tell me will be the truth, and there's a chance the way you wish to end the civil war won't be in my best interests. So what incentive is there for me to accept the duel?"

"If you want something more concrete, then..." I hold out my upturned palm, and a plate of meat appears atop it. "I'll tell you why I can do this."

The aroma of freshly cooked steak fills the meeting room. With the delicious smell, there's no way that the plate of food could be confused with something like the [Transform] spell, since turning an object into cooked meat is pretty much impossible.

The sudden appearance of the steaming hot steak makes all the beastkin gathered here widen their eyes, as it's not a spell that can be accomplished even with the Lost Magics. As they watch on, the plate vanishes, but the smell continues to linger.

"What a surprise," the king says. "I've seen street magicians fool others with their sleight of hand, but that was no trick."

"It's a real steak, and it's not the only thing I can summon at will. So, interested in the duel now?"

The king looks to one of the soldiers. "Prepare the arena."

*Alright! It's time to fight a king!*

*…Again.*

----------

"Since it's my first time dueling in your lands," I say, "can you go over the rules so there aren't any mishaps?"

"It's simple. No offensive magic or weapon skills. Anything else is fair game."

"Alright. So support magic is fine, including spells like [Earth Wall]."

"Yes, along with personal enhancement magic. Though you're only allowed to enhance yourself."

"Makes sense. It's a duel after all, so asking powerful allies to buff you would be bad form. As for equipment, I assume there aren't any restrictions."

"None. We consider items you've managed to procure through your battles as part of your own strength, since you had to risk your life to obtain them."

"Agreed. And from the looks of it, you managed to find quite a powerful set of gear."

"It's only natural for a beastkin king to have some of the strongest in the kingdom. It's the combination of me and my equipment that allowed me to take the throne, after all."

"Interesting. I'm learning a lot of things already."

As expected of a king who's trapped in a besieged city, he was wearing his full set of enchanted gear from the moment I teleported in. And it's not just any old set of items, either. Their strength can be considered the top of the top among everything I've seen in this world.

Other than my own, of course.

Our recent dungeon dive allowed me to rank up my crafting and enchanting skills even further. I used those upgraded skills to power up all our equipment, and I even recrafted most of it, adding things like adamantium threads to our clothes to enhance their potential even more.

When all was said and done, our items became what could only be described as ridiculously overpowered. If a craftsman were to get his hands on them, he'd surely believe that they were made by the Goddess herself.

Even with this beastkin king's world-class equipment enhancing his already high stats, it simply can't be compared to me as I am now.

Despite that, I still have more room to grow. I've only achieved four of the five tiers of magic and crafting skills, making me wonder just how much stronger we can become if we unlock the final tier.

*No use thinking about it now. I've got a fight to enjoy.*

*But overwhelming him with pure numbers would be boring, so why don't I take a page out of Laya's handbook.*

I obliterate the enchantments on a few of my items and replace them with weaker versions. My [Sense Mana] spell has gotten so precise that I can basically estimate the strength of the king's items, so I bring mine down to match.

*With this, the match should be roughly even. I wonder if I can still win.*

The excitement of my upcoming battle courses through me, causing a smile to form on my lips.

"I see you've come to enjoy combat," the beastkin king says. "Perhaps you'd fit right in here in my lands."

"You may be right, but I have no intention of planting my roots just yet."

"It wasn't a suggestion. Merely an observation." The beastkin king holds his arm out, and a soldier plants a weapon in it.

"Oh? This is a surprise. It's rare for me to fight another powerful spearman in single combat."

"I was a soldier before I became king, and the spear was the weapon of choice on the battlefield."

"True. It's great when combined with a formation of well-trained troops. Though it's just as effective in a duel as long as you have room to swing it."

Being an arena, there are no obstacles to prevent us from using our full suite of techniques, no matter how wide the swings are.

"Have fun, Master!"

"Thanks, Alisha. Maybe you can have some duels later."

"Yeah, yeah! I want to duel again!"

"I figured. But for now..." I ready myself. "I've got a job to do."

The king gives a nod, so I return it. With that, we're both ready to battle. All we're waiting on is...

"Begin!"

The king vanishes.

My spear twirls, ending up behind me. No sooner did it disappear behind my back than the sound of clanking metal rings out.

I turned as I spun the spear, so by the time I finished deflecting the attack, I'd already done a full one-eighty. What I see is the king regaining control of his weapon after I'd knocked it aside.

It's too late to counterattack, as by the time I'm ready to strike, he's already in a defensive stance, prepared to intercept me. But that's fine with me, as banter between clashes is one of the best parts of a duel.

"[Accel], huh? Pulling it out at the very start of a duel is quite rude, isn't it?"

"Perhaps, but so is requesting to duel a king when you've not proven yourself worthy."

"So it was a test. If I'd fallen to that attack, then I wasn't worth fighting. But it seems the plan backfired, didn't it? After all, [Accel] has quite a long cooldown."

"That may be so, but I don't particularly need it to defeat you."

"Heh. Guess you need that kind of confidence to be a king. Maybe you two aren't so different, all things considered."

"And who might you be comparing me to?"

"Just an arrogant man I've unfortunately been forced to work with on a few occasions."

The king understands that there's no use pursuing the topic. Or rather, he seems to want to continue the battle, so I oblige him by telegraphing my intent to attack.

My spear whips out, probing at his defenses. Normally, I can use my weapon's longer range to safely attack at a distance, but that strategy doesn't work when my opponent has the same reach.

After deflecting my pierce, the king returns the favor. But he only finds the shaft of my spear as I step forward, my weapon a blur.

"Let's see what you've got up close!" I yell to him.

He calmly blocks my whirlwind of strikes. "Not content with the safety of distance?"

"Not today!" I duck a counter as I speak.

A constant clanking fills the arena as our two spears clash time and again. The weapons are moving so quickly that they'd likely be virtually invisible to people whose levels were too low to track them properly.

But to me and the king, this speed feels just right.

Neither of us are giving it our all yet. Overextending would give the opponent an advantage, were either of us to make a mistake. So, we're still testing out each other's fighting style, trying to find a way to land a clean hit.

*He's good. No wonder he became the king of a race known for their love of battle.*

*To think he gained this much skill without the use of cheating like me. It's really quite amazing.*

*I won't apologize for being a cheater, though.*

Even though I put my stats roughly equal to the king's, there's still one discrepancy between us. No matter how good he is, the knowledge granted to me by the Mana Network is absolute. All things equal, nobody can challenge my spearmanship.

"Tch." The king finally releases a frustrated noise when he's forced to retreat from my assault.

"You're a talented warrior. One of the best I've ever fought. But it's no use. Just give up."

"If I backed down just because of one poor engagement, then I wouldn't have the right to rule Belfast."

"Nice. I was hoping you'd say something like that."

"I'll admit I'm surprised at your strength. I can count on one hand the number of people who can best me in a duel. However, if this is your limit, then I suggest you give up trying to end the civil war in my country."

"Because one of those people who can beat you is Riona, the general leading the army sieging the city?"

"Yes. You would be a good match for her, but she has thousands of troops to back her up, while you have four companions. It's simply not enough."

"Well, you're right. This amount of strength isn't enough. So, it's fortunate that I still have more in reserve."

"What? Are you holding back?"

"No, I'm giving it my all. It's just I'm not enhanced by much support magic, and the enchantments on my equipment have been reduced. However, if I do this..."

I concentrate on my battle outfit, maxing out the enchantments as much as I can for my current level. The surge in strength is enough to push me up a power tier, but that's not the end of my growth.

"[Empower]. [Haste]. [Stoneskin]. [Gale]. [Enhance]. [Blessed Aura]." I call out the names of all my physical enhancing buffs as I cast them.

"What!? Don't tell me you just cast each of those spells!"

"Sure did."

"[Blessed Aura] is the Heroic-Class Light Support Spell that raises all status for the caster and his allies! Are you saying you have access to such powerful magic despite being a warrior!?"

"Whether it comes to weapon techniques or magic, they're all easy to master for a cheater like me. Now then, still want to fight?"

"Kuh..." The king's expression turns grim. "A true ruler won't back down, no matter how dire the situation may be."

"Well said. In that case, let's continue."

I vanish. At least, that's what it must look like to almost everyone here. However, unlike the king, I didn't use [Accel]. It's just that my speed has risen so much that even most of the veteran warriors would have a hard time keeping up.

Among the ones who keep track of my movements is the king. His eyes follow me, but that doesn't mean his body can do the same. The spear he swings is even faster than before since he's obviously given up on holding back and is putting everything into his attack.

But it's not enough.

The sharp sound of metal. A whizzing of air. And finally, the clattering of a spear hitting the floor.

"It's my loss," the king says, my spear pointed at his chest.

His weapon lies across the arena grounds. Besides that, he understands just how futile it would be to continue the battle. That's why he went for an all or nothing attack as soon as he realized how outmatched he became. He was hoping for a miracle.

A foolish decision on the battlefield, and one that I'm sure he wouldn't make. But when it's a duel where he can't rely on tactics like retreating or teaming up on his opponent, it was really his only chance.

"Thanks for the fun battle," I say. "I think I could get used to this country's tendency to rely on duels to settle things."

"Hah..." The king shakes his head. "We have enough trouble already. We don't need a human running around challenging our best warriors to duels."

"Don't worry. Once we solve this little civil war, we'll be on our way. We've got more important things to worry about than a single country."

The king raises an eyebrow. "You speak as if you hold the world's fate in your hands."

"Well, you're not wrong. But why don't we get comfortable before we get into such a long discussion."

"The condition for my victory was information on you and your strange skills. But I lost, so there's no need to reveal them."

"Oh, right. I was planning on telling you anyway, so it was all the same to me, win or lose."

"So I was fooled into accepting a win condition that didn't even matter..."

"Haha. Don't think about it too deeply. Just go with the flow."

"Well, it matters not. Though I suppose if you plan to spill some details, we'll use this estate's reception room since it offers comfortable accommodations."

The king motions for us to follow. So, onward we go to reveal the truth to Belfast's ruler about who we are and why we're here.

And to get some refreshments, of course.

# Chapter 13: Hatching a Plan

## ----- Lutz -----

"[True Blessing of the Goddess]?" the king, Kuro Zidane Ballard, says. "Are you saying that you were summoned as a Great Hero?"

"Yep." I release his hand now that I've completed the [Scry] spell for him.

"But I don't recall any of the three heroes being so young and ... no wait! Could it be that you're the False Hero!?"

At the mention of my title, the air grows tense. Even if I'm not being hunted to the same degree in the beastkin lands as I was in Orakio, that doesn't mean my reputation hasn't preceded me.

Even the elves knew of my summoning, thanks to King Edgar sending letters out to all the major nations on this continent, so it's no surprise that I get many hostile glares.

"Master's not a bad person!" Alisha seems particularly determined to reiterate her feelings these days.

"I'm inclined to agree, based on everything I've seen since his arrival," Kuro says. "He even rescued my only daughter, so I suppose I owe him the time to explain his situation more clearly."

"He saved me from slavery in the human lands, then beat up some bad vampires, then built a hotspring, then helped the elves, then beat up an army of fiends, then met the Goddess, then beat up the guys chasing your daughter, then came here to meet you!"

*Hey, why are you emphasizing everything I beat up during our journeys?*
*And I think you skipped some details in your explanation...*

"That's quite a lot of disconnected events." Kuro says exactly what I was thinking. "But we can go more in depth later. For now, I'm curious about the magic you showed me earlier. Can you teach it to others?"

"About that..."

I give King Kuro the rundown on my [Inventory] skill. He's disappointed to learn that I can't teach others, but he perks up when I hand him a ring enchanted with the skill.

The usual conversation follows, with me giving various explanations about many things, both on my strange abilities and my adventures. I've told the stories so many times now that I almost fall into a trance with each retelling.

Of course, I only tell him the things that aren't secrets. Stuff dealing with the Immortal Beings or details on some of the people helping me, like Lumina and King Edgar, are left out. I can't reveal the true identity of the other three heroes yet, either. At least, not until the time is right.

My connection to the Mana Network is also off limits. There's no telling what people would think if they knew I was essentially a walking Great Cathedral. Best to keep that one to myself until I can figure out how to strengthen my connection and access some of its features.

"And that sums it up." I take a sip of tea.

"Quite a tale." Kuro sits back in his seat. "If it's true, then Chaos has truly played us all for fools."

"Yeah, pretty much. But I'm slowly clawing my way up. Once I get the strength I need, I'll be putting an end to this war myself."

"That's some confidence. Do you really think you can defeat the army of fiends with just this small group?"

"No. Actually, I was pretty much told that I needed the support of the people before I had a chance of winning."

I leave out the fact that the reason I need their support is more for unlocking my final Heroic Skill, rather than their help on the battlefield. Since I'm not sure how much having them fight alongside me in the final battle would help, it's best to assume me and the girls will be doing most of the heavy lifting.

*I should grind up some more people before then. Kalyn and the others, maybe. Kymil and Galan, perhaps. Even Lumina's brothers, Lyle and Rhys, might be a good option.*

Having a few other high levels to lead the main battle while I take on the Lord of Chaos might be a huge help. The cooperation of the other nations is a must-have, as well. More national scale armies means more pressure we can put on the fiends. And if I grind up each nation's most powerful warriors, they can hold their own, even against full strength Archfiends.

"Anyway," I say. "I've told you about who I am, so how about telling me about yourself. More specifically, why you've been dethroned and who took the crown."

"I made a grave mistake. I received a request to duel by someone who by all accounts had no right to challenge me. And I accepted it."

"Uh, what? Where's the mistake, exactly?"

"He was seeking the crown, so when I lost the duel, I lost the throne."

"Wait, you were dueling over the right to be king!?"

"Yes. Although it may seem strange to humans, beastkin kings often receive such challenges. However, very few have the right to demand I accept the duel, so there's no shame in denying most of them. That should have been the case with Rei, but I foolishly accepted, believing I could easily defeat him."

"So this Rei guy is the new king?"

"Correct."

"And he's even stronger than you? There can't be many people in Belfast who could beat you in a duel, so was this guy a mysterious adventurer or something?"

"No, he's..." Kuro looks to Princess Keiko and her brother, whose name I still haven't checked. "He was the crown prince."

"He's your son!?"

The revelation that the king was dethroned by his own son was something that I never expected. Considering how badly Rei wants to get rid of the old king, it's still hard to believe, even after hearing it from Kuro's own mouth.

"It seems this Rei fellow would be right at home in my lands," Tylith says.

"Mmm. A vampire's most threatening adversary is often their own son."

"Yes. My brother took his position of power after overthrowing our father. Though at the time, I could only see it as a boon considering how bloodthirsty that man was."

"But I thought the duels beastkin love so much were steeped in honor, not desire. How is it that your son was allowed to seek the throne and even send the army to hunt you afterwards?"

"It's a long story," Kuro says. "Suffice to say that my rule had been growing unpopular as of late. Many saw me as weak, especially since I had plans to form an official alliance with King Edgar of Orakio in an effort to defeat our shared enemy."

"You were going to team up with the humans?" I ask. "I can see how that'd be unpopular, but isn't now the exception? I mean, there's the whole impending end of the world and all."

"If it's the fiends, then I'll have you know our war efforts against them have been quite successful. We even managed to recapture a bit of our land. Perhaps that's why many fail to see how perilous our situation is. Though there are a few more grievances that likely had a bigger impact on many of my nobles' decisions to rally behind my son."

"What could be more important than the war that requires the summoning of the Great Heroes?"

"It was precisely the summoning that they detested. Or rather, who was summoned."

As I think upon the king's words, I recall a comment made by the Astral Dryad the last time I saw her. She teased me with a bit of information to get me to think about why humans have been allowed to conquer most of the continent.

*The Goddess is biased toward humans. During this summoning, each hero was a human, after all. Even me, and I'm not even from this world.*

*Though what they don't know is that it wasn't the Goddess who picked the other three heroes.*

*Still, most heroes have been human, with only one elf, two beastkin, and not a single vampire. That means out of the 16 people who've been picked as Great Heroes during the four summonings so far, 13 of them have been human.*

*Something's definitely strange about that...*

"Yeah," I say. "I bet there were a lot of frustrated beastkin who thought at least one of their kind should have been chosen."

"Indeed. Add onto that the recent invasion of our lands from the father of one of the Great Heroes and the picture becomes even more clear. There was no way I could dispatch a force to push him from our lands, not with his close relation to one of the heroes."

"I attempted negotiations, allowing him to keep the territory for now, if he granted safe passage out of the land for my people. But the man rejected the offer and even claimed that he wouldn't stop with just reclaiming his old territory. So, I was forced to send troops north to protect our border, pulling them away from the battle against Chaos."

"Ah, him." I nod, remembering the vile man. "Well, he's dead now, and I forced his army to retreat. Though I didn't stay long enough to make sure they didn't regroup and retake the city."

"You ... killed him? One of the Great Heroes' own father?"

"Yeah. I gave him a chance, just like you did. When he turned my offer down—well, he barely had time to regret it."

King Kuro looks conflicted. We managed to take back his territory, but we did so by potentially causing irreparable damage to their relationship with Cedric, one of the Great Heroes.

Something I've been holding back from Kuro is that Cedric is actually working for Chaos. It's too much to take in without any sort of evidence to back it up, and it'd only make me seem like I'm conspiring against the Great Heroes, which isn't a good look considering my title of False Hero.

So, explaining why I went so far as to slay the man's father is difficult.

"I know what I did seems rash," I say. "But you'll have to trust me that it wasn't out of revenge or anything like that. Well, maybe a little. But I really would have let the man go if he cooperated."

"If you're trying to convince someone, you shouldn't say that even a small part of it was for revenge." King Kuro sighs. "But what's done is done. We'll have to work through this turn of events one way or another."

"Right. About that. If you want to do anything about it, you'll need to be king again. But I have two questions I need answered before I can make any moves. First, why were you so caught off guard about your son's strength when he demanded a duel? Shouldn't you have a good grasp on how strong he is?"

"I did. At least, I thought so. But when the duel began, he brought out strength surpassing even my own. Even now, I still don't understand where he obtained it in such a short time."

"Hmm. If it's a sudden surge in strength, then it's possible he power-leveled in a dungeon or got his hands on some super powerful enchanted gear. Maybe both. And if it's knowledge on how to farm dungeons or create world-class items, there's only one culprit..."

"Chaos," Laya says.

"Yeah. I mean, look what happened after the kid took the throne. Civil war. That can't be a coincidence. This is likely a scheme to destroy Belfast from the inside. I've seen the fiends do it many times now."

"Find the son and solve the problem?"

"I'd like to secure the real king's safety first. Maybe we can teleport him far away for now, then solve the problem ourselves."

"I don't think that's a good idea, Master."

"What's wrong with it?"

"Beastkin won't follow a man who fears for his life so much that he hides while a group of unknown adventurers solve his problems. Even if he regains the crown, it will only be for a short while."

"Ah. Beastkin culture is still new to me, so I didn't think about that. I suppose we have no choice, then. We'll have to put King Kuro front and center as we retake the throne. Anyway..." I look back to the king. "My second question was about the one leading the army sitting outside the gates, Riona. Can we reason with her?"

"Riona has always followed the word of the king without question. When the crown was set upon my son's head, her allegiance switched in an instant. Getting her to give up the siege without a fight will be a difficult task."

"I thought so, from what I heard about her earlier. Guess I really do have my work cut out for me, then."

"What do you plan to do?"

"I'll try talking to her first. Who knows, maybe I can bring about a miracle."

"And when that fails?"

"Ouch. Not even an ounce of confidence, huh? Well if that fails, I'll hatch a scheme of my own. Though I'm still working out the details..."

"What about us, Master?"

"You four can do whatever you want for a bit. Just don't leave the city unless you're teleporting. I don't want to cause a commotion if they catch sight of you."

"Alright! I'm going to go help some of my people while you're gone!"

"I figured you'd say that. Then, I'm off to meet this Riona. I'll be back in a while."

"Have fun!" Alisha sees me off with a wave.

After stepping out of the reception room, I turn toward the powerful source of mana that sits outside the castle walls.

*I wonder what kind of ears she's going to have...*

----------

*Hmm. Is my luck that good today? Riona's all alone right now...*

After leaving the mansion, I walked to the western edge of the city, stopping on top of the wall that separates us from the army of troops outside.

Well, walked might not be the right word. I was chased by soldiers not long after leaving the manor, so I basically fled capture all the way here. Several times.

But it's no big deal since King Kuro said he was going to inform the soldiers that we're here to help. Maybe by the time I get back from my meeting with Riona, I'll be able to walk around without getting yelled at to halt and other commands.

Even though my [Sense Mana] spell can detect presences for several miles in all directions, I have a hard time picking out individual presences when they're packed together so tightly. Getting closer helps, just like how a person can see objects in the distance but may have to get closer to make out the finer details.

As for my [Minimap], it only shows dots for those in areas I've explored. While the entire landscape around the city is revealed on my map, there are a few dark spots.

Enclosed areas won't be revealed just by leaping around the sky, so I'll have to get closer before they show up on my map. That's why all the tents and such the army has set up are still dark to me. And unfortunately, Riona has been in one of those dark spots every time I've checked my map.

*Well, since she's alone in her tent, this is the perfect chance for me to talk to her.*

*But should I take a more diplomatic route by walking up to someone strong and asking to meet her?*

*Nah. Sounds annoying.*

"Hey, you!" I hear a man's voice call out from below. "What are you doing up there!?"

I look down at the wall below, where a pair of soldiers stand in the middle of the walkway they use to patrol. Normally, they'd only have to look up at the watchmen standing in dedicated towers, but seeing as how I'm standing on the roof of one such tower, they have to turn their heads up to me, as well.

"Oh, how's it going?" I wave down at the soldiers. "Good job on the patrol. Keep it up for a little longer, alright?"

"Who are—"

The man's words cut off there, as do all sounds. My vision warps at the same time, while my senses go numb.

However, the teleport ends quickly, and when the light returns, I find myself in a tent adequately lit with candles. It's so large that there's even room for a full-size command table surrounded by a dozen chairs, atop which sits a map of the city and surrounding land.

From a cursory glance, I can see that they've been marking the locations of all the troops, no doubt preparing for a potential invasion of the city.

But I'm not here to spy on their battle plans. If everything goes the way I want, there won't even be a need to fight. So, I tear my eyes from the map, and they fall on this tent's sole occupant.

Riona is tall for a woman. Nearly as tall as me, and I've got several fingers over most men in this world. However, she has all the curves one might expect for a woman. As for her ears...

*Floppy and brown? Looks like dog ears, though it beats me what kind of breed it might be.*

Although it might not be accurate to call her young, neither would it be right to call her old. She's sitting somewhere comfortably in-between, which I'd expect from such a powerful warrior.

Checking her status, I see that she's 37, though she looks about a decade younger than that. Maybe it's from all the exercise, as her body is quite toned, with sun-kissed skin not only on her arms and legs but also her nape, shoulders, thighs, and stomach.

As for how I know what the bare skin on her stomach looks like...

*Huh. So she wears white underwear.*

*No, wait. That's not what I should be thinking right now.*

*I wonder if her murderous glare is because I barged in on her while she's getting changed.*

"Assassin." Riona says, not even attempting to hide her body.

*Guess not. She's probably just getting ready to murder me, like normal. Hmm. When did that become normal?*

I pull my mind back from that line of thought. "Hello, Riona. It seems I intruded on you at an inconvenient moment. I'd be happy to wait while you dress yourself, if you want."

"Fool! I don't need my armor to defeat an assassin!"

"I'm not an assassin, though? I mean, I'm not even carrying a weapon." I show her my empty hands and waist.

"It'll take more than that to get me to drop my guard. Assassins are known for their hidden weapons."

"What, you want me to strip down, too? I didn't know the general in charge of Belfast's army was such a deviant..."

"A-as if I would want such a thing!"

"Haha. Don't worry, I'm not much of an exhibitionist. But seriously, we can't have a conversation with you looking like that, so get dressed already, would you?"

Riona glares at me some more, but she does grab a cloak and drape it around her body. It seems covering herself improves her mood because her death stare subsides just a bit.

"You have one sentence to explain yourself before I run you through." Riona points her sword toward my heart.

"I'm a summoned hero who just happened to be in the area and got dragged into this civil war thanks to rescuing Princess Keiko and bringing her back to King Kuro, who lost to me in a duel and was forced to tell me everything and go along with my plan to end this war and get Belfast back into the battle against Chaos, which is where you come in since convincing you to stop the siege is vital to getting the two sides to make peace, and now that I'm here, I want to talk to you about how we can achieve that. How's that? It was one sentence."

Riona frowns. "You sure are relaxed, even after spitting out so many lies. Don't think you can get away. [Teleport] has a long time between casts, and you're surrounded by thousands of my men."

"Hey, what part was a lie?"

"All of it, of course! How ridiculous! Do you expect me to believe you were summoned by the Goddess!? The three heroes are all in Orakio, fighting at the behest of the king!"

"Hmm. You're partly right, but I can't give you full marks for that answer."

"Then it's good that this isn't a lesson. Unless you count the lesson you're going to learn about how I came to be Belfast's Grand General."

"Woah, fast!" I barely manage to twist my body out of the way of her piercing attack. "Could it be that my charming personality backfired?"

"Who'd be charmed by a creep who teleports in while a woman's changing!?"

"Hey—" I duck a swing. "—it's not my fault. Who gets changed in the command tent, anyway?"

"Silence!"

*Well this didn't turn out like I hoped...*

The truth is that Riona isn't someone I can defeat in an instant like most others in this world. Even without her equipment, her strikes are scary quick. If I were to take a hit directly, I'd actually sustain some damage.

If her offense is this high, then her defense should be roughly similar. It wouldn't be a simple matter to restrain her or defeat her without a prolonged battle.

Back when Alisha was retelling our adventures, she kept talking about all the people I beat up. But that's not why I came here. In fact, fighting back would probably only hurt our chances of ending this conflict without bloodshed, so all I can do is dodge her assault.

"Stop moving!" Riona yells.

"I will when you stop swinging that sharp piece of metal around!"

"I'll stop swinging my sword after you're dead!"

"Don't you think that condition is just a little one sided!?" The blade passes right by my ear.

"Complain to the Goddess when you meet her!"

*What to do...!*

*Escape? But I haven't really made any progress. No, I just made things worse, didn't I?*

*I can't leave like this!*

*C'mon, think. How can I calm her down, just for a minute?*

A plan blooms in my brain. One so genius that I have to struggle to keep the smirk from my lips.

*Hah. Let's do it!*

Riona's sword closes in, but unlike every time before, I make no attempt to avoid it. She realizes that it's too late for me to dodge, so a frown appears on her face, as if she's expecting a trap.

"[Accel]."

"Kuh...!" Riona lets out a sound as I whizz by her. "...Huh?"

She turns and meets my eyes "You didn't attack? What a wasted opportunity. I won't give you another chance!"

"Oh, I attacked." I hold up my hand. "And I got exactly what I wanted."

Riona looks at the cloak in my hand, then down at her exposed body. "K-kyaa—"

She forces her mouth shut before more than a tiny snippet of her scream escapes. But it's enough to reveal the truth.

"I knew it! You were trying to act like you didn't care that you were in your underwear, but when you had the chance to bundle up, you did so in a hurry and even looked relieved after!" I point my free hand toward her. "You're actually really shy, aren't you!"

"H-how uncouth! Undressing a maiden in the midst of battle! I won't forgive you!"

"Try saying that again after wiping those tears from your eyes."

"There aren't any tears!" She wipes them anyway.

"So..." I twirl the cloak. "Feel like having a civil discussion now?"

"As if I would ever talk to a barbarian like you!" She seems to realize something. "The guards. Certainly they've heard the commotion, yet..."

"Oh, I paralyzed them with fear after teleporting in. They're a bit strong, so I'll be feeling the physical effects of [Hypnosis] soon. I'd like to end this dance quickly, if you don't mind."

"But you just used [Accel]! Are you saying you can dual cast!?"

"Bingo."

Although I provide no proof, the simple fact that the guards haven't rushed in during our battle adds weight to my words. That's enough of a crack for me to pry open.

"I'm going to end this civil war, Riona. And I need your cooperation to do so."

"I follow the orders of the king, not some human who shows up when he pleases!"

"Yeah, so I've heard. But don't you think this situation has gotten out of control? I mean, you're going after the former king on the order of the new one when the world is on the brink of disaster. Isn't that a little strange?"

"..."

"So you do understand. Look, I don't have time to play mediator with everyone. I'm going to end this civil war, and I'm going to do it with your help. Do you want to know how?"

"I ... wouldn't turn down the opportunity to hear the plans of my enemy."

"Excellent. Then..."

I give Riona the quick version of my plan. Even though I only speak a couple sentences, that's all it takes for her to understand. But it's obvious she has absolutely no faith in my idea.

"I won't turn your offer down. However, you'll fail. Honor dictates that I fight with everything I have."

"I was hoping you'd say that. But as for whether or not we can succeed—well, just look forward to it." I toss the cloak back to Riona. "Here, get dressed. It's not proper to go around looking like that."

"And whose fault is it!?" She puts the cloak on during her retort.

"Anyway, I'll be going now. Try not to think about how embarrassing this was when you're going to sleep tonight."

"As if I'll spare this encounter even a single thought when you leave!"

"Haha." I give her a wave. "Cya soon."

The world's light vanishes once again. However, [Teleport] is still on cooldown, so I'm actually using my [Shadow Step] spell to warp through the tent's ceiling, where I land on an [Air Step]. Leaping higher with [Shadow Step], I reach a height where I can't be easily spotted, so I allow my Dark Magic spell to come to an end.

*Hmm. I wonder how long she stared at my shadow clone before realizing it was fake.*

*Eh, not my problem.*

Turning, I take off through the skies, heading back to the estate where King Kuro still resides. The man is back in the meeting room where we first met, so I drop down onto a balcony that's close to it and barge right in.

There are guards, but word about us has already spread, so they don't attack. They do insist on escorting me, though. Since I don't have a reason to refuse, I let them lead me to Kuro.

"That was rather quick," the king says. "Did you fail?"

"Yes and no. I didn't manage to get her cooperation outright, but I did get her to agree to a plan that will lead to our victory."

"Oh? And what is this plan of yours?"

"King Kuro." I point at the man. "You are going to duel Riona!"

Silence fills the meeting room. The officials, soldiers, Princess Keiko, her brother, and even the king himself look at me with disbelief.

"That's your plan!?" Kuro yells. "Riona would never throw a duel! And despite my strength, even I cannot defeat her in single combat!"

"I know. That's why I'm here. With my help, you'll be strong enough to face her—and maybe even win!"

"You don't sound very confident!"

"Haha, sorry. I only have until tomorrow afternoon to get you ready, but I'm sure it'll work out."

"Barely half a day. What do you expect to accomplish in such a short time?"

I raise a single finger. "We'll start by beating up some dungeon bosses! Tylith."

"Hmph." She appears as soon as I speak her name. "I'm prepared to teleport us at any time."

Kuro looks between the two of us. "What have I gotten myself into...?"

# Chapter 14: The Beastkin City

## ----- Alisha -----

"Keiko, Keiko!" I smile at the black-haired princess who has a set of cat ears like me. "Where to next!?"

"Um, let's see. We brought food to the orphans, medicine to the sick, and healed the injured. I'm not sure what else we can do, but perhaps we could visit a church to reassure the worshippers."

"Oh, a church! People who are the most worried will go there to pray, right?"

"Yes. By showing my face there, I'm hoping that I can relieve some of their anxiety."

"Then let's do it! To the church!"

After Master went to meet with that Riona person, the rest of us went out to help lots and lots of people. We did our usual rounds at all the important places, doing our best to make everyone smile.

Somewhere along the way, Master returned. Because things didn't go the way he wanted, Tylith had to leave and help him teleport the king, Keiko's brother, and a few of the most powerful beastkin soldiers.

They're going to the dungeon where we beat up lots of monsters a couple weeks ago so he can grind King Kuro some levels. I wanted to go, too. But I also wanted to keep helping people here, so it was hard to decide!

Since Laya and Belle were staying, I built up my resolve and stayed behind, too. I was surprised that only Master and Tylith were going. I understand why Belle wanted to stay, but Laya usually follows Master everywhere, so I knew there was a reason.

Before he left, Master gave Laya a mission to check the city for any strange sources of mana or Dark Magic. The places we've been going to help people have brought us all over the city, so it was the perfect chance for her to complete two missions at once!

But so far everything has been normal. We haven't even met a single bad person. Though some of them have been really rude, especially to Belle! It makes me mad, but that's just how it is here.

Actually, there is one strange thing in the city, but it's not something that's a threat. Besides, Master already knows about it, though we're not sure what to do about it yet.

"We're here," Keiko says. "I wonder how many people are inside."

"Lots! Ah, but there's still room for us, so don't worry!"

"That so? Then shall we all go inside?"

"We'll sit this one out," Belle says. "We spent a lot of time in a church recently, and I'm sure they'd rather hear from their princess, rather than a group of mysterious adventurers."

"I suppose you have a point. We couldn't share all the information with them, so they don't know the full truth. That makes things a bit difficult."

"Yeah, and this gives me the perfect opportunity."

"To do what?"

"Hehe. Don't worry, just focus on cheering those people up!"

Princess Keiko looks between us, but since Laya and I have no idea what Belle's talking about, we can only shrug back at her. Ah, I'm the only one who shrugged, though.

Keiko quickly gives up on us going inside with her. Since she understands we don't plan to do anything bad, she and her guards enter the church, leaving me, Laya, and Belle alone on the street outside.

"We sure do go to a lot of churches these days," Belle says. "And I have a feeling that's only going to increase in the future..."

"Mmm. Even after the war, we may visit them often, depending on what Lutz decides to do."

"Yeah. He should have quite a reputation afterwards, huh? Though I don't see him letting anyone to parade him around like a trophy."

"I agree. It would be best if we could live a simple life after the war."

"Ohhh!" Belle smirks. "We, huh? Who's going to be living with him, exactly?"

"W-well…"

"Ah, I want to stay with Master! Laya should stay, too! And everyone else!"

"I don't mind at all," Belle says. "It sounds like things were different where he came from, but in this world, it's quite normal, isn't it?"

"Laya, you're staying, right?" I show her a sad pair of eyes.

"Of course she is. Her reason for being so reserved all this time was because she thought her lifespan didn't match up with Lutz's. But now…"

"Still doesn't match," Laya says. "He's an Immortal Being now."

"The situation may have reversed, with him now having a longer life ahead of him, but that doesn't change the fact that his increased lifespan shattered the one wall that stood in your way."

Everyone in our party knows how Laya feels, even Master. But because it was impossible, nobody pushed the issue. Now that impossibility is gone, like all the monsters we beat up.

Ever since we found out the truth about Lutz's new lifespan, Laya has been quieter than usual. She gets like that when she's thinking a lot, so we all left her to sort out her feelings.

But it seems Belle thinks it's been long enough. She wants to know what Laya decided, and now's the perfect chance to ask.

"I … don't intend to do anything," Laya says after a long silence. "We have too many responsibilities and too many people depending on us. We can't afford to let anything distract us from our goals because if we fail, there won't even be a world left for us to live in.

"So we have to get stronger. Strong enough that we can protect everyone without fail, strong enough that all of us live to see the smiles on the people's faces once we defeat the Lord of Chaos. That's the only future I care about right now.

"But even as we seek that strength, we can't let anything prevent us from helping the people who are suffering, just like the ones here in the beastkin lands. If we simply leave the people within arm's reach to their misery, then we don't even deserve to be called heroes.

"It's only by focusing on those two goals that we can defeat Chaos. Strength and faith. We must acquire them, no matter what personal desires we have to give up in the process. That's why I won't be saying anything to Lutz.

"But ... I'm not his daughter. I'm Laya Emilia Sylphrena, and after this war, I intend to tell him clearly."

*I've never heard her speak so many words at once!*

Her long speech only goes to show just how much she's thought about the subject and how much she cares to make the right decision, one that will leave a smile on everyone's faces, including her own.

"Wow!" Belle's eyes shine. "From one battlefield to another! Ohhhh, but fighting for love isn't like fighting monsters! I hope you're up to the task!"

"Ah..." Laya's rosy cheeks turn away. "I'm sure I can figure it out..."

"Well, don't worry! Just leave it to big sis Belle! I've already got it all planned out, so get ready for quite a show once the war is over!"

"Ah, teach me, teach me!" I wave my raised hand.

"Of course! And the same goes for the shy vampire and reluctant princess. Oh, and the battle-maid! Can't forget about her!"

"Yay! I can't wait!"

"Oh, but don't think we'll put everything on hold for you, Laya! Some of us don't have time to sit around for decades!"

"Mmm. I'm aware. But it's fine. It's simply the result of our circumstances. However, I'll always be number one, even if I'm last in line."

"Wow. When did you get so confident in these kinds of matters?"

"I've been giving it a lot of thought, so it's only natural."

After another round of lively conversations, Keiko finally steps out of the church, somehow looking both satisfied and sad at the same time.

Since I don't know what she's thinking just by looking at her face, I just come right out and ask!

"Hey, hey. How did it go in there?"

"About as well as I could hope. Many of them are worried. Not only about the civil war but about the fiends and the arrival of so many refugees."

"Eh? Are refugees that bad? It's normal during wars, isn't it?"

"Yes, but for some reason, many of the refugees have become Forsaken. It's thought that they've turned against the Goddess due to losing their livelihoods during the war, so we've had no choice but to lock them away."

"A-ah..."

Hearing that so many others with the same curse I carry have been showing up makes me a bit sad. It's not their fault that they were cursed any more than it was mine.

But it's not easy to convince people that the curse doesn't mean they've turned against the Goddess. It's a deeply ingrained belief, after all. Even I used to believe it, until Master told me otherwise.

"Forsaken," Laya says. "We felt their presence when we arrived, with many of them being held in what we assumed was a prison."

"Yes." Keiko nods. "We're not sure what to do about them because they don't seem dangerous. But it's not like we can let them roam freely."

"Yes, it's the same everywhere. Even we elves do not allow Forsaken to live freely. Though it's not something I agree with now."

"Eh? But aren't they enemies of the Goddess?"

"No, the truth is far different. Or so we believe. But it would be best to have this discussion later."

"Hey," Belle says. "If there are so many Forsaken, then do you think it has something to do with the Great Cathedral?"

"Mmm. We should probably stop by on our return trip to make sure there's no repeat of what happened at the eastern cathedral."

After hearing Belle and Laya mention the battle against the High Priest in the east, it makes me wonder if Chaos really is trying to take control of the Great Cathedral in Belfast.

According to Master, the fiends can only fight at full strength when near one of the cathedrals they control. So if they manage to take over the one near here, then this whole region would be overrun with Chaos.

"Anyway," Belle says. "Not much we can do about it now. Let's just keep doing our best for the people of this city until Lutz and the others get back."

"Yeah!" My excited nature overrides my negative thoughts. "I want to help them even more!"

"In that case," Keiko says, "let's walk around and see what other help we can offer."

The tour of one of my homelands' larger cities continues, led by none other than my very own princess.

# Interlude 2

## ----- Lumina -----

"What a surprise that was." I pour a bottle into the cauldron. "To think my uncle was alive all this time."

"Indeed," Elise says. "According to public records, he was executed after the civil war two decades ago."

"Yes. But Father managed to keep the truth hidden until now."

"After your grandfather's passing, the two of them fought for the crown. The loser of such a conflict will often find his head separated from his body to prevent another civil war from breaking out."

"That's true." I add the final ingredient and stir the goopy mixture. "Then I wonder why Father secretly exiled him..."

"I'm not sure, Princess. Maybe you should simply ask him."

"Perhaps. Though the reasons aren't too hard to deduce."

Two decades ago, my grandfather suddenly passed away from illness. The unexpected death of Orakio's king left a vacuum of power, which both my father and uncle attempted to fill. Since a nation can only have one ruler, it was obvious that conflict between them was inevitable.

My uncle had the support of many powerful nobles, but Father was the older of the two and was first in line to the throne. Because of that, he was able to rally most of the kingdom's army behind him.

According to the history books, the civil war was an attempted coup by my uncle. But reality is often different from the records written by the winner. Without having experienced the war with my own eyes, I can't say for sure which side was actually in the right.

"More importantly," I say as I stare into my cauldron. "I was surprised to see grandfather's former advisor make his return. According to my studies, he's a political genius."

"Yes. My own father admired him for his ability to navigate the treacherous landscape of politics. He never understood why the man retired so early, but now we know why."

"He left after the civil war, along with my exiled uncle. Though that doesn't tell us why. Regardless, he's made his return. Perhaps that will tip the scales in our favor when it comes to dealing with Duke Bradley and the three heroes."

"Speaking of the three heroes," Elise says. "They've been more active in the city as of late, but getting information on the details has proven difficult."

I begin the process of bottling up my mixture into potions. "It's frustrating, but we can't get involved with them directly. We've already made ourselves targets, so we can't afford a confrontation. Not while Sir Lutz is still seeking the power he needs."

"We'll have to hope that none of them make any major moves until he returns. Placing our hopes in the hands of fate is risky, but unless a door opens for us, it's the only path we have right now."

I finish filling up the final bottle, then send the remnants of the goopy mixture to my [Inventory]. It's the easiest way to clean the cauldron, and I can quickly dump the contents from my storage the next time I'm outside.

The day has been long, as most are for me now. Ever since I obtained the title of Prime Oracle, my responsibilities have gone from virtually zero to never ending.

I've become a symbol of humanity's resistance against the fiends, just like the three heroes. It's a little daunting, but this is the path I chose when I first decided to leave the safety of my private chambers to seek out Sir Lutz.

In the past, I had so much free time that taking on a new hobby like alchemy on a whim was simply a matter of deciding to do it. There was no sacrifice and no need to find a way to fit it into my busy days.

But it's different now. I spent most of today on my new duties, only allocating this short reprieve between tasks to enjoy my new hobby. But now the moment has passed, and it's time to get back to work.

Elise and I exit the atelier, locking the door behind us. The castle hall the room sits in is rather close to my personal room, as was my request, but that means it's also a bit distant from the main facilities we use when performing our official duties.

However, it's just a single castle, so even if the walk is a bit long, the difference in time is negligible.

"About the agenda for the rest of the day, Princess—do you have any candidates in mind for the position of High Priest?"

"Do you think they'd entertain the idea of elevating Miri?"

"A nice jest, Princess. Though I don't think the clergy would see the humor in it."

"Haha. I know, I know. But really, it's difficult to give my support to anyone but her, considering her role in this world now. Perhaps it would be best to abstain from the discussion until the time is right..."

After Sir Lutz defeated High Priest Melina in the far east, it left us with only a single High Priest. Since we control two of the Great Cathedrals, we've always had two High Priests to match.

Though in truth, we now control no Great Cathedrals. The one in the far east was destroyed during Sir Lutz's battle, while the one on the western peninsula is under the control of Chaos. In this situation, perhaps it'd be accurate to say we shouldn't have any High Priests.

But pride won't allow us to admit to such a thing. Not to mention the boost to morale we'd gain by elevating someone to High Priest. Under these circumstances, even I can't deny that choosing someone—anyone—would be a boon for our kingdom.

"I suppose they'll be pushing to elevate the priest in charge of Cedric's church," I say. "As much as it irks me, I can't see any others contesting his claim, considering he was handpicked by one of the Great Heroes."

"Indeed. But perhaps we can find at least one candidate to contest his claim. There are many priests who have done far more to help the people than him. By some miracle, maybe we can—"

Elise cuts her words off when we reach a four-way intersection. The reason for that is...

"Good afternoon, Princess Lumina." A man in an extravagant outfit gives me an elegant bow. "How fortunate we are to meet you here."

"Duke Bradley." I somehow manage to keep my voice even. "It's rare for you to grace us with your presence as of late."

"Ah, I'm a busy man, you see. Isn't it only natural that I'd be hard at work, rather than involving myself in the endless games of lesser nobles?"

"I see. When put that way, I suppose I can't argue. We can only hope that your days remain filled with work. For the sake of our kingdom, of course."

Duke Bradley smiles. "There's no need to worry about the future of our kingdom. I'll see to it that we continue to have a long and prosperous future."

"With allies like her by your side, it's only natural that you'd leave your mark on our nation's history books." My eyes move to Duke Bradley's companion.

"My, what an understanding child," Collette says. "It's no wonder you were chosen for a daunting position like Prime Oracle."

"Yes, and my connection to the Goddess has been very enlightening. Perhaps in the future, the world will come to understand, as well."

"Ah, the optimism of youth. Unfortunately, as long as they can continue living their lives, most people will believe whatever's most convenient for them."

"I have faith that those who are fighting to save this world will emerge victorious." I hold Collette's eyes. "And that those who stand in our way will get the end they deserve."

"It would be great if the world worked the same way it does in fairytales. Perhaps when you grow older, you'll realize that nothing is without sacrifices."

"Ladies," Duke Bradley says. "If we dally here any longer, we'll be late for the meeting. And as I'm sure you're aware, I'm quite the stickler for appearances."

"Then let's get moving. Since we're going to the same meeting, would you like to accompany us, Princess?" Collette gives me a knowing smile.

"I would love to walk with the two of you," I say without delay.

The four of us step into one of the four hallways and fall in line. Elise puts herself between me and the two agents of Chaos, with Duke Bradley coming next and Collette walking on the far end.

Most would never dream of walking alongside their bitter enemies. But it's still the afternoon. In high society, nobles get along while the sun still gives light to the world. It's only after darkness falls that we must fear the blade.

For now, the three heroes seem content to follow those rules. Though we can't be sure how long it will stay that way, hence why Elise put herself between me and them. It seems Collette is also signaling her intent to continue playing the game, as she walks at the furthest point from me.

I turn my head slightly, taking in the two of their faces. "I assume you're here to seek the advancement of Cedric's priest to the position of High Priest."

"It is so," Duke Bradley says. "Isn't it the natural conclusion? The Goddess would be pleased, I'm sure."

"Yes. Very pleased." I don't hide the sarcasm in my voice. "But if you wish to appoint him, why bring Collette and not Cedric?"

"Cedric is … preoccupied, you might say."

"Oh? It seems like he has plenty of time to preach at his church, so I'd be interested to hear what's so important that he couldn't make it to this meeting."

"I bet you would. However, the affairs of the Great Heroes shouldn't be spoken of lightly, even to the Prime Oracle herself."

"I see. In that case, I'll just wish him luck in whatever endeavor it is that's proving so difficult."

We finally arrive at the meeting room. Inside are some of the most influential people in the capital, including my father. Together, we will decide who will claim the currently vacant title of High Priest.

"After you, Princess Lumina." Duke Bradley gives me another one of his perfect bows.

"How gracious." I step into the room, with Elise on my heels.

*I wonder how long we can keep up this charade. Surely, whatever they're planning cannot stay hidden much longer.*

*Sir Lutz. I hope you will have a quick and uneventful journey…*

# Chapter 15: A King and His General

"And ... done!" I hold up a light green spear.

From just looking at it, anyone can tell this weapon is special. No metal gives off the same shine as adamantium, and when mixed with orichalcum, it becomes an unmistakable shade of green that embodies the highest class of equipment.

Stepping back from the crafting table, I give my body a nice stretch. With my obscenely high physical attributes, something like an hour or so spent heating and hammering this legendary-class spear into a proper form is nothing to me, but stretching still feels good, no matter what kind of shape a person is in.

The door in front of me opens, and King Kuro steps into the forge. In stories, these kinds of timings are always extremely convenient, where the person needed to move the scene forward just happens to walk in at the perfect time.

But in this case, there was no happenstance about it since I sent him a telepathic message telling him that his spear was ready. If there was anything I could label convenient, it'd be how quickly he arrived. Though that's likely because he understands just how important it is to go into battle fully equipped.

"Almost noon," Kuro says. "You certainly cut it close."

"Just makes it more dramatic, right? No harm in that. Anyway..." I motion to the spear laid out on the table. "I managed to get it mostly ready in time."

"Mostly? Is the weapon missing something?"

"Don't worry about it. All the important bits are finished. Sure, I wanted to add some sagestone to it, but I didn't have the time to completely revamp this forge to make it capable of smelting it. I'm sure you'll do just fine with the spear as it is."

King Kuro lets out a sigh. He's an intelligent and contemplative man, allowing him to react to nearly any situation with an appropriate response. That helped a lot when I teleported in with his daughter in tow.

He is a bit rigid, however. I guess that's to be expected of royalty, since they have to deal with so many formalities, but it means he has a hard time dealing with people who are outside his command.

*Come to think of it, I haven't even seen him crack a smile this entire time.*

Dropping that line of thought, I bring out several more items and place them on the table. A couple rings, a pair of boots, and a shirt to name a few. It's nearly a whole set of equipment, and each one radiates a powerful mana.

But in terms of pure strength, the only item other than the spear that really sticks out is the shirt. It has a few embroideries, but in terms of elegance, it can be considered lacking when compared to something a powerful noble would wear.

That's not much of a problem, though. It's technically an undershirt, meant to be worn beneath a highly decorated coat or robe. Since it won't be seen, even someone like a king can wear it without damaging their public image.

That's precisely why I chose it. We got it on our recent outing to the dungeon, The Beast Warrens, so of course it's a powerful piece of equipment. But just getting it from a chest isn't enough, which is why I recrafted it by adding some adamantium threads.

Although I'm still a little fuzzy on the finer details, changing an item's material composition in such a way makes it count as a crafted item, which means I can add my powerful buffs onto it, just like I do when I craft weapons or armor from scratch.

It's not like I can just add a single thread to it, though. I had to spend nearly an hour on this single shirt before the system recognized it as being recrafted. But that's still far better than making an entire shirt from a spool of thread.

All that said, I did hold back quite a bit on the shirt's enchantments. There's a reason for that, of course. Or rather, it was because of a request from King Kuro himself. The beastkin sense of honor is really strange.

I motion for Kuro to try on the equipment. It requires him to get changed, but people in this world aren't nearly as self-conscious about things like that, so his guardsmen and I don't even leave the room.

I still turn my head away, though. Just because he doesn't care doesn't mean I want to see another man undressing. Unfortunately, I can still clearly hear the sound of his ruffling clothes.

When he's done, I turn back to him and see that he looks almost exactly the same as before. That's to be expected, considering the enchanted clothes I gave him are worn beneath his extravagant attire.

But there are a few differences. The rings on his hands have changed, as have his boots. Like the shirt, they're items I got from the dungeon and are enchanted with powerful buffs, making them strong when compared to nearly anything else in the world.

Although I wasn't the one who enchanted his items—most of them, anyway. He wanted to leave the original buffs on them that they had when we found them in the dungeon chests. That's the only way he would use them in the upcoming duel.

Since Kuro managed to gain 5 levels in the dungeon, that brings him to level 63. He's still a full 5 levels behind Riona, but his equipment might make up the difference.

That said, I could feel a powerful mana coming from Riona's items. What little she wore during our meeting, that is. No doubt they came from a dangerous dungeon, just like the ones Kuro will be wearing.

I felt firsthand just how much skill Riona has with the sword. Kuro's no pushover, but Riona lives on the battlefield. If her skill and combat instincts are good enough, it's possible that she could defeat the king, even if his items are better than hers overall.

"I'll ask one more time to make sure," I say. "Do you want me to enhance you with magic?"

"Absolutely not." There's not an ounce of hesitation in Kuro's voice. "Duels are to be fought with one's own strength."

"You sure have some strange sense of honor. You'll let me grind you some levels and get you powerful equipment from the dungeon, but you won't let me enchant them or enhance you with spells before the duel."

"Victory should only go to the one who fought and won with their own strength. I was there with you, battling those fearsome guardians in the dungeon. Therefore, I have every right to lay claim to these items. However, if you were to enchant them with powerful magic beyond the scope of other mages, they would cease to be in the realm of equipment I can confidently claim to have earned with my own strength.

"Riona delved deep into many dangerous dungeons, where she obtained the strength she needed to become our country's Grand General. Were I to step onto the dueling grounds against her wearing equipment enhanced by a Great Hero, I couldn't claim victory, even if I defeated her in combat."

I nod. "Yeah, I get it. I've been there before, but I didn't think you'd still adhere to that sense of honor when your very kingdom is at stake."

"If I fail, even with the strength I've allowed you to grant me, then I don't deserve to rule Belfast." Kuro holds the newly crafted spear up.

When he told me I couldn't shower him with overpowered equipment, I bugged him until we came to a single agreement. As king, or former king now, it's common for people to offer gifts. So I told him that I, Lutz, was giving him the gift of a new spear as thanks for accepting me here in the city.

It was a weak argument, but it was just enough for Kuro to set aside his strict sense of honor. In the end, he allowed me to craft it and even agreed to use it in the duel against Riona.

To be honest, I wouldn't be so sure of his chances of victory without it. Even with it, there was enough doubt in me that I secretly recrafted that undershirt he's wearing and placed a few more buffs on it. He didn't notice when he put it on, so he probably thinks that's how strong it was when we got it from the dungeon chest.

Unfortunately, he can't wear his enchanted overcoat on top of the undershirt. Buffed equipment that's too close together will interfere with each other, which is why we only wear one enchanted ring on each hand.

Artifacts are an exception, though. Equipment that contains no buffs, like our [Inventory]-enchanted rings, can sit right beside our powerful items without issue. That means we can, and do, wear artifacts that contain spells, ready to use whenever needed.

It's helpful for rounding out the girls' spell list, like giving [Accel] to Belle, allowing her to cast it, even though she can't use it naturally. However, Kuro rejected even that. He does have some artifacts, a few of which we found in The Beast Warrens, but he wouldn't let me enchant him any new ones. He wants the duel to be between him and Riona.

Since we're finished with preparations, we step outside, where Alisha and the others are waiting. There's nothing else for us to do, so we're all just counting down the minutes before the scheduled start of the duel.

"Master! It's noon, it's noon!"

"Is it, though?" I look up at the sky.

"Yeah! The sun is just being a little slow today!"

"I don't think that's how it works, you little rascal." I give her hair a nice ruffling.

"Hehe~" She leans into my hand. "I got a reward."

"There's less than a half-hour before the duel," Kuro says. "I'm going to the wall, where we agreed to meet."

I give a shrug. "Might as well join you. Not much else to do right now, and it's a good chance to pick your brain."

The king begins walking westward, toward the wall. "Pick my brain?"

"Don't let his weird way of talking get to you," Belle says. "He just wants to dig for information."

"If it's questions, then don't expect answers if any are national secrets."

"No, no," I say. "It's nothing like that. I'm just curious about a few things. For example, will this army really just leave if you beat Riona in a duel? That's a huge investment of their time and resources they're putting on a single battle's outcome. Not to mention the current king—your son. Will he accept something like that?"

"Our ways may seem strange to foreigners, but this wouldn't be the first time a decisive battle has been determined by the generals of each side. Any who refuse to accept the outcome will lose a great amount of honor in the eyes of our people.

"However, even if I obtain victory here, that doesn't mean I can simply walk to the capital and take the crown. Once my son receives news of the duel, he'll likely redeploy the army in a defensive position and order them to prevent me from marching on the city. Such a move wouldn't violate the sanctity of the duel, but it would stop any retaliation."

I nod after hearing Kuro's words. "We could work with that, if that's how it ended up."

We reach the base of the wall, right where a guard tower sits. It's actually the very same tower I stood on before my own little duel with Riona.

Following the king, we climb the spiraling steps, eventually ending up on the wall's walkway.

I can't help but wonder if any of the guards happen to be the same ones who were surprised to see me atop the tower yesterday. But I didn't care enough to memorize their faces or mana signatures, so it'll forever remain a mystery.

"You know," I say, placing my hand on one of the crenellations and looking out over the enemy army. "I can't help but notice that they have you outnumbered at least 5 to 1. Even if you have these walls, there should be enough of them to take the city, if they really wanted."

Kuro joins me, running his eyes over the troops in the distance. "Riona follows orders to a fault, so she must be obeying my son. Perhaps he wishes to avoid a full-scale battle because of the fiends. Though from how he was acting before I fled, I have to wonder if he has the restraint to continue this stalemate."

"Perhaps. But if the usual suspects really are pulling the strings, they would have this army inside the city already. Makes me wonder if we're overthinking things."

Kuro focuses on some unusual movement in the enemy troops. From the thousands of soldiers, a small group steps out into the flat grasslands between them and the city.

"Seems she's ready." Kuro activates [Air Step]. "I'm going. I don't want to keep her waiting."

"Alright." I follow his lead, jumping off the wall. "I can't wait to see this battle!"

It'd be too suspicious if all of us go, so the girls are going to watch from the wall. With their enhanced eyesight, they won't have any problems making out the details, though.

Kuro, his guards, and I come to a stop in the center of the grassy field between the city and the besieging army. Riona and her men are already here, so all the pieces have been gathered. All that's left is to let the main contestants battle it out.

*Hmm. I really should make some popcorn for moments like this...*

"It's been a while, Riona," King Kuro says after coming face to face with the general.

"Indeed it has, Your Majesty. I didn't expect our reunion to end up as a duel. Are you sure you want to place the hopes of your resistance on such a match?"

"The fates have dealt me a hand, and it's one I intend to play."

"Fate, huh?" Riona glances at me for a brief second. "Recent events have been quite … peculiar. But it's not my place to question them, nor will I let some unseen current guide my hand. If you wish to challenge me to a duel, know that I will not show mercy, even to you."

Kuro nods. "That's precisely what I expected to hear, and I would have it no other way. However, don't think I'll be defeated as easily as the last time we fought. The fates have also seen to it that I have the strength to retake my kingdom."

"I noticed." Riona eyes the king's new spear. "Adamantium and orichalcum alloy weapons are a rarity, even in dangerous dungeons. Yet you've acquired one while stuck in a besieged city."

"It's not the only way I've grown recently. If you don't begin the battle giving it your all, you may soon find that you are the one lying defeated on the ground."

"Of course I will strike with the intent to win, even from the start. To do otherwise would be a dishonor to everything the duel stands for."

Seems the two of them have said everything they want to say. They give each other some sort of salute, then step back, allowing the gap between them to widen.

I'm not the only one who accompanied Kuro. His son and daughter came to watch the duel, as did his most powerful commanders.

I listen silently as those people all wish the king luck in their own ways. Since they've gone all-in on the chance he can regain the crown, it's no exaggeration to say their very livelihoods depend on the outcome of this duel.

*I wonder what kind of fate awaits them if Kuro were to lose.*

*Would they be executed as traitors? Or maybe just demoted and forcefully conscripted into the new king's army?*

My time in the human lands conditioned me to lean toward the most brutal outcomes in situations like this, but the beastkin culture has surprised me a few times now, so I can't say how it would end up.

Even though their cities closely resemble that of humans, there are some noticeable differences, such as the architecture used to construct their buildings.

The structure of their society is likewise similar to humans, but the finer details paint a different picture. For one, individual strength is far more important. Even King Kuro was once a soldier in the army. He wasn't born into a position of royalty and instead earned it by facing the previous king in a duel, which he won.

It seems everyone else is finally done talking. Since I don't want to be the only one who didn't wish him luck before the duel, I take this time to do so.

"You should have just let me cheat so you can easily win." I end up saying what's on my mind instead.

"We've been over this, Lutz."

"I know, I know. It just kinda slipped out." I don't even try to hide the smirk. "Anyway, I can tell you that your chances of winning are 50/50 if I'm being generous. Your spear is way better than her sword, but your other equipment is about equal. And since she has 5 levels over you, she has higher base stats."

"Riona was always powerful, even when she was young. It's not a surprise to hear that this weapon is only just able to help me close that gap."

"Yeah. So because of that, I won't be wishing you luck. Instead, I'll just tell you to have fun. That's more important, isn't it?"

"You sure are relaxed," Kuro says. "Considering this battle could determine the fate of an entire country, isn't a bit more prudence called for?"

"I couldn't help but notice you didn't deny the fact that you're enjoying this."

Kuro looks toward Riona on the other side of the clearing. "I wouldn't have become king if I didn't love the thrill of battle."

"I thought as much. My little beastkin companion is the same way. Well, minus the whole becoming the ruler of a nation thing."

Riona steps into the clearing, sword in hand, so we cut the conversation there. Kuro matches her steps with his own, leaving me, his family, and his guards behind.

The two warriors meet in the middle. There's enough space in the makeshift arena for them to move about as they please, without worry of stepping out of bounds. To an extent, of course.

With how quickly high level fighters can move, even this rather large area can be traversed in a single leap if they really wanted to. But there's no purpose in doing so under normal battle conditions.

"Sir Lutz," Princess Keiko says. "Can Father really win against Riona? She's one of our country's most powerful warriors..."

"Well, not only did I duel your dad, but I also saw him fight several powerful bosses in a dungeon. So I can say with certainty that Kuro is ... competent."

"Competent?" Keiko looks worried. "Isn't that just a nice way to say he's lacking?"

"It's all about perspective. I'm comparing him to the best of the best that I've seen in this world, like Laya. Among them, Kuro can only be considered competent, not exceptional. No matter how powerful he gets and what kind of legendary equipment he wears, it won't help things like his battle instincts."

"I see..."

"Don't look so disappointed. Compared to the average warrior, he could still be considered a genius. But he's not fighting an average warrior. You said it yourself, he's going up against one of the strongest warriors in your country.

"Some people are so far above others that they seem out of reach to the average person. When you try to compare yourself to them, it's hard to even know where they stand. But to another genius in the field, it's not so uncertain. And once the two geniuses clash in a winner take all competition, their limits become much more defined."

"Are you saying that Riona and Father can see each other's limits, even if I cannot?"

"Yeah. Which means your dad knows that he's at a disadvantage in this fight. Yet he still held true to his honor for a fair duel. So while he might not be the best warrior in the world, perhaps he could be the most honorable one. I wouldn't know, though."

Keiko refocuses on the two warriors. Or rather, she never actually looked away from them. It was only her thoughts that drifted.

*Honor, huh? It's commendable, but...*

It's easy to claim someone has honor because they stick to their beliefs, even when things are difficult. But like anything else, honor is subjective.

Riona is honoring her beliefs, just like Kuro. She's obeying the king, as she's always done. Were the ruler someone acting in good faith, then her dedication would be seen as admirable.

But what happens when they're a tyrant? That rigid way of thinking can only lead to enhancing the tragedies in a tyrant's wake.

Following that line of thinking, it's easy to say that sometimes, abandoning your personal beliefs for the greater good is the better course of action. But in that case, when does it become just a convenient excuse to do what you want?

How is anyone supposed to know if their version of honor is correct? And if you're met with a difficult decision where your morality conflicts with your sense of honor, which one do you abandon?

Riona is struggling with that very question. I saw it in her eyes when we fought in that command tent. She understands that the new king's orders are questionable at best, yet she continues to follow them because that's what her honor dictates.

Kuro knows that it's up to him to bring this country back from the brink of disaster. He even has a hero summoned by the Goddess by his side, yet he refuses to take the easy path to victory because of his honor. If things go poorly, it won't be only him who suffers but an untold number of his citizens. Perhaps the whole world.

If someone were to ask me which one of them was in the right, I wouldn't be able to give a definite answer. Perhaps Riona thinks this is the best path for her kingdom. Kuro himself ousted the previous king in a duel, so this is just the way of her people. What right does she have to decide that this time is different?

As for Kuro, maybe he thinks the only way to legitimize his rule is to follow the codes of honor that he's lived by his whole life. I don't know what drove him to duel the previous king for control of the country, but from what I can see, it wasn't a lust for power. By giving up his honor, he might worry he'll eventually become no better than the man he replaced.

Such matters are never so easily categorized as good, bad, moral, or just. That's just how people are. Messy, imperfect, hypocritical, and a host of other ailments plague each and every human.

Some deal with it by closing their eyes each time they look in the mirror. Others recognize their shortcomings, but just knowing they have flaws doesn't mean they understand how to fix them. If it were that easy, humanity wouldn't have made so many mistakes over the centuries.

*Those two really need to take others into consideration when thinking about their honor...*

I mentally release a sigh.

*After all, I'm the one who's going to have to put in the overtime to make sure both of them can keep their honor intact.*

# Chapter 16: Duel of Honor

## ----- Kuro -----

*What a frightening aura. It's even more overwhelming than the last time we dueled.*

Although I recently became stronger and received more powerful equipment, Riona still feels like a mountain in my path, one that I had failed to climb many times before.

*Lutz said I had a nearly 50% chance of victory. But is that really true?*

I don't have the ability to perceive mana like that hero, so judging my chances is quite difficult. But there's one thing I'm sure of.

*When it comes to skill with a weapon, Riona outclasses me.*

*But it doesn't matter. I'll defeat her and anyone else who stands in my way. I won't stop until I've reclaimed my throne from that honorless coward.*

My son was a talented warrior. I had high hopes for him in the future, but he still had much growing to do. So when he challenged me to a duel with the crown as the reward, I thought it a good chance to teach him a lesson.

I never imagined I would lose the fight.

*He must have had help. But from who?*

*No, I can worry about that when the time comes. For now...*

"I'm ready," I say to Riona.

"As am I."

A horn bellows, and the duel begins.

My spear whirls, seeking Riona's flesh. When fighting against someone with a sword, my weapon's extended reach allows me to be more aggressive in my assault. Using that advantage, I poke and prod her, looking for an opening.

However, Riona isn't just a master of the blade. She's our kingdom's finest soldier, and the sword is more an extension of her body than a weapon she wields. Even with my extra reach, I slowly find that I'm the one taking a step back.

"Fast," Riona says. "But I'm faster."

"Tch!" I click my tongue as my spear is deflected at an awkward angle.

The downside of my weapon is that even the smallest of mistakes can be exploited, thanks to the time it takes to reposition it for the next attack. Riona was waiting for that. Or rather, she brought that future into reality with her movements and timing.

My instincts flare up, and I quickly backstep. The edge of her sword whizzes by my face, coming within a blade's width of hitting flesh.

Riona's assault doesn't end with one attack. A second strike follows, then a third. Both miss, but...

*At this rate...!*

With each attack, my stance crumbles further. Each dodge or deflection only increases the difficulty of avoiding the next until it feels like I'm dancing on her blade's edge.

*No choice...! [Accel]!*

At the same time as I mentally yell out the spell's name, the world blurs.

My defense which was on the verge of crumbling transforms into a devastating attack as I seemingly vanish from sight.

"Ow." Riona releases a single word, but there's little pain in her voice.

"You managed to deflect some of my attack, even when it was fueled by [Accel]. Just how quick is your reaction speed?"

"Not quick enough." She points to the blood flowing down her side. "And I didn't react to your [Accel]. I predicted it."

"So that's it. You knew I had no choice but to activate it to get out of that assault."

"It was one of the options I considered, so when I saw you forego defense and prepare an attack, I knew it was coming."

"How fearsome. No wonder you lead our armies into battle."

Riona levels her sword at me once again. "Since you've used [Accel], you won't be able to cast it again for a long while. However, mine is ready to use at any time. Now, I wonder how many other cards I can force you to play."

*Not good. She knows a high level duel like this can go on for quite a while. By forcing me to use my aces, she can whittle my hand down while keeping hers intact.*

*If I'm not careful, I'll run out of options and be overwhelmed all at once.*

"If you think you can defeat me while holding back..." I ready my spear. "...Then let's put that to the test!"

The distance between us shrinks in an instant, and the sound of clashing metal fills the air as our duel continues.

----------

"Hah ... hah..." I tighten my grip on the spear.

No matter how firmly I hold it, the weapon still threatens to slip each time it clashes with Riona's sword. It's not just the sweat. A cut on my forearm has coated its shaft red and acts as a grease that prevents me from maintaining a proper grip no matter how much I try.

The battle between us has been going on for a good ten minutes now, and it's been a brutal one. Even now, I can feel my blood flowing from numerous wounds, despite my [Cure] spell doing its best to heal me.

But I'm not the only one bleeding. Riona's dealing with many of the same problems as me, with her fatigue and injuries finally beginning to slow her down.

Unfortunately, it feels like it's too little, too late. She may be getting winded, but I'm reaching my limit. By now, it should be clear to everyone that at this rate, I'll lose the duel.

*I can't afford to fail here. My family, my citizens, and my entire kingdom needs me. If my son keeps the crown, it'll be the end of this country.*

*Should I have taken Lutz up in his offer to grant me an easy victory through his mysterious powers?*

At the time, I was so sure I was making the right decision. Accepting an unfair advantage in a duel is something only honorless cowards do. People who will do anything to win don't deserve to lead a kingdom.

But now...

*Is it okay to sacrifice my honor if it's for the good of the people?*

*Or would that make me no better than the disgraceful man who ruled before me?*

I've tried my best to live by the codes my teacher instilled in me, and this way of living had always ended up beneficial for me.

My teacher was so impressed by my dedication that he personally took me under his wing. The extra lessons allowed me to excel in the army when I came of age, where I continued to live as he taught me.

After making a name for myself, I quickly climbed in the ranks until I was summoned by the king himself. That's where I first realized just how much of a disappointment he was.

Most of the generals and officials had always spouted only good things about our ruler. He had honor, they said. He always did what was right. He was a man of the people who only wanted to do what was best for them.

Lies. All lies.

Not long after having my expectations shattered, I achieved a great victory for our kingdom. As a reward, I asked to duel the king for the crown.

Normally, such a request would be laughed at. But I knew what was brewing behind the scenes. The generals and officials were fed up with his incompetence, so the king sought to defeat the new upstart commander who dared challenge his right to rule.

He had the kingdom's most powerful equipment, none of which he obtained with his own hands. And to this day, I'm sure he had powerful mages cast enhancement magic on him before our battle began.

A true coward, he was. But in the end, none of it mattered. By a hair's breadth, I emerged the winner. And my reward was the entirety of the kingdom.

Now, I find myself in the same seat as that honorless coward. My rule slipping from my grasp, with the tantalizing fruit of outside help willing to lift me to victory.

Even now, I'm sure I could win, if only I were to activate the [Mental Link] spell embedded in my ring and ask for his help.

And yet...

*I won't throw away everything I've stood for all my life, even if it means my path ends here!*

*No, it's Riona who should abandon her honor! Doesn't she understand that my son took the coward's path to the throne!?*

*It's obvious that he had help, so why does she still obey him!? Is she an idiot!?*

*Yes, that's it! She's simply too stupid to realize that she's the pawn of a coward!*

I can feel my knuckles crack as they squeeze the shaft of my spear tighter than ever before. But that's just an afterthought as I look upon the worthless general who dares stand against me when all I'm trying to do is save the very kingdom she serves.

"Give up," Riona says after our short breather. "The victor is already clear."

"Give up!?"

"That's right. I don't know if you intend to fight until the bitter end, but I'd rather not take the life of my former sovereign."

"I'll never give up! If you want this battle to end, then come force me to obey, Riona!"

She gives me a strange look. "What's gotten into you? I've never seen you lose your composure like this."

"It's because of you! If you would only listen to my commands like you used to, then I wouldn't have to fight my way back to the throne!"

"You know I can't—"

"Shut up! I don't want to hear any excuses! All I want to hear..." I ready my spear. "...Are your cries for mercy!"

I close the distance in a blink. Even Riona wasn't expecting the space between us to vanish so quickly. She barely manages to get her guard up before my spear reaches her.

"What!?" She lets out a shout of surprise.

"It's you who will be giving up!" My weapon blurs as I speak.

It's satisfying to see that look of surprise as she struggles against my assault. For the first time since the duel began, her confident and composed face shows just a hint of unease.

*It's not enough! Struggle! Suffer! Just like I am!*

"Impossible!" Riona shouts, narrowly avoiding an attack. "You're faster than me!?"

"How pitiful! Is this the limit of our Grand General!? You should be ashamed! Calling yourself the strongest soldier in our kingdom when you're this weak!"

"Kuh...!" Blood flows from a fresh wound on Riona's body. "[Accel]!"

She vanishes, and a searing hot pain flashes across my chest. However...

"H-how absurd..." Riona says from behind me.

Turning, I see a fresh wound on her, nearly identical to my own.

"If I place my spear in your path when you use [Accel], then you'll skewer yourself on my weapon as you pass by. Common sense, isn't it?"

"It's a logical conclusion, but to actually pull it off in battle—" She coughs, interrupting her words.

"Accept it, Riona! You're too weak to defeat me!" I ready my spear again.

"How...? I should be ... stronger than you..."

*How?*

*Yeah ... how?*

*No, that's not important! I'm on the verge of winning this duel!*

"If you want to know the answer," I yell, reigniting the fading flame, "then defeat me and I'll tell you!"

Riona ignores her injuries and holds her sword before her. "Then let's settle this."

She doesn't wait for me to attack. But neither do I wait for her. Our feet move at the same time, both of us intent on ending the duel in the next attack.

The whizzing of blades, a splash of red, and the soft thunk of someone hitting the grassy ground.

The silence goes on for several heartbeats. Or perhaps I'm just too exhausted to hear. Either way, someone eventually yells out the duel's final conclusion.

"W-winner ... Kuro!"

It feels as if hearing those words sapped the last of my strength. The ground grows closer, but there's nothing I can do to stop myself from collapsing. However...

"Nice job," a young man says as he catches me.

He lays me down, and I feel a powerful healing energy flow into me. Looking up at Lutz, I see the brilliant light of [Cure All] radiating from him, no doubt so he can heal Riona, as well.

"What did you...?" I trail off.

"Me? I just watched. It was a very entertaining battle."

"I felt ... a powerful rage. Somehow, it made me strong enough to win..."

"Ah, that. Well, you see—"

"He must have cheated!" I hear a man yell, cutting off Lutz's words. "There's no way he could come back from that! Not against Riona!"

"I agree!" another says. "Magic! He must have had someone cast magic on him to enhance his abilities!"

"It was him! It has to be!"

All eyes fall on Lutz. A human being here to witness a duel that could determine the fate of our kingdom is strange enough. But now that Riona's commanders suspect foul play, they're latching onto that oddity in an attempt to avoid living up to their end of the bargain.

"Actually," Lutz says in his usual, casual tone. "There's a perfectly good explanation as to why Kuro was able to defeat Riona."

"Yeah, right! And why is a human even here to witness this duel!?"

"Anyway. Kuro has a Unique Skill called [Berserk]. It increases all his stats when he gets angry, but it also causes him to go … well, berserk."

"Unique Skill? What kind of nonsense is that!? You just made it up, didn't you!?"

"Have a little faith, would you? Or that's what I'd like to say, but I guess I should show some proof." Lutz turns to Riona. "You just going to pretend to be asleep?"

"How rude." She gets a hand beneath her and pushes herself to a sitting position. "I am neither asleep nor pretending to be so."

"Then how about helping me out here? I'm about to be strung up just because I'm a human, you know?"

"Are you always so overdramatic? No, forget it. I heard what you said about this Unique Skill. I assume you have a way to prove its existence?"

"Here, give me your hand."

Riona raises her bloody hand, which Lutz grabs without hesitation. A few seconds go by, then a look of surprise slowly forms on her face.

"Cast it on Kuro," Lutz says.

Riona looks to me, but her eyes seem to be looking at something only she can see.

"T-this spell...!"

"Yep. It's the [Scry] spell, but it's much stronger than the orbs used by the Adventurer's Guild. It's rank 3 to be exact, which means you can see the Unique Skill listed in Kuro's status."

"[Berserk]. It's really there." She looks to Lutz next, and her eyes grow even wider.

"Rank 3 also adds an AOE effect, so you can see anyone's status for as long as the spell lasts. So, what do you think of mine?"

"[True Blessing of the Goddess]..." She gulps. "Does this mean..."

"Guilty as charged."

Just as he did with me, Lutz gives Riona an explanation of who he is and why he's here. By the time he's finished, her face has become grim.

"Are you suggesting the fiends are playing us for fools?" Riona asks.

"Yeah. They probably have their hands deep in Belfast's civil war, though I'm not sure how."

"It's ... probably him."

"Him? Who?"

"Jun, the king's new advisor. He appeared after Kuro was chased out of the city, and he seems to have much influence over the young king's decisions."

"Jun, huh?" Lutz rubs his chin. "Guess we'll start there. But we have to get into the capital first. And since you lost the duel, you'll allow us in, right?"

"Did you forget? The condition in case I lost was to end the siege and return to the capital. There was nothing said about allowing anyone to invade."

Lutz sighs. "You sure are rigid, aren't you? You know, if you loosen up a bit, maybe you could have won the duel."

"I don't see what that has to do with anything."

"Just saying. Maybe you could have come up with a tactic to win. Like, I don't know, fighting in your underwear to distract your opponent?"

"As if I would ever...!"

"Ah, of course not. What was I thinking?" Lutz shows her a mysterious smile. "Jokes aside, we're going to the capital. What you decide to do now that you know the truth is up to you. But if you wish to join us, then you're more than welcome to tag along."

"It'll take the army at least a week to march back to the capital, but something tells me you're not going to wait that long."

"Nope. We're heading out as soon as we're finished here. I don't have time to sit around, so I'll be finishing this sidequest today."

"Hmm..." Riona seems to be considering something. "To tell the truth, I had my own suspicions that something wasn't right. So, I have someone watching Jun already. I'm interested to hear what they managed to find."

"Oh? That's convenient. Let's go meet them together then, shall we?"

Lutz reaches his hand out to Riona, who's still sitting on the grassy ground. After eyeing it for a long second, she takes it and uses it to get to her feet.

"Fine. But I need an hour to prepare. Are you okay with that?"

"Sure, we can spare an hour."

"Then I'll come to the city gates in an hour and we can begin the journey west, to the capital." Riona looks to me next. "And Kuro ... it was a great battle."

"I'm honored to hear that from our kingdom's Grand General. And please, forget anything strange I said during the duel..."

"It's too late to forget. And with that Unique Skill, you should prepare for more such outbursts in the future."

"N-no, surely that won't be the case."

*I hope...*

# Chapter 17: Monster Hunter

## ----- Laya -----

*"He's definitely going to lose,"* Lutz's telepathic voice fills our minds. *"Guess I'll have to do it after all."*

*"Mmm. It's better than dealing with the consequences after he loses."*

*"Yeah. I just hope he doesn't figure out that I cheated. Ah, well. Not like he can prove it."*

*"Isn't that why you haven't taught him any of the Lost Magics yet? So you can more easily pull their strings?"*

*"Exactly. But I was hoping it'd be just a precaution that I wouldn't have to rely on. Still, it's good that I thought of it. After all, if anyone here had the [Sense Mana] spell, they'd be able to detect what I'm about to do.*

*"I wish I didn't have to do this, but I just don't have time to deal with the consequences of Kuro losing the duel. If that means forcing him to cheat against his will, then so be it. I'm fine with being labeled as an honorless coward if it means I can save the world."*

After his words, Lutz begins channeling for a spell.

The match between Kuro and Riona has been going on for a long while, but by now, Kuro's chances of victory have fallen to practically zero. It'd take a miracle for him to win, considering his condition.

But we're not placing our hopes on such a miracle, even if it means tainting the sanctity of the duel the two warriors are so proud of. That's why...

Lutz releases his [Hypnosis] spell, with Kuro as his target. The man has a Unique Skill called [Berserk] that increases his stats when he's brought to anger, so of course Lutz is filling him with a sudden rage to activate it.

As I watch, Kuro's face goes from resigned to frustrated, then to unfiltered hatred. According to Lutz's rank 5 [Scry], which shows a person's stats, his strength has drastically increased along with his rage.

However...

"Isn't he a little too angry?" Belle asks. "Are we sure he's not going to do something crazy?"

"Uh..." Lutz's voice lacks his usual confidence.

"Just how much rage did you force on him?"

"Not this much, I swear. But once he reached a certain point, it was like he just snapped."

"Do you think ... it's because of his Unique Skill?"

"Probably. Maybe when it activates, it actually makes him go berserk, as the name implies."

During the conversation, the battle between Kuro and Riona had begun again. With his heightened status, the former king manages to gain the upper hand for the first time since their battle began.

But with how much rage that's leaking from him, the five of us begin to worry what might happen if he wins while under the effect of his Unique Skill.

"No choice," Lutz says. "I'll have to calm him down with [Hypnosis]."

Even though he was the one who filled Kuro with anger, Lutz starts reversing it by forcing a feeling of peace and relaxation into him. Just a little at first, so he doesn't accidentally deactivate the Unique Skill and cause him to lose.

It's a delicate balancing act, and I can see a look of pure concentration on Lutz's face as he fights to keep Kuro under the effects of [Berserk] without letting him go overboard.

Fortunately, the battle was almost over, even before Lutz intervened. Before long, the two warriors are preparing for a final clash to decide the winner.

Their figures blur, and...

"Whew." Lutz lets out a telepathic sigh of relief. "That was a little dicey. But in the end—ah."

He cuts his words when Kuro begins to collapse. With the Unique Skill no longer boosting his stats, the accumulated injuries and fatigue is just too much for him.

Since there's no need for us to get involved, we let Lutz take care of the post battle negotiations.

"Finally," Tylith says. "We can head to the capital and put an end to this disaster."

"Mmm. But I suspect we'll meet even more resistance there, if the fiends really are involved with the prince's coup."

"That's true. Though that can be considered a good thing if the alternative is a web of politics with no real enemy to defeat."

Now that the duel's over, there's no reason for us to stay on top of the wall. We leap down to the ground, hitting the grassy plain that surrounds the city.

Lutz is still engaged in some negotiations, but he's keeping us updated on what's being said so he doesn't have to explain it to us later. Thanks to that, we're not in a rush to get to him for any particular reason.

By the time we make it to him, all the relevant conversation has been taken care of, meaning we don't have to stand around listening to them work through any of the details.

"Well," Lutz says. "That's that. Now it's just waiting for an hour until Riona's ready to go. Then, we'll be off to Belfast's capital city!"

"I don't know about anyone else," Belle says, "but I'm going to relax for the next hour."

"Ah, me too!" Surprisingly, Alisha agrees with Belle.

*No, she probably just wants to spend more time with Princess Keiko. Those two seem to get along rather well.*

They're both beastkin and also the same age. I suppose it's only natural that they'd become friends.

"As for me," Tylith says, "I shall be taking a final tour of the town. Care to join me, Laya?"

"Mmm."

With our destinations settled, we split into two groups, with Lutz, Alisha, and Belle heading back to the estate with Kuro and his children.

In my case, I just follow Tylith down whichever road she wants to walk. I'm not sure why Tylith wants to explore, but her reasoning is likely similar to mine.

We've been rushing through the beastkin lands with haste, so we haven't had the chance to just explore like we did when we visited my homeland.

Although I don't enjoy the company of random strangers, the architecture and culture of these beastkin is another matter.

It'd be a shame to not take in the sights of their cities when given the chance, so an outing like this gives me the perfect opportunity to do so.

When I run my eyes over one of the buildings, I can see a hint of elven architecture in it. Though whether that's coincidence, I can't be sure.

Either way, the roof of the building has the distinctive peaks and design that are common in the elven lands, but the tile that covers it is far different. It's placed in such a way that the roof appears rippled, like gentle waves in an ocean.

Unlike the more economical design of most elven buildings, the ones here have a bit of flourish, with eaves jutting out, held up by decorative, wooden pillars.

When Lutz saw the design of their houses, he said it had an 'asian feel' to them, though that didn't explain much to me. When he said it was a reference to a certain culture back on Earth, all I could do was accept it.

Our steps take us to a particular building. It's familiar, yet slightly different than I'm used to. We didn't come here on purpose, so it's just coincidence that we ended up at this city's Adventurer's Guild.

A man standing outside the guild lets out a long sigh, looking as if he's disappointed in someone's ridiculous decision. He's rubbing the end of his bow as he sighs, which pokes out from behind his back.

Normally, our eyes would run right past this man, as there's nothing weird about him, other than his level being slightly higher than average. But there's something strange about him, despite everything being seemingly normal.

He's a human.

"Not worth it, they say?" He voices his frustrations. "They're the ones who posted the request in the first place, and now it's suddenly not worth helping me get my items back?"

He turns from the guild door and suddenly realizes that we're watching him. At first, his face gets even more sour, but after taking in our features, it shifts to surprise.

"Are those elf ears?" He eyes my pointed ears. "And I thought I was the strange one, being human in the beastkin lands and all."

"Elf." I spare him a single word.

"I hope you weren't planning to ignore me," Tylith says.

"Huh? Is there something strange about you—woah! Are you a vampire!?"

"Finally noticed, did you? What was it? The long, purple hair? The elegant fangs? Or perhaps the crimson eyes?"

"Uh, all of them, I guess? No, wait. That's not important! Why are an elf and vampire here? And you're together? That's more than a little strange!"

"Don't sweat the small stuff. You'll just end up going bald early."

"Hey, I've still got all my hair!" He runs his hand over his head, as if to verify that fact.

"Human." I speak a single word to get them back on track.

"Huh? You mean why is a human here in the beastkin lands? Well, I'm an adventurer. Adventuring to new lands isn't that strange, is it? Though I'll admit there aren't many of my people here. There's a reason for that." He looks back at the Adventurer's Guild.

"Problem?"

"Took a quest to gather scales from the lizards that live in the swamps to the south. But when I got back to the city, I found it surrounded by an army! There was no way they'd just let me in during a siege when I'm carrying a huge bag of scales, right?"

He sighs, remembering the moment. "So, I went into the woods to hide the scales until the battle was over. But that's when I ran into them! Those giant ants! I don't remember bothering them, but they didn't care. They came at me by the dozens, the hundreds! I had no choice but to toss my bag and run!"

"And now you're requesting help from the Adventurer's Guild to get those scales back?"

"That's right." He sighs again. "But they tell me it's my responsibility. That may be true, but the guild usually helps its members during extraordinary circumstances like this. But not me."

"Because you're human."

"Yeah. Things got worse when some idiot noble decided to invade while Belfast's army was busy fighting the fiends. What kind of moron uses a world catastrophe to capture land, anyway?"

"You don't have to worry about that anymore."

I have a feeling this human will continue to find things to worry about, despite my words.

Another sigh escapes his lips. "Guess I'll just go back there myself since I can't afford to issue a guild request to help me complete the quest I started. If

I did that, I'd just end up as the laughing stock of the other adventurers, anyway."

"No teammates?"

"I used to, but they were being harassed for teaming up with a human, so I left the party."

"I see."

"Guess I better go now so I don't get stuck outside the city walls after dark. Good luck with whatever you want from the guild."

He lets out a final sigh, then begins walking away.

It seems he thought we came here to make a request, but the truth is that we just happened to walk by. We have no intention of stepping foot inside.

"Stop," Tylith says.

The man turns back to us. "Huh? Did you need something?"

"No, it's not us who's in need. It's you."

"Yeah, but I already told you that those idiots won't help."

"They may have turned you down, but are you just going to ignore the fact that an elf and vampire are standing right in front of you?"

"That's strange, sure. But what are you getting at?"

"I'm saying we've got enough time to help you."

"No way. You're one thing, but I can't ask a kid to go fight those ants!"

"Not much younger than you," I say.

"Ah, that's right. Elves do look younger than they really are. But still..."

"Half an hour."

"Half an hour? What about it?"

"We've got half an hour before we need to return, so let's get moving quickly."

"There's no way we can even get there in that time, much less find the scales and make it back!"

"No problem." I pull a map of Belfast. "Name?"

"I'm Hunter. And you two?"

"Laya."

"Tylith. A pleasure."

I hold the map so Hunter can see it clearly. "Where did you drop the bag?"

He sighs but points to a spot on the map. "Here. But this map's scale is too large."

He searches through a pouch on his side and pulls out a piece of parchment. After he unrolls it, I realize that it's a map of the land just south of the city, meaning that the details of the area are far higher than the one I'm carrying.

"This is the exact spot where the bag is sitting."

I look to where his finger is pointing. "You're quite confident."

"Of course. I always meticulously prepare everything I need before each quest. That's how I survived so many missions on my own."

"And what of the ants? Didn't they surprise you?"

"That's exactly the problem! The infestation wasn't known until I told the guild! They should be thanking me for finding them before they can wreak havoc, but instead, they're content to just let them be!"

"Decisions dictated by emotions instead of logic. They'd rather see you fail than deal with the ants in a timely manner."

It's a scene I've seen play out many times during my trips through the human and beastkin lands. Prejudice can often bring out the worst, even in an otherwise good man.

*Even my own people aren't any different in that regard. No, we're even worse than humans or beastkin...*

"Hmph." Tylith eyes the map, right where his finger is pointing. "If it's only that far, then it's not a problem."

"Not a problem?" Hunter asks. "Even if we hurry, we might barely make it before your half-hour time limit."

"By normal standards, yes. But we're far from normal."

"What do you mean by–"

Hunter's words are cut off by the shifting of the very world itself. All light, sound, and even sensations are cut off as we travel through the strange space that we can visit only when teleporting.

*Hmm. This place is becoming oddly comfortable.*

Lutz said the same thing, though the details are so hard to describe that it makes comparing my experience to his rather difficult.

Soon, the world reforms, and we're standing in a lush, green forest. As usual, the trees are massive, but their size isn't really the most important matter here.

"What the!?" Hunter yells. "You *teleported* us!? And right into the ant infestation!?"

He removes the bow slung around his shoulders and takes a stance between us and the giant ants that are quickly gathering. Although they look fearsome, with mandibles large enough to behead a man in a single attack, their average level is only in the low 20s.

Compared to me and Tylith, who are level 71 and 70 respectively, they can only be considered weak.

Hunter doesn't realize just how much we outclass these monsters, so he no doubt intends to take the front line for himself. But I'd rather not deal with an annoying battle, so I release my own magic.

A torrent of wind tears through the forest, centered on the colony of ants. The storm is violent enough to create multiple small tornadoes, each of which spew their own blades of wind at nearby enemies.

Hunter stands between us and that raging storm, as still as a statue. All he does is watch on as my [Windstorm] spell completely eradicates the swarm that was forming ahead of us.

"Bag," I say.

"H-huh...?"

"Where is your bag of scales?"

"Oh ... right." He tears his eyes away from the now dying magic. "That way!"

We follow Hunter as the raging wind finally recedes behind us. I wasn't able to get each and every ant, but Tylith is currently dashing through the woods, taking care of any that get too close.

That leaves me and Hunter free to focus on finding his bag. If it were full of enchanted items, perhaps I could sense the magic emanating from it, but if it's just monster parts, then I can only rely on my sight.

Fortunately, Hunter seems competent at his job. He confidently leads me through the forest, seeming to get more certain of our destination with each passing second.

"There!" He points to a wool bag.

"Mmm. Nice job."

Hunter swoops by, picking up the bag in one smooth motion without stopping. Now that he's got what he came for, he focuses on the surroundings, looking for any potential threats.

But Tylith has done her job well. There's not an ant to be seen anywhere around us. Though I can feel more heading our way, probably following our scent.

My vampire companion appears, having slain the few remaining nearby monsters. As soon as she falls in line with us, she matches my pace.

My hand comes up, and she grabs it. Immediately after, I feel her vampiric mana coursing through me. She uses it to create a spell formation with a combination of her mana and mine, slowly crafting the magic.

Finally, it's complete.

"Prepare," I say.

"For what?" Hunter asks.

"For this." I release the magic, and the world warps.

For the second time in just a couple minutes, I find myself in that strange space between worlds. It goes by just as quickly, and when it's over, we're standing in an alley just beside the Adventurer's Guild.

"Again!?" Hunter says. "You two are nuts, using magic like that without care!"

"Hmph. If it's us, then things like national bans on Dark Magic mean nothing."

"If it's you? Who are you two, exactly? You're obviously not in the army, so are you adventurers, like me?"

"Yes, but that's not our main profession."

"Our primary objective," I say, "is to fight alongside the Great Hero, Lutz, and defeat the forces of Chaos."

"Uh..." Hunter looks between us. "You're serious..."

"Mmm."

He sighs. "Don't tell me that rumor about a hero being here was true..."

"Yes, but not for long. We're leaving to put an end to this civil war and get Belfast back to the battlefield to fight the fiends."

"The fiends, huh..." Hunter shows us a look of contemplation, but it turns into another sigh. "Well, in any case. Laya, Tylith, thanks for helping me get my bag. Now I can afford to buy the equipment I need to visit the nearby dungeon."

"You're going to such a dangerous place?"

"I need to get stronger, and a dungeon is the best place to do that."

"True." I look to Tylith and she nods. "In that case take these."

Several items appear in my hand, like a pair of rings, a mantle, and bracers. I hold them out to Hunter, but he's reluctant to reach for them.

"Take," I say.

"I'm not even going to ask where they came from, but by the looks of them, they're enchanted equipment. I can't accept something like that."

"It's fine. They're just leftovers that we have no use for. I keep them on hand precisely for moments like this."

He sighs. "Well, it'd be rude to turn down a gift."

He takes them from me, then proceeds to equip them without reservation. With each piece, his eyes only grow wider.

"What is this!? Legendary equipment!? I thought you said they were useless leftovers!"

"Mmm. Weak. But compared to your own items, they're several times stronger. They came from a dungeon, after all."

"Amazing..."

"Hmph." Tylith raises her hand, and one final item appears. "If you're going to upgrade your equipment, then it only makes sense for your weapon to have comparable strength."

"A bow..." He takes it from Tylith's outstretched hand. "Such power. I can't believe this is what you consider weak."

"It's all about perspective. Ah, but it seems our time is nearly up. I suggest you find some trustworthy companions for your trek through the dungeon. Reliable allies can be the difference between life and death."

"Thanks, Tylith. I'll try to find such people."

"Hmph." She turns and begins walking toward the mouth of the alley.

"Don't expect your new equipment to bring you victory," I say. "If you want to achieve your dream, then you have to keep working hard."

"Yeah. You're right. Thanks, Laya."

"Good luck on your trek through the dungeon." With that, I turn and follow Tylith.

"I..." Hunter's voice comes from behind me. "I'll absolutely make my dream into a reality with my own two hands."

And so, our little adventure through this beastkin city comes to an end. We saw some interesting sights and had some fun.

But more importantly, we managed to help the human named Hunter in his quest to find the strength he needs to follow his dream.

# Interlude 3

## ----- Lumina -----

"What do you think?" I ask. "It's quite a nice restaurant, isn't it?"

My second brother, Lyle, doesn't even glance around the establishment. Even the food sitting in front of him is untouched. Though it just arrived, so I suspect that will change soon enough.

"I've eaten at places just as fancy as this before," Lyle says.

"Yes, but have you eaten at *this* one?"

"No."

"Then you should try to enjoy it a bit more."

Lyle finally picks up his fork and stabs it into a slice of pork. "What's your deal? You invite me out to eat, then go on about having fun. What're you planning?"

I hold back a sigh. "No tact, as usual. But that's to be expected from you."

Lyle doesn't even humor me with a retort, deciding to continue eating his food instead.

"Well," I say. "I do have something to speak to you about, but half the reason I called you out is simply to enjoy our new freedom."

Lyle looks at the guards which surround our table, Elise included. "Freedom? If we were really free, Father wouldn't have sent babysitters along."

"You know how dangerous it is for us, especially now. Shouldn't you just be happy that we're able to visit the city whenever we desire?"

"I'll be happy when I'm on the battlefield, fighting the army of Chaos."

I take a sip of my water to wash down the chicken pasta I've been eating. "You've begun extensive training for that precise purpose, haven't you?"

"Worthless monsters and bandits. I'll never gain the strength I need by wiping out such weaklings. I should be out on an adventure, battling real opponents, like the False Hero!"

"Haha..." I hide my dry laugh by taking another bite of my pasta.

"You should have seen him! All high and mighty, acting like he's invincible! Then I did it! I used Master-Class magic and nearly killed him in one spell! If he hadn't used some strange teleportation artifact to flee, he'd be dead right now!"

I resist the urge to sigh. "You know, Lyle. Things aren't always as simple as they seem. People often hide the truth behind a facade, and it's up to each person to see through that illusion."

"Whatever. I'm not interested in your philosophy, Lumina."

The meal continues in silence for a short while. Despite his new freedom, Lyle still can't break his habit of falling into a bad mood whenever things don't go the way he wants. It's a little frustrating, but that's just how he's been for so long thanks to Father's poor parenting.

*Well, he's getting better little by little. Maybe by the time the war is over, I'll even get to see him smile.*

*But until then, I have to be careful. Telling him the truth about Sir Lutz would be dangerous. There's no telling what he'd do with that information.*

*Besides, he'd never believe me, not with his attitude. But perhaps I can set the stage for the day I can reveal it to him...*

"Lyle, did you know Elise and I were planning on taking a trip to a dungeon soon?"

"What!?" Lyle nearly drops his fork. "Does Father know?"

"Of course. I already got his approval."

"That bastard...! When I said I wanted to visit a dungeon, he flat out denied me! But you get to go!?"

"There are special circumstances involved."

"Like I give a damn!" Lyle stands from his chair. "I'm going to go have a word with Father right now!"

"Are you sure you want to do that?"

"Why wouldn't I?"

"Because I told you about my upcoming trip for a reason that I've yet to reveal. If you leave now, you may never know why."

Lyle hesitates. "Hurry and spill it, then."

"Certainly." I hold back a smile. "Lyle, I want you to come with us to the dungeon."

For the first time in a long while, Lyle stares at me with a look of pure shock, his mouth hanging open without reservation.

*This is the reaction that Sir Lutz is always looking for when he gets up to his antics. It's...*

*...Rather fun.*

"To a dungeon..." Lyle frowns. "But Father..."

"Father has already given his permission."

"Of course he would, if you asked." Lyle sits back down. "Which dungeon?"

"The Beast Warrens."

"Are you insane!? That's one of the most dangerous dungeons in the kingdom!"

"I'm aware. But it'll be fine. Trust your little sister, would you?"

"Tch. Don't try to act like an innocent little girl when it's convenient. Now that I can cast [Scry], I can see just how strong you are. You may be a far higher level than me, but there are still people stronger than you. Father has you beat by 6 levels, and even he fears that dungeon."

Lyle is level 18. Seeing as how I'm level 71, he can't even be considered a threat.

Under the guidance of Sir Lutz, I've had my level changed to 42 within my Status Screen. He said that the time to reveal our true strength will arrive shortly, but it's best to not appear overly powerful right now.

That's why Lyle believes that I'm six levels lower than our level 48 father. The strange mana-changing artifact Sir Lutz gave both me and Elise helps us align the strength of our mana to our fake level, allowing us to fool the [Sense Mana] spell, as well.

"You haven't answered my question," I say. "Would you like to come with us to the dungeon?"

"I..." Lyle looks out the nearby window. "If it means getting the strength to defeat the False Hero once and for all, then I'll go, no matter how dangerous it is."

"Excellent! Then prepare to travel at any time because the day may arrive on short notice."

After finishing our meal, we exit the restaurant, surrounded by our usual retinue. Elise stays at an unusually far distance from me in order to give me and my brother a sense of privacy, though it's only for appearance's sake, as I intend to tell her all the important information with telepathy.

Since I managed to get Lyle to agree to join us on the dungeon dive, my early morning mission has been accomplished. I want to visit the orphanage on the way back to the castle, but it'd probably be best to avoid bringing Lyle to such a place. I wouldn't want him to frighten the children with his scary eyes.

So, the only thing left for us to do is get into the carriage and go back to our home at the castle.

At least, that should have been the case.

"What's he doing?"

I follow Lyle's eyes and see the back of a cloaked person. They even have their hood up, making it impossible to tell if it's a man or woman. But Lyle has already assumed them to be male, so I do the same.

"Is there something strange about him?" I ask.

"Haven't you noticed? He's strong. Stronger than me."

"Ah, well he's certainly above average, but I wouldn't call him strong. He's only a few levels higher than you."

Lyle gives me a sidelong glance. "Well sorry for being weak, oh great Prime Oracle."

"That's not what … no, nevermind." I openly sigh. "But I still don't see what so strange about this man."

"I've been tracking his mana while we were eating, and he's been hanging around here ever since we arrived. Isn't that a little suspicious?"

I also felt his mana when I did a scan of the area, but since he's only a little stronger than an average guard, I didn't feel any danger. If someone with any actual knowledge of my situation were trying to spy on me, they'd likely use someone with a more inconspicuous level of strength.

"I do agree his attire is rather suspicious, but I don't believe that to be enough to investigate him."

"You're too soft. You're supposed to be someone important now, aren't you? Try to be a little more cautious."

Lyle steps away from the carriage, heading toward the cloaked man. With no recourse, I follow his lead.

Since the mysterious man's back is turned to us, it's an easy enough task to close the distance without alerting him. However, before we can truly get near him, he turns his head, as if suddenly alerted to our presence.

Turns out, Lyle was right about him being male. But when I look into his eyes, I don't see anything that makes me feel threatened or even uncomfortable. Although there is a strange sparkle in them, as if incomprehensible thoughts were running through his mind.

"Good day, my dear guests!" The man gives us a flourished bow. "The pleasure is mine."

"What?" Lyle looks on with a confused face. "How is the pleasure yours when we haven't expressed any pleasure for meeting you?"

"A formality, I assure you." The man snickers to himself. "But forget about the details, there are important matters here!"

"What are you talking about? Is something wrong with your head?"

"I can almost assure you that I'm sane."

Lyle and I look at each other, neither quite sure what to make of the man's words.

"Anyway!" he says. "It seems I found that man's targets."

"Targets?" Lyle asks. "And who's this man you're referring to?"

"Why it's the man I've been following, of course!" His arm snaps up, pointing across the street.

I follow his finger. "There's … nobody there."

"I know that. He fled when you started walking this way."

"So that's how you knew we were coming."

"You sure follow along quickly!"

I inspect the man again, but no matter how much I look at him, I can't find anything that seems dangerous. Just … strange.

*Even his name is odd. I've never heard of anyone named Boron.*

*Could it be he was destined to be an oddity, even from birth?*

*No, there's something more important right now…*

"This man you've been watching, you say he's been spying on us?"

"That's exactly right! He's a member of a gang that prowls these streets, looking for high class victims like yourselves!"

"I see. Are you perhaps an undercover guard?" I have my doubts considering his unusual behavior, but I have to ask.

The man puffs out his chest. "Nope!"

"Ah..."

"Tch." Lyle makes an annoyed sound. "Whatever. I'm getting tired of looking at him."

Lyle turns, as if he's about to leave, but Boron speaks up before he can take his first step.

"Don't worry, Your noblenesses! I'll hunt him and his gang until they're too scared to even stalk these streets at night!"

"Uh, right..." I end up going with the strange man's flow.

*"Princess,"* Elise says telepathically. *"Perhaps we should apprehend the one who was watching us. He may have ties to Duke Bradley."*

*"That's true, but the man has already fled, and I didn't take note of his mana signature."*

*"I'm afraid I didn't sense the presence of anyone suspicious enough to track, either. But it may still be a good idea to send someone to investigate the gang."*

*"True, but..."* I look at Boron's strangely confident face. *"The one who knows most about them is already in front of us."*

"Boron," I say. "How much do you know of this gang?"

"I know..." Boron snickers. "...Absolutely nothing!"

Silence fills the side of the street we're using to hold our conversation. Nobody—and that includes me—expected him to look so confident while claiming to know nothing about the people he's supposed to be hunting.

"Perhaps this was a mistake, after all..." I say as I shake my head.

"Hmm?" Boron seems clueless. "Anyway! If you're done here, I'm off to follow that man to wherever it is he plans to lead me!"

"You're going to follow him? But he's been gone for at least a minute now."

"Child's play, my dear nobleness! I clearly saw the street he fled to, and I know the best paths to take when trying to stay hidden! And since he left one minute and ten seconds ago, I can easily estimate how far he's gotten since then. After adding in the time it will take me to catch up, I know exactly where to go to find him!"

"That's quite an intricate tracking technique. So what you're saying is that you know where to find this man, correct?"

"Indeed I do! But I must leave quickly, so pardon me for my abrupt exit!" Boron turns and runs across the street, to the spot where the spy was supposedly watching us.

*How ... interesting.*

"Let's go," I say.

"About time," Lyle grumbles.

"No. I mean let's follow Boron and see if he can find this spy for us."

"What!? You really believe that nutjob? There's obviously something wrong with his head!"

"Maybe. But I have some free time, and this could end up being important."

"Tch, whatever. I'll just be happy if I get to beat up some gang members."

"Don't you mean bring them to justice?"

"Sure, why not."

This time, we're the ones running across the street, chasing after Boron. The strange man has already slipped into an alley, but that's not a problem for us. We've already memorized his mana signature, after all.

After a couple turns through the city streets and alleys, we reach a transitory zone where the noble district meets a neighboring district. At the same time, we catch up to Boron, who's silently watching a group of three young men walking down the street.

"Huhuhu." A strange laugh comes from his mouth. "Come to watch the action, my noblenesses?"

"How did you know it was us?" I ask. "You didn't even turn to check."

"A mystery, indeed!"

"In any case, from how you're looking at those young men, am I correct to assume one of them is the spy?"

"Your mind is as sharp as ever, nobleness. The one on the right was your watcher. The other two, his accomplices."

"Okay, but are you sure?"

Boron finally looks at me. "Do ratmen stink?"

"I believe they do have a reputation for their smell."

"Then your question is answered." He turns back to the gang members.

*What a strange person.*

The thought runs through my mind once again, just as Boron steps forward. His targets step into yet another alley, giving him the freedom to move without drawing their attention.

"This is ridiculous," Lyle says. "Let's just apprehend those men for questioning. I'm tired of this charade already."

"Not yet, Lyle. I'm quite intrigued with how this is going to turn out." I start following Boron.

"Are you serious?" Lyle catches up to me. "The guy's insane. We should take him into custody, too!"

"Is that your answer to everything?"

"Only when my patience is wearing thin!"

"But aren't you always lacking in patience?"

"Yeah, so what!"

"So I worry that you'll bring us some bad karma if you go around arresting everyone you don't like."

"Give me a break..."

We turn into the alley, just on Boron's heels. To my surprise, the strange man picks up a stone and tosses it further into the alley. It hits the ground just behind the three men, bouncing into the back of the suspected spy's boot.

The gang members all turn at once, taking in the sight of Boron, along with me, Lyle, and our entourage of guards.

"W-what the hell!?" The spy yells.

"Ladies and gentlemen!" Boron says, despite all three of them being males. "Please be seated. The presentation is about to begin!"

The three men now look confused on top of worried.

"What's this guy talking about?" Another of the criminals asks.

"I ain't got a clue!" The spy turns. "And I ain't staying to find out!"

"No, no, no." Boron's hand rustles around inside his overcoat. "We can't have our guests of honor leaving so soon!"

"Stick it up your—hey!" The spy narrowly avoids a bottle thrown at his head.

The shattering of glass fills the alley as the bottle breaks on the stone wall just ahead of the three criminals. At the same time...

"Slime!?" the spy yells. "It's everywhere!"

Right when the bottle broke, a huge glob of slime exploded out from the shattered remains, covering the entire alley ahead of the men in a green, goopy mess.

"Screw this!" One of the other criminals runs right through the slime. "I'm outta—"

"Huhuhu." Boron laughs as the man collapses into the goopy mess. "The audience should just watch quietly."

*Are they the audience or guests of honor?*

Boron can't seem to make up his mind about what role the men are supposed to be playing, but I suppose it's not a big deal.

"What is that stuff!?" The spy yells.

"Oh, that? Don't worry, there's no pain while it slowly drains your life until you're nothing but a shell."

"Ughhhh..." The collapsed man lets out a strange groan.

The spy's eyes widen. "There's pain! There's definitely pain involved!"

"Oh, shoot." Boron ruffles through his overcoat. "Seems I used the wrong potion. Ah, I'd be careful of touching that stuff."

"You damn freak!"

"How hurtful! I am just a normal, everyday alchemist!"

*No, no. You're definitely not normal.*

"Hmm. Looks like I'll need to teach you a lesson after all."

Boron opens his overcoat in a swift motion. Lined up in his inside pockets are potions of every shape and color. Dozens of them. So many that I can barely see the fabric of his inside coat.

He reaches to one of his pockets and pulls out a brown potion. As he inspects it closely, the remaining two criminals watch on with horrified faces.

"Explosions sure are fun." Boron looks from the brown bottle to the terrified men. "Don't you think so?"

"Y-yeah...?" The spy ends up agreeing.

"I knew it. I knew you understood! Then..." Boron readies his arm. "I'll let you experience one closely."

"No! We don't need to—"

*Kaboom!*

A shockwave erupts within the narrow alley, centered directly on the two remaining criminals. Shards of rock accompany the explosion, clinking off the walls and ground with modest force.

We're also close enough for the shrapnel to reach us, but Boron put up a [Shimmering Shield]. Since the bits of rock are imbued with magic, the barrier blocks them from pelting us.

Of course, I had my own spell ready to do the same, but when Boron's appeared, I canceled mine.

When the potion's effect ends, both of the men are lying on the ground.

"Another magnificent performance, if I do say so myself!" Boron nods at the scene in front of him.

"How interesting," I say. "I've never heard of potions like those."

"Ah, my nobleness. That's because it's an original creation by yours truly!"

"That's quite an achievement. What process did you use to imbue the stones with paralysis magic? And how did you get the slime to expand from the broken bottle?"

"Oh? You're interested, are you?"

"I'm somewhat of an alchemist myself, so I'm always willing to learn new recipes."

"In that case!" Boron pulls another potion from his overcoat. "Perhaps we'll meet again, nobleness!"

He throws the bottle at his own feet. When it shatters, a large puff of smoke completely obscures his figure. It only lasts a few seconds, but when the breeze carries the smoke away, Boron is gone.

In his place is a single sheet of parchment, slowly floating to the alley floor like a feather. However, rather than watching it fall, my eyes are tracking something else.

*A potion that creates a smoke diversion. But the actual effect is a short burst of speed.*

*Clever.*

Boron used that speed to dash out of the alley, completely leaping over the goopy mess and turning the corner before the smoke cleared.

I walk over to the parchment that now rests on the dirt ground.

"Hmm?" I scan the scribbled text. "A recipe for a potion? But ... what's a plajig?"

I store the paper in my [Inventory]. I'm sure I'll find the time to craft the potion one day.

"What an idiot," Lyle says. "We should have arrested him, too."

"Oh don't be like that, Lyle. I thought the whole thing was rather fun."

"Whatever. Let's just get these criminals and go back to the castle."

Lyle turns and begins walking out of the alley, leaving the three men to the guards.

*It sure is fun coming out to the city.*

*I wonder if Sir Lutz will be paying a visit soon...*

Turns out, the three criminals weren't even after us. They're just opportunists, looking for a chance to steal from any oblivious nobles that enter their territory.

The whole affair ended up leading nowhere. But at least a few more criminals are off the streets.

# Chapter 18: The Beastkin Capital of Kava

## ----- Lutz -----

With a flash, the world's light returns to my eyes, revealing the rocky hills I expected to see upon our arrival.

Beside me are the usual suspects, namely my party members who accompany me nearly everywhere. But we brought Riona, Kuro, and even his two children along with us this time.

The commanders who led the two opposing armies weren't happy to be left out of the teleportation, but each person we bring means more mana cost, and since we're entering enemy territory, I'd like to keep as much of our mana as possible.

I did make an exception for the kids, though. Kuro said he needs his son here for the plan, and I can agree with that. But I'm not sure what use Princess Keiko has. I guess he just wants his daughter nearby now that he's moving to retake his throne.

Everyone steps out of the teleportation circle's area of effect, some with more haste than others. The magic has a bad reputation because it's prone to be misused by nefarious people. But in reality, it's just another spell. When the Lost Magics become widespread, its usefulness to criminals will fall dramatically.

Kuro looks around, eyeing the rocky landscape. "These are the hills just east of the capital, aren't they?"

"Yep. They're only a few minutes' walk from the city, but since nobody lives around here, they were a convenient barrier to hide my teleportation circle."

"Indeed. But now that we're here, shouldn't we eradicate the spell?"

"Nah. It might come in handy when we're done here, so I'm going to leave it."

"I see. I suppose there's no harm since only the caster can activate it."

"That's not exactly true. If someone with [Manipulate Mana] and more magical strength than me were to find it, they could override my mana within the circle and take control of it. But the likelihood of that happening is about as close to zero as you can get."

Since teleporting somewhere I've never been is extremely difficult, I had no choice but to rush to the capital on my own and set this circle up for us. Warping around ate up quite a chunk of my mana, but Tylith helped carry the burden.

Currently, around 10% of our mana is gone, and it won't come back until the backlash from [Teleport] runs out. For me, that's an hour. For Tylith, it's four hours. But since we have something to do before the showdown with Belfast's new king, there's a good chance mine will recover. Tylith will likely have to deal with only having access to 80% of her mana, though.

"Anyway," I say. "Let's go meet this informant of yours, Riona. I'm interested in what he found out while you were off playing with Kuro."

"There was no playing involved. I'm always serious when it comes to my duty." Riona gives me a sidelong glance. "But I'm also eager to hear what she has to say. If Rei's new Minister truly is behind his rise in strength, then that's grounds to dismiss his duel against Kuro."

*So the informant is a girl, then.*

"No duel, no crown. And it goes back on the head of the former king."

"Yes. But only if we can prove that Rei used strength he obtained through cowardly means."

"Like powerful equipment he didn't earn, or if someone brought him to a dungeon where he just sat around as others defeated the monsters."

Riona nods. "Finding such evidence usually proves difficult, but with [Scry], we can check the quality of his equipment and his so-called level. Perhaps that will be enough to convince the nobility to rescind the duel's outcome."

"I'm not going to get my hopes up."

While it'd be great if things worked out so easily, people usually fight for the outcome that most benefits them. If the nobility benefits from having

Kuro's son in power, then they'll likely conveniently ignore a lot of
inconsistencies to keep him on the throne.

*Kuro did say his rule was getting unpopular because of a few decisions, like
forming a proper alliance with King Edgar.*

*If Rei's easier to manipulate due to his young age, then the nobles may rally
around him, even if we can prove he essentially cheated during the duel.*

In Orakio, I've seen firsthand just how selfish those in power can be when it
comes to keeping hold of their authority. Somehow, I doubt the beastkin's
culture of honor really amounts to more than an empty formality for most of
them.

In fact, most of the commanders and officials I met in Kuro and Riona's
armies were vocally opposed to any outcome that didn't benefit their side.
Right after Kuro won the duel, Riona's commanders tried coming up with
reasons why it was invalid. I doubt they would have done anything but smile
had she won.

I mean, I did cheat, so they weren't wrong. But that's beside the point.

"Ah, I see the city!" Alisha rushes to the top of the hill we're climbing.

"The capital, Kava," Keiko says. "I didn't think we'd be returning so soon.
Accompanied by a summoned hero, no less."

"Hehe! You never know what to expect around us!"

"Yes, I've come to realize that. Though there's something I've been
wondering, Alisha. Sir Lutz picked you up in the human lands, right? Why were
you living there and not in Belfast?"

"Ah, well..." Alisha looks to me, and I nod. "I was born in a village on the
western edge of Belfast, but..."

"That's where Chaos began their invasion." Keiko makes a complicated
face. "But if you were displaced, why flee into human lands?"

"Because ... I was cursed."

"The [Curse of the Forsaken]!? You're carrying such an affliction!?"

"Yeah."

"But you're with one of the summoned heroes, right? How can someone
cursed by the Goddess be fighting to save the world?"

"It's not like that at all. The curse didn't come from the Goddess. It came
from Chaos."

"What? The fiends can place the curse on people?"

"That's what Master said."

"I deduced it from a multitude of events," I say. "It may be hard to believe, but it's true. The curse is a weapon used by Chaos, though I'm still not sure how or why."

"The curse weakens the victim," Kuro says. "Perhaps it's simply to lower our fighting strength."

"True, but Alisha's entire village was cursed. Why put it on random villagers? That doesn't seem like a very efficient use of the curse to me. And stronger people can resist it pretty easily, so it's not very useful for weakening anyone who's already strong."

"Hmm." Kuro rubs his chin. "Maybe a way to limit the growth of any future warriors. Curse them while they're young and either they'll be arrested or simply too weak to threaten the fiends in the future."

"Maybe, but something's still bugging me about the whole thing. I should have asked the Goddess when I spoke to her, but I had so many other questions, and our time was limited."

"You *spoke* to the Goddess!?"

"Oh, yeah. I had a little chat with her. A whole city heard her voice, too. When you take the throne, look into what happened in the human city of Silvia, just north of Orakio's capital."

"Things just keep getting more outlandish..."

"Anyway," I say. "I'm curing Alisha of her curse. In a couple weeks, she'll finally be free. Maybe sooner!"

"Cleansing the [Curse of the Forsaken]? I suppose if anyone can do it, it'd be a Great Hero..."

"Yep! And just wait! When she's cured, she's going to be the most powerful beastkin in your nation's history! Great Heroes included!"

"I'm going to be that strong!?" Alisha looks at me with sparkles in her eyes.

"You know it! That Unique Skill of yours is no joke! I can't wait to see what your uncursed stats look like after it activates!"

"Yay! More grinding! More harem!"

*Uh, why is grinding suddenly coming up? And I'm not even going to acknowledge the other one.*

What goes on inside Alisha's head is a mystery that simply can't be solved. Thinking about it too much will only cause my sanity meter to drop, so I let it go.

We're still standing atop the same hill, looking at the city in the near distance. By now, each of the girls have felt the overwhelming presence of mana emanating from behind those walls. Even Alisha knows, despite the low range of her [Sense Mana] spell.

"How strange," Tylith says. "Is it a coincidence that the capital city of Belfast is sitting on top of a Mana Spring?"

"No idea. But it's really disruptive to our ability to sense mana. We should be careful."

"A Mana Spring?" Riona says.

"Basically a fountain of mana that erupts from the ground. You'd never know it was there without the ability to sense mana."

"Then, do you feel it, Kuro?"

"No. Maybe I need to get closer."

I nod. "I only taught you rank 1, so your range is limited."

Kuro would have to get closer, so sometime during our walk to the city, he'd be hit by the feeling of that overpowering mana. If we planned on walking there, that is.

When I came here to set up the teleportation circle, I made sure to leap around the sky, high above the city. That revealed most of its terrain in my [Minimap], meaning I can see dots from all the people inside.

But more importantly, I can see areas without dots. That means areas without people, which is exactly what we need.

"Well," I say, "let's get moving."

"It'd be best to remain hidden at least until we meet with my informant," Riona says. "But sneaking past the walls might be difficult."

"Oh, I wasn't going to even try doing something annoying like that. Sure, we could use [Transform] to hide our identities, but we'd have to come up with a convoluted story to get in. Maybe we could hop the wall, but who knows how long it'd take to find a spot without a sentry. No thanks, I'm taking the easy route."

"Easy route? What did you have in mind?"

"This." I release my magic.

A familiar darkness cloaks me, dampening my senses and emotions. However, since our destination was practically within eyesight, the feeling fades before I even have a chance to enjoy it.

When my vision returns, I'm treated to the sight of a well-kept yard, complete with a flower garden, a fountain, and even a small pond with little fish in it.

As I look around, I see that the home the yard belongs to is a massive building, practically a mansion. No, definitely a mansion. If I were to compare it to what I've seen in the human lands, then I'd have to say that it belongs to someone with a lot of money and power, like a high noble.

"Are you mad!?" Kuro yells softly. "This is the estate of Kuge Hoshi! If we're spotted, the whole city could be put on alert!"

"Ah, that doesn't sound good. I guess a little more reconnaissance would have been a good idea..."

I teleported us to a spot without any people, but I didn't consider what kind of area that might put us in. Now that I think about it, a large estate owned by a powerful noble is actually quite likely to be where we end up.

"Well luckily for us, nobody's in the yard. So let's just sneak out while—"

"Hey, you!" A voice shouts in the distance.

Turning, I see a figure standing quite a ways away. His dot on my [Minimap] is so far away that I assumed he wouldn't be able to see us. But because this yard is so flat and wide, we're actually well within his line of sight.

"How ... unfortunate."

"That's all you're going to say!?" Kuro yells again.

"This kind of thing happens sometimes, so I guess I've just gotten used to it. Ah, but we really should run before he gets close enough to recognize you or Riona."

"I'm way ahead of you!"

As he stated, Kuro has already begun running, ushering his children with him. The rest of us fall in line, following the king through a beautiful flower garden.

"Make sure not to step on the flowers!" I yell to the others.

"Is that really what's important here!?" Kuro seems to find some fault with my priorities.

"It'd mean more work for the gardener, right? I don't want to ruin his day!"

Kuro's actually carrying Keiko now, since her level is too low to keep up with us. His son is rather strong though, so he's fine on his own.

I can hear the yelling of more people now, most likely guards or workers who are trying to help find the intruders. But none of them can match the speed of our party.

Thanks to the fact that the king knows this estate, he manages to lead us to a spot where we can hop the wall. But when we get to the other side, we're met with the gazes of other affluent people who live in the area.

Seeing a shady group of people leaping out from inside a powerful noble's estate doesn't make for a great first impression, which is probably why they're eyeing us with obvious suspicion.

"This way!" Kuro dashes off again.

The estate is on a well-constructed road, with fancy little decorations flanking it with no other purpose than to display the wealth of the ones who can afford to live here.

But that's not important. What is important is the pair of guards who come from around a corner and spot us fleeing.

*Is this my unlucky day, or is it divine punishment for messing with that honorable duel?*

*Goddess! If you're messing with me, just know that I'll be getting my revenge next time we meet!*

It's been a while since I blamed her for my misfortunes, so I take this opportunity to throw all the responsibility for our current situation onto her.

Even though the guards start yelling at us to do things like 'stop' and 'get back here', we ignore them. Now that we're on an open road, our feet can outpace the speed of information in this world.

Back on Earth, a cop might radio ahead in the direction a suspect is fleeing, but the guards here can only reach the ears of anyone in the range of their voice. And that's not good enough.

"Whew," I come to a stop beside Kuro. "What an ordeal."

"Why are you acting like this was someone else's fault? It was thanks to your sudden and unplanned teleportation, wasn't it?"

"Hey, don't get too caught up on the past. Let's look forward to the future instead."

"In that case, I hope you learned your lesson and don't make the same mistake in the future."

Riona steps forward, scanning the street from around the alley's corner. "My informant resides in the next district. We should hurry and speak with her."

This time, everyone follows Riona instead of Kuro. She takes us down some streets, then some alleys, then more roads. We're still a suspicious group, so it's best to avoid crowded areas.

In the end, we wind up at a building that looks no different from the rest. If I had to say one notable thing about it, it'd be that the one who lives here has a liking for potted plants because there are quite a few sitting out in the yard.

*Well, here we are. Now it's time to find out about this mysterious minister who helped Rei take the throne from Kuro.*

After entering the informant's house, we find it completely empty. I knew that before we entered, of course. But I wanted to get off the street since we caused quite a ruckus due to a ... miscalculation.

I look around the living room. "If you think about it, the chances of your informant being home in the middle of the afternoon is pretty low. They'd be out doing their job, right?"

"Yes," Riona says. "I expected this, but we had to check first, just in case. And this gives you a safe place to stay while I go out and find her."

"You're going alone?"

"Who do you take me for? I'm the strongest beastkin in Belfast's army. I don't need a babysitter to tag along with me."

"Ignore him," Belle says. "He's just being overprotective, as usual."

"I can only imagine the hardships that must bring to you and the others."

"Tell me about it! With how much worrying he does, I'm surprised he still has a full head of hair!"

I hold back a sigh. "We're not going down that road again. I still haven't forgotten how you girls teamed up on me back before we entered our first dungeon, you know!"

"Serves you right!" Belle shows me her tongue.

"While you two settle this," Riona says, "I'm going to go find my informant."

Without another word, she leaves the house, and I watch her dot on the [Minimap] as she heads back to the west, toward the castle.

Since we've been given the exciting mission of holding down the fort, we make ourselves comfortable using the furnishings sitting in this rather nice room. There are a few too many of us though, so I have to bring out a couple accommodations of our own.

Looking around the interior of the house, I once again confirm my thoughts when it comes to the similarities between beastkin architecture and old-style Japanese houses. Mats cover the floor, made from some kind of straw, while the interior walls are constructed from a light wood so thin it seems like I can almost see through them.

*There's even a sliding paper door! I wonder what's behind it...*

*No, it's probably just the informant's bedroom, so I shouldn't pry.*

The entire house is rather small by modern Earth standards, but it's probably worth a lot, considering it's in a good neighborhood in the middle of the beastkin's capital city.

Tearing my eyes away from the decor, I turn toward the former king, who's making himself comfortable on a small couch.

"So Kuro, what do you think of the mana around here?"

"It's as you said. Overwhelmingly powerful. It makes it difficult to discern individual sources of mana outside a very short distance, like mist clouding my vision."

"Yeah. It's a little easier for us since our [Sense Mana] spell is a higher rank, but we're facing the same general problem. We've got other magic to make up for it, though."

"These Mana Springs, are they rare?"

"Yeah, stumbling across one isn't very common, though I've found several during my adventures."

"So it's strange that there'd be one in a city, then."

I bring out some snacks and refreshments. "Definitely. So strange that I can't help but wonder if there's a reason for it."

"How could there be when we couldn't sense the mana when the city was founded?"

"I don't know, but there could be another reason. Was the city built on a landmark of some kind? Or maybe there was an abundance of some mineral?"

"Records don't indicate that minerals were involved with the capital's construction, but the city was built around an ancient temple, one of the oldest in our lands. It still stands to this day, though it's been through several renovations over the centuries."

"A temple, huh?" I take a sip of tea. "I'd definitely be interested in seeing it once you're back on the throne."

"That's not a problem. Our ancestors once believed that our people were created there, which is why they gave it the name Temple of Origins. It still holds an important place in our kingdom's culture, but it's not as revered as it once was."

"Created? By the Goddess?"

"Yes. That's only natural, isn't it? Where else would we have come from if not the divine being herself."

"Yeah ... true."

I can't spread the true origin of the beastkin as a weapon of war, created through genetic manipulation by pre-devastation humans. Not only would it be controversial, but I was told in secret by one of the Immortal Beings.

Maybe one day, the world's true history will be revealed, but I definitely won't be the one to get the ball rolling. I've got too many enemies already. I don't need fundamentalists coming after me for spouting heresy.

Well, more heresy than I already spout on a daily basis.

We end up waiting the better part of an hour, but eventually, Riona's dot reaches this house. She's accompanied by a relatively powerful person, though that's only by the standards of an average soldier.

The door opens without even a knock. Of course, I already spoke with Riona telepathically while she was on her way back here, so there's absolutely no surprise about who's stepping through the doorway just behind her.

Riona motions to the beastkin girl beside her. "This is my informant. As I mentioned before, she's been investigating the king's new minister, Jun."

*What kind of ears are those? Squirrel? She even looks a little like a squirrel, what with that brown hair and tiny body.*

*But why would the humans from 10,000 years ago try to make supersoldiers out of human-squirrel hybrids...?*

There's no way for me to ask what they were thinking when over ten millennia have passed, so all I can do is shake my head and hold back a sigh.

The informant gives a small bow, which only reinforces my perception of her squirrelly heritage. "It's a pleasure to meet you. And I'm glad to see you're in good health, Your Majesty."

Kuro nods to her. "Thank you for your hard work. I hope you can enlighten us on who this mysterious advisor is and what he's been up to."

"About that. Ever since Prince Rei took the throne, the advisor, Jun, has been a close aide to him, rarely leaving the prince's side. The few times he's not acting as advisor, he's often seen praying in the Temple of Origins."

"The temple? Why there?"

"I'm not sure. He always enters one of the private praying chambers, where he spends many hours at a time."

"Private praying chamber?" I ask.

"There are rooms at the temple where believers can pay to pray to the Goddess privately."

"So once he enters, nobody sees him until he leaves the room."

"Yes, as is tradition."

*Alone at the temple for hours at a time. What exactly is he doing in there? He's not actually praying, is he?*

There's still no proof that this advisor is up to no good. So far, all we have is a convenient timing for his appearance and some suspicious activity.

But the informant isn't done with her report yet.

"Go on," Kuro says. "What else have you found?"

"Unfortunately, I've not had much contact with the advisor due to his close proximity to Prince Rei, so detailed information on his personality and objectives is lacking. However, rumors are circulating that he's a religious zealot, which is supported by his long hours at the temple.

"During my few encounters with him, I managed to pick up on his general persona, at least the one he displays in public. He speaks with a passionate tone, as if he believes his goals were of the utmost importance to the future of this world. I can definitely see where he got his reputation as a fanatic."

Kuro looks thoughtful. "A passionate and zealous man, spending most of his time with my son and the rest praying at the Temple of Origins. It's strange, but there's still no proof he had anything to do with Rei's sudden rise in strength."

"My apologies for not being able to confirm it."

"No, it's fine. The information is enough to stoke my suspicions even further. I'm more confident than ever that this advisor needs to be confronted, one way or another. Only then will we find the truth. Do you know where he is currently?"

"He's within the temple, no doubt in one of the private rooms."

"Hmm. An interrogation, is it?" Brown cat ears and a tail sprout from my body. "I think I can handle that. What's this man look like?"

"He's a dog-kin, with dirty blonde hair and fur. Green eyes, somewhere between his late 40s and early 50s."

"Alright. Should be easy enough to find."

"Remember," Kuro says, "there's no guarantee he's the one we're after."

I grab my own tail and look at the brown fur covering it. "What do you take me for? When it comes to getting the truth, I'm very gentle."

"I can attest to that," Riona says. "Though it'd be great if you weren't so perverted during your search for the truth."

"Oh?" Belle immediately speaks up. "Tell us more about how he was so perverted."

"When we fought in the command tent, he tore the cloak right off my body so he could–"

"And I'm gone!" I release my spell.

*"Hey!"* Belle's voice follows me. *"Don't just teleport away when we're about to expose your foul deeds!"*

I ignore the voice, of course. Because I'm in the middle of a mission and not at all because it's convenient for me.

*Now then. According to my [Minimap], the temple should be just a few blocks south of here.*

Having the terrain show up on my map is really nice. Even if I don't know where a landmark is, I can usually find it just by zooming in and looking around.

*I should do that next time I teleport somewhere risky, like when I brought everyone into the city.*

*Don't wanna accidentally warp into a noble's garden again.*

I step out of the alley I teleported to and onto a road. Following it south will put me almost right next to the temple, so all I have to do is keep walking.

I'm hiding my identity, of course. Not only do I have a pair of furry, brown cat ears and a tail to blend in, but I'm dressed in casual clothes. It's way better than wearing a suspicious cloak.

Since I've got a few blocks to go, I use this opportunity to take in the sights of this city, Kava. As expected of a capital, the buildings are constructed with the highest quality, using the most modern techniques and materials.

Although they bear more similarity to human architecture than elven, there's a bit of both in the design. Though whether that's due to coincidence or outside influence, I can't say for sure.

Compared to the buildings I saw in the few towns I visited during my rush through the beastkin lands, there seems to be a trend of homogenizing the construction here. The flourish and creative designs have been dialed back, making these houses look even more similar to the ones in the human lands.

Still, it doesn't take an architect to see the differences, though I can't help but wonder if the beastkin's construction methods will eventually fully prioritize function over form, as modern Japanese houses often do when compared to their older counterparts.

After making it to the final intersection, the Temple of Origins comes into view. It's strikingly different compared to the surrounding buildings, with white stone making up its outer wall. The pillars that support the roof along the walkway to its entrance are made of similar stone and are carved with artistic depictions that mean nothing to me but are at least pleasant to look at.

*The architecture for the temple is wildly different from the rest of the city. Almost as if it were built by entirely different people.*

Kuro did say the temple went through several renovations, but they likely tried to mimic the original style, which is why it still looks so unique to this day.

Since it was built so long ago, it makes sense why it was made with stone, rather than more modern materials like wood or brick. Since the inhabitants that rule this world have a history spanning 2,000 years, construction methods have obviously evolved in that time. It could be that ancient beastkin really did build the temple during the beginning of recent history.

Either way, there's no wall or guards preventing me from entering, so I confidently step onto the temple grounds, walking beneath the white stone roof and between the rows of carved pillars.

The walkway makes me feel like I'm in a tunnel of sorts, transitioning between the modern world into an ancient one. I can't help but wonder what purpose the temple used to serve to those who originally built it two millennia ago.

When I reach the entrance, I stop and look at the carvings that flank the doorway. One is a lion, while the other is a wolf. Both of them are humanoid and carry a staff, though their features are much more animalistic than the beastkin race.

I don't know what they symbolize or even if these carvings are part of the original design. But they certainly remind me of other ancient archeological sites on Earth.

Since the doors are wide open, I walk through.

The inside is made of the same white stone as the outside, making it quite bright, despite the relative lack of light. Among the first things I notice is just how high the ceiling is. It didn't look so big from the outside, but now that I'm in it, it seems to have grown several times over.

It's just an illusion, of course. The temple is rather tall, but not compared to something like a castle. The reason it feels so small outside and so grand inside is because there's only one floor in this temple. As I stare up, I'm looking at the bottom of the roof far above my head.

*How high is it? Even if 20 people stood on each other's shoulders, I doubt they could reach the ceiling.*

As my eyes crawl down the walls, they take in the sight of two great statues, one on each of the side walls. From the looks of them, they were carved directly into the stone, and their heads nearly touch the temple's ceiling.

Like the carvings outside, they're humanoid animals, but rather than holding staffs, their arms are simply crossed along their chests. Their garments are strange, as well. At least, what little is left of them. There's a lot of wear on the statues, and it looks like they weren't renovated with the rest of the building.

The temple's main hall isn't just tall, it's also wide. The entire space is so open that it makes me feel small in comparison, with the walls and ceiling so far from touch. Here, I can see the hand of a more modern renovation, as the weathered stone has been painted, likely to prevent more destruction from the visitors who frequent the temple.

About three-quarters of the way to the back of the temple is a massive set of stairs. Like the statues, they were carved directly from the stone. At the top is a platform, where an altar is displaying a large, ornamental chalice.

Behind that is a ridiculously large door, the only one I can see in the entire temple. I can feel several mana presences behind the door, including one that sticks out from all the others in here.

Since there's no other place the private praying rooms can be other than behind that door, I continue my walk toward the massive set of stairs.

"Blessings be upon you, child," an old beastkin priest says when I approach the steps. "Have you come seeking guidance during these troubling times?"

"Yes. I have many problems, and I wish to voice them to the Goddess alone."

"If that's what you want, then I can lead you to a chamber at this very moment. Though only those who donate can access them."

*Is it really a donation, then?*

"Of course," I say, keeping my thoughts to myself. "I brought this."

Two gold appears in my hand, and I hold them out to the priest.

"Thank you, child." He takes them, perhaps a little too eagerly. "Please, follow me."

The old man leads me up the massive staircase, past the altar and chalice, and into the room beyond. Here, the modern touch is even more obvious. Since this is how the temple brings in coin, it likely gets the most attention out of all the areas in and around the building.

He brings me to one of many doors that line the hall behind the altar. Although the door has an ancient look to it, it's obvious that it's nowhere near 2,000 years old, as the temple is supposed to be. They likely just built it to match the rest of the design.

The priest leaves after wishing me well, so I take a look around the small praying chamber. It has a padded mat for kneeling, placed just in front of another altar, though there's no chalice this time.

*Hmm. Somehow, I doubt the Goddess can hear anyone praying in these rooms.*

*Actually, I'm sure of it since she told me she can't hear the voices of the people anymore. With the exception of me and Lumina.*

*But if she can hear my voice...*

I kneel on the mat and get into a generic praying position, putting my hands together beneath my chin.

*Hey, you can hear me, right? I've got a few things to say to you.*

*First off, stop being biased toward humans. The other races are really interesting and deserve to be picked as Great Heroes, too!*

*Secondly, make up with the Immortal Beings already. Maybe then, we wouldn't have any more of these world-ending threats!*

*Ah, and third, I guess help us out a bit when you can. You know, on our journey to save the world and all.*

After my amazing prayer session, I stand and nod at my own words. It always feels nice to push responsibility onto her whenever I have the chance, and that hasn't changed, despite being on good terms with her now.

Since I can't very well barge in on the advisor during his private prayer, I can only sit around in my own room and keep an eye on his mana signature, so to speak.

Ten minutes go by, then twenty. I'm not just sitting around, of course. Instead, I'm working on one of my recent inventions, though it's not one that takes a lot of mental effort since I don't want to get too involved, only to be pulled away at the worst time.

It's good that I picked such an easy project because about half an hour after I entered the praying chamber, the mana I've had my eye on begins to move.

I leave my room at the same time, looking as casual as possible. A few doors down, I see another man step into the hall. He's got dirty blonde hair, dog ears, and green eyes.

*Yep, that's him alright. And man, he sure looks relaxed.*

The look on his face can only come from a place of peace, as if he found his own personal meaning in this life and has no regrets about it.

I'm not going to complain though, as such a face makes it easy for me to strike up a conversation as he approaches me on his way toward the large door that leads back to the temple's main room.

"I hope you found what you were seeking," I say.

"Oh yes, I did. Each time I come here, I grow closer to the truth."

"Truth? You understand such a thing?"

"Ah." He shows me a wide smile. "If only you could hear her as I do. Alas, only I have been chosen. Though you can rest easy, my friend. I will bring this world back from the brink of destruction."

"Is … that so? I'm a little confused, but if you were chosen, then that's good right?"

"Yes. Very good! It means the Goddess is leading us to salvation. And King Rei is the one who will bring about the end of this chaotic era. Of that, I am sure."

I nod along with him. "That sounds fantastic. Do you think these hard times will end soon? So many are suffering."

"Yes, very soon. We need only wait until the appropriate time, then all will be made right again."

We pass the altar outside the prayer hall and start down the steps.

"Is there anything we can do to help you?" I ask.

"No, this mission is mine and mine alone. That was clear. You need but wait. And pray, as you have today. Perhaps that's the most important of all."

The new king's advisor looks even more content, as if talking about this mission of his only increased the feeling of joy for being chosen.

I keep the conversation going until we reach the temple's entrance, but I only receive more fanatic responses from a man who seems to truly believe he's been chosen by the Goddess to fulfill some divine mission.

After we exit, we part ways, and I watch as he walks off with light steps.

*You poor fool. I don't know who's talking to you in that prayer room, but there's one thing I'm sure of.*

*It's not the Goddess.*

# Chapter 19: Twin Doppelgangers

## ----- Lutz -----

"He's hearing voices at the Temple of Origins?" Kuro asks.

"Yeah. I doubt he's actually crazy, so it's probably from someone using [Mental Link], pretending to be the Goddess."

"You said before that this civil war may be a scheme by Chaos to destabilize our kingdom. So does that mean an Archfiend is behind this?"

"Maybe, but even someone as powerful as an Archfiend has limitations. There's no way they can use the [Mental Link] spell from as far away as their territory on the western peninsula, so whoever's behind it is likely much closer. In this very city, even."

"But you said Archfiends lose their power when too far from their lands."

I nod. "It makes me wonder if they sent one of their lackeys instead. A beastkin that they turned to their side, perhaps. I've seen them do the same with humans."

Some of my first major opponents in this world were humans doing the bidding of Chaos. Marquis Lars who was running Silvia into the ground, then that mage Geld fanning the flames of the revolution in Reim, the city where Karina used to be mayor.

The fiends even managed to turn the entire race of vampires against the other three races. Something like getting a single beastkin to manipulate the king's advisor would probably be an easy task.

As usual when we're dealing with Chaos, things aren't going the way I'd like. If we were anywhere else but in the middle of this Mana Spring, maybe I could feel where the mage is casting [Mental Link] from. But it's hard enough to feel nearby mana presences, so tracking down a spellcaster would be really difficult.

And it's made even tougher by another interesting fact.

"When I was at the Temple of Origins, I realized something. I said the capital was built on top of a Mana Spring, but that's not really true. It was the temple that was built on the Mana Spring."

"The temple? Are you saying the center of the spring is directly beneath the temple?"

"Yeah. The flow of mana is strongest in the center of the temple, which tells me that whoever built it knew exactly what they were doing."

"It was our own ancient ancestors who constructed it, and I don't see how they would know where the Mana Spring is, especially back when civilization was so rudimentary."

I look around the room at the faces of Riona, Kuro's children, and my companions. Each of them look back to me, as if expecting me to have the answer to the mystery.

By this world's standards, I've got an advanced education. Just having fundamental knowledge of things like math and history doesn't help much, but all the years I spent learning and problem solving has given me a vast understanding of so many subjects that it makes it easier to connect dots that seem unrelated to those who don't have such an education.

Add to that all the time I spent playing videogames, and my advantages only grow. Although many people say games are a waste of time, there are some clear skills to be learned by playing them.

For example, each game is bound by a set of rules, known as the game mechanics, which defines how you interact with the game world. If your character has a sword, then the game mechanics include how your character swings it. Wide, slow attacks that leave you open to well-timed counters? Or perhaps lightning-quick strikes with a long string of combos?

Depending on how the game mechanics are set up, it can drastically change how the game needs to be played. And there are other forms of game mechanics, as well. Does the game have a leveling system? Are currency and drop items integral to progress? What about a crafting mechanic? Each of these can play a role in defining a game.

Every mechanic added together form the game's system. Enemies, puzzles, and traps are what most people see as their opponent in videogames, but the true final boss is the system of game mechanics that make up the world on which the game is built.

By understanding that system, players can optimize their builds, reduce down time, and defeat powerful enemies under restrictions that the average person would believe to be impossible.

Indeed, the process of understanding a game's system, and then learning how to pick it apart, is a skill that has much real-world use. After all, the entire world runs on systems. From rules that define a job to physics that define the laws of the universe, everything can be boiled down to a system of mechanics.

Those who spend countless hours going from one videogame's system to another, constantly learning and eventually exploiting them to their advantage, are in fact practicing a valuable skill that if honed will allow them to understand the many real-world systems that make up our everyday lives.

It's this skill to recognize, adapt to, and overcome these systems that's allowed me to thrive in this world. But even I can't figure out the answers to each piece of the puzzle.

"I don't know how they managed it, either. Even if you consider the fact that the Goddess could guide them to build it here, that still leaves the question of why. Is there a purpose to having a temple sitting on a Mana Spring? Or was there some artifact that used to take advantage of the power flowing through here? I just don't know.

"But no matter why they built it here or who's behind the manipulation, it doesn't change what we need to do. This kingdom needs to be back in Kuro's hands. If we can accomplish that, then none of the other stuff matters. We just have to be a little more careful with our plans, just in case there is a powerful mage behind it all who can use the massive amount of mana in the city."

"But Master, why not capture that advisor and have him tell us?"

"I doubt a religious fanatic would be willing to spill the truth, no matter how nicely we ask. He believes he's doing the Goddess' work, so he'd likely die before going against that voice."

"Ah, I guess that's true."

"Also, I didn't want to ruin things. I'm still not familiar with beastkin culture, so I wanted to talk to Kuro about our choices before I made any moves that would lock us onto any one path."

Alisha tilts her head to the side. "What else can we do?"

"We've got a couple choices. Kuro, what are the chances of you being able to request a duel from Rei like he did to you?"

"Not good, I'd say. I'm in no position to force his hands, having lost to him only a week prior. It'd be completely up to Rei on whether or not to accept it."

"The beastkin culture is limiting our options again, huh? I still don't quite get it, but I'll just take your word for it. There's also the option of investigating who's talking to the advisor. I marked Jun on my [Minimap] so we can find him anytime. But with the Mana Spring clouding our ability to sense mana, I'm not sure how long it'd take to find the mage behind the curtain."

"You said you were in a hurry, didn't you? Do you have time for such an endeavor?"

I sit back in my chair. "I don't have time to be cautious and careful. That means I'd have to take some risks, and I'm not sure how well it'd turn out."

"Hmm. If it were a simple matter, then I'd like to take that route. But if there are unknown risks, then I think another path might be best."

"What about taking the throne back by force? Is that out of the question?"

"Such a path carries no honor. They'll never accept me as the true ruler if I abandon even the pretense of tradition to retake the throne."

"So no good, huh? I thought so..."

"Even if I force the nobles to accept such a method, it'll only invite their animosity and opposition in the future. They may even stage their own rebellion by claiming me to be a usurper, allowing a powerful noble to ascend to the throne."

"Yeah, I've seen what a power-hungry noble can do to a country. It'd be bad to repeat that here."

"Hero," Laya says.

"Looks like I'll have to do it, huh?"

"You mean use your position as a summoned hero?" Kuro asks.

"Yeah. At the very least, I should be able to force something like a duel by using my authority. If you win and have my backing, that should be enough to secure your throne, right?"

"Perhaps that's our best option. I'll likely be ridiculed for seeking the help of an outsider to retake my throne, but as long as I can hold onto power until the end of this war, it's worth doing."

A moment of silence fills the room. All the ideas we managed to come up with have their own drawbacks, but they're the best ones we can think of.

It'd be nice if there was some perfect solution, but life doesn't always provide an easy path to what we want. Sometimes, you have to grab an axe, harden your resolve, and chop your way to the future you want.

"Well," I say. "If we're going to confront Rei directly, then we can at least come up with a plan that gives us the best chance of it working out in our favor."

"Like how?" Belle asks.

"By trying our hand at asking for a duel the old-fashioned way first, maybe? Even if there's only a slim chance he'll accept, it leads to the best outcome, so it'd be good to try at least."

"I guess it can't hurt. If people see that we tried, then it might help us win them over afterwards, even if only a little."

"It's settled, then," Kuro says. "We'll go in with the intent to duel for the throne. If he denies me, then we'll have to rely on your title as a summoned hero to compel him to accept. With Riona backing me, the soldiers will likely take our side in the aftermath, which will let me force the nobility's hand in the immediate future, in case they try to scheme."

"We need to make sure the advisor is there, too," I say. "If things get crazy, there's a chance he'll accidentally spill something that might help us."

With this plan, we're basically combining all our ideas into one. Going for the best route of a victory through a duel, with the advisor present to make sure all the major players are there. And if we can't make anything happen, we use my title and see if we can force their hands. With Riona's support, things should work out afterwards.

*How messy. Is this really the best plan we have?*

*If only I could find the mage manipulating that advisor...*

There's nothing I can do about a person I can't find. Before I left the Temple of Origins, I checked the mana sources and the dots on my [Minimap], but I didn't see anything suspicious.

The mage has to be nearby to use [Mental Link] to talk to that advisor, yet I couldn't find anyone with any substantial power. With the Mana Spring overwhelming my ability to sense mana, it adds another layer of difficulty to locating them, and if they're somewhere like an underground hideout, even my [Minimap] won't pick them up until I explore it.

*There's just no time left. I've already spent a full day on this sidequest, and I can't afford to spend who knows how many more on an investigation that may or may not lead anywhere.*

*Even if it's sloppy, we'll just have to put Kuro back on the throne by any means necessary.*

*The most important objective is to ruin whatever plans Chaos has for Belfast, after all.*

"If we're going to do this, then we're going to do it right." I wave my hand, and several items appear atop a table.

"Powerful enchanted equipment?" Kuro asks.

"Yeah. I'm not asking you to use them in the duel, but if the fiends are involved, we may end up in a fight, even if you win."

"That's true. I'll keep them in my [Inventory], then."

"And these..." More items appear. "Are for you, Riona."

"You have my gratitude." She puts them into her [Inventory].

With that, preparations are basically complete. I was worried that we'd have to wait around until the advisor decided to go back to the new king's side, but it seems that won't be a problem. After he left the temple, he went straight back to the castle.

Unfortunately, the inside of the castle is still dark on my [Minimap]. Things like shacks and small houses are revealed just by getting near them, but the same isn't true for large buildings. They won't show up until I step inside and explore them.

However, if he's in the castle, then he's probably with Rei. At the very least, we can call for him when we meet the new king.

"We'll need a plan to get in," I say. "If Kuro just shows up at the castle, won't they try to throw him in a cell?"

"I think I have a solution for that." Riona turns to Kuro. "My Liege, I'm hereby placing you under arrest."

Kuro smiles. "So that's your solution. Rather than letting them arrest me, do it yourself."

"This way, I can control your destination. As the Grand General, nobody will question me if I say I'm bringing you to Rei as a captive."

"Then so be it." Kuro sends most of his powerful items to his [Inventory]. "This magical storage space is proving quite useful already."

"Then how about this," I say. "Tylith, Belle, and I will join you as guards, while Laya and Alisha pretend to be your kids. With a little Dark Magic, we can make them nearly indistinguishable."

"I'm going to be a captive!" Alisha sounds a bit too happy about it.

"I'm going to have cat ears again..."

"You look cute with them, Laya!"

"Mrrr."

It seems Laya's remembering that time in the elven lands when we forced her to fight with cat ears and tail, meowing with each attack. It was hilarious.

And like Alisha said, she looked cute with cat ears. That's not why I chose this setup, though. Well, maybe just a little.

"Ahem." I clear my throat for no reason whatsoever. "If everyone's clear on their roles, then we can head out anytime. We'll need to make a stop to get some armor, though. Much easier to wear it than fake it with [Transform]."

"No problem," Riona says. "I can acquire a few sets."

"Excellent! Anything else we need to do before we get started?"

Kuro turns to the informant who's been with us the whole time. "Take care of my children while we're gone. We'll be back with good news before the day's out."

"Understood, Your Highness."

"Then..." he turns to me. "Let's go."

Just like that, we leave the informant's house, heading toward the castle to finally put an end to this civil war.

----------

"I'm a boy!" Alisha's overly excited voice fills the air.

"Hey," I say. "You are most certainly not a boy. We just took out some of the softness from your facial features and changed your hair. Nothing else."

"Ah, but I'm taller, too!"

"Oh yeah. That's true."

"And I'm a boy!"

"Hah…" A sigh escapes me. "Maybe this plan was a mistake."

"Eh? No way! This is fun!"

"You were the one who thought of it!" Belle says. "Don't try to act like it's someone else's problem now!"

"Yeah, yeah. It's just gender bending was never my thing, so I guess I shoulda seen this coming…" I look to the other girl who's under the effects of [Transform]. "Laya's got some cute cat ears though, so I guess it was worth it."

She stiffens at my words. "It's not that cute or anything…"

Her reaction causes her tail to rise straight into the air, the black fur standing on end. Although her words are as monotone as ever, her body's new additions give away her embarrassment.

"Huh? What kind of nonsense are you talking about? Of course it's cute! Who doesn't like furry little cat ears poking out through a head of hair? Am I right?"

I look to the others who are walking with us. Alisha is nodding furiously, while Belle visibly holds back a sigh. Tylith avoids my eyes, but I clearly saw her watching Laya's fuzzy little ears just before.

As for Kuro and Riona, the two of them have been surrounded by beastkin their whole lives, so it's only natural that they'd be numb to seeing something like cat ears. That's what I expected at least, but it seems Riona understands where I'm coming from because she unconsciously nodded at my words.

"Anyway," I say. "You're Kuro's kids for now, so don't forget to react to your new names if they're called. That means you're Keiko for now, Laya. And Alisha, you're … wait, what's the prince's name again?"

"Don't just suddenly forget his name!" Belle shouts.

"I'm joking, I'm joking. Haha…" Nobody laughs with me. "Anyway–"

"And stop saying 'anyway'!"

"Hey, it's my go-to for when I'm shifting the conversation. Really useful word, isn't it?"

"Only because you keep having to pivot after your jokes fall flat."

"Eh? Does that ever happen?"

"You've got a very convenient memory, as usual."

"Anyway." I look over our group. "We're all set now, so might as well get the party started, right?"

We've already changed into the armor Riona brought back from wherever it was she got it from. And since we've perfected Laya and Alisha's transformations, we can start the mission anytime.

Neither Tylith nor I want to hold such a large [Transform] any longer than we have to, so we only activated it after getting close to our destination. In other words, the castle.

With Riona leading us, the castle quickly comes into view. It stands so tall that the wall around it can't even begin to hide its majesty.

We've been spotted already, but that's what we expected. The guards at the wall's eastern gate are already preparing for our arrival, though they don't seem to have realized who it is that's approaching them.

When we finally get close, their hardened faces are covered in surprise. They probably never imagined their Grand General would show up so suddenly.

In fact, the unannounced visit is quite a problem.

"H-halt," a guard says. "General Riona, is that you?"

"It is. And as you see, I've captured the former king." Riona motions behind her, where Kuro stands.

The guard looks between Kuro and Riona. "That's ... definitely His Maj–I mean the former king. But we haven't received word of your arrival. When did you return to the city?"

"Just now. We were in a hurry, so we made it here before my own messenger."

The guards look between each other, obviously suspicious. One of the most common uses of [Transform] is to take the appearance of someone powerful in order to gain their authority for whatever foul deeds the Dark Mage has planned.

When someone shows up without an announcement and wants access to a secure place like the castle, it's bound to draw suspicion. That goes double for people who are supposed to be several days' march away.

However, there's one thing we have going for us.

"I'm going to bring the former king and his children to King Rei." Riona motions toward Alisha and Laya this time, who are still transformed.

The hesitation in the guard fades a bit, and he finally salutes his general. "Understood, Grand General. Please, allow us to escort you inside."

"That would be much appreciated."

*Alright. That went about as well as we could hope for.*

It's one thing to have a single Dark Mage transformed to trick a guard. But when there are four recognizable faces, the chances of each of them being under the effects of [Transform] drops dramatically. Laya and Alisha are actually transformed, but that's not important.

Either way, the guards don't trust us entirely, which is why three of them decide to 'escort' us to the castle. The fact that two of the three flank our party is just a coincidence, I'm sure.

They're not in a hurry, either. The biggest drawback with using [Transform] is its insane mana cost. Copying someone's features well enough to fool people will drain the mage's mana quick.

But we're not too worried about a short delay. Tylith and I have so much mana regeneration that a few extra minutes isn't a big deal. We anticipated the guards would use this strategy, which is why we only transformed Laya and Alisha at the last possible moment.

Still, my mana is taking a beating since I had to change so many things about Laya. Giving her cat ears and a tail, turning her hair black, changing her facial features, and making her taller. A normal mage would probably be drained in under a minute, but I can hold it for an hour or so.

Fortunately, I don't need to take drastic measures because we arrive at the castle's main entrance with plenty of time to spare.

At first glance, the beastkin castle seems to be made completely of wood, unlike the stone castle in the Orakian capital of Roshar. But when I look closer, I notice that it's actually a mixture of stone and wood. I'm no architect, but from a quick examination, it seems the stone forms the foundation and main walls, while the wood is mainly for aesthetics.

Before I have time to admire its construction further, we're stepping inside. As expected, the artistic design doesn't end at the door. Compared to Lumina's castle, this one definitely has a lot more flourish.

Down a hall, around a corner, up some stairs, and repeat. It'd be much more convenient if they put the stairs right next to each other, but that'd also mean invaders would have a much easier time getting up them. Lumina's castle has a similar layout for the same reason, so it takes a bit of time to get from the entrance to the important places.

Not long after we reach the third floor, we run into a small crowd in the hall. From their finely crafted outfits and confident faces, I'd put my money on them being nobles, not servants.

Sure enough, Riona stops when we get close to them, though from the slight frown that covers her face for a brief second, it seems she'd rather not have run into them.

"Grand General," a beastkin noble says. "I wasn't informed of your return."

"Nobody was informed, Kuge Hoshi. We rushed back here with haste, even beating my own messenger."

*Wait, that name sounds familiar...*

*Wasn't he the noble whose garden we teleported into when we came into the city?*

When Kuro first mentioned him, I thought Kuge was his first name and Hoshi was his last. But I found out later that Kuge is a noble rank, the highest in the beastkin lands. If compared to human nobles, it'd be equivalent to the rank of Duke.

Hoshi looks to Kuro. "So it's settled, then..."

*Hmm? He doesn't look very happy. Was he one of the nobles who was supporting Kuro?*

*If so, why did he stay in the capital instead of fleeing like many others did?*

"Yes," Riona says. "The civil war is over."

"I suppose we should just be happy that our kingdom can be reunited so quickly. But..."

"Is there a problem, Kuge Hoshi?"

"No." He steps aside, opening a path. "I'm sure King Rei will want to speak to his father. You should make haste."

"Indeed." Riona motions to us. "Let's go."

Turns out, the throne room is on the third floor. The magnificent double doors have their own set of guards protecting them, but they're not an obstacle to us. They open like all the others before them, granting us access to the room that holds Belfast's highest seat of power.

*Huh. I remember the first time I stepped into the king's throne room back when I was first summoned.*

At the time, I was overwhelmed with its size, with the weight of what it represented nearly stopping me in my tracks.

But now...

*...Kings are just people, like any other.*

I step into the room, taking in the sights with a casual turn of my head. It's fancy, as expected, but somewhere along the line, I grew used to places that would make a normal person gawk. If anything, I'm more concerned with how it compares to Orakio's royal castle more than anything else.

But I didn't come here for that. As my eyes scan the room, I'm actually searching for anyone suspicious who could really be pulling the strings behind Rei and that advisor. Unfortunately, nobody sticks out, either in looks or strength.

So, I'm forced to focus on the two major players who are here.

Rei—or rather, Belfast's current king—is sitting on the throne, as expected. He's Kuro's eldest son, so of course he would share his features, like black hair and cat ears. But he didn't seem to inherit any of the man's temperament.

His posture on the throne screams impatience, as if he were fed up with how things are going and wants to get up and take care of things himself. What those things are, I can only guess. It'd be an educated guess, though.

*Is it the stress of being king? Can't be easy for a kid who just usurped the throne from his own dad.*

*Or is there another reason for his obvious anxiety?*

My eyes fall on the advisor standing beside Rei. The man has the same enlightened smile as when I saw him at the Temple of Origins. It's a bit creepy to see someone be so confident in their beliefs when they're actually just a pawn in someone's game.

*Nothing I can say will ever get through to that man. I'm sure of it.*

We come to a stop well before reaching the throne. There are guards everywhere. They flank us, they stand between us and the throne, and a few are even guarding the door on the inside. We're completely surrounded, despite having arrived with literally no notice.

*Does he keep this many guards around him, even when he's on the throne?*
*Is he afraid of being assassinated?*

"Riona!" Rei shouts from the throne. "Why didn't you send word of your arrival!? Walking in here with Father in tow ... what if I wasn't prepared!?"

"My apologies, Your Majesty. We arrived so quickly that—"

"I don't care!" Rei grits his teeth. "I swear, if only everyone would just do their job properly...!"

"Your Majesty," the advisor says. "As frustrating as her methods may be, it seems in the end, you got what you wanted."

"Yes … yes, I did." Rei focuses on Kuro. "You should have come quietly like I demanded, Father. Things would have been so much easier."

"The easy path usually leads to a dead end, Rei. As tempting as it may be to take it, those who persevere through the perilous path often find the reward for their efforts far outweighs the difficulty of walking it."

"More of your philosophical ramblings? I've heard enough of them for one lifetime already! You're in my custody now, so stop acting like you're in control!"

Kuro shakes his head. "You want to be the ruler so badly that you're willing to start a civil war with your own family. You always were hot headed, but never like this."

"It's because of you! Talking about an alliance with the humans!? They just invaded us again! We'd be throwing away every ounce of our pride if we came crawling to them for an alliance right now!"

"Diplomacy isn't easy, son. Would you rather sacrifice your pride or the lives of your subjects to another war, even as the battle against Chaos continues?"

"The fiends aren't a threat anymore. We're winning, or weren't you paying attention?"

"Are we? Or have they simply changed tactics?"

"Enough! I don't care to hear any more of your so-called wisdom." Rei smiles. "I already sent a force north. Not only will they retake our lost territory, but they'll march even further, taking more of the human lands for Belfast!"

"You're starting a war with Orakio? Rei, how foolish."

"Your Majesty," Riona says. "I am in agreement with Kuro. A war with Orakio isn't feasible in our current state. We have soldiers on the borders of Chaos and many men are still not back from the short civil war. Even when they return, it will take a while to arrange the strategy and get all the nobles in line. These kinds of things should be done with care."

"You too, Riona!? I don't care about any of that. I'm the king, and the soldiers will obey. You will obey too, as you always do."

"Your Majesty, there has never been a time when I have disobeyed the throne. You know that very clearly. However, that doesn't mean my allegiance belongs to the king."

"Huh? I'm the king, and I sit on the throne. That means you answer to me."

"My apologies, Your Majesty, but I disagree."

"What do you mean you disagree!? Riona, have you betrayed me!?"

"She didn't betray you," Kuro says. "She's just following her sense of honor, as always. Perhaps you never understood her in the first place. But enough of that.

"Rei." Kuro summons his equipment, covering his body in powerful, enchanted gear. "I hereby challenge you to a duel! To the winner, goes the throne!"

"Are you mad!? I bested you once already, Father! I have no need to accept a challenge so soon! You know our ways better than that!"

"You're right, son. But in this case, I think you'll find the duel not so easily avoided."

*And here it comes. He's not willing to duel, so time for me to force his hand with my title.*

*I wonder if–*

"Your Majesty," the advisor says, cutting off my thoughts. "You should accept the duel."

"""What!?""" Several voices shout in unison.

"There's no need to worry. This was foreseen by the Goddess herself."

"There you go again..." Rei looks hesitant. "But if you're sure this will benefit me..."

"Oh, yes. The nobles who've begun to plot against you will be forced to recognize your supreme power once again."

"Yes ... yes, they will." Rei's eyes harden again. "Fine. I accept your challenge, Father. But after I defeat you, know that I won't accept any more disobedience! From anyone!"

*Well, that went way differently than I thought.*

*But hey, at least I get to enjoy the duel as a nameless soldier instead of a central figure!*

*Still wish I had that popcorn, though...*

# Chapter 20: Twin Duels

## ----- Lutz -----

*Hmm. I guess that really seals the deal. He's definitely being manipulated by an agent of Chaos.*

My eyes rest squarely on the advisor that confidently told Rei to accept the duel. Most people need a reason to show such confidence, like a lifetime of skill or the support of powerful individuals.

When I first met the advisor, I assumed his unwavering belief in his actions was the result of his supposed connection to the Goddess. Certainly, that's a large part of it, but now I realize that it's not the only reason for his arrogant smile.

*A spell orb, most likely. A strong one, too.*

*And the mana feels familiar. Deep, powerful. Just like the one I took from that mage Geld several months ago.*

Part of me wants to bring that spell orb out to compare it with the one I feel beneath the advisor's robes, but it'd be dangerous to suddenly call a powerful item out right now. After all, the advisor could have the [Sense Mana] buff on him.

*If he's got a powerful spell orb, then there's no doubt that the fiends have their hands in this mess.*

*But where are they?*

"Master, what are we going to do about him?"

"Nothing. Not yet, at least."

"Does that mean you have a plan for later?"

*"Well, plan is a strong word. I really just want to see what he's going to do. Maybe he'll reveal something if he thinks he's still a hidden mastermind."*

*"Ah, I see! But what if he interferes in the duel?"*

A smile forms on my lips. *"There are a few spells I've been wanting to try out, so maybe that wouldn't be so bad."*

I felt the advisor cast [Scry] when we walked into the throne room. With it, the strength difference between Kuro and Rei should be obvious to him.

Not only is Kuro ten levels higher than his son, but Rei's stats are rather average for his level. Kuro may not be able to compete with a pure genius on the battlefield like Riona, but he's far from average. He wouldn't have become king, if he were.

The advisor should know that the battle won't be easy for Rei, yet he doesn't have a shred of hesitation on his face.

*"Ohhh!"* Belle lets out a frustrated sound. *"That man's face really ticks me off!"*

*"Mmm. Arrogant."*

*"I know, right!? And he's so confident that he's doing this for the good of the world. Get real!"*

*"If he truly thought himself a hero, then he would stop and look at all the people who are suffering because of his actions."*

*"Exactly!"* Belle gives a small nod, her helmeted head barely moving in the corner of my vision. *"Starting a civil war at a time like this! I don't care what reasons he has, he's no good!"*

I can't help but agree with the girls. I've sacrificed my fair share of people in order to survive, so perhaps it's hypocritical of me to condemn this advisor, but I just really don't like the way he's doing things.

During this moment of downtime, Kuro and Rei have been getting ready for the duel. Though both sides were already fully equipped, so it was actually more about preparing the arena and gathering the nobles to witness the event.

Even the noble we met in the hall is here, Kuge Hoshi. Since the capital is obviously filled with those who support the new king, I expected to see him and his buddies eagerly awaiting Kuro's final defeat here in the arena.

But that's not the feeling they're giving me.

*"I can smell it,"* Tylith says. *"Their fear."*

*"Fear? Why would the nobles be afraid of a duel like this?"*

*"Perhaps it's not the duel itself but the outcome."*

*"Afraid of Kuro regaining power? Or..."*

My eyes fall on the advisor. He's on the far side of the arena, his figure nearly blocked by Rei, who stands in the center of the dirt ring.

An unfamiliar magic begins to flow from the man. It's so strange, I can't even figure out which elemental school it belongs to. And of course, it's being cast through that powerful spell orb.

*"Get ready for anything,"* I say to the girls.

*"Mmm."*

He completes the magic, and I feel the energy he's gathered burst from his body. However...

*Nothing? Did he cast some kind of debuff on Kuro?*

Kuro's still in my party, so I check his status through the menu, but I don't see anything strange.

I turn back to the advisor, and as I watch him, I can clearly see his lips moving. However, none of the nobles here seem to want to get close to him, so there's nobody near him. That makes me wonder...

*Who's he talking to?*

Because Rei is clearly in my vision, I catch sight of his face as it twists in some combination of pain and anger.

*What's going on? Strange spells, odd whispering, and Rei oozing with hatred.*

*Could it be?*

I risk casting a spell, [Scry]. As expected, the advisor picks up on it, and his eyes fall on me. It would have been nice to stay hidden, but I need to know.

Checking Rei's status confirms my theory.

*So that's it. This advisor is...*

"Rei," Kuro says. "You always were too arrogant for your own good. But I never thought you'd resort to overthrowing me in a time of relative peace."

"It's because you're too weak, Father! Peace and trade, even while the humans attack?" Rei lifts his warhammer. "I won't stand for it!"

"Still won't listen to reason?" Kuro falls into stance. "Then I'll have to let my spear do the talking."

The battle begins with the spectacle of Kuro's spear meeting Rei's warhammer. And no sooner do they clash, the cheater reveals himself.

*"That advisor's being bad!"* Alisha says.

"Yeah. The spell he's casting is easy to recognize this time."

"[Enhance], right?"

"Yep. He's going to use it on Rei, probably followed by many more buffs to make sure his man wins."

"Then are we going to cheat, too?"

"Not exactly. I'd rather leave matching his buffs as a last resort. Instead, let's try this..."

The fourth-tier Arcane Spell [Disrupt] activates the same instant the advisor releases his [Enhance]. The two energies clash, producing the equivalent of a fireworks show for anyone who can sense mana.

Since it was centered on the advisor's own body, the man nearly leaps into the air as the crackling energy explodes around him.

Immediately, his eyes fall on me. I'm on the other side of the arena, but I can clearly see his self-righteous expression.

*Don't like it when people get in your way, do you? Well, deal with it.*

*More importantly, [Disrupt] worked. I love it when new spells come in handy.*

I tested it out with my allies, but this is the first time I used it in a battle, so to speak.

As the name suggests, the magic will disrupt spells cast by the targeted mage. It's a counterspell, in other words. The cooldown is only a few seconds, but the downside is that it takes a lot of mana to disrupt high level spells, so a counterspell mage would run out of mana quickly.

But when countering average spells, it's manageable, which is why...

*Give it up.*

My [Disrupt] obliterates the advisor's next magic spell.

*Heh, look at him. He's getting mad now.*

Several more buffs flow from the advisor's fingers, but each one is intercepted by my counterspell, with the exception of one that manages to break through.

However, even when [Disrupt] doesn't fully stop a spell, it can still reduce its power. In this case, the buff the advisor manages to get through becomes so weak that it shouldn't affect the outcome of the battle too much.

Of course, both Kuro and Rei cast buffs of their own before the battle, but neither of the two royals can really be considered a powerful mage. Their magic is sporadic and low rank, while the ones from the advisor are powered by that spell orb.

On top of that, Rei has powerful equipment that's stronger than even Kuro's best items, his spear not included. Without a doubt, they were given to him by someone that stands above even the kings of this world.

The prince's level has obviously been boosted, as well. They probably took him into a dangerous dungeon and power leveled him. The combination of his levels, items, and buffs gave him the strength he needed to defeat his father last time.

But Kuro has gained five levels and has a spear crafted by none other than me. His other items have gotten stronger, too. Not to mention the undershirt I secretly recrafted for him.

By disrupting the advisor's buffs, I can take away one aspect of Rei's unearned power. And with Kuro's increase in strength, the match should be much fairer compared to last time.

"Do you know why I fled and rebelled against your rule!?" Kuro yells as their weapons clash.

"Because you were too cowardly to obey!" Rei raises his warhammer.

"Fool! It wasn't because of your ridiculous orders!" Kuro deflects the oncoming attack. "It's because you're not acting like yourself! You've lost your wits, ever since the day you first challenged me to a duel!"

"No, I ... I'm not insane!"

The battle heats up, forcing both of them to focus. At the same time, the advisor finds a new tactic.

*He's channeling that strange magic again? And from how he's looking at me, it looks like he plans to hit me with it.*

*In that case...*

The fourth-tier Light Spell, [Anti-Magic Field] appears around me and my companions. Appear isn't quite the right word, as the spell has no visual effects. But with the [Sense Mana] spell, I can certainly feel its presence.

When the advisor releases the spell, I feel it hit my barrier. [Anti-Magic Field] will attempt to disrupt any magical effects that enter its zone of protection. In the cases where the magic is too powerful, it will simply be reduced in strength.

The spell the advisor used isn't just any run-of-the-mill magic. It stands outside even my knowledge, meaning it must either be a spell from before the Devastation or one made using Spellcrafting.

Either way, it's not to be taken lightly, which is why I put up the [Anti-magic Field]. The downside is that magic can't be used from within the field, either. But I can step out of it if I need to cast again.

Since my stats completely overwhelm this advisor's, his magic has little chance of actually harming me in any meaningful way, but I can't be too careful. However, when the spell he used hits my [Anti-Magic Field], even my defensive magic can't fully stop it.

The remnants of the mysterious magic hit me, and its name, [Torment], appears in my Status Screen.

*"Hate him,"* a deathly voice whispers in my head. *"Make him suffer."*

It sounds like the voice is coming from beyond the grave. Or from a creature who has returned from such a place. But rather than making my skin crawl, I find the sound pleasant.

My eyes have been on the advisor as he whispers to himself, but I feel them slowly drawn to someone else. Kuro.

Anger rises in me, directed at the cat-eared man that I've been helping until now. Several thoughts occur to me, ways to ensure that Kuro loses the duel. It'd be quite an easy task, actually.

*"Pain. Agony. Torment. Show him. Show him true misery!"*

The hatred reaches a peak, and I suddenly realize the best and most humiliating way for Kuro to lose.

*All I have to do is make him get caught cheating. Not only would it cost him the match, but it'd completely destroy his honor.*

The path to make that into reality forms in my head nearly on its own. As the ideas flow, I turn my gaze back to the advisor. He's not whispering anymore. Instead, he seems completely focused on the duel.

My foot moves forward, and the rest of my body follows. One step. It was all I needed to get in range.

The advisor releases his magic, [Haste], I cast mine at the same time.

The buff the advisor planned to use on Rei fizzles just as it leaves his body, obliterated by my [Disrupt].

*"Stop!"* the whispery voice says. *"You will obey! Torment him, show him—gah!"*

My next spell slams into him. It's only [Mental Link] though, so it doesn't do any sort of damage. But when overpowering an opponent's magical defenses to forcefully connect our minds, it can be quite a shock.

"Obey you?" I ask. "You'll have to do better than some mind-altering magic like [Torment]."

I already used [Restore] to remove the spell. It was a little annoying to have voices and feelings forced into me. I played along with them to see how strong the feeling would get, but as expected, my magic resistance protected me from most of its power.

"You poor fool." He casts [Scry] on me for the first time, but I've already stepped back into my [Anti-Magic Field]. "I don't know who you are, but if you've come to stop me, then you can only be an enemy of the divine!"

"Don't just make up something so convenient. Maybe you're the one on the wrong side here."

"Hah! If you had even a fraction of my knowledge, you'd never say something that ridiculous!"

"Yeah, yeah. I knew talking to you would be useless. You're already too far gone."

"This isn't over! Even if my hands are tied here, Rei can still win! Just watch! He's going to–"

"Kuh...!" Rei spits blood after taking a punch to the abdomen.

"You should have trained more, son." Kuro twirls his spear, catching Rei square in the chest.

The young king hits the floor, the warhammer dropping to the stone with a clank.

"W-winner ... King Kuro!"

At the referee's announcement, cheers erupt from many of the onlookers. It's kind of shocking, since I thought most of them were backing Rei in the fight.

So Tylith was right. They were afraid. Afraid Rei would win, and they'd have to deal with an incompetent king again.

"How!?" the advisor yells out loud.

Heh. Weren't you paying attention? Kuro was gaining the upper hand little by little the whole time.

Or were you too busy dealing with me?

Sadly, the advisor already severed the telepathic connection, so he can't hear my words.

The truth is that I used my [Party Management] skill to rank up Kuro's spear skill. The knowledge that filled his mind gave him an even better understanding of how to wield the spear.

Combined with his level advantage, it was enough to give him a clean victory. If the advisor had been able to buff him, it could have been a very different battle.

"Ugh..." Rei slowly stands.

"It's over. The crown is mine again."

"No ... this wasn't supposed to happen...!" Rei looks to his advisor.

The man has already sunken into the crowd while most are still focused on the two men in the arena. But he's tagged on my [Minimap], so there's no escape for him.

*"Master, should we capture him?"*

*"No. Let him go."*

*"Eh? Why?"*

*"Because if there's a time when we might find the man behind the curtain, it'd be when this advisor is desperately trying to escape."*

*"Ah, he might lead us to the one who's controlling everything?"*

*"Exactly. Riona, Kuro, you two can handle the rest here, right?"*

*"Not a problem,"* Riona says. *"The nobles seem relieved at the outcome, rather than angry."*

*"Good, then I'll let you two play your political games. We're going to have ourselves a little hunt."*

*"Alright!"* Alisha voices her excitement. *"Leave the hunting to me!"*

# Chapter 21: Cat and Mouse

## ----- Lutz -----

*"So that unknown magic is called [Torment],"* Belle says.

*"Yeah. Nasty little spell, too. I could hear that advisor's whispering, and he was able to not only manipulate my emotions but also draw my focus to whatever he wanted. He tried to get me to make Kuro lose the match. But the spell was too weak to control me."*

*"But for someone like Rei..."*

I lead the girls around a corner as we continue following the advisor. *"Yeah, there's no telling how long Rei's been tormented by that magic. No wonder he always sounds like he's one step from a cliff's edge."*

*"But Master, you told Kuro about the spell. That means he'll understand, right?"*

*"Politics is messy ... but Kuro doesn't strike me as the kind of guy who'd execute his own son after finding out he's a victim in all this, too."*

*"Aww. I hope so..."*

Since Kuro and Riona are intentionally letting the advisor escape, none of the guards even try to stop him on the way out. We're still in disguise, so the same is true for us.

He's fully aware that we're following him since he can sense our mana. But since it's the fake mana signature from my artifact, we feel much weaker than we really are.

Finally, we leave the castle grounds through one of the gates in the surrounding wall. The city opens up before us, with roads filled with everyday citizens going about their day.

"As expected," I say. "He's going to the Temple of Origins."

"Again, Master? Is he going to pray to his Goddess?"

"Probably. Chances are, he just doesn't know what to do now that his plan has fallen apart."

"That's stupid! He should really learn how to think for himself! You're doing the work of the Goddess, and you don't go running to her for advice every time something goes wrong!"

"Well, that's true..."

*I'd love to push off a bit more work onto her if I could, though...*

Ignoring my thoughts, we step onto the grounds just in time to see the back of the advisor as he dashes through the ornate doors that lead inside.

He's caused quite a ruckus on his way in, shoving aside temple visitors and even one of the priests. But since he's the king's primary advisor and visits the temple daily, nobody calls for any of the guards.

We might not be so lucky. Even though we're still disguised, nobody here knows us. And since I don't want to make trouble yet, the girls and I decide to keep our pace leisurely.

By the time we reach the same temple door the advisor took, the man has already climbed the massive set of stairs leading up to the altar. Without even sparing a single glance at the priest up there, he dashes right by him and through another door.

The only thing beyond the door is a hall full of prayer rooms. There's not even another way out, besides the way he went in. So unless he tries something crazy like blasting his way out with magic, then the advisor has already been cornered.

The man knew this from the beginning, yet he still chose to run into that hall because he truly believes his salvation can be found in one of those prayer rooms. That's just how deeply he's been hooked by whoever it is that's pulling the strings.

"I wonder if I'll be able to sense their magic this time," I say to nobody in particular.

"You mean the one fooling this advisor?" Tylith asks.

"Yeah. Last time I came here, he was already praying, so I couldn't detect the magic when it was cast."

"But this time, we're already here. Though the Mana Spring makes detecting magic difficult."

"Difficult, but not impossible. Ah, he's just stepping into a prayer room. Focus. Find the spell."

A storm of mana flows from beneath our feet, like a reverse waterfall. It's enough to power some incredibly strong magic, if it were to be harnessed. But I didn't come here to test my new artifact that's capable of capturing this mana.

All magics have an effective range, and only supremely powerful people like the Astral Dryad can do things like start a telepathic communication from across the continent. Chances are, the man behind the curtain is nearby, well within our range to detect under normal circumstances.

*The advisor stopped moving. He must be starting his prayer.*

The unstoppable current of mana continues, almost feeling as if it's washing over my physical body as it passes through me. Within the torrent, I feel little blips, the presences of the people within the temple. They may be weak, but even the mana that naturally leaks from them can be felt, albeit just barely.

Nobody here is strong enough to catch my attention. If one existed, I doubt he could hide, even within the Mana Spring. Yet there's nothing, not a single person strong enough for me to suspect as the mastermind.

All I can do is let the mana wash over me, looking for something–anything– that stands out.

A ripple, in the distance. Not far, yet so weak against the massive amount of ambient mana. But it's enough.

"I felt it," I say. "It was definitely a spell. But there's one problem."

"Underground," Laya reveals it for me.

"You felt it too, huh? Yeah, it's underground. I didn't know this temple had a basement. Where would the entrance even be?"

"Ask Kuro?"

"Guess so. I don't really want to wait for permission, though. We'll be entering the basement as soon as we find out where it's at."

As I'm about to send Kuro a telepathic message, a sudden change causes me to pause.

*The advisor's done praying already?*

*And wow, he's in a hurry. Where does he think he's going to go when we block the only exit?*

The man appears from behind the door at the top of the steps. His eyes meet mine, but rather than desperation...

*He's smiling? Why do I have a bad feeling?*

The man starts channeling for a spell. It's one I've used countless times myself, so it's easy for me to figure out which magic he's about to cast. But even if I know what, I don't know why.

*What's he think he's going to do with [Fireball]?*

*Should I [Disrupt] it? But he doesn't seem to be targeting any of the other people in here.*

*If he uses it on us, we can just shrug it off. Or rather, it'll never reach us because of [Shimmering Shield].*

We ready our defensive magic, just in case. If he throws the fireball at the temple visitors or priests, we'll need to be ready to intercept it.

But that doesn't seem to be this advisor's plan. His focus changes from me to something else. Not another person, but the altar right in front of him, the one at the top of the steps with the decorative chalice sitting on it.

A deafening boom reverberates through the temple's main room. The large, open space sends the explosive sound back at us as echoes bounce around, reflecting off the stone walls time and again.

Some people run, others freeze in fear as they look to the top of the stairs where the explosion occurred. But whichever way they react, it has no impact on their safety.

A blue tinted barrier encloses the entirety of the upper platform, the [Shimmering Shield] ensuring that no spells can make it to the crowd. But it only stops magic, which means there's nothing preventing the bits of stone from pelting us.

*Hey, I just washed these clothes, now they have stone dust on them. You'll pay for that.*

I didn't technically wash them because the girls won't let me, but that just makes it more of a crime for this man to get them dirty.

Nobody seems to have been hurt by the flying stone, so I refocus on the altar. Right now, there's a dust cloud just on the other side of our magical barriers. But with each second, the dust thins.

I can still see the advisor's shadowy figure in the dust. But as I watch it, the shadow begins to move. It seems to step nearly right on top of where the altar should be. But as soon as he reaches it, the shadow begins to shrink.

Smaller and smaller it gets, until the shadow's head sinks right into the ground.

*No, he's not shrinking. He's...*

The dust finally clears, revealing the platform on top of the stairs.

The advisor is gone, as expected. But so is the altar. Well, most of it. Some of the foundation survived the explosion, but the rest was blown to pieces.

I brush off one of those pieces that had landed on my coat. "Seems there was another door in this room after all."

Laya follows me as we begin climbing the steps. "Mmm. Though rather than calling it a door..."

My feet stop just in front of the altar's remnants. "Yeah, it might be better to call it a secret passage."

In the center of the floor, where the altar once stood, is a set of stairs leading down into darkness.

"Let's go." I ignore the noisy priests around us. "But be careful. There's even a chance we'll run into an Archfiend."

Since Alisha's [Protector] isn't active right now, my foot is the first to take a step down the stone staircase.

With my Light Magic orb lighting the way, the formerly dark path down is revealed. All around us is the same white stone, with the steps having been cut straight from the rock.

Now that I'm a few steps down, the end of the staircase becomes visible. As far as I can tell, there aren't any traps, so we continue on.

The noisy priests have finally been silenced, too. They were yelling at us about who we are and what we're doing. That kind of annoying stuff. So, I put an [Earth Wall] at the entrance once we all got inside the passage.

It also has the added benefit of preventing anyone from following us. Wouldn't want them to get caught up in a battle, if we end up fighting.

My feet touch the floor at the bottom of the steps. It's just a small carved out section of rock, big enough for maybe a dozen people. But there's one object of interest here.

In fact, it's very interesting indeed.

"Is this..." Tylith says. "...A research facility?"

I look at the door, which seems stuck in a half-open state. "Looks like it. At least, it has the exact same type of door. Not to mention that unmistakable look on the inside."

We step through the doorway and into the facility. There's strange, highly advanced equipment everywhere I look, just like the facility we explored with Rin and Kiah.

However, there's something noticeably different about this place.

"No power," I say, looking around the room.

"Is that good or bad?" Belle asks.

"We can get through any door, so that's helpful." I look down a hallway. "They're just down there. I can feel him now, the man behind the curtain. But..."

"They're weak." Tylith just comes out and says it.

"Yeah. But be careful anyway. We're in the center of a Mana Spring."

I lead them into the hall and past the first intersection, my eyes set on a door at the far end. It's closed, but that's not an obstacle if there's no power in the facility. No mana in the walls means we can even blast our way through them, if we want.

But when I reach the door and push, it opens easily. Just inside are the mana presences of the advisor and the puppet master, waiting for us.

Not seeing anything strange, we step into the room.

The advisor looks just the same as ever, the confident smile back on his lips. But standing beside him is someone new.

*So that's what they look like. Or more like, they sure do wear a thick cloak.*

As if he were waiting for this moment, the mysterious mage living beneath the temple brings his arms up, grabbing the hood of his cloak and slowly lifting the cloth.

"It's been a long time..." His hood falls. "...Tylith."

"Ashton!" Tylith can barely contain her bloodlust. "Why are you here!?"

"Is that how you intend to greet me every time, dear sister?"

"Answer me! Why are you messing with these beastkin!?"

"Perhaps I came here for my own pleasure? Wreaking havoc in other kingdoms is something I'm quite good at, wouldn't you say?"

"Always, always with those ridiculous answers! But it doesn't matter! Because we're going to stop you!"

"H-hey," the advisor says from beside Ashton. "What's going—eep!"

The man lets out a yelp when a blade presses against his throat.

"Silence." Ashton's eyes never leave Tylith. "Now, dear sister, let us have a little chat."

"You want to chat!?" Tylith shouts. "After everything you've done!?"

"Must you be so loud, dear sister?"

"I'll be as loud as I please! Now hurry and speak! But if I don't like what I hear, you'll be answering to these." Tylith extends her nails.

"Oh my, how threatening. These past few months of adventuring haven't dulled your violent tendencies, I see."

Ashton von Phyress, the Vampire Lord ruling over the strongest of the five Great Clans, the Coven of Dusk. As Tylith's brother, she obviously has unfinished business with him, but there's one problem.

He's the most powerful living vampire.

Ashton eyes Tylith's nails with a smile. "Sister, don't you think it's about time you gave up your foolish tantrum and accepted your fate as a servant of Chaos?"

"Are you mad!? Did you not hear my vow the day I left the mansion?"

"Mere words. I expected you to be stubborn, but the reprieve from battle is nearly over. If you stay opposed to us with that level, you will certainly fall."

"What!? What do you mean the reprieve is almost over? What do you have planned, Ashton!"

"I only follow the orders of my lord. If it's his plans you wish to know, then you need only give your allegiance to his rightful rule."

"Never! I'd rather die fighting than live in servitude!"

Ashton shakes his head. "As foolish as ever, I see. Well, perhaps I could tell you the next step in his plan, if you tell me one thing in return."

Tylith gives her brother a skeptical look. She knows that anything he tells us could be a lie, so giving up any information in a trade is dangerous. Knowledge really is power, especially in war.

But it can't hurt to ask. After all, just knowing what topic he's interested in could be useful.

"What is it you want to know?" Tylith asks. "And be quick! No games!"

"And that's why you were never good at politics, dear sister. But no matter. What I seek is the answer to a single question." Ashton's eyes fall on me. "How did the False Hero survive that day?"

*As expected, it's about that.*

A few weeks ago, the Archfiend Vrazruk ripped my heart clean from my chest. Nobody could survive something like that, not even a summoned hero. Until recently, the Lord of Chaos probably thought I was dead. Who wouldn't after hearing his minion tore my heart out?

Yet here I am.

Of course, the reason is because my genetically modified body has emergency features to help in the case of my immediate demise. But the only ones who would ever consider such a possibility are those with detailed knowledge of the distant past, before the Devastation.

*There's no way we'll tell him something like that.*

*He must know that, so why even ask?*

"Hmph! I have no need to play the game as you wish. And I never expected you to take such an interest in Lutz."

"Why wouldn't I? If it means I can enjoy a little entertainment, then it's only natural to be interested." He looks to me again. "Yes, I know all about you. The [Inventory] and [Minimap] skills are quite useful, aren't they? We've had to remove many of the spells you use to locate us with your little map, including one you put on me. Quite useful, indeed."

*As expected, the Lord of Chaos is the one removing the tags I put on him and the Archfiends I met.*

Normally, anytime I tag someone, they will always stand out on my [Minimap] when they're nearby. But that isn't the case for Ashton. Right now, his dot is just like anyone else's. I don't know when it happened, but one day, I was checking his location, and I couldn't find him.

I even thought he might have died, since that was the only way I knew of that the tag would be forcefully removed. But then it happened again when I tagged the Archfiends. As soon as they went back to their lands, their dots vanished.

*Well, every magic has a limit. That's true, even for my Heroic Skills.*

I shake my head. "You really did your homework–is what I'd like to say. But you weren't the one who figured all that out were you?"

"As much as I loathe to admit, I was merely told. But the information is correct, of that I'm sure."

"Shouldn't you spill a few of your own secrets, just to make things even? Like maybe why your mana feels so weak right now?"

"There's nobody in this world who would agree to such reasonings."

Like us, Ashton's mana is moderately strong, at best. If I had felt his overpowering strength before we entered this room, we wouldn't have walked in so casually.

But he's not willing to tell us whether it's a spell or artifact that he's using to match the effects of my custom-made mana manipulation orbs.

"If you refuse to share any information," Tylith says. "We'll find the answers we seek, even without you!"

"That so, dear sister? Then I guess there's nothing left to be said."

"I was thinking..." Tylith spreads her feet. "...The same thing!"

With a blur, Tylith appears in front of Ashton.

"Useless." He catches Tylith's nails with his own. "Didn't you learn from our last encounter? You cannot defeat me."

"Yes, I learned. But not the lesson you assume!"

A burst of speed, and a flurry of strikes. Yet none of them hit their target.

*It's going as expected. Does this mean he doesn't know our full power?*

We're all still using the artifacts to hide the true strength of our mana. But I didn't pick just any setting for it, I chose to make our mana signatures roughly the same strength we were before our recent dungeon dive.

In other words, when Ashton checks our mana, he thinks we haven't gotten any stronger since the last time we fought him. And since I edited all of our status to match, Tylith currently shows up as level 40 to anyone who casts [Scry] on her.

Since she's actually level 70, Ashton has seriously underestimated her strength.

"I'm growing bored." Ashton casually reaches up and swats away Tylith's nailed hand. When his hand makes contact with hers, it...

"An illusion–gah!"

Ashton twirls, blocking the second strike. "This magic ... it's [Shadow Step]."

"How observant." Tylith's voice is laced with sarcasm.

"Your level..." Ashton backpedals, dodging more swipes. "...isn't high enough to cast Heroic-Class magic."

"Oh?" Tylith pauses and looks at her red-tipped nails. "Then how did I draw your blood?"

I can practically see a flurry of thoughts pass through Ashton's head in an instant. Could it be some unknown magic that doesn't show up on [Scry]? Or maybe her equipment has improved so much that it's closed the gap to this degree?

His eyes even flicker toward Laya, no doubt remembering the last time we fought, where she suddenly started powering up.

But he rejects each one, knowing that none of those situations can bridge the wide gap between their levels. Since Ashton is level 84, he thinks Tylith is 44 levels below him. That's not a difference that can be bridged in any feasible way.

Ashton releases [Scry] for a second time. "Ridiculous. To think that the level displayed in your information would be faked. And I thought only gods possessed the power to manipulate what appears inside."

"Hmph. Are you saying the Lord of Chaos is a god? It was he who renamed the other three heroes' Unique Skills to prevent the masses from finding the truth, wasn't it?"

"Him? A god?" Ashton lets out a genuine laugh. "He's powerful, but he's no god any more than you or I."

"You didn't answer my question."

"Yes, I did." Ashton looks to me. "Speaking of heroes, I hadn't heard of this skill that allows you to change your mana signatures and edit your information. I wonder what else I'll find out before this battle is over."

"Well," I say. "Before the end, you're going to find out that you made a huge mistake challenging us alone."

"Confident, are you? I'm beginning to miss that look of desperation the last time we met, when you realized your teleportation wasn't working."

"I hope you took a picture because there won't be another chance to see it."

"And to think I was kind enough to let you escape." Ashton smiles. "Not even going to give me a simple thanks?"

"Idiot. If you knew that we were enemies, you wouldn't have just let us walk away that day. When did they tell you? Before or after I stopped the Archfiend from summoning the army of Chaos on the elves?"

"Hm? What led you to believe I was uninformed that the False Hero was our adversary? It was made clear to me the moment you escaped your dungeon cell."

"What?" I can't help but show a bit of surprise. "You knew, even back then? Then why did you let us go?"

"Simple." Ashton reveals his fangs. "It was far more interesting to watch everyone's struggles."

"That's it? Just to watch us having a hard time trying to survive?"

"Not just your little group. The havoc you brought about for all was a savory sight. Like a storm within a storm, you moved about the war-torn land, upending carefully laid plans and bringing about true chaos."

Ashton shakes his head, but the smile never leaves his lips. "For a race called Chaos, they certainly do not live up to their namesake. No questions, no uncertainty. Only orders from above passed to the servants below."

His blood-red eyes fall back onto me. "What fun is that? Watching the war unfold in carefully planned steps would be a bore. You don't even realize just how much we've been forced to change plans because of you. And now, the finale is nearly upon us."

"You're insane," I say after listening to his rant.

"Isn't it normal to seek excitement? Take this very moment. Can you truly tell me you're not enjoying yourself?"

"..."

"As I thought. Before calling others insane, perhaps you should start with yourself."

"Ashton!" Tylith yells. "We're going to make you pay for everything you've done!"

"Is that your plan? Then I suppose I should take this battle a little more seriously." Ashton unleashes his mana.

"Eek!" The advisor falls on his rear, his eyes wide as he looks at the source of the overpowering mana.

A mountain, with sheer cliffs and twisted peaks. Back then, I was but a hill sitting in that mountain's shadow.

But I've grown. My level is much higher, I've crafted legendary equipment, and I have nearly all the strongest buff spells enhancing me further. Compared to the me at that time, I can also be considered a mountain.

Now, when standing beside Ashton's fully released power, my mana is...

*He's still that much stronger than us?*

*This may just be our toughest battle yet...*

At level 84, Ashton has a full 12 levels over me, and his items are obscenely powerful, just like our own. Since I fought him once before, I already know that he's a fearsome warrior.

"If you're going to go all out, then we'll do the same." I revert my mana signature back to normal.

All the girls follow my lead, filling the room with six individual mana sources so powerful that even the Mana Spring can't hide them.

"W-what is this!?" the advisor yells. "Why are there so many powerful people here!?"

I grab the man by his collar. "You have a lot to answer for, so try not to get yourself killed."

I toss the man toward the only door in the room. It leads back to the hall, which connects to the main entrance. Of course the advisor takes off, heading back toward the secret passage to escape back to the surface.

Unfortunately for him, I blocked off the exit. Even if he blasts his way through, I've already notified Kuro of what's going on. The advisor has suddenly become a wanted man, so he'll find that getting around the city won't be quite as easy as it was before.

"You girls ready?"

Tylith nods. "I'm going to put an end to his plans here and now."

"Then there's nothing else that needs to be said."

The true battle against Vampire Lord Ashton begins.

# Chapter 22: The Strongest Vampire, Ashton von Phyress

## ----- Lutz -----

Out of habit, I run my eyes along our status screens.

*[Empower], [Haste], [Stone Skin], [Regeneration], [Gale], [Enlighten], [Frost Skin], [Amplify Magic], [Cure], [Enhance], [Resist], [Barrier], [Blessed Aura], and [Absorb Mana].*

*Good. Everything's here.*

Since we can't afford to hold anything back, all the buffs I have available are enhancing us.

Ashton's mana is nearly equal to a dungeon boss. But unlike a dungeon boss, he's a real, thinking person.

And that makes him dangerous.

Beasts, no matter how powerful, are predictable. Even trickster-type enemies like the Assassin Mantis we fought in the misty dungeon were only difficult until we found out their weaknesses.

But people are different. Technique, tactics, and cunning are all skills that can be learned, trained, and honed to near perfection. It's precisely those skills that allowed us to defeat many of the bosses in the dungeons.

And now, we're facing off against someone who has the power of a dungeon boss and the intelligence of a Vampire Lord.

*That's why we're starting this battle off strong!*

"Tylith!" I yell for her to attack with me.

Ashton's already fully buffed himself. He just watches with a smile as the two of us take the initiative.

My spear zips out, striking at his face as soon as I'm in range. It hits only nails, but the greenish-yellow shaft blurs into a flurry of attacks.

"Hmph." Ashton looks disappointed. "Too predictable."

"Predict this! [Crescent Wave]!" I swing my spear, and a blue-white wave of energy flies from the tip.

The first-tier Weapon Skill specializes in knocking opponents back, even if they block it. That means...

"Got you!" Tylith slashes at her brother who'd been knocked into her.

"Like I said." Ashton catches her nails. "Too predictable."

A foot slams into Tylith's midsection, sending her flying. With the wall not far behind her, she quickly hits it, sending a loud crack through the room.

"Tyli–" A set of nails cuts me off.

"You're stronger than before," Ashton says, his nails pressing down on my spear's shaft. "But if this is the best you can do, then give up. You can't win."

The pressure increases further as the nails being held back just above my head inch closer.

"Don't decide that on your own!" I push back against his nailed hand. "What's wrong? My spear's not so easy to break this time, is it?"

"Hmph. You may have gotten your hands on some adamantium, but the weapon isn't anything special."

The nails retract to their original length, meaning they're no longer pressing down on me. However, his hand is now coming toward my chest, the nails already back out and gleaming in the scant light.

Like the time he broke my spear, Ashton seeks to sink his nails into my unprotected chest. A clean hit, dealing massive damage, and one that can greatly shift the momentum into his favor.

After what feels like a long wait, his nails finally make contact.

"Hmm?" Ashton looks to Alisha, who stands between me and his nails. "I was sure I used enough power to knock you away ... no, you've grown far stronger."

"Now..." Alisha says. "... I'm strong enough to fight, too!"

She swings her sword, forcing Ashton back.

"So your Unique Skill activated. No wonder you were able to keep up with the others, despite your curse. But why did it activate? Simply by being attacked? Or is it because..."

Ashton's eyes fall on me as I stand behind Alisha.

"I'll never tell you!" Alisha swings at him again.

He dodges the strike, putting enough distance between us to reset the match. Now that we've gotten warmed up and activated Alisha's [Protector], the battle can truly begin.

"Dear sister," He looks to Tylith, who stands beside me with a smile. "Even your pitiful performance was part of the act?"

"Hmph. It's only natural for us to work together in such a fashion, not that someone like you would understand."

"I alone am enough. That is how it has always been."

"Then I'll make you regret your arrogance!"

Tylith grabs the arm offered to her. My arm. Even as I stare at Ashton, I feel two fangs sink into my wrist.

With a satisfied sound, Tylith releases my arm. "Dear brother. For so long, you stood at the top. A Vampire Lord so powerful that even the other lords feared him. But those days are about to end. Once we defeat you, I'll claim your empty seat and force the others to kneel. Not just my subjects but all vampires, even the lords! I'll rule them all and make my desires into reality!"

Ashton runs his hand through his hair. "How absurd."

"Is that all you have to say!?"

"It's all that needs to be said."

Despite her suddenly violent attitude, Tylith isn't the one to strike first.

"I'm going!" Alisha leaps at Ashton.

I look to Laya and see that she's ready. Since this room is small, it limits her airborne fighting technique, but she's still deadly, especially when paired with me.

My spear appears from behind Alisha, heading straight to Ashton's face, but his nails swipe away the tip, and my weapon veers off course.

From above, a chain sickle falls. With one hand dealing with me and the other Alisha, Ashton has no way to block the attack. His eyes turned up, he simply watches as the blade draws closer.

*A spell!?*

It was over in a flash. Whatever spell he used has a virtually instantaneous cast time. But there's no effect that I can see.

However...

Ashton moves at the last possible instant, and the chain sickle that should have been a direct hit finds only air.

*What kind of movement was that? It was a perfect dodge, but if he had made one mistake, he'd have taken a direct hit.*

But our plan won't fall apart from a single miss.

Without a shred of noise, Tylith appears behind her brother just as he's dodging Laya's sickle. She's even hiding her mana to make sure he can't detect her, and with his focus on us, this gives Tylith the perfect chance to strike.

"No way!" Tylith stares at her nails, blocked by Ashton's own.

"Still not good enough." Ashton retaliates, forcing Tylith back.

*"Now!"*

While his focus is on his sister, the three of us who've been channeling magic release our spells.

A dozen blades of wind burst forth, seeking Ashton's flesh. With Laya on the Vampire Lord's far side, near Tylith, Ashton finds himself completely flanked by our oncoming magic.

As soon as he sees the spells, he stops his attacks. But it's too late. Not even he can dodge these heat seeking missiles when they're released at such close range.

The blades converge right where Ashton stands, nearly completely covering his figure. At that moment, Belle's [Scorching Ray] reaches him, with the beam of fire joining our [Wind Blade] spell.

A sound similar to shattering glass fills the room. With it, the first layer of Ashton's defense falls.

A second high-pitched crack rings out, then a third.

*How many layers does he have!?*

Finally, the fourth [Shimmering Shield] gives way, and the blue tinted barrier shatters and disappears. With it, a path to his body opens.

Most of our wind blades were expended just to get past his defensive magic, and Belle's [Scorching Ray] is already over halfway through its duration.

But what's left of our spells hits Ashton. Three blades of wind and four seconds of Belle's beam of fire, each powered by our obscenely high magic stats.

"Hmph." Ashton slashes at the remaining wind blades, using his nails to dissipate two of them into harmless gusts.

With his other hand, he perfectly tracks the [Scorching Ray], catching the beam with his palm. No matter how much Belle moves it around, she can't get it past his defense.

Soon, her spell also comes to an end. When it's over, Ashton stands nearly exactly where he did when the battle first started. Despite taking all of our attacks and magics, we have almost nothing to show for our efforts.

*But we did manage something.*

Even if it's just a little, the palm of Ashton's hand is burnt. And the single blade of wind that made it through left a small cut on his shoulder.

*He took damage, even from our second-tier spells.*

*And if he bleeds, he can be defeated.*

"Is that all?" Ashton asks. "I gave you a chance to show me what you're capable of, and this is all I get?"

"Don't think you can figure out our strength with just one clash."

"Then allow me to push you to that limit." Ashton blurs.

"I won't let you!" Alisha meets his attack, then releases her Shield Skill, [Taunt].

"Trying to draw my attention?" He smiles at her. "You may want to consider otherwise."

His counterattack hits Alisha's shield with such force that her blurred figure passes right by me just before I hear her slam into a wall. On the ground are scrape marks, leading all the way along the floor and ending at Alisha.

Our party's tank lowers her shield, her back pressed against a shattered wall. A trail of blood flows from her lips, but there's still a smile on her face.

*What power. Even Alisha can barely defend against it.*

Ashton smiles. "Let me show you what true strength looks like."

Ashton blurs. It's not magic, it's just his physical speed is so high that even my eyes have a hard time keeping track of him.

My spear comes up, clashing with a set of nails that seek my throat. As quickly as they appear, the nails vanish along with their owner.

"Where's that confidence now, little hero?" Ashton holds up a hand, fresh blood dripping from its nails and flowing down his fingers.

I look at my shoulder, where a wound now sits. "Don't get arrogant just because you managed to hit me once."

"The first of many, I assure you."

"Let's put that to the test!"

Alisha's already back at my side, so we attack together. Spear and sword strike at the same time, even as a sickle zips toward Ashton's body.

Blood spills. Unfortunately, it's mine and Alisha's.

The Vampire Lord seems even quicker than before, his figure a constant blur.

*Not good. His equipment is even stronger than ours.*

Ashton uses that strength to dash between me and Alisha. The next thing I know, the room begins to spin.

I hit the ground, using my momentum to spring back to my feet. Laya and Tylith have taken up the assault, giving me a precious second to gather myself.

Immediately, I'm back in the melee, another wound added to the last.

A sickle appears, but it's knocked away by Ashton's nailed hand.

My spear seeks the opening Laya provided me, but even with it, my weapon only slices the air beside him.

Alisha charges back into battle, the tip of her sword aimed at Ashton's body. But the Vampire Lord sends her flying with a kick.

Just as Alisha lands on her feet next to me, Tylith strikes from behind him. But Ashton already saw her coming, as if he had eyes on the back of his head.

After nearly each attack, Belle has been weaving in her spells. Lances of ice, balls of fire, blades of wind. She's using all her quick casting magic to exploit openings.

Among all of us, she's having the most success, with a few of her spells landing undefended. But although the magic is quick, it lacks power. She was using those spells to provide us an opening, but Ashton saw through the strategy and decided to ignore her magic, knowing it can't cause him any real damage.

*"We're changing tactics!"* I say telepathically. *"Alisha and I will engage, the rest prepare powerful magic!"*

The assault on the Vampire Lord lessens as Laya and Tylith take a back seat, only striking when we need help. Instead, the two girls focus on completing their spells.

Ashton isn't a fool. He knows what we're up to. But just because he can see through our plan doesn't mean he'll be able to stop us.

That doesn't prevent him from trying, though. When he sees an opening, he dashes toward Laya, intending to put on enough pressure to interrupt her spellcasting.

"No you don't, Mr. Vampire!" Alisha steps in front of Ashton.

"You again. Do you think you can stop me?"

"I'll do it, even if I can't!" Alisha throws out one of her usual logic-defying statements.

Like several times before, Alisha's sent flying after taking a direct hit from Ashton's fully powered attack. But despite losing ground against him, she still keeps herself between him and Laya.

*"Ready,"* Laya says.

*"As am I."* Tylith adds.

*"Same!"* Belle says.

*"Good. Then let's hit him with our special attack!"*

Alisha smiles at Ashton and releases her [Taunt]. "This game is fun, Mr. Vampire!"

"Another taunt? Didn't I already tell you how worthless that skill is against me?"

"Like I care what you say!"

*He hasn't realized? Then that'll make this easier!*

Despite his words, Ashton has given extra focus to Alisha each time she uses [Taunt]. Even if it's not holding his aggro, it does draw his attention for a few seconds.

And that's enough.

*"Go!"*

My spear misses its mark, as does Alisha's follow-up attack. But that was expected. After all, our goal was only to force him off balance to set up for the real attacks.

Belle's [Flame Pillar] is the first to appear, engulfing the Vampire Lord in a raging inferno. The heat from the spell is enough to make me want to shield my face, so I can only imagine how scorching the center must be.

Just as the fire springs to life, a crack of energy splits the air, bright enough to overpower even the light of the inferno. Laya's [Lightning] spell travels straight through the center of the pillar of flames, right where Ashton stands.

At the same time, Tylith swings her scythe from just outside the [Flame Pillar], her weapon glowing with dark energy from her [Life Drain] spell. It vanishes into the fire, the tip seeking Ashton's flesh within.

"What!?" Tylith looks at her scythe after it emerges from the flames. "I missed!?"

I turn to her weapon and don't see a drop of blood on its tip. It went through the pillar of fire, from one end to the other.

*The only way for her to miss Ashton would be if...*

The [Flame Pillar] dies down, revealing Ashton's figure. He still stands exactly where he did when we first started casting. Even his expression is the same.

"An illusion!?" I look at the Vampire Lord who still stands in the center of those dying flames.

"[Shred]." Ashton's voice comes from somewhere behind me.

"Kyaa!" Belle yells.

Alisha makes it to her friend even before I do, and the screeching sound of nails on metal rings out. The rest of us catch up a heartbeat later, pulling Ashton into another fierce melee.

"Are you okay, Belle!?" Alisha asks, still protecting her.

"Y-yeah. The [Barrier] absorbed most of the attacks, but some made it through."

I spare a glance at Belle and see a wound on her side. Not enough to even slow her down, but with her [Barrier] down, the next time she's hit by a skill like that, she'll take far more damage.

*This is bad. He's starting to go for our most vulnerable member.*

Attacking backliners is common sense in a battle. Taking out the ones who have the hardest time protecting themselves can tip the scales in a big way.

With dungeon bosses, it's easy enough to control the battlefield with proper positioning and aggro skills. But that tactic doesn't work on someone like Ashton.

*"Alisha, protect Belle for now."*

*"Yes, Master!"*

*"Tylith, let's see if we can give Laya an opening!"*

*"Leave it to me!"* Tylith immediately goes all-out against her brother.

"A futile effort, dear sister." He meets Tylith's nails with his own.

"Act arrogant while you still can, Ashton!" Her hands blur, and the air fills with the sound of nails clashing against nails.

*Damn! Missed again!?*

Ashton dodges my strike, despite attacking from behind.

*My spear...!*

Ashton finds an opening to grab my weapon and give it a solid pull.

A flash of red and white. Blood coated nails.

The pain hits me a second later. As I leap back, I glance at my chest, where a fresh wound now sits.

"Kyaa!" Tylith's scream is followed by the crash of her body hitting a research table.

"Again!" I lunge at Ashton, my spear as quick as a snake's strike.

"Weak." The Vampire Lord catches my weapon, just behind the tip.

With a smirk, I release my Master-Class Spear Skill, [Gale Stab].

The energy explodes from the tip, hitting Ashton and piercing him right through the chest. The arrogant smile falters for a fraction of a second, and blood begins to flow down his torso.

I pull my spear free from his loosened grasp and swing it directly at his face.

"You trash." Ashton knocks my weapon aside. "You'll regret—"

His words cut off just as the whizzing of Laya's sickle reaches our ears.

The weapon sinks into his raised forearm. Although he blocks it from reaching his head, it still manages to draw blood.

As he watches, a red light flows from the sickle, indicating the activation of her Weapon Skill.

"[Dominion]." Ashton says.

He leaps away just as Laya's sickle seemingly comes to life, zipping around like an angry wasp. Unfortunately for him, he jumps right into Belle's oncoming spell.

The [Waterblade] is wide, covering the entire area Ashton chose to escape to. Or rather, that's exactly where we wanted him to go.

"Kuh!" The Vampire Lord grunts as the massive blade of water hits him.

"More." Laya's sickle catches up to him, and this time, it finds his body.

My spear joins Belle's magic and Laya's sickle, sinking into Ashton's flesh and stacking up the damage.

Tylith's scythe lands cleanly as well, the dark energy adding even more damage on top of her attack.

"Enough!" Ashton roars.

A surge of mana prickles my skin, and my weapon is nearly knocked from my hands. Like mine, all the girls' weapons are thrown back.

Bloodied, Ashton stands in the center of our encirclement, his expression already back to neutral.

"It's been a while since I've had to use this." Ashton turns to Tylith. "You seek my seat of power, dear sister. But you're still too weak. If you wish to see why the other Vampire Lords truly fear me, then allow me to give you a glimpse."

I immediately check his status and see something new.

*A buff? [Shroud of Darkness]. I haven't seen it, even amongst the fourth-tier spells.*

*Could it be a special magic? Maybe something granted to him by the Lord of Chaos? Or is it...*

*...fifth-tier magic?*

"You really are a monster, Ashton." Tylith speaks with gritted teeth, having felt his rise in strength.

"No." He shakes his head. "You haven't seen a true monster."

"You mean the Lord of Chaos?"

"Hah. Still trying to get information out of me, even now?"

"Hmph. Many opponents blabber on when they're confident in their victory."

"Fools, then." Ashton widens his stance. "Just like all of you."

"Ah...!" Tylith's the first to get blown away.

We were waiting for Ashton to attack, but nobody could react in time, not even Tylith herself.

"No you don't!" Alisha uses [Taunt] again.

"I tire of you." Ashton knocks her sword aside, then sends her flying.

Alisha flies right by me, so I reach out and grab her. Her momentum pulls me several paces, but I manage to keep her from crashing into the wall again.

While I'm busy with that, Laya hounds Ashton. But the little elf girl is having a hard time landing a clean strike, even with [Dominion].

When I watch Ashton dodge one of Laya's attacks, I'm once again shocked at just how efficiently Ashton moves. It's as if he has complete confidence that he'll avoid her sickle, despite how close the blade is to sinking into his flesh.

After only a few attacks, the vampire manages to catch the chain, halting the sickle just in front of his face.

It's a scene that played out once before. Laya atop her [Air step], with Ashton's hand around her weapon's chain. Last time, all it took was a single yank and Laya came crashing down to the ground.

"You've grown stronger," Ashton says. "But I don't feel that mysterious power emanating from you this time."

"I don't need it to defeat you anymore!"

"Such confidence." Ashton pulls on the chain, forcing Laya to struggle against him. "Let me bring you back down to reality."

With a quick motion, Ashton yanks on Laya's weapon, intending to pull her from the sky. The chain sickle flies toward Ashton, pulled by the vampire's ridiculous strength. And Laya...

"You look surprised," Laya says, still standing on her [Air Step].

"Hmph." Ashton looks at Laya's chain sickle, which rests in his hand. "Letting go of your weapon is certainly one way to avoid being pulled. But it was a foolish choice. Now that I have your–Gah!"

Ashton's words are cut off, and the chain sickle clatters to the stone floor. As soon as it hits the ground, it rises back into the air, then zips to the ceiling, where it's caught by a pair of small hands.

"This weapon..." Laya looks at her chain sickle, [Arc of the Crescent Moon]. "...Always returns to my side."

I felt Ashton use [Scry] on the chain sickle as it flew toward Laya. From the expression on his face, I can tell that he saw something that surprised him.

"A Divine Armament..." Ashton's voice is soft.

*There's a classification for weapons with names?*

"No matter," Ashton says. "In your hands, even that weapon won't be enough to defeat me."

"And what about mine!?" My spear narrowly misses his face.

"Worthless." He intercepts my jabs, one after another.

More weapons come flying at him, enough that I'm sure any other opponent would be completely overwhelmed.

Although we manage to land a few hits, he always seems to avoid the deadliest attacks. As such, the amount of damage we're doing is far too low.

That's when Tylith comes in, completely sacrificing any semblance of defense in an attempt to land a powerful blow.

"Got you!" Tylith shouts.

"Yelling when you attack is–" Ashton's eyes widen just a bit as Tylith's nails pass right through his defenses. "–An illusion!?"

"[Shred]."

"Gah!" Ashton yells in pain as Tylith's nails slice into him from behind.

The Vampire Lord turns, his own nails seeking her blood. But thanks to the burst of speed provided by her Weapon Skill, Tylith just barely manages to avoid his counter.

"[Shadow Step]," Ashton says. "But your illusion moved nearly as well as you do."

"Hmph." Tylith swipes with her hand, sending Ashton's fresh blood splattering to the floor. "I'm not the [Master of the Dark Artes] without reason."

"Your Unique Skill. So it improves your [Shadow Step] to such a degree."

*Actually, she practiced really hard to make her illusion move like that.*

I keep my thoughts to myself. There's no harm if Ashton keeps believing it's all thanks to her Unique Skill. It definitely helps, though.

"Now who's the arrogant one here?" I say.

Tylith, Alisha, Laya, and I all have him surrounded again. Belle's spell is ready, and the rest of us are channeling our own.

"You may have powered up." I look at the fresh wounds we just gave him. "But we're already getting used to your new strength. And from what I can see, we can still win."

Ashton smiles. "Let's put that confidence to the test, then."

In a flash, the Vampire Lord reaches me. My spear lashes out, but like many times before, he manages to narrowly avoid the weapon.

However...

*So that's what you're doing.*

Ashton looks to capitalize on my miss, his extended nails already closing in on me.

I release a spell, and Ashton's nailed hand slows to a crawl, cutting the air at a quarter the speed it was before. It's not the only thing that slows down. Laya and the other girls are moving at a snail's pace, too. And the same is true for me.

The only thing that's changed is my perception. [Slow Time] is a fourth-tier Arcane Spell that lets the caster see the world in slow motion. It doesn't let me move any faster than I can normally, but by slowing everything down, I can move more efficiently.

For example, dodging attacks by a hair's width with ease.

Ashton's claw passes through the air beside me, missing me by the slimmest of margins. At the same time, my spear twirls, the tip arcing toward Ashton's vulnerable flank.

Still in slow motion, I see him frown for the briefest of moments, his eyes accurately trailing my weapon.

*As I thought, he's using [Slow Time].*

*To him, we're all moving in slow motion. No wonder he's dodging our attacks so effortlessly.*

There's a reason why I haven't been using the spell. And that reason is starting to show itself already.

My spear finds only air, with Ashton dodging it like the many times before. As soon as our little engagement comes to an end, I cancel [Slow Time].

*What a hungry spell...*

Everyone talks about how mana hungry [Transform] is. It's true that the spell eats energy quickly, but it can't be compared to [Slow Time]. If I had the spell on me since the beginning of the battle, I'd have already been drained of all my mana.

But Ashton's been mitigating that downside by activating the spell only when he's met with an attack he can't dodge with his normal perception. By only using it right when he needs it, the mana cost is manageable over a longer battle.

As I adjust our plans to the new information, I'm treated to the sight of Ashton being forced to hold his [Slow Time] spell active in order to dodge Laya and Belle's combined assault.

Knowing how much mana he must be eating through makes me feel satisfaction, even as he dodges their entire barrage.

*We can do this.*

*We can beat Ashton.*

----------

After nearly half an hour of fighting, the battle's end is finally in sight.

With one heavy breath after the next, I take a look around at my teammates. Without exception, each of them look as injured and tired as I feel.

We've been giving it everything we have. But there's simply not much left to give.

As for our opponent...

"Give ... up." Ashton says with heavy breaths.

"We're the ones who should be saying that…"

"Hmph." He stands up straighter and pushes the sweaty hair from his forehead. "You're a fool if you think you can win. All it would take is for one of you to fall, and the rest will swiftly follow."

"Isn't that what you said five minutes ago?"

"And it's even more true now."

The battle is certainly coming to an end. The problem is that the winner still isn't clear.

The girls have already gotten into position for the next engagement. This little breather was good for us since we were able to decide on a new tactic and prepare the things we need.

But the same can be said of Ashton, and it seems he's not willing to wait any longer. His hand comes up, the nails still extended well past his fingertips. But he's not looking to use them to draw our blood. At least, not yet.

Instead, he's holding a spell at the ready. However, the spell he's using isn't really a threat. And it's not one that's even suitable to use to start combat, so I can't help but wonder what he has planned.

Finally, he releases the magic, and a massive ball of fire erupts from his extended hand. It flies wildly off course, not even coming close to any of us.

After passing us by, I hear it explode on one of the unbroken walls behind us. From the sound of clattering stone, it seems like that particular wall can't be classified as unbroken anymore.

*What's his deal? Is he trying to bring the facility down on top of us?*

We've all had to be careful not to destroy the facility during our battle. Even Ashton has been avoiding tossing magic at certain walls.

Having the massive amount of stone and dirt come down on top of our heads would be … inconvenient, to say the least.

Purposefully destroying the facility was always a plan in the back of my mind, but if we were that desperate, it'd be best to just escape with [Teleport] rather than going through with such a risky plan. Which means…

*Did he destroy that particular wall … on purpose?*

None of us want to take our eyes off Ashton and turn around. It would give the Vampire Lord the perfect chance to strike.

But something feels off.

*"Alisha, protect me. I'm turning around."*

*"Understood, Master!"*

Slowly, I twist my neck, keeping Ashton in sight. But the Vampire Lord just keeps to his casual stance, as if he's not even worried about taking advantage of an opening.

In one quick motion, I turn the rest of the way, looking directly at the wall hit by his [Fireball]. Or, what's left of it. It did crumble, revealing the inside of another room.

And what I see leaves me speechless.

*A spell orb!? And it's massive!*

The large orb sits atop a pedestal in the center of that other room.

But it's not the only dangerous thing in the room.

*That's...*

*...A teleportation circle!*

*I've got to destroy it!*

I dash through a crumbling wall, heading to the one Ashton blew open with his [Fireball]. As I run, I channel the same spell. I've already destroyed one teleportation circle with this very spell, so as long as I can hit it, I can prevent anyone from activating it and teleporting here.

My arm's already pointing toward the circle, so as soon as I finish the spell formation, a ball of flames leaps from my hand.

It travels seemingly in slow motion, its path taking it directly at the glowing circle on that room's floor. Inch by inch, it grows closer to obliterating it from existence.

"Futile." Ashton catches my [Fireball] with his bare hands.

The spell explodes in his face, covering his figure with a flash of light and a cloud of smoke.

*He used [Shadow Step]!?*

*Don't think you've stopped us!*

The girls have already realized the situation. Laya's spell is the first to follow my own, her [Wind Blade] tracking the teleportation circle with absolute precision.

"Begone." Ashton's voice comes from within the smoke cloud.

All seven of Laya's blades vanish into harmless gusts just as they enter that room.

*[Anti-Magic Field]!? And a strong one!*

Tylith's [Blood Spray] hits Ashton's defensive magic next. Her spell specializes in destroying magical barriers, but its unique effect doesn't work against an [Anti-Magic Field]. The blood vanishes, just like the blades before it.

Finally, Belle's [Scorching Ray] arrives. Among all our spells, hers is the strongest. On top of that, it also has an extended effect, meaning it can put pressure on magical barriers over many seconds.

That pressure is apparent, as the magic is crawling ever closer to the teleportation circle, as if the [Anti-Magic Field] can't quite eliminate the spell's power.

All the while, I haven't stopped moving. Even if Belle's spell ends before destroying the circle, I'll do it with my spear.

Ashton doesn't even try to block my way, giving me a clear line to the teleportation circle.

As expected, Belle's [Scorching Ray] fizzles out just before it reaches the pattern on the ground. That just leaves me and my spear.

I finally reach the teleportation circle, my weapon cutting through the air in a single, powerful strike.

A burst of energy, and a flash of light. As my spear is repelled by a powerful force, I feel it. The presence of someone powerful.

"Kuh!" My hand wraps around something just in front of my chest.

"Oh?" A familiar voice enters my ears. "This was unexpected."

Archfiend Vrazruk looks down at his arm, which points at my heart like a spear tip. Wrapped around his wrist is my hand, stopping him from piercing me like he did weeks before.

"I won't fall for that again!" I throw his arm aside and leap back, joining the girls.

"Unfortunate." Vrazruk fixes the sleeve on the arm I grabbed. "It would have been far easier had it ended immediately. Easier for you, of course."

*This is…*

Vampire Lord Ashton von Phyress now stands beside another one of the most powerful creatures in the world, Archfiend Vrazruk.

And unlike us, Vrazruk is at full strength.

*…Really bad.*

# Chapter 23: Turning Tides

## ----- Lutz -----

*Should we run?*

That's the first thought that goes through my mind when I see Vampire Lord Ashton and Archfiend Vrazruk standing side by side.

The battle had already been a close one. Even now, I can't say whether it would have been us or Ashton who emerged the victor.

But one thing's clear. If we have to face them both, it'd take a miracle for us to win.

*Vrazruk's mana is draining, but not fast enough.*

Like every time before, the fiend is having his mana and stats sapped away by the debuffs that hit him whenever he's too far from their Great Cathedral. Unfortunately, the Mana Spring seems to be limiting the draining effect due to the saturation of ambient mana in the air.

*We're nearing our limit, especially Alisha. Even I'm starting to feel the effects of exhaustion, so I can only imagine how bad it must be for the others.*

Each of us have our fair share of wounds. The constant releasing of spells has slowed our mana regen, and the same is true of our physical stamina.

Because of Alisha's curse, she can't really keep up with the rest of us when we go all out. I even rotated her out of battle several times so she could rest. But even with that, she can't fight much longer.

Ashton looks to be nearing his limit too, but Vrazruk doesn't have a scratch on him. With such a huge discrepancy in our conditions, there's a real chance we could get wiped out by their combined assault.

*They've got an anti-teleport artifact, too. That means I'll need the girls to buy me some time before I can break through it.*

Both of our enemies will know the second I start channeling [Teleport]. That means I need to commit to it, as it'll likely be a signal for them to attack, knowing they'll have an opening.

Part of me wants to start channeling now so we can get out as quickly as possible. But there's one thing that's holding me back.

*They're not attacking.*

*Does that mean I can get a bit of information from them before we go?*

It's only been a few seconds since Vrazruk arrived, but I expected a quick and violent continuation after the strike at my heart. Yet he's only been watching us with a smile as the girls and I regroup a short distance from him.

"I can see right through you," Vrazruk says. "You're wondering whether or not you should escape, aren't you?"

"And what if I am?"

"Then of course we'll stop you. I wonder if you can finish your teleportation spell while enduring our attacks."

"Don't worry about me. I'll complete it, no matter what."

"That would be quite a bad ending for me. You see, our Great Lord has tasked me with ending your life, little hero. And I won't fail him again." Vrazruk's smile turns sinister. "If you did get away, I might even be angry enough to take out my rage on this city. How many thousands of beastkin live here, I wonder."

*Tch. He's taking this whole city hostage to keep me from running.*

Months ago, back when I had just met Alisha and Belle, I was ready to abandon a city to a terrible fate in order to protect the girls' lives. At the time, I had no real friends or deep connections to this world other than the girls themselves.

I would have sacrificed any number of cities, if it meant keeping them safe.

But things are different now. I have friends from all over the continent. I've finally made this world into my home, and it's my responsibility to save it.

*I can't just leave them. Kuro, Keiko, Riona. I only just met them, but they're already people I decided to protect.*

*Can I take them with me if we run?*

*No, something tells me Kuro and Riona would stay and fight, even if their opponent is an Archfiend.*

*And what about the others? The thousands of everyday beastkin who'd get caught up in the battle? Can I just leave them to their fate?*

I find myself at a fork. In one direction is almost certain defeat and the consequences that come with it. There's no telling what would happen to us. Death would likely be the best outcome of them all.

In the other direction is nearly guaranteed survival for me and the girls. We could flee, recover, and live to fight another day. The only thing it would cost is...

*...Everyone else's lives.*

Countless stories are based on heroes who stood and fought, despite knowing they're destined to lose. Nearly everyone who has something worth fighting for can resonate with such tales, and I'm no exception.

But I'm no hero.

*Kuro and Riona might be willing to keep to their honor until their dying breath.*

*But not me.*

*"We're getting out of here,"* I say telepathically.

*Donning the persona of a hero when it's convenient.*

*And throwing it away when it's not.*

*Maybe my title of False Hero is fitting, after all.*

People I care about are counting on me to defeat the ones trying to destroy this world. It'd be easy for me to use such an excuse.

But the reality is...

*I'm not going to let the girls die in a hopeless battle.*

I look at Ashton and Vrazruk, coming up with a plan and several fail-safes to ensure we can get out of here alive.

I'll need the girls to buy me some time, but they should have at least recovered enough to hold them back for a single minute. That's all the time I need to cast [Teleport] and break through their anti-teleportation artifact.

But as I'm looking at our two, powerful opponents, the smile on Vrazruk's face fades. I prepare for him to attack, but to my surprise, he turns his eyes to Ashton.

"What do you mean you're leaving?" Vrazruk frowns at the Vampire Lord.

I suddenly realize that the two of them must have been talking telepathically. I didn't detect the casting of the [Mental Link] spell, so they were either connected already or they're using some other method of telepathy.

"I've no interest in a battle where the outcome is already decided." Ashton scans our party. "Look at them. Barely an ounce of strength remains. All it would take is one good push, and they'll fall."

"You'd disobey our Great Lord, simply because you've lost interest!?"

"Disobey? I've achieved the goals he set for me already. Bring about a civil war, lure in the False Hero, and spring the trap. There was never any mention of defeating him with my own hands."

"Fool! It was obvious that we'd battle them together, even if it wasn't said!"

Ashton smiles. "Are you afraid? I wonder what our Great Lord would think if he heard you begging for my help to defeat injured prey."

Vrazruk finally turns his entire body toward the Vampire Lord. "When I return, I'll make sure you regret those words."

"A mere Archfiend is too weak to threaten me."

Vrazruk reaches for Ashton's throat, but his hand goes right through the Vampire Lord.

"Do enjoy yourself, Vrazruk." Ashton's voice comes from behind us. "And dear sister, it's a shame I couldn't bring you to the winning side, but perhaps this was just how it was destined to end."

"Ashton!" Tylith yells back. "I don't care how long it takes me! I'm going to take your power for myself and become the strongest Vampire Lord in our people's history!"

"Is that so?" Ashton casually straightens his outfit. "Then do your best to survive the day, dear sister."

As we watch Ashton, he releases his teleportation spell and vanishes. A quick look at my [Minimap] shows me that he's not anywhere in the city or surrounding area.

How he managed to use teleportation magic with the artifact still blocking the spell is a mystery. But it's one I can worry about later.

*He really did leave, which means...*

I turn back to the Archfiend.

*...We only have one opponent.*

This short rest was exactly what we needed. Although we're still in terrible shape, we did manage to recover a little. At the same time, Vrazruk is also getting weaker.

The gap separating us from victory is still wide, but it shrinks with every second. Vrazruk knows that too, but I don't see a shred of anxiety on his face.

"Never trust a vampire," the Archfiend says.

"I can't agree with that." My eyes flick to Tylith.

"I wasn't speaking to you." Vrazruk places his hand on the large spell orb. "I was reminding myself."

I stare at his hand. "Maybe if you didn't use fear to control people, they'd be a little more trustworthy."

"Perhaps. But I'm not interested in placating my lord's subjects. I only care about achieving his goals."

"And what is that goal?"

"At it again, are you?" Vrazruk smiles. "But I won't spill his secrets so easily this time."

"A shame. I guess I'll have to try harder."

"The only thing you'll be trying to do..." Vrazruk's fingers begin tapping on the orb. "...is survive."

A spell erupts from the orb, one like I've never felt before. A wave of energy passes by me, sending a shiver coursing through my body. Not because of the spell's strength, but just due to the uncomfortable feeling it gives me.

*No, wait! I've felt this kind of magic before!*

A memory surfaces in my mind. A wave of energy that pricked my skin and sent a similar shiver through my body. That was months ago now, back when we fought...

*...High Priest Melina!*

"Kyaaa!" Alisha's shriek shatters the silence.

"What's wrong!?" Belle yells.

"M-my heart...!" Alisha falls to her knees, her hand on the scale mail, right in front of her heart.

I check her status, even as I cast every healing magic I possibly can. Just as I'm bringing out a powerful potion that cures most debuffs, I see it.

I see the words that confirm my greatest fear.

*No...! How is this possible!?*

Alisha gained a new Unique Skill. Or rather, one of her two Unique Skills got replaced. [Curse of the Forsaken] is gone. Normally, that'd be cause for a huge celebration, but any thoughts of celebrating fade when I see the Unique Skill that took its place.

*[Touch of Chaos]!*

With each second, the strength of her mana rises, as if she were powering up. But at the same time, her status is starting to change on its own.

Her name and race are nothing but garbled text, as if the system responsible for the status information doesn't know what to display.

*Alisha, she's...*

I think back to High Priest Melina, who went through a similar change.

*...turning into an Archfiend!?*

# Chapter 24: The Fate of the Forsaken

## ----- Lutz -----

"Alisha!" I yell her name as she collapses.

Belle catches her and slowly lowers the young girl to the ground.

"I-I'll be ... fine." Alisha says through pained breaths.

Alisha hates it when her physical condition drags her down. Even now, Alisha doesn't want to worry us, despite being in pain from a mysterious magical effect.

But this is different.

I know from experience that Unique Skills can't be messed with lightly. The fact that whatever Vrazruk used can tamper with her Unique Skills directly means it's either a supremely powerful spell, or...

*It's using the energy from the Mana Spring.*

*Does that mean if I get her away from here, it'll stop!?*

We faced a similar situation when fighting High Priest Melina. While she was near the Mana Spring, she absorbed more energy from it and slowly lost her humanity.

Back then, we were too late by the time we realized what was happening, but now...

"Alisha, listen closely. Just concentrate on staying awake. We're going to get you out of here and heal you right up!"

"U-understood, Master..."

I lift Alisha's body and waste no time running to the exit.

*The faster we can get her away from the Mana Spring, the quicker we can—ugh!*

*W-what the? She's getting heavy!?*

Even if I'm tired, my Strength is high enough that carrying a single girl in armor is nothing to me. Yet somehow, with each step, it gets harder to keep hold of Alisha.

*No, she's not getting heavier! She's being pulled back to the Mana Spring!*

I can feel it tugging now, like a cable that's been stretched past its limit. The enormous amount of energy from the Mana Spring is acting as a tether, preventing me from carrying Alisha away.

*In that case...!*

I get ready to activate [Teleport], targeting all of the girls. There's only one problem...

*I can't target Alisha!?*

No matter how much I try, the spell simply won't work on her.

"Hahaha..." Vrazruk's soft laughter fills the air. "Did you really think it'd be so simple?"

"Shut up!" I put Alisha back on the ground.

"Oh how brusque you've become, little hero. You can merely think of this as payback for all the times you thwarted my plans." Vrazruk lets out another laugh. "Did you never wonder why the number of Forsaken has grown so rapidly since the Great War began?"

I put my hand on Alisha's shoulder and send my mana into her body. "You've been cursing people and looking for candidates to become Archfiends."

"It's true that only those who've been cursed can join us. But it's not just for Archfiends."

My mana flows to Alisha's Mana Core, right where her Unique Skill, [Curse of the Forsaken] was embedded. "Are you saying that..."

"Indeed. Only those marked can join our ranks, becoming part of our Great Lord's plans. Or to put it more accurately, any who bear the curse are destined to obey, whether as an Archfiend or Berserker.

"So all the fiends, they're..."

"Precisely. Without exception, every single fiend was once human. Or beastkin, in the case of your little teammate."

*Good. All his talking gave me some time to study what's happening to Alisha.*

The Unique Skill, [Curse of the Forsaken] is changing, becoming something different. Something that will turn her into an Archfiend.

The process that's taking place is so advanced that I don't even know where to begin when it comes to stopping it.

An exorbitant amount of mana is involved too, making it hard to even use my usual technique of controlling my mana within Alisha's body. It's getting overwhelmed by the energy flowing into her from the Mana Spring.

*Dammit! I was so close to ridding her of that curse! Just a couple more weeks, and now…!*

I look to the Spell Orb sitting on a pedestal next to Vrazruk. He used it to cast the spell, so there's a chance I can cancel it by destroying the orb, like I did when we fought High Priest Melina.

The Archfiend must know exactly what I'm thinking because he plucks the orb from the pedestal, as if planning to protect it from me.

What I didn't expect was for the orb to suddenly vanish from his hand.

"What's with the look of surprise?" Vrazruk asks. "Did you think yourself the only one capable of producing artifacts enchanted with [Inventory]? Perhaps it's time you realize just how powerful our Great Lord truly is."

*This is bad. If the artifact's gone, then that means it's not controlling the spell that's turning Alisha into an Archfiend.*

"Her transformation won't stop until it's complete," Vrazruk says. "Once it's begun, the only way to end it is to kill her."

I refocus on my mana circulating inside Alisha. I can feel the Unique Skill that used to be [Curse of the Forsaken]. Even though it's changing shape at this very moment, it's still recognizable thanks to the many hours I spent trying to remove it.

*There's got to be a way! Some way to stop it!*

"Do you finally understand?" Vrazruk says. "Soon, you will be facing two Archfiends, one born from your very own companion! Unless you put an end to her yourself."

I ignore his mocking voice, closing my eyes and focusing all my attention on the transforming Unique Skill inside Alisha's body.

*How!? How can I stop it!?*

I'm doing my best to fight back against the mana that's flooding through Alisha and causing her transformation. But no matter how much mana I have, it's still just a speck compared to something like a Mana Spring.

"The transformation may take a bit of time," Vrazruk continues. "And I'm not one to sit idle and wait."

I feel him begin to channel for a powerful spell.

"Laya," I say with my eyes still closed. "I need time."

"I won't fail." She steps between us and the Archfiend.

Belle and Tylith follow her, the three girls preparing to battle an Archfiend at nearly full power. As for me...

*They'll protect us. That means I can focus on helping Alisha.*

I've already learned almost everything I need about what's happening to her. The spell Vrazruk used created a connection between her and the Mana Spring, and it's powering the change of her Unique Skill.

The only way to stop it is to cut that connection. But there's a problem...

*I'm just a drop in a bucket compared to a Mana Spring. There's no way I can overpower it with brute force.*

Messing with someone's Mana Core is dangerous. Normally, it's hard to even get close to it because the other person's mana will protect them. But when the person relaxes their defenses, it's possible to get access to it.

That's exactly how I'm able to work on curing Alisha's curse each night. She allows my mana to flow inside her without restriction.

But right now...

*Her mana is fighting back!?*

*No, this mana is different. It's not her mana anymore!*

The change has already begun. I can see Alisha's moderately tanned skin start to shift in color, taking on a bluish tone.

It's just like what was happening to High Priest Melina when she started to transform into an Archfiend. The transformation was subtle at first, but once it reached a certain point, Melina lost her humanity.

*I can't let that happen to Alisha!*

I try sending my mana to shield the transforming Unique Skill from the spell's influence, hoping to cut off the supply of energy that's fueling the spell's effects.

But no matter how much I try, the mana won't stop flowing in, further morphing the Unique Skill and turning it—and Alisha—into something else.

*There's got to be something! Something I can do!*

I've learned a lot during my hours of practice removing Alisha's curse. But in the grand scheme, my skill level can only be considered basic when compared to someone like the Astral Dryad.

And whoever created the spell that transforms the Forsaken into fiends is far above me. Finding a way to fight back against the magic is looking more and more futile.

*Do I ... have to do that?*

Among the many lessons the Astral Dryad taught me while I was learning how to cure the curse, one of them was a dire warning. She said that if I ever try to forcefully remove the Unique Skill before I'm finished healing Alisha, it could damage her Mana Core.

If that were to happen, the worst-case scenario would be Alisha's sudden death.

A distant feeling of pain hits me. My body lurches forward, but I barely pay it any mind. Whatever attack struck me got through the girls' defense, which can only mean one thing.

They're struggling against Vrazruk, just like I am against this spell. If I don't hurry, not only will we lose Alisha, but the girls fighting the Archfiend may actually be defeated.

*Dammit...!*

I open my eyes, looking down at the young girl who's become an even darker shade of blue. "Alisha, I'm thinking of doing something really dangerous. So dangerous that if I mess up ... you could die."

"Ugh..." She struggles to focus on me. "I-if it's Master, then there's nothing to worry about..."

"No, this time, even I'm not sure how it will turn out. But it's the only way I can think of to stop the transformation."

"I ... don't want to become a monster. I don't want to be made to hurt people..."

"I know." I wipe her sweaty forehead. "I won't let that happen."

"I don't care how dangerous it is." Alisha squeezes my hand. "I want it to stop..."

"Then close your eyes and leave it to me."

She does as I ask, and I take a single second to look at her face. A girl with boundless energy and enthusiasm, whose sole desire is to help the innocent people of this world.

She believed in me when almost nobody else would, becoming an irreplaceable part of my life.

That girl is putting all her trust in me to help her. To save her from the fate that's been hounding her ever since the day she was cursed as a young child.

*Alisha. I'll absolutely protect you.*

I send a torrent of mana into her body, directly at the Unique Skill.

"Give Alisha back!"

The energy slams into the Mana Core, right where the Unique Skill is embedded. There's a surge of mana, alongside the feeling of something cracking.

Alisha gasps, having had her vulnerable core hit with such extreme force. Her body, formerly tense and trembling, finally relaxes, the muscles going limp all at once.

I feel around the Mana Core, looking for the Unique Skill. It's nowhere to be found, obliterated by my wave of mana.

I succeeded. The [Touch of Chaos] is gone. But...

*She's ... she's not breathing!*

I...

...Killed Alisha.

*No...! This can't be happening!*

The destruction of the Unique Skill wasn't the only consequence of what I did. There's a reason the Astral Dryad warned me not to use such a method.

*I damaged her Mana Core...!*

Right where the [Curse of the Forsaken] used to be is a crack.

*Can I fix it!?*

*No, I don't know anything about how to fix a Mana Core! Then what do I do!?*

*All this magic, but there's nothing that can help with this!*

There aren't any spells that can heal Mana Cores or revive the dead. Despite all my potions, artifacts, and knowledge gained from the Mana Network, none of it can help me bring Alisha back.

*I ... I can't do anything!?*

*Dammit! I can't help her!? Me!? The only hero to have ever been summoned from another world!? I'm going to fail—*

My thoughts come to an abrupt halt.

*Wait ... Earth...*

I send Alisha's scale mail to my [Inventory], leaving her in just the undershirt she wears beneath.

Normally, it's impossible to forcefully store equipment while someone else is wearing it. But right now, nobody is wearing the scale mail.

After all, Alisha is dead.

Holding back a tremble, I place my hands on her ribcage, feeling the bones just under the thin layers of clothes and skin.

Then, I push.

*Please...! Please!*

I push down again and again, counting each one. After reaching 30, I tilt Alisha's head back to open her airway.

Two breaths. One second each. Then back to pushing on her chest.

*Come on! Please!*

I go through the entire CPR rotation a second time, exactly as how I remember it from the classes I had to take back on Earth.

And yet...

*Still nothing!?*

In many cases, CPR is performed until a trained medic arrives. But this world doesn't have such professionals on standby, much less things like defibrillators to restart someone's heart.

*Defibrillators...*

I reach out, placing my hand right over Alisha's heart. "[Shock]."

A jolt of electricity courses straight through her body. Even though I held back, it's still powerful enough to severely injure any normal human on Earth.

Alisha gasps. "Ughhh..."

I throw my arms around her. "Alisha! Thank God!"

"M-Master...? What happened?"

"I ... I thought I killed you..."

"Huh? But ... I'm alive?"

"Yeah ... you're alive, Alisha." I hold her a little tighter.

"Master, I'm being squeezed—Ah, wait!" She suddenly sits up. "Weren't we fighting!?"

I finally take a look at the other girls. They've been doing their best to hold back the nearly full powered Archfiend this entire time.

Since they've had no choice but to protect us, it left them at a huge disadvantage against Vrazruk. That's instantly apparent from the extra wounds they've accumulated in just a short time.

Likewise, their mana and physical stamina have been pushed to their limits. They were already exhausted before, but after giving it their all for several minutes, it's nothing short of a miracle that all three of them are still standing.

"We have to help them!" Alisha scrambles to her feet.

"Easy." I help her up. "You're in no condition to fight. Your Mana Core's been damaged. I don't know what will happen if you push yourself."

"I don't care. I'm going to help my friends, no matter what."

*Well, that's Alisha for you.*

*At least her [Protector] is still active. That'll make it—no, wait!*

I already checked her status. When she died, all of her buffs vanished, including [Protector].

Yet when I look at Alisha's stats, I see that all of them have doubled from her unbuffed state. The reason is obvious, but seeing it still shocks me.

*Removing [Curse of the Forsaken] made her this much stronger?*

*She's as powerful now as she used to be after activating [Protector]. Which means, if we activate it now...*

"Ready, Alisha?"

"Yes, Master!"

"Then let's put an end to this battle together."

Alisha and I stand side by side, both of our gazes locked on the Archfiend who attempted to take her away from us.

*It's time to pay, Vrazruk.*

# Chapter 25: Shackles Unbound

## ----- Lutz -----

*"Now,"* I say telepathically to Laya.

The three girls fighting Vrazruk go for a reckless attack. Even if the girls are at their limit, the Archfiend can't take their coordinated strike lightly. Rather, it's at moments like this that desperate warriors can pull off a surprising upset.

Unfortunately, that reality doesn't play out. Vrazruk defends against an assault so deadly that nearly anyone else in this world would have fallen.

But Vrazruk still stands.

"A foolish attempt at a desperate att–kuh!" Vrazruk spins, his claws passing just in front of my face.

The Archfiend turns and looks at me with surprise, then to Alisha who stands beside my illusion.

*[Shadow Step] really is a useful spell.*

"How!?" Vrazruk yells. "She was caught in our Great Lord's spell!"

"Maybe this lord of yours isn't so great after all."

"You annoying little hero. I'll put an end to all of you myself."

"I won't let you." Alisha says, stepping toward Vrazruk. "I'll make sure you won't be able to hurt anyone ever again!"

"Like I care what a failure like you wants. Now that you're no longer useful to us, you'll meet your end with the rest of them."

"Useful..." Alisha comes to a stop just out of attack range. "Is that why you cursed my village? So we would become useful servants of Chaos?"

A sickly smile forms on Vrazruk's face. "What other use could such lowly creatures have? Becoming part of our army is the highest honor they could receive."

"You destroyed my hometown just to make everyone into your pawns!? My parents fled to a human country because of the curse, and I watched as they died to a curable disease! All because of you!"

"How frustrating that so many managed to escape before we could bring them to our lord. I'll make sure the next time we curse a village, we capture each beastkin without fail."

Alisha readies her sword. "There won't be a next time for you."

"You're still no match for me, and they..." Vrazruk eyes the other three girls. "They've got nothing left. Once I defeat you and this wretched hero, I can finally bring some good news to my lord."

*Well, he's right about one thing. Laya, Tylith, and Belle don't have any strength left. We can't expect them to recover enough to fight again, even if we buy some time.*

*That means it's up to me and Alisha to finish this.*

*Fortunately, Alisha's recovered a lot of her strength.*

*Is it because I removed the curse? Or maybe it's a result of the transformation she was going through.*

Either way, Alisha's suddenly the only one here in real fighting shape. Though I'm still not sure what kind of affect her damaged Mana Core might have on her.

As for me, I need a good night's sleep to really recover. But the short break while the girls held Vrazruk back helped a little.

I was already in the best shape among all of us, even though I never once rotated out of the battle against Ashton like the girls did. The strength given to me by the Goddess really does put me in a tier of my own.

"Looks like the girls managed to give you a nice dose of the mana draining poison already." I make a show of looking at his few wounds, each given to him with weapons coated in that special potion.

"An annoyance, at best." He turns squarely to me.

"That so? Well, don't be surprised when that arrogant attitude comes back to bite you."

*I did make the potion stronger, you know.*

Vrazruk's no fool. He knows Alisha is our party's tank, and anyone with a basic understanding of battle knows not to go out of their way to attack the tank.

Add in the fact that I'm still just a few paces away from him, and it only makes sense that I'd be his target.

Yet I don't even attempt to evade as Vrazruk's clawed hand falls from above, seeking to add yet another wound to my body.

"[Accel]," a soft voice says from nearby.

The grinding of nails on metal fills my ears the same instant a set of lavender hair covers my vision.

Alisha angles her shield, deflecting the claw and sending the attack off course.

At the same time…

*Woah. She's ridiculously strong.*

I knew [Protector] would boost her stats by a lot, but feeling the power increase for the first time is still a little surprising.

"Accursed defect." Vrazruk is openly angry at having been tricked into activating Alisha's [Protector].

"No, I'm not cursed anymore."

"You'll soon wish you were."

Vrazruk goes on the offensive, starting with a spell.

A stone spear erupts from the ground just in front of Alisha. It hits her shield, just as Vrazruk's claws did a moment ago. But the force of the impact can't be compared to before.

Alisha's knocked from her feet by the third-tier Earth Spell, [Impale]. As she flies through the air, more spears appear, attacking her with precise strikes.

I was on the receiving end of that magic back when I battled Prince Lyle at the capital, so I know just how much force those stone spears carry.

But being the focus of attacks is exactly what Alisha wants.

I don't let the chance go to waste. A pillar of fire roars to life at the Archfiend's feet, engulfing him in its searing flames. From within, I see his figure leap, trying to escape the spell's AoE to limit the damage he takes.

Seeing which direction he chooses, I dash to the edge of the flames where he will be emerging, making it there just as he bursts through the [Flame Pillar].

"[Gale Stab]!" A piercing energy covers my spear tip.

"[Bulwark]!" A barrier appears in front of Vrazruk.

My spear hits his magical shield, powered by my momentum and enhanced by my Spear Skill.

For a split second, the two forces battle it out between us. But in a blink, the winner is decided.

*Crap!*

I twist my body, trying to dodge Vrazruk's claws. But my failed attack leaves me open, and the Archfiend takes advantage of that.

With no other alternative, I summon my shield. Vrazruk's claws hit me with enough force to send me flying, but I manage to catch myself on an [Air Step].

*That was unexpected. [Bulwark] is a Shield Skill, but he doesn't have a shield.*

*We'll have to be careful. There's no telling what other surprises he has for us.*

Alisha's already back at my side. Although she took a direct hit from Vrazruk's third-tier spell, she's barely any worse off than before.

Her equipment is geared almost solely for defense. It was a necessity back when the curse was sapping her stats, but her lopsided enchantments aren't exactly doing us any favors right now.

"Alisha, we're changing tactics."

I place my hand on her shoulder, replacing the enchantments on her scale mail. Next is her necklace, then bracers and rings.

"Wow! I'm getting stronger!"

"Yes, but at the cost of your defenses, so be careful."

"Understood, Master!"

As she was, Alisha still wasn't much of a threat to Vrazruk because of her lack of offensive buffs. It would have been simple for him to ignore her and focus on attacking me, knowing that taking me out would eliminate most of our offensive potential.

But that's not the case anymore. Although she's still primarily geared for defense, I've increased Alisha's offensive potential enough to threaten even an Archfiend. We'll need that power if we want to take him down.

*Now, let's really get this battle started.*

# Chapter 26: Rebirth

## ----- Alisha -----

For the first time in my life, I'm free.

Master released me from the slave seal months ago, but the curse remained, like a collar that nobody could remove.

Until now.

*I feel so much stronger. And my head is so clear.*

I had almost forgotten what it was like to feel normal. Even though I had gained so many levels, I could still feel the weight of that curse dragging me down the whole time.

I look around at the ones who've been protecting me ever since we met.

Belle, my best friend who helped me, even though I was a beastkin slave.

Tylith, the best hunting partner I could ask for.

Laya, who's always looking out for me.

All three of them fought with everything they had while Master was healing me. Not to defeat Vrazruk, but to protect me while I was down.

They believed that Master would succeed. And right now, they believe that he and I can win.

*I won't let them down!*

"Ready, Alisha?"

"Yes, Master!"

"Then let's use that in a real battle for the first time."

"Okay!"

That's all we need to say.

Like always, I take the front, my adamantium shield held between me and the powerful Archfiend. Even as strong as I've become, I can still feel the difference between us. Winning by myself would be impossible.

But I'm never alone.

"We're going to stop you this time!" My sword arcs.

"Foolish girl!" He catches my attack with his nails. "You could have gained power. You could have helped rule this world. But you chose to die a pitiful death beside this worthless hero!"

Even as Vrazruk speaks, he doesn't stop attacking. Even with Master's [Wind Blade] and spear hounding him, I can only take a step back under his assault.

"I want to get stronger." A powerful blow nearly sends me flying. "Stronger than anyone! I'll keep fighting and fighting until nobody can beat me!"

I plant my feet and raise my shield, taking the full force of Vrazruk's magically-enhanced attack. "Because I'm going to stop you and all the other fiends who only know how to hurt people!"

"Enough!" Vrazruk raises his hand. "I won't have you speak ill of my brethren!"

A burst of energy explodes from him, and my vision goes blue as a torrent of water slams into me.

The [Maelstrom] is like nothing I've ever felt. Even Belle's can't match the powerful currents pulling at me, dragging me along against my will. It's like being in the center of a small hurricane, one whose water can cut like glass.

Despite my efforts, my feet keep scraping along the stone floor as the spell's power drags me. All the while, cuts and scrapes appear on my body, given to me by the shards of water.

But the spell isn't known for its damage. It's far more useful as a way to disable the opponent.

From the murky depths of the [Maelstrom], a hand appears. The blood covering it mixes with the water, darkening it with a muddy red.

The nails on the hand are glowing, and when they reach me, magical energy bursts from them.

My body explodes from the [Maelstrom], flying through the air. Vrazruk's attack struck me before I could put up a defense, and I already know it's the deepest wound I've gotten since the battle started.

A pair of arms catches me before I crash into the wall, and in a blink, my feet are back on the ground.

"Thanks, Master." I give him a smile.

"No problem." He steps in front of me, his spear held defensively. "Ready?"

"Yes."

"Good. Let's get started, then. And Alisha—make sure to return every ounce of pain right back to him."

"Leave it to me."

He rushes back into battle—alone.

I drink a potion as I slowly step back toward their fight. It's one of the most powerful potions Master gave me, but if there was ever a time to use it, it's now.

I come to a stop, still far from the battle. Right now, Master's still fighting Vrazruk alone.

And losing.

*Not for long.*

Master's eyes meet mine, and I raise my hand into the air.

Vrazruk's not dumb. He's been watching me, wondering why I've stopped at this particular range when I'm a melee fighter. When he sees my raised hand, realization enters his eyes. However...

"Magic?" Vrazruk scoffs. "We know all of your strengths and weaknesses. Even if you're no longer cursed, the strength of your spells is still nothing compared to the others."

"It's true that even now, I can't match someone like Belle or Laya in magic. But..." I activate the spell formation. "I'm a cheater, too!"

Massive globs of acid burst from my hand. The first time I saw this [Acid Spray] was during our battle against this very Archfiend. Back then, we could barely survive it, even when we used every defensive ability we had.

Now, that power belongs to me. I watch as the green acid arcs through the air, heading straight toward the Archfiend.

In his face, I see not just surprise, but shock. The globs are every bit as big as the ones he used against us that day. But now, they're raining down on him.

"Gah...!" He raises his arms as the acid showers him. "How!? There's no way you should have such magical strength!"

Vrazruk tries to flee from the area of effect, but Master cuts him off, his spear a wall preventing his escape.

"She already told you," Master says. "She's cheating!"

In truth, Master is the real cheater. When he caught me just now, he replaced every single enchantment on my equipment. Without exception, each buff is now maximizing my magical power at the expense of everything else.

That was the only way for me to release such a powerful spell. And it's why I can't engage in melee until the enchantments are changed back.

*Master was right. Investing in the future was a great idea.*

I was surprised when Master said he wanted to raise my fourth-tier Earth Spell, [Acid Spray] to the maximum rank. Back then, I was still cursed, so my magic was painfully weak. I didn't think I'd get any use out of an offensive spell, even if it was Heroic-Class.

But Master said he was 'investing in the future', and that one day, the spell would be very useful.

And today, it is.

My magic comes to an end, the last globs of acid hitting the floor on the other side of the room. Vrazruk is covered in the green slime, but even a powerful fourth-tier spell can't defeat him in a single cast.

Which is why Master is here.

"It sure is hard to fight when dual casting," Master says with a casual tone. "Especially when they're both fourth-tier spells. Frankly, I'm exhausted."

"What...?" Vrazruk focuses on Master and seems to realize something. "Two of them!?"

"It's good that [Acid Spray] lowers the target's Constitution and Intelligence stats. Because it makes follow-up attacks that much stronger." Master raises both of his arms. "[Windstorm]. [Shardstorm]."

As soon as he says the spells' names, magical energy explodes from his hands.

A raging storm, accompanied by an explosion of icy shards. Vrazruk's body if fully engulfed by the spells, his yells barely reaching my ears over the roar of magic.

Unlike me, Master is a powerful mage, even without changing his enchantments. Watching the magical display, I can only imagine how painful it must be for anyone caught inside.

Master comes back to my side, placing his arm on my shoulder and reverting the buffs to normal.

"Good work, Alisha."

"Thanks, Master!"

"Vrazruk won't fall from just this, but the battle's turning in our favor."

"That just means I have time to make him regret every single evil thing he's done."

Master smiles. "True. Then, let's remind him together."

The magic ends, with Vrazruk standing bloodied on the far side of the room.

Yet despite the damage he took, there's not a shred of fear in his eyes as he glares at us.

*I'm going to put an end to you, Vrazruk!*

# Chapter 27: Disrupt

## ----- Lutz -----

"Guh!" Vrazruk grunts as Alisha's sword gives him another wound.

The battle has been raging for a good ten minutes now, and the tide has finally shifted.

The Archfiend has several deep wounds, each of which were inflicted with weapons coated with the mana draining poison. With each drop of mana he loses, we come that much closer to victory.

As his mana drains away, so do his stats. The speed and strength he had at the beginning of the battle is nowhere to be seen.

While the same can be said of us, we're not on nearly as much of a timer as Vrazruk. He's far from the Great Cathedral that supplies him with power, meaning he's been fighting against the clock the entire time.

"Impossible," Vrazruk says. "You should have fallen by now!"

"We won't give up until we defeat you!" Alisha is still energetic, even though we're reaching our limit.

"This is all the fault of that damn Vampire Lord! If he had stayed as he should have, then...!"

"It's because you're a bad person. Nobody likes you, even the ones who should be your allies."

"Shut it! I don't need people to like me! I just need them to obey!"

"Never."

"Grrr." Vrazruk grits his teeth. "To think I'd be forced to retreat again. You damn hero. I'll get my revenge next time we meet!"

"Isn't that what you always say?" I ask.

"Don't think our lord will let you do as you please forever! If it's him, then all it would take is a single spell to wipe you from this world!"

"I'd like to see him try."

The smile returns to Vrazruk's face. "In that case, I will certainly work to arrange such a meeting. I hope you don't regret it once he appears before you."

The Archfiend begins channeling [Teleport]. As expected, he intends to warp away and make his escape like he did back when we first met him in the elven lands.

Back then, we were glad to see him go since we didn't have the strength to take him out. But things are different now.

"You won't get away!" I release my own spell, and an [Anti-Magic Field] fills the entire fighting area.

"Such a weak spell can't stop my teleportation," Vrazruk says.

Despite the spell's name, powerful opponents can still cast magic inside an [Anti-Magic Field]. It will just lower the strength of the spell, essentially making the field into an area-wide debuff for mages.

"You're right the spell won't stop you. But don't think it's all I have up my sleeve!" I lunge at Vrazruk, grabbing him.

"Wretched hero!" He struggles to break free, but he doesn't have a huge stat advantage over me like last time we grappled.

While we struggle, I send mana into his body and attack his spell formation, trying to prevent him from casting [Teleport].

As always, using this technique on a powerful enemy isn't easy. The strength of his mana is too much for me to obliterate the spell formation, but I can at least create imperfections in it and lower its effectiveness.

But eventually, Vrazruk completes the spell.

"When we meet again, it'll mean your end." He releases [Teleport], the massive amount of energy flowing from him in a burst.

"[Disrupt]." A single word escapes my lips.

Vrazruk's body vanishes...

...is what he expected to happen. But all the mana he spent on his [Teleport] spell simply joins the already saturated room, mixing with the boundless energy as it erupts from the Mana Spring.

"W-what..." Vrazruk's eyes widen.

"It's true I can't stop you with [Anti-Magic Field]. Nor can I stop you with [Disrupt] or by destroying the spell formation with raw mana." I smile at him. "But if I use all three? Well, even a spell from an all-powerful Archfiend can fail."

"Impossible! Cancelling my spell!?"

"And since [Disrupt] only works on spells that are used, it means you don't get your mana back from your cast. Ah, and the cooldown is in effect of course, so don't think you can just try again."

"Mr. Archfiend." Alisha approaches him, step by step. "It's time you paid for all the suffering you brought to this world."

"I won't fall here," he says. "Not to a bunch of fools like you!"

Vrazruk looks toward the only exit. Laya, Belle, and Tylith have been standing near it ever since Alisha and I took up the fight. But now he realizes that those three girls no longer block his path out.

That doesn't mean he's free to go, though.

"Surrounded!?" Vrazruk looks around him, where Laya, Belle, and Tylith are channeling their spells.

"The battle's been going on for quite a while," I say. "Did you not think they'd at least be able throw out a few spells by now?"

"Curse you! I won't be—" His words are cut off by the deafening roar of magic.

The crack of lightning mixes with countless shards of ice and a massive blade of water as the three girls cast all at once.

From the outside, it's a dazzling display of magical effects. But for anyone caught in the middle of those powerful spells, it's anything but pleasant.

Despite his normally reserved attitude, even Vrazruk lets out a scream as the third and fourth tier spells hammer him. Eventually, the spells play out their effects, and by the time we lay our eyes on him again, he's already fallen to the ground.

Alisha takes the final couple steps separating her from Vrazruk. "The pain of those who've suffered. Me, my family, my friends, and all the people of this world. I'll return it to you!"

Her sword falls, piercing the Archfiend directly in his heart.

"Kuh..." Vrazruk spits up blood. "You ... you will all perish. My lord, he ... he's destined to rule this world..."

With those words, the light fades from Vrazruk's eyes.

"Hahhh..." I resist the urge to collapse right where I stand. "We did it. We beat one of the Archfiends."

"Amazing," Belle says. "We're actually strong enough to win."

"Yeah. It might be a different story if we fight them in their own lands, but now we know that if an Archfiend starts causing problems outside their territory, we can take them out."

With the teleportation circle destroyed during the battle, that only leaves one item left to retrieve. The [Inventory] artifact Vrazruk used to store the Spell Orb could be anywhere on him, but since I'm not too keen on stripping him down right now, I just send his entire body to my own [Inventory].

*The equipment he's wearing might come in handy, too. It's powerful, even compared to my own.*

While I'd love to grind more and surpass even the items worn by Ashton and the Archfiends, I have an important task that needs to be done first. That means I'll have to settle with taking the spoils of this battle for now.

Next, I turn toward the girl who was pivotal in us winning against Vrazruk. Alisha looks satisfied at taking out one of the Archfiends who helped destroy her village and ruin her childhood, as evidenced by her subdued smile.

I was going to praise her for it, but someone else takes the initiative before me.

"Alisha!" Belle throws her arms around her friend. "Your curse is gone!"

"Haha, that tickles." Alisha pushes a few strands of Belle's hair away from her nose. "But yes, Master got rid of the curse and stopped the transformation."

Belle pulls back just enough to speak comfortably. "How? When I looked over, you even looked like you were ... um, dead."

"Ah, I did die, I think?" Alisha tilts her head.

"Huh!?"

Several faces turn to me, each carrying the same question in their eyes.

"She wasn't breathing, but she was fine, otherwise." I try to weasel out of their glares.

"Nobody's fine if they're not breathing!"

"Well ... you got me there."

"And what of that strange spell?" Tylith asks. "The one that brought her back to life. I've never seen a spell that required ... something like that."

"It wasn't a spell. It's called CPR, and it's a technique that specializes in keeping people alive after their heart stops. Though it only works when there isn't a lot of damage to the body."

"And this CPR requires a … k-kiss?" Tylith pointedly looks away.

"Hey!" Belle shouts. "What exactly did you do to Alisha!"

"Eh?" Alisha looks thoughtful. "Did something like that happen?"

"It wasn't a kiss!" I try to make that fact clear. "It's a necessary part of the technique to keep fresh oxygen circulating through the respiratory system! Without it, the chest compressions would become useless as all the body's oxygen gets used up!"

"Ah, I get it!" Alisha smiles. "Does that mean I can count on Master for more oxygen in the future?"

"Absolutely not! Breathe on your own from now on!"

Thanks to Alisha's playful response, I'm able to weasel out of that particular conversation for now. But the look on Belle's face tells me she's going to use it to her advantage later.

*I really screwed myself this time…*

"Anyway," I say. "Why don't we get out of this abandoned research facility before the whole thing collapses on top of us."

"Mmm. Stuffy."

"Yeah, not a fan of the stale air and cramped space, either. Though it helps that most of the walls were destroyed during the battle."

There's only one exit, and it's the same way we came in. Stepping back out, we find ourselves on the landing platform with a set of stone steps leading up.

As we walk up the stairs, I see that the [Earth Wall] I used to cover this entrance has been destroyed. I already knew that though, and the culprit is obvious.

That advisor fled through here after the battle with Ashton began. That was over half an hour ago now, so of course he would break through during that time.

But just when the advisor thought he was free, he was hit with quite a surprise.

My foot lands on the final stair, stepping back into the temple that was built atop the research facility. When I look around, I see exactly what I expect.

"Thanks for guarding the entrance," I say to Kuro.

"As you said, it would only be a burden for you if others entered the secret passage."

"Yeah, we had our work cut out for us already. Having to protect someone who wandered into our battle would have been annoying."

"So it's over, then?"

"It's over. There are a few loose ends, but that's something I'll be leaving in your hands."

Kuro looks to the advisor, who's being held captive by guards. "This kind of business isn't that uncommon for kings. Many people seek our authority, so dealing with usurpers simply comes with the position."

"Good because I've had my fill of dealing with civil wars for now."

"That may be so, but I hope you'll at least stay for a day. It wouldn't do to have the one who saved our kingdom vanish before the celebration. I'd also like to discuss a few things in private."

I turn to the girls, who look just as tired as I feel. "We're not going anywhere today, that's for sure. But we need to get back on the road tomorrow, so can we hold the celebration in the morning?"

"I think we can work with that."

With that, all our business at the temple is finished. The battle against Ashton and the defeat of an Archfiend were important moments for us. But there's one thing that trumps both of those events.

My eyes fall on Alisha.

*Finally. Finally, the curse is gone.*

# Chapter 27: Ceremony

## ----- Lutz -----

"And so," King Kuro says after a long speech. "It is my honor to introduce Sir Lutz, the Great Hero who helped resolve our civil war and defeated the Archfiend who sought to destroy our kingdom."

The large dining room erupts with voices, each demanding answers to their own set of questions.

Most of the nobles gathered here had no idea what was happening behind the scenes. Many thought it was just another change of rule, so after hearing the whole story, of course they'd want answers.

It didn't help that I was recognized as the False Hero before Kuro could even mention who I was. So when told that I'm actually the one who saved the kingdom and that I'm battling against Chaos, the number of questions multiplied.

As I listen to the roar of voices that are too chaotic to make out, I can't help but see a stark difference between the high society here compared to in the human lands.

*They sure do like their meetings to be lively, don't they?*

Human nobles are usually more reserved, paying close attention to their place in the hierarchy of high society. But the beastkin are far more outspoken, regardless of their rank.

*Hey, hurry up and speak in an orderly fashion already.*

I continue waiting while the nobles are still making a ruckus.

When Kuro said there'd be a celebration, I thought I'd be paraded through the streets. I was even hardening my resolve to deal with huge crowds of people.

But it seems I misunderstood Kuro's plans. He said bringing me out in front of the people would be a huge risk, so we should focus on letting the nobility know the truth first.

That makes sense to me, and I'm more than happy to reduce the number of people I have to deal with from thousands down to a couple dozen.

*These couple dozen are some of the most powerful people in Belfast, though...*

Finally, the commotion dies down, actually giving us a chance to explain a few things.

The usual scene unfolds, with me revealing the truth about who I really am and proving it by showing some of them my Unique Skill, [True Blessing of the Goddess].

Even after seeing that, there are sometimes skeptical people, and this time is no exception. But I've already taught Kuro and a couple others how to cast the Lost Magics, so as the Arcane spell tree spreads and people get familiar with [Scry], they should realize that Unique Skills are permanent and beyond the ability to add or remove, bringing those skeptics to my side.

However, there is one problem.

*With the right knowledge and setup, Unique Skills can be changed.*

*That means I can't rely on it as my only way of convincing people.*

The three heroes had their Unique Skill, [Blessing of Chaos] changed to [Blessings of the Goddess]. Once people start ranking up their [Scry] to show Unique Skills, they'll think the other three heroes are fighting for our side.

A confrontation with the other heroes is inevitable, so when that day comes, I may need more than my Unique Skill to convince people to put their faith in me instead of them.

*For now, it's good enough to just help people and spread my name, like I did today.*

It'd be nice to say I went through the trouble of solving this civil war without a shred of selfishness. But that's just not the case.

Belfast is an important kingdom, since it borders the lands of Chaos. If they were to fall, it'd be disastrous for the overall war effort.

Of course, I also planned on spreading my name like this from the beginning. In the end, I got everything I wanted out of this conflict. In a way, the civil war even ended up benefiting me since it gave me a chance to play the hero.

*I just hope someone like me is enough to win their faith.*

I'm not the smiling, selfless hero most people might imagine when thinking of the summoned heroes. But I can pretend to be when it's necessary.

Whether or not I can use that fake persona to fool the world into thinking I'm someone worthy of being recognized as a Great Hero is questionable. But it's a question that we need to find the answer to sooner, rather than later.

After far too long dealing with Belfast's nobles, the so-called celebration comes to an end.

It definitely felt more like a punishment than a reward, though.

----------

"Whew." I let out a breath as a door closes behind me. "I'm just not cut out for life as a noble."

"Oh, come on!" Belle says. "It wasn't that bad. Actually, wasn't it kind of fun?"

"I don't think our definitions of 'fun' are really lining up."

I look around our new room. It's extravagant, as expected for a king's personal chambers. A couple months ago, I'd probably gawk at all the excessive decoration, but I don't feel like a tourist in a strange land anymore.

This world is my home now, and I've been in too many throne rooms and royal chambers to feel anything other than admiration for whoever decorated this room.

*They really did do a good job.*

But I didn't come here to admire the artist's talent.

"Now that we've got some privacy," Kuro says. "I wanted to discuss something of importance."

"Sure. But I have a question of my own first. What do you plan to do with your son who tried to take your throne?"

"Rei." Kuro says his name with disappointment. "He may have been manipulated by that advisor, but that doesn't absolve him of his actions. He will face punishment for his part in the near destruction of our kingdom."

"What kind of punishment?" Alisha asks, obviously worried.

"I suppose I'll say it now if it's all of you. I plan to exile him to the eastern edge of the kingdom, somewhere he won't be able to use whatever influence he may have remaining."

"Ah, he gets to live!"

"Yes, though he will find himself living a more humble life in a large village, lacking the convenience found in our capital city."

*Well that's not a bad outcome, all things considered.*

Having felt the [Torment] spell myself, I can say with certainty that someone with a lower level or a weaker will could easily be influenced by the magic.

But it's not a spell that controls people. It only influences them, meaning Rei's still responsible for at least part of his actions.

At least that's the way Kuro feels about it. What I think doesn't really matter, as the outcome is acceptable to me. Besides, I'm not really in the business of telling kings how to run their own countries. Getting involved too much would just be a major headache.

"Anyway," I say. "That's all I wanted to know so go ahead with whatever you wanted to talk about."

"In that case, I wish to ask for your support in getting the king of Orakio to agree to work together to defeat the fiends. I believe it's more than apparent that they pose a threat to the survival of our very world."

"King Edgar, huh? I don't really want to get involved with the politics of war, but I guess I don't have much of a choice. Working together is exactly what we need to do right now."

"I'm in agreement. Our enemies are far too coordinated, while each kingdom in this world only seeks to keep their own borders secure. At this rate, we'll fall one by one."

I sigh, already imagining the annoying meetings I'll be going through later. "Then I'll speak to him and set up a way for you two to meet in person and discuss it."

"Excellent. I'll prepare everything I need for the meeting, so simply send a message when you're ready." Kuro holds up his hand, which has a [Mental Link] enchanted ring.

"Will do. But I'll be rushing to the Dragon Isles for the next day or two. Gotta make up for lost time."

"Understood, but before you go..." Kuro looks to Alisha. "I haven't said this until now, but I'm happy that one of our own is fighting alongside Lutz."

"It's fun, so I'm happy too." Alisha gives him her usual smile.

"I see. Then please continue to bring honor to our people by helping save this world."

"Okay! I'll keep doing my best!"

Kuro visibly shifts gears. "Also, congratulations on becoming the first person in history to break the [Curse of the Forsaken]. A well-deserved outcome, without a doubt."

"Thanks! I feel like a whole new person now! My head is finally clear, too. I wonder if I'll eventually be recognized as a genius!"

*Uh, Alisha. I don't think that's going to happen. Your Intelligence stat is still really low, you know...*

Her base stats nearly doubled, but her Intelligence was so low that even after removing the curse, it's still below average.

On the other hand, her Constitution and Agility are both really high. Especially her Constitution, which is nearly equal to mine.

Overall, her stats are still a bit on the lower end when compared to me, Laya, and Tylith. But she's ahead of Belle, at least. And when she activates [Protector], her stats grow frighteningly high.

*[Protector] adds about a 50% increase to her stats.*

*Compared to before when the buff used to double them, it seems like it's been nerfed. But that's not really the case.*

Her [Protector] always gave her a 50% increase. It just did its calculations based on her uncursed stats, meaning nothing has really changed about it.

*With how she is now, Alisha may be our strongest member after activating [Protector].*

*That's actually incredible...*

In a real battle, I don't see me or Laya losing to her. But it'd certainly be quite a fight now.

"Well," I say, "we need to get going. Got nearly half your kingdom to travel through before we reach the southern ocean, so I want to get started."

Kuro nods. "Thank you again for your help. I will surely repay it one day."

"As long as we win this war, I'll consider the debt repaid."

"In that case, I'll have to work even harder toward that goal."

I hold my hand out, and Kuro takes it. With a single shake, we solidify our commitment to working together and putting an end to the war.

The girls each say their goodbye's as well. Soon, there's nothing left to be said. The five of us huddle close, and with a quick cast of [Teleport], we vanish from Belfast's capital city, leaving Kuro with one last wave.

Shortly after, a wide landscape fills my vision. We didn't teleport far, just a couple hours walk south of the capital. But it's enough to get us started on our trip to the southern ocean.

"Alright," I say. "Nothing can stop us from meeting the dragons now."

"Don't jinx it," Laya says.

"Ah, oops."

Belle gives me a strange look. "No more princesses."

"Hey, it's not my fault we keep running into royal girls."

"No, you're definitely causing it somehow!"

"Hmph." Tylith swishes her hair back in her usual fashion. "At least Keiko didn't attempt to join him on his quest."

"Yeah! Imagine if she said she wanted to come with us. Mr. Princess Collector over here would probably have said yes!"

"Hey! I'm very selective about who I bring with me!"

"Ah." Alisha makes a noise. "It's been a while since you've added to the harem, Master!"

"What harem!?"

"Hehe~" Alisha steps close, not even trying to hide her intentions.

"Alright, alright. You deserve lots of headpats for your hard work today." I run my hand through her hair. "And Alisha. Congratulations on being free."

"Yeah," she says in a far more mature voice. "Thank you."

# Epilogue

## ----- Lumina -----

"You want me to accompany you to a dungeon?"

My eldest brother, Rhys, can't hide the surprise on his face.

As the crown prince, he's had some of the best training available to the people of this world. Thanks to that, his level is already at a respectable 35.

But compared to the dangerous foes we'll be facing soon, it's simply not high enough.

"Yes," I say. "Increasing your strength would lift a heavy weight from my mind."

"It's true I'm lacking compared to our kingdom's top warriors, but dungeons are dangerous. It'd be foolish for the general to risk entering one. Were we to perish, it could give the enemy an opportunity to strike."

"Dungeons are certainly as dangerous as the stories say. But there are ways to mitigate that risk. Even I became a Conqueror, you know."

"That's true, but Father would never allow it."

"Actually..." I take a sip of tea. "Father is the one who suggested it."

"He did what!?"

"Father sees the wisdom of grind—I mean of increasing your strength. And since he's going as well, I suppose he wanted to make it into a sort of family outing. Ah, Lyle's going, too."

Rhys sits back in his chair, contemplating my words. "I'll be needing a detailed explanation of this dungeon trip, along with the names of everyone attending."

"Certainly. As stated, all of our immediate family will be going, along with Elise. We're also being joined by an adventurer and his companion to ensure we have the strength needed to defeat the most powerful guardians."

Rhys throws more questions my way, each of which I answer to the best of my ability. My eldest brother has always been a meticulous strategist, so it only makes sense that he'd dig into the details.

Eventually, even he runs out of things to ask. In the end, he decides to join the rest of us in the dungeon. When he heard we'd be going tomorrow night, he sighed, mentioning the lack of preparation time.

While I agree, this is just how things are. We have to take the opportunity when we have it, and tomorrow night may be the last chance we have for a while.

Leaving Rhys to start his preparations, I step back into the castle halls. Elise has been waiting out here, not wanting to rudely listen in to a conversation between siblings.

While I wouldn't mind, the same might not be true for Rhys. He doesn't know the whole truth yet, so he has no idea just how embroiled Elise is in the quest to save this world.

He doesn't even truly understand how deep I'm steeped in that quest, either. After all, we haven't yet told him that Lutz is actually our world's one and only true hero.

Soon, we arrive at the door to my personal chambers. Turning, I look to Elise and see her still steadfastly protecting me, even in the heart of the castle.

However, this is where her duty ends for the day.

"I believe I'll be resting early tonight," I say. "It's been a while since I've read at length, so I'm going to indulge for a couple hours before bed."

"Understood, Princess. In that case, I shall make preparations of my own for our upcoming trip to the dungeon. If you require anything, simply send me a message and I will bring it."

"Thanks, Elise. But you should relax, as well. It would be good for your mental health."

"I'll consider it."

With an exasperated smile, I wish Elise a good night and step into my room. The maids keep it clean while I'm out, but I'm someone who prefers cleanliness and organization, so I never leave the maids much work to do in here.

Just beside my bed is a soft chair sitting next to a small table. It's perfect for reading, which is precisely why I set it up in such a fashion.

I take a seat, sinking into the thick cushion.

*It sure is nice to relax like this from time to time.*

*Maybe one day, every night will be so comforting.*

For now, I've still got too much work to do, so nights like this are going to be a rarity into the foreseeable future.

My grimoire, [Ballads of the Unremembered], appears in my hands. I fought many battles in the dungeon while wielding this mysterious book, yet I've still not been able to unleash its next spell.

The first story that appeared inside granted me the unique magic, [Balefire of Purifying Light]. But since then, there's been no progress no matter how much I fight.

With the grimoire open to the final passage of that first story, I flip the page, and...

*Still nothing.*

Blank page after blank page fills my vision, no matter how much I flip through the grimoire.

*It seems I'll need to battle even more before I can further unlock its secrets.*

Giving up on the grimoire, I bring out a typical book. Its pages contain a simple story, but that's precisely what I wish for, something that will further relax me during my down time.

As I dive into the world contained within, hours pass in mere minutes. My bedtime has come and gone, but I'm so close to the book's end that I continue reading, determined to see the story's conclusion before I lay down.

*Ah, I thought I broke this bad habit...*

Reading late into the night is one of my guilty pleasures, and I've paid the price for it the next day many times. Sitting in a stuffy meeting with some nobles when I only had a couple hours of sleep the night before is never a fun experience.

*Just a few more pages. I won't be too late for bed ... right?*

I consciously avoid estimating the time, not wanting to know how far I've already passed my bedtime.

*Just a few more pages, and–*

The soft rattle of metal startles me, my eyes immediately darting to the source.

*The doorknob?*

It's locked, of course. But if that noise really came from the doorknob, then there's a problem.

*Nobody's out there.*

Not a drop of mana can be felt outside my door.

*No, wait...*

I pull out a special orb. Looking at its surface, I see the terrain of my room, along with the castle hall outside my door.

The [Minimap] enchanted orb can pick up the presence of anyone in its range, even when...

*Someone is hiding their mana.*

I've already stood and swapped to my battle outfit, the grimoire held in my left hand. Whoever's outside my room hasn't left, nor have they made any moves.

Finally, the rattle of metal returns. With my eyes now firmly on the doorknob, I see that someone is indeed turning it.

Even though the door is locked, that won't stop someone with any real strength. So there's no surprise when the rattle turns into grinding metal.

Despite the lock, the doorknob turns, the mechanism inside giving way to the intruder's strength. Finally, it gives, and the door creaks open.

A sliver of the outside hall appears, revealing a shadowed figure standing outside. That sliver widens, revealing the intruder.

*A maid?*

*No, that's...*

The supposed maid steps into my room, her eyes holding my own. Despite seeing me fully prepared for battle, there's not a single shred of surprise or hesitation in her gaze.

The reason for that is...

"Hello, Princess." The intruder cancels their [Transform] spell, revealing their true identity.

"Collette. I didn't expect you'd be the one who'd come to assassinate me."

The Hero of Chaos shuts the door behind her. "You assumed it'd be Rolf, didn't you?"

"Considering he's an assassin, yes."

"Sorry to disappoint you then, but this mission is personal."

"Personal?" I give her a questioning look. "Have I ever done anything to anger you?"

"No, you misunderstand me. I couldn't care less about you. The reason I'm here on my own is for the future ruler of this world."

"Pardon, but I don't follow."

Collette shakes her head. "You still have no clue, Princess. There's nobody in this world who can stop him, not even that little hero of yours. Even the Goddess can't overcome his power, or haven't you noticed?"

"There are … complicated reasons for the Goddess' influence being sealed. I'm sure of it."

"No, it's not complicated. When faced with his strength, she's simply too weak. That's why..." Collette readies her wand. "...I will kill you here and earn his favor. More than the other heroes, more than the Archfiends. I will become his favorite, no matter what it takes."

"So that's what you meant." I shake my head. "Willing to bloody your hands just to earn his favor. How pitiful."

"I don't need your pity." Collette clenches her wand. "I just need you to die."

A spell bursts forth from Collette. The [Waterblade] covers the width of the entire room, its sharp edge able to slice most creatures in half with ease.

But thanks to Sir Lutz, I'm far above a common creature.

The blade of water slams into a translucent barrier that protects my body. Just a hand's length in front of me, that razor sharp edge threatens to slice through the [Shimmering Shield].

With a crack, the barrier shatters, Collette's spell overpowering even a shield that specializes in defending against magic.

Fortunately, I have three more barriers between me and the [Waterblade].

The second [Shimmering Shield] suffers the same fate as the first, the blade proving too much for it to handle.

As I watch Collette's spell hit my third barrier, the water that makes up the blade deforms, with small waves rippling through the length of its body.

With a splash, the [Waterblade] covers my vision, splattering onto my magical barrier. Streams of water flow to the ground, quickly clearing my vision.

What I see is Collette's surprised face.

"You ... defended against my attack." Her surprise turns into wariness. "At your level, the spell should have overpowered any defensive magic you used."

"Yet here I stand." I raise my hand, putting it straight through the remaining barriers protecting me. "And I'm also a Water Mage."

A [Waterblade] erupts from my hand, growing to nearly the size of the room.

When Collette sees the magic she used cast back at her, she quickly raises her own barriers.

With so many magical shields between us, her figure takes on a deeper shade of blue, as is always the case when looking through so many translucent barriers.

My [Waterblade] hits her first [Shimmering Shield], and within a breath, it shatters. The blade moves a hair closer to her body, hitting her second shield.

My offensive magic against Collette's defensive magic. Considering she has the strength of a Great Hero, the fact that I'm able to stand against her at all is nothing short of amazing.

But it seems the difference between us is still too large.

My [Waterblade] becomes no more than a splash on Collette's second barrier, failing to penetrate.

"Hah." Collette grins. "I don't know where you got such strength, but it's obvious now. Between us, I'm stronger. One more spell, and your barriers will be gone, while mine will still protect me. It's over."

"It's true that you're still above me, but I'm okay with that. After all..." I raise my Grimoire, opening it to the first story. "... I'm not fighting this war alone."

"Guh...!" Collette turns, swinging her wand.

Elise blocks the attack with her bloody sword, then kicks at the supposed hero.

Collette avoids Elise's foot, leaping to the far side of the room.

As for me, I've made my way to Elise's side, near the door that leads out to the hall. It's the only way out, as there's not even a window in my room.

"Hiding your presence, you damn attendant."

Elise takes a half step forward. "I don't want to hear that from someone who used the same tactic."

"Don't act so confident just because your numbers doubled. You're still no match for me."

"Perhaps. But you've been in our trap since the moment you touched Lumina's doorknob, so I wonder if you're the one who's being arrogant."

"And," I say. "The guards are already on their way. Our spells have made quite a ruckus."

"Tch." Collette looks at a wall, tracking the mana of the approaching guards.

"I wonder what the Lord of Chaos would think if you were spotted here. Surely that's not the path to earning his favor, is it?"

"Fool. Still so naive." Collette lowers her wand. "This isn't over. Your day will come, whether by my hand or another's. Enjoy what little time you have remaining."

With that, Collette releases [Teleport] and disappears.

"Whew." I let out a breath. "That was quite a shock."

"Yes. It's good that we prepared for such an attack. But it also means the farce of peace between us and the heroes is coming to an end."

"We're not ready. Sir Lutz still hasn't obtained the power he seeks."

"Then we should do all we can to delay the battle until he's ready. As we are now..." Elise looks to her sword, which has only a few drops of blood despite scoring a direct hit on Collette's unprotected back.

"Yes. A battle against even a single Hero of Chaos would be dangerous, much less all three."

*Sir Lutz, please hurry. Time is running out.*

# Extra Chapter 1

## ----- Lyle -----

"You're teleporting us?" My eyes fall on my younger sister.

"Correct, Lyle," Lumina says. "I set up the teleportation circles myself, so I have to be the one to cast the spell."

"Thought you said you didn't like Dark Magic."

"Someone eventually managed to change my mind about the Spell School."

Lumina's the first to step onto the softly glowing pattern. Her attendant follows without a word, and even Father walks into the circle like it's normal for Lumina to do something like cast [Teleport].

*Dammit. Why am I so far behind her?*

Our destination is several days away by foot, and the further the distance, the more draining it is to teleport. Yet Lumina will be taking five of us along with her, as if it's no big deal.

Rhys walks onto the pattern. "Isn't it dangerous for you to cast [Teleport] just before going to a dungeon?"

"You mean because of the spell's backlash?"

"Yes. For an entire day, it prevents you from recovering the mana spent to cast it. Won't you need all your strength for the battles ahead?"

"Ah, there's no need to worry. I have more than enough mana to spare. Besides, we'll be meeting up with a couple adventurers who will be helping us, so our overall battle potential won't be greatly impacted."

My sister's words remind me of an incident that still upsets me to this day.

Five years ago, I challenged Lumina to a contest. We'd both cast magic at a pile of dirt until one of us ran out of mana.

Even though she was only 7 years old, people were already talking about how much potential Lumina had as a mage. But I wanted to show her that she still had a ways to go to catch up with me.

I was 10, and people also praised me for my magical talents, so it should have been an easy victory.

But I lost.

No, it was worse than that. Lumina forfeited after realizing that I was reaching my limit, saying she was feeling the effects of mana exhaustion.

It was a lie to help me save face in front of the crowd. Maybe I should have been grateful. But at the time, all I could feel was anger.

Magic was the only thing I was ever good at. It was the one skill I had over our eldest brother, who was constantly praised.

Yet Lumina had beaten me in a contest of magic.

Back then, I wondered how. How can someone have so much mana?

But now I know.

I step into the teleportation circle, coming to a stop beside Lumina.

*Her Unique Skill, [Mana Fountain].*

Lumina activates [Teleport], using the enormous amount of mana given to her by that Unique Skill to power the teleportation. The backlash that would drain nearly anyone else doesn't even cause her to miss a step.

As soon as we arrive at our destination, Lumina's practically bouncing out of the circle and down a grassy slope. Elise is her shadow, like usual.

I look down that slope and her destination. "The adventurers."

"Only two," Rhys says. "And they're so young."

"Can we really trust them? Who are they, anyway? You'd have to be an S-Class adventurer to go to a dungeon like The Beast Warrens."

"Perhaps we should inquire about their identity." Rhys looks to our father.

"No need," he says. "I've already confirmed their identities myself."

Father starts walking down the slope, heading toward Lumina and the two adventurers. Rhys walks off too, leaving me alone in the teleportation circle.

"Whatever." I follow along with the rest.

"...been a while since I've been to an ocean," the male adventurer is saying when I walk up. "The sea breeze really does enhance the sense of adventure."

"And!" the young, female adventurer says. "If there's an ocean, there's lots of fish! So we ate at lots of great seafood restaurants!"

"Hey, you were the only one eating at all of them."

"Oh yeah~"

I've been paying far more attention to the adventurers themselves than whatever it is they're going on about. But I didn't have to look hard to see something strange.

*She's a beastkin.*

The young adventurer girl has white cat ears poking through her hair. It's rare to see beastkin work their way up to S-Class in human lands, but it's not unheard of.

The way she speaks so familiarly with Lumina is strange, though. It's as if she doesn't care a single bit that she's currently standing in front of Orakio's entire royal family.

"Ah." Lumina seems to realize something. "Everyone, this is Rune and Tama. They'll be fighting with us in the dungeon."

"It's good to see you again, Your Majesty." Rune turns to us. "And it's good to meet the two princes for the first time."

"Yeah!" Tama says. "Meeting new people is always fun!"

"Rhys." My elder brother gives a small bow. "We'll be in your care for today."

"Let's just get started," I say. "I'm tired of standing around."

"Then you're in luck," Rune says. "I'm in a bit of a rush, as is usual these days. So, I planned to start right away."

I feel him begin channeling for a spell. From the feeling of the mana, I can tell it's Dark Magic, but I don't know which spell.

*No, there's only one choice.*

For the second time in just a few minutes, my vision warps. When the world reappears, I'm in a strange hallway like I've never seen before.

"Where are we?" Rhys looks around the hall. "This place looks ancient."

"Yeah, it's old," Rune says. "Really old. But ignore the deteriorating interior. Dungeons never change, so this is just how it's always been."

"I thought The Beast Warrens was a forest dungeon," I say. "Why are we inside a building?"

"It's because I teleported us to the very center of the dungeon, inside this Biological Research Facility."

"Wait. The center of the dungeon? Do you mean...?" I look to the door that sits just in front of us.

"Yep. One of this dungeon's final guardians is inside. If we're going to level everyone up, then of course we're going to start with the juiciest enemies."

"Hey! There's no way we can fight a guardian that strong! Isn't this one of the most dangerous dungeons in our kingdom!?"

"I assumed we'd merely be staying near the dungeon's entrance," Rhys says. "Did you know, Father?"

"Of course. Just stay out of the way and let them handle the guardian."

As if without a single worry, Tama pushes the door open and steps inside. Rune, Elise, and Lumina follow with the same relaxed movements, leaving me, Rhys, and our father still standing in the hall.

*I don't know what the hell's even going on anymore, but I don't care. If it means I can get stronger, then I'll face any enemy.*

I walk in behind the other four. The room's wide, with a high ceiling. Perfect for combat.

"You three stay here, next to the door," Rune says. "We'll keep its focus."

Before anyone can respond, a loud crack fills the room. On the far wall, a blue light leaks from a fissure.

As I watch, the massive head of a beetle bursts from it, shattering more stone as it emerges. A huge, round body follows, so big that I fear the wall it's coming from will crumble completely.

Somehow, that doesn't happen. When the creature crawls out of the fissure, the crack glows and disappears, leaving nothing but a solid wall like before the giant beetle appeared.

*This is...!*

Now that I can sense mana, I know the general strength of everyone around me. Father is powerful, as is Lumina and Elise. The same can be said of the two adventurers.

But none of them can even begin to compare to the guardian now standing before us.

*We're dead. There's no way any of us can stand against that thing.*

Rhys has the same look of impending doom on his face as I feel on mine. Even my father is frowning, despite being the strongest person here.

"Guess there's no need to hide our strength here," Rune says.

Lumina nods. "I'm in agreement."

Four bursts of mana fill the room. Rune, Tama, Elise, and even Lumina are now leaking so much energy that even the guardian's mana is getting overpowered by it all.

"What the..." I can't help but stare at them, lost for words.

Lumina looks back to us. "Like we said, just stay there. Leave the guardian to us."

She releases a spell, and several magical barriers surround us. With that, she turns and joins the other three as the battle begins.

*It can't be. How did she get so strong?*

Back when Lumina beat me at my own challenge, I thought she was just lucky to be born with an absurd amount of mana.

But according to her, I obtained my own Unique Skill, [Ascended Magic], when I battled the False Hero back during the siege. Ever since that day, I've felt much stronger and can cast Master-Class magic at will, something I shouldn't be able to do at my level.

But my Unique Skill makes it possible.

*Nobody gave me my Unique Skill. I earned it. Which means Lumina has earned not just one, but two of them.*

Lumina and Elise seem to know exactly how to coordinate with the two adventurers, as if they'd fought together many times.

As someone who enjoys battle, I can say for certain that such flawless teamwork isn't easy to obtain. Yet they make it look easy.

Seeing my little sister battling this absurdly powerful guardian, I'm hit with a realization.

*I was wondering why you were chosen as the Prime Oracle. But now I understand.*

*You've been working hard for a long time, too.*

As the four of them claimed, the guardian falls without a single casualty.

"One down," Rune says. "Many more to go."

"That was fun!" Tama leaps into the air, as if the battle was just a warmup.

*Who the hell are these people?*

Unfortunately, my internal question would remain unanswered.

# Extra Chapter 2

## ----- Belle -----

"And that's it for the food." I cross it off the checklist. "It's important to follow the list."

The large bag of food still sitting on the counter vanishes. My [Inventory] might not be able to stop time like Lutz's, but it slows it enough to store food for a day.

We leave the shopkeeper staring at us in confusion.

"Grinding all day and night," Tylith says. "How enviable."

"You should have gone with them to the dungeon."

"There was already going to be a crowd, what with the entire royal family going. And another member wasn't necessary as long as he has Alisha, Lumina, and Elise with him."

"Also," Laya says, "you wanted to give Alisha room to shine now that she's been freed from the curse, didn't you?"

"Well, of course."

While Lutz and Alisha went to go level up Lumina's family, the three of us have been buying supplies at this beastkin city. Compared to battle, it's a bit boring. But I love a lively march through the city streets, so it suits me just fine.

Plus, this is a port city on the southern ocean, so there are a lot of interesting sights to see.

"Let's see." I look back at the list. "Next we need to pick up about a hundred empty potion bottles. Gah, we're always going into alchemist shops!"

"More ingredients, more potions," Laya says.

"I get it. If he's going to pick up a lot of drop items from the dungeon, then he might as well put them to use."

"Mmm. And some will be sold at your family's shop."

"That's true. And Celine said they're selling out of lots of items really quick, so anything Lutz can pick up in the dungeon will help restock their shelves."

The shop has been a huge success. That's great and all, but it also means we'll need a reliable way to restock the shop's supplies without having to spend too much time in the dungeon ourselves.

*But that's something Lutz can worry about! He says he has a plan, after all!*

On our way to the alchemist shop, a sign catches my attention. It's one that I've seen many times throughout my life, even as a young kid.

"Ah!" I come to a stop. "Now that's what I'm talking about!"

"A clothing shop," Tylith says.

"If we're gonna be out shopping, then of course we need to buy something in this city's style, right?"

"I guess that's to be expected from the daughter of a tailor."

"Yeah! I can't wait to show my dad this crazy fashion!"

We step into the shop and see racks of clothes all over the place. With a quick scan, I take note of the store's layout. As expected of a shop in a major port city, the place is organized and tidy.

The areas of most interest are in the front, telling me the owner believes in putting their best foot forward when it comes to attracting customers.

During my scanning, I see a rack of clothes that's way different from the rest. Even though the fashion here is strange, I still recognize what kind of dresses are hanging on that rack.

*Wedding dresses.*

"Hey," I say as we enter the shop. "You ever thought about how you want to get married?"

"M-married?" Tylith asks. "I don't particularly see how such a thing matters..."

"Of course it matters. Aren't you excited for your big day?"

"A little, I suppose..."

"Hehe." A snicker escapes my lips. "As shy as ever, huh? Just admit it already. You plan to marry Lutz when this is all over."

Tylith turns her face away. "It'd be a lie to say the thought never occurred to me."

"Then just say it clearly! Sheesh, with all the embarrassing lines you say when you're in that dominating personality, you'd think admitting something like this would be easy. And don't even get me started on what you do to get into that mood!"

"This and that are entirely different matters." The vampire princess runs her hand through her long, purple hair.

Without a doubt she's imagining all the times she's drunk Lutz's blood. She never hesitates when it's time to drink it, but she always gets embarrassed about it when it's brought up later.

"Forget about all that," I say. "We should figure out if we're going to get married all at once or if we're going to each have our own ceremonies."

"Is that something we should be deciding on our own?" Tylith asks.

"It's just a discussion for now, so it's fine."

"Is this about the … technique he used on Alisha?"

"Well of course that got me thinking about a few things. Wasn't it the same for the both of you?"

Tylith avoids my eyes. "Perhaps…"

My gaze falls on the silent Laya. She looks back at me with her usual, cool expression, but she doesn't say anything.

That's not uncommon for her, but after months of traveling with her, I understand her well enough to see under that mask.

*If that incident didn't make her think of a few things, then she would have calmly denied my question.*

*The fact that she only stared blankly at me means I was right.*

"Seems we're all on the same page, then!" I march them over to the wedding dresses. "You better start thinking about what style you wanna wear that day because it may come sooner than you think!"

With a trip to the clothing store, our little shopping trip takes a sudden turn. But it gives us a chance to lay the foundation for our eventual future.

"What happened to following the list?"

I think I hear Laya's soft voice, but I decide that it must be my imagination.

# Afterword

Hello after quite a while! It's hard to believe that I actually finished and published 8 volumes of The False Hero already. In my original vision, the series would have been ending around this point. But the scope has expanded a bit, so we're not quite there yet. The ending is drawing closer, but we're only about 2/3 of the way there so far.

But let's talk about the book itself for a bit. We finally got some answers to a lot of the questions that have been building up for a long time. The truth of Lutz's body, a glimpse into the distant past, and the revelation that he may very well be an Immortal Being himself.

The picture is becoming clear, but there are still quite a few mysteries remaining. I'm looking forward to revealing them in the upcoming novels.

Oh, and don't you think a carriage rescue scene is just so iconic? I mean, sure I did it in Volume 1, but you can't rescue enough nobles riding in their carriages, right? Especially when it's a princess! Anyway...

Skipping all the stuff in the middle, let's talk about Ashton! It's been a while since we've seen him. All the way back in Volume 4, to be precise. I was excited to finally bring him back into the story, and I think his scenes came out really well. I hope you will read between the lines and figure out what he really wants.

Also! Vrazruk is dead! Finally, progress against the main baddies. It was a long time coming, wasn't it? To be honest, writing that scene felt great, heh.

But more importantly, Alisha is cured!!!! Wow, for the past several books, I've had so many people asking when she was going to be cured. Of course I couldn't answer them, but I hope the people who were waiting for this moment are satisfied with the results. Was it worth the wait?

Well, that's it for their journey for now. Thank you for reading, and I hope you will continue the series until the grand conclusion!

Until next time!

## Social Media

**For early access, extra content, and updates, follow me at:**

Website: http://www.thefalsehero.com/

Patreon: https://www.patreon.com/MichaelPlymel

Facebook:

https://www.facebook.com/michael.plymel.79

Twitter: @Michael_Plymel

Discord: https://discord.gg/Wc2cYpPMt3

Reddit: https://www.reddit.com/r/TheFalseHero/

# Copyright

Made in the USA
Las Vegas, NV
30 January 2025

17197001R00193